MW01487248

Also by Scarlett St. Clair

When Stars Come Out

HADES X PERSEPHONE
A Touch of Darkness
A Game of Fate
A Touch of Ruin
A Game of Retribution
A Touch of Malice
A Game of Gods
A Touch of Chaos

ADRIAN X ISOLDE
King of Battle and Blood
Queen of Myth and Monsters

FAIRY TALE RETELLINGS
Mountains Made of Glass
Apples Dipped in Gold

FAIRY TALE

RETELLINGS

VOLUME ONE

SCARLETT ST. CLAIR

Bloom books

Published by Bloom Books, an imprint of Sourcebooks
P.O. Box 4410, Naperville, Illinois 60567-4410
(630) 961-3900
sourcebooks.com

Printed and bound in China.
OGP 10 9 8 7 6 5 4 3 2 1

For the fuck of it.

Content Warnings

This book contains themes of physical abuse of humans and animals, mental abuse, suicide, and violence.

If you are a victim of domestic violence, please call the National Domestic Violence Hotline at 1-800-799-SAFE (7233) or visit thehotline.org

If you or someone you know is contemplating suicide, please call the National Suicide Prevention Lifeline at 1-800-273-TALK (8255) or go online to suicidepreventionlifeline.org.

Are you a survivor? Need assistance or support? Call the National Sexual Assault Hotline at 1-800-656-HOPE (4673) or go online to hotline.rainn.org

Have you witnessed or experienced child abuse? The Childhelp National Child Abuse Hotline Crisis can help. Call 1-800-422-4453 or go to childhelphotline.org.

Glossary

This glossary serves to offer insight into the origin of the creatures and entities in *Mountains Made of Glass* and *Apples Dipped in Gold.*.

Crone/Witch: In fairy tales, a crone or a witch is often an old woman. She can have evil intentions, but I find she can take on a more ambiguous role. She sometimes curses or gives tasks to the hero, who then must overcome the obstacle by demonstrating their morality. She is usually the catalyst to the hero's change, which makes her a very powerful creature in stories.

Red Caps: A type of goblin. In MMOG, these goblins are called red caps because they soak their hats in the blood of their victims. However, in other fairy tales, they are called red caps only because their hats are red. There are variations of redcaps depending on the origin of the fairy tale and not all are malevolent.

Sprite: A type of fairy. Sprites are very tiny and are usually attracted to water. They are temperamental and can inflict madness upon a person.

Pixie: A type of fairy. Pixies can be household fairies and are sometimes described as mischievous. They often like to play tricks.

Brownie: Brownies are described as spirits, often those of a dead relative. They are sometimes classified as fairies or hobgoblins, which is why I used them in this retelling. They are usually male, but there are a few females, and they are said to keep house.

Magic Mirror: A reference to the story of Snow White. In particular, it is said that the tale was based on a real person, Maria Sophia Margaretha Catharina von Erthal, who resided near a glass-making region. It was said that the mirrors they made were of such "extraordinary quality, with the glass being of such excellence that people said the mirrors 'always spoke the truth.'"

Elves: A type of fae. I used two types of elves in this story: basically "human-like" elves and "fairy-like" elves, meaning small ones. Both seem to exist within folklore depending on origin. I identified the creatures in the wardrobe as elves as a reference to "The Elves," which is a fairy tale about a shoemaker who is very poor and helped by little elves who make shoes.

Selkie: The Selkie comes from Irish myths and legends. Their true form is that of a seal, but on land they can shed their skin and become human. If they do not have their seal skin, they cannot return to sea.

Faun: A half-human, half-goat creature. They are more like nature spirits, especially in reference to Greek mythology. In this retelling, I considered them a type of fae.

Fairyland: Reference to Irish fairy tales by W.B. Yeats in which he refers to the land of the fairies as Fairyland. In *Mountains Made of Glass*, all land inhabited by fae is considered Fairyland.

The Glass Mountains: The Glass Mountains take on various roles in fairy tales across the world. They sprout trees with golden apples, offer refuge, or serve as an obstacle to the hero who must overcome them to obtain a princess (usually). Within Grimm fairy tales, they appear in "The Iron Stove," "The Seven Ravens," "The Raven," "The Drummer," and "Old Rinkrank."

The Enchanted Forest: In fairy tales, the Enchanted Forest is a symbol of change and transformation.

der Kingdom

𝕸ountains

𝕿he Kingdom
of 𝕱oxglove

𝕶ingdom
𝕿horn

𝕿he Kingdom
of 𝖂illowpin

𝕬spen

hanted 𝕱orest

𝕾hroud

𝕵uniper

𝕷ark

𝕽en

𝕰lk

𝕽ose

𝕭riar

𝕱ox 𝕳ollow

𝕳awk

Mountains
made of
Glass

The Seven Brothers & Their Seven Kingdoms:

The Seventh, Casamir: The Kingdom of Thorn
The Third, Lore: The Kingdom of Nightshade
The First, Silas: The Kingdom of Havelock
The Sixth, Eero: The Kingdom of Foxglove
The Fourth, Talon: The Kingdom of Hellebore
The Second, Cardic: The Kingdom of Larkspur
The Fifth, Sephtis: The Kingdom of Willowin

CHAPTER ONE
The Toad in the Well

GESELA

he goose hung suspended by its feet from a low limb, bleeding into a bucket. Each wet plop of blood made me flinch, the sound inescapable even as I chopped wood to feed my hearth for the coming storm. The air had grown colder in the few minutes I had been outside, and yet perspiration beaded across my forehead and dampened all the parts of my body.

I was hot and the blood was dripping, and the strike of my ax sounded like lightning in the hollow where I lived before the Enchanted Forest. I could feel her gaze, a dark and evil thing, but it was familiar. I had been raised beneath her eyes. She had witnessed my birth, the death of my mother and father, and the murder of my sister.

Father used to say the forest was magic, but I believed otherwise. In fact, I did not think the forest was enchanted at all. She was alive, just as real and sentient as the fae who lived within. It was the fae who were magic, and they were as evil as she was.

My muscles grew more rigid, my jaw more tense, my mind spiraling with flashes of memories bathed in red as the blood continued to drip.

Plink.

A flash of white skin spattered with blood.

Plink.

Hair like spun gold turned red.

Plink.

An arrow lodged in a woman's breast.

But not just a woman—my sister.

Winter.

My chest ached, hollow from each loss.

My mother was the first to go on the heels of my birth. My sister was next, and my father followed shortly after, sick with grief. I had not been enough to save him, to keep him here on this earth, and while the forest had not taken them all by her hand, I blamed her for it.

I blamed her for my pain.

A deep groan shook the ground at my feet, and I paused, lowering my ax, searching the darkened wood for the source of the sound. The forest seemed to creep closer, the grove in which my house was nestled growing smaller and smaller day by day. Soon, her evil would consume us all.

I snatched the bucket from beneath the goose and slung the contents into the forest, a line of crimson now darkening the leaf-covered ground.

"Have you not had enough blood?" I seethed, my insides shaking with rage, but the forest remained quiet in the aftermath of my sacrifice, and I was left feeling drained.

"Gesela?"

I stiffened at the sound of Elsie's soft voice and waited until the pressure in my eyes subsided to face her, swallowing the hard lump in my throat. I would have called her a friend, but that was before my sister was taken by the forest, because once she was gone, everyone abandoned me. There was a part of me that could not blame Elsie. I knew she had been pressured to distance herself, first by her parents and then by the villagers who met monthly. They believed I was cursed to lose everyone I loved, and I was not so certain they were wrong.

Elsie was pale except for her cheeks which were rosy red. Her coloring made her eyes look darker, almost stormy. Her hair had come loose from her bun and made a wispy halo around her head.

"What is it, Elsie?"

Her eyes were wide, much like my sister's had been at death. Something had frightened her. Perhaps it had been me.

"The well's gone dry," she said, her voice hoarse. She licked her cracked lips.

"What am I supposed to do about it?" I asked, though her words carved out a deep sense of dread in the bottom of my stomach.

She paused for a moment and then said quietly, "It's your turn, Gesela."

I heard the words but ignored them, bending to pick up my ax. I knew what she meant without explanation. It was my turn to bear the consequences of the curse on our village, Elk.

Since I was a child, Elk had been under a curse of curses. No one agreed on how or why the curse began. Some blamed a merchant who broke his promise to a witch. Some said it was a tailor. Others said it was a maiden, and a few blamed the fae and a bargain gone wrong.

Whatever the cause, a villager of Elk was always chosen to end each curse—some as simple as a case of painful boils, others as devastating as a harvest destroyed by locust. It was said to be a random selection, but everyone knew better. The mayor of Elk used the curses to rid his town of those he did not deem worthy, because in the end, no villager could break a curse without a consequence.

Like my sister.

I brought my ax down, splitting the wood so hard, the blade cracked the log beneath.

"I do not use the well," I said. "I have my own."

"It cannot be helped, Gesela," Elsie said.

"But it is not fair," I said, looking at her.

Her eyes darted to the right. I froze and turned to see that the villagers of Elk had gathered behind me like a row of pale ghosts, save Sheriff Roland, who was at their head. He wore a fine uniform, blue like the spring sky, and his hair was golden like the sun, curling like wild vines.

The women of Elk called him handsome. They liked his dimpled smile and that he had teeth.

"Gesela," he said as he approached. "The well's gone dry."

"I do not use the well," I repeated.

His expression was passive as he responded, "It cannot be helped."

My throat was parched. I was well aware of how Elsie and Roland had positioned themselves around me, Elsie to my back, Roland angled in front. There was no escape. Even if I had wanted, the only refuge was the forest behind me, and to race beneath its eaves was to embrace death with open arms.

I should want to die, I thought. It was not as if I had anything left, and yet I did not wish to give the forest the satisfaction of my bones.

I gathered my apron into my hands to dry my sweaty palms as Roland stepped aside, holding my gaze. Elsie's hand pressed into the small of my back. I hated the touch and I moved to escape it. Once I had passed Roland, he and Elsie fell into step behind me, herding me toward the villagers, who were as still as a fence row.

I knew them all, and their secrets, but I had never told them because they also knew mine.

No one spoke, but as I drew near, the people of Elk moved—some ahead, some beside, some behind, caging me.

Roland and Elsie remained close. My heart felt as though it were beating in my entire body. I thought of the other curses that had been broken. They were all so different. One villager had wandered through the Enchanted Forest and picked a flower from the garden of a witch. She cursed him to become a bear. In despair, he returned to Elk and was shot with an arrow through the eye. It was only after he died that we learned who he was. The next morning, a swarm of sparrows attacked the hunter who had killed the bear and pecked out his eyes.

There was also a tree that had once grown golden apples, but over time, it ceased to produce the coveted fruit. One day, a young man wandered through the village and said a mouse gnawed at its roots. He claimed if we killed the mouse, the fruit would thrive, so our previous mayor killed the mouse, and the fruit returned. The mayor picked an apple, bit into it, and was consumed with such hunger, he gorged himself to death.

No one else touched the fruit of the tree or the mayor who died beneath its boughs.

There were no happy endings, that much I knew. Whatever I faced after this would surely lead to my death.

The villagers spilled into the center of town like phantoms. They kept me within their ghostly circle, surrounding the well, which was open to the sky and only a cold, stone circle that went deep into the ground. I approached and looked down, the bottom dry as a bone.

Roland stood beside me, too close, too warm.

"Who will you sacrifice when everyone you hate is dead?" I asked, looking at him.

"I do not hate you," Roland said, and his eyes dipped, glittering shamelessly as he stared at my breasts. "Quite the opposite."

Revulsion twisted my gut.

I had known Roland my whole life just as I knew everyone in Elk. He was the son of a wealthy merchant. That money had bought him status among the villagers and placed him at the mayor's side, which gave him power over every woman he ever laid eyes on and ensured he never had to face a curse.

My own misfortune had never deterred Roland. He had often offered to *help my case* if only I'd fuck him.

"You are disgusting."

"Oh, Gesela, do not pretend you despise my attention."

"I do," I said. "I am telling you."

Roland's face hardened, but he drew nearer, and it took everything in me not to push him away. I hated how he smelled, like wet hay and leather.

"I could make this go away. Say the word."

"What word?" I asked between my teeth.

"Say you will marry me."

I shoved him.

It was not as if he were serious either. He had made many proposals to women under the guise that he would save them, only to shame them later for believing he was serious.

If anyone was a curse on this land, it was Roland Richter.

"That is more than one word, idiot," I seethed. "But I shall give you one—never!"

Roland ground his teeth and then pushed me toward the well.

"Then you will face this curse."

I stumbled, catching myself against the side of the well,

6

my palms braced against the slimy stone as I faced the endless darkness below.

"The crone in the wood says there is a toad in the well. Kill it and we will have water again."

"And did the crone say what will happen to me?"

"I gave you an out and you refused."

"You did not give me an out," I snapped. "You offered another curse."

"You think marriage to me is equal to what the forest would do?"

"Yes," I hissed. "I might consider it if I found you the least bit handsome, but as it is, I would vomit the moment your cock entered my body."

Roland snapped. I knew he was capable of violence. It was a truth that moved in his eyes.

He pushed me, and as my knees hit the back of the well, I tumbled over the edge and fell. The air was cold against my back, and I hit the bottom with a loud crack. I lay, quiet and stunned, blinking at the bright light streaming in from the round opening above. It seemed so far away, though my fall had been quick.

Elsie was the first to peer down, and when she caught sight of me, she covered her mouth and disappeared. Then there was Roland, who spit into the well.

"Elven bitch," he hissed.

I flinched at the words, which were just as painful as my fall.

Then they were gone.

I groaned and tried to sit up, but my back hurt and each breath I took was painful. A high-pitched trill made me jerk, sending a spasm of pain down my spine. I turned to find a large, bulbous toad staring at me, its round eyes glowing like lamplights in the dark.

I mourned that I had not killed the toad during my fall. At least then it would have been an accident.

7

"This is all your fault," I said.

The toad's answer was a shrieking call before it jumped.

I screamed, thinking it was about to leap on me, but saw that it landed on a piece of stone jutting from the side of the well.

I sat up slowly, groaning as the pain in my back constricted my lungs. The toad screamed again, throat bubbling. I considered killing it and looked at my feet, searching for a loose stone I might use to smash it, though the thought sent a wave of nausea through me. I might slaughter geese to eat, but a toad was different. This toad was different. It was the victim of this curse just as I was.

Another screech echoed loudly in the compact space, and I cringed.

When I looked back at the toad, it had moved farther up the wall, perched on another rock, waiting.

"Are you trying to escape me?" I asked.

Its answer was to turn, its webbed feet squelching against the rocky surface, and jump to another ledge. Once it was secured, it turned to look at me and offered another high-pitched shriek. I cringed at the sound as it surrounded me, my muscles tightening.

I suddenly wondered if this toad was trying to help me out of the well instead.

I approached and placed my foot on one of the rocks, gripping two others over my head. My heart raced as I searched for foot and hand holds, gripping frantically at slimy stones. The reach hurt my sides and stole my breath, but I managed to lift myself. As I did, the toad moved on, finding another ridge. I followed carefully, fingers freezing, legs shaking as threads of pain skittered down my spine.

The higher I climbed, the harder I clung to the stones for fear I would fall again. The weather had worsened since I'd been in the well, and sleet stung my face.

The toad reached the top before me, turning to stare with

its large, yellow eyes before hopping out of sight. I was not far behind. Gripping the edge of the well with numb fingers, I managed to peer over and found the center of town deserted, likely because the storm had already arrived.

I was relieved, fearing that if Roland caught me climbing out of the well, he would only push me in again.

I let my stomach rest on the stone lip before sliding to the icy ground. There I lay, still and quiet, body racked with pain. Absently, I wondered what parts of me were broken. At the very least, I was badly bruised.

The toad waited patiently nearby, and as I stared up at the pale, gray sky, I wondered if anyone was watching me from the warmth of their home. Would they inform Roland? Had he assumed I was dead?

A now-familiar croak drew my attention, and I let my head fall in its direction, watching as the toad hopped onto the ledge of the well.

"No!"

I scrambled onto my knees and stumbled to my feet, bolting toward the toad, managing to grab its leg as it was about to jump back into the dark hole we had just left.

I threw it, and it soared over my head and landed on its back in the muddy square behind me. As if it felt no pain, it righted itself and started toward the well.

"I am trying to save you, you bastard," I said through my teeth, reaching for it again. Its body was slippery, which did not make it easy to hold as it wriggled in my grasp. "I'll keep you in a cage if I have to!"

I'd rather that than kill it.

The toad gave a keen cry just as my foot hit a patch of frozen ground. I fell onto my back again. I hardly had time to register the pain because the toad was free and already leaping frantically to the well.

A sharp twist of frustration spurred me on, and I shifted onto my knees, crawling to reach it, but it was one hop ahead of me. I tried to get to my feet, but the ground was too slick, and I crashed to my knees.

I gritted my teeth, scowling as I moved over the ground, my palm slamming down on a sharp rock. I did not even care that it hurt. My fingers curled around it. It was heavier than I thought it would be, bigger too, and just as the toad returned to the well, I reached for it, yanked it to the ground, and brought the rock down on its head.

A heavy silence followed, pressing into my ears, filling my body with a strange sense of shock as I stared at the lifeless toad, its legs still twitching. I did not remove the rock because I did not want to face what I had done.

It wouldn't stop. Why wouldn't it stop?

But I knew the answer.

It was cursed. We were all cursed.

I vomited and the rancid smell continued to turn my stomach, even as I pulled off my apron and wrapped the toad and the rock in the fabric. I rose to my feet and stumbled home. The goose I had slaughtered earlier was long gone, likely pulled from its place by wolves.

I could not find it in me to care.

I grabbed my ax, still lodged in the log where I'd left it, and walked to the edge of the Enchanted Forest where I chopped into the hard ground, scraping mounds of dirt aside until I had formed a deep enough chasm to fit the toad inside. Once I covered its body in the hard dirt, I sat there on my knees, letting the sleet strike my body like small, sharp needles. It reminded me that I could feel.

After a while, I rose, and despite the cold, I made my way to the rain barrel outside my house, breaking the sheet of ice that had formed over the top, and used the pan I kept inside to douse myself in water, washing my face and arms.

I brought the ax inside, leaving it on my bedside table before tending to the fire. I stripped off my sodden clothes and pulled on my nightgown before crawling into bed.

My head throbbed and my body ached as I curled into myself, shivering until I grew warm beneath my blankets.

I wondered if I would die in my sleep.

I hoped.

Because I knew something worse was coming for me.

CHAPTER TWO
Five Elven Princes

GESELA

 woke up shivering.

Peeling open my bleary eyes, I saw the shutters were open and ice had gathered on the ledge. Despite the howling wind, my curtain hung stiff, frozen.

I frowned, confused. I had definitely latched the window.

The hair on the back of my neck rose, and gooseflesh trailed down my arms as a deep sense of fear ran my blood cold.

I was not alone.

I reach for my knife, which I kept beneath my pillow, but as my fingers brushed the hilt, it disappeared.

"Fuck!"

"Tsk, tsk, tsk," said a voice. "Such language."

I rolled onto my back, intending to reach for my ax, which rested on the bedside table where I left it, but my eyes caught on a figure leaning against the wall of my room. He was tall, thin, and ethereal. The tips of pointed ears peeked out from his long black hair, which slipped over his shoulder, as shiny as moonlight on dark water.

He wore a black wool overcoat trimmed in gold, leggings, and heavy black boots, the foot of one propped flat against the wall behind him.

He was an elf, and judging by the finery of his clothing, a lord.

"Fuck," I said again.

This wasn't good.

He, like all types of fae, had come from the Enchanted Forest. I had no doubt he had come to seek retribution for the toad I had killed.

A hand gripped my chin hard as something sharp trailed down the side of my face. Blood welled.

"Foul human," said another voice, a wet tongue skating over the wound. "Foul mouth."

I tried to move but couldn't and only managed to sink my nails into the arm of my attacker, dragging them downward.

I felt his skin gather beneath my nails, and the creature hissed, his hand tightening on my face as he jerked my head back.

Now I could see his face, which was similar to the other elven lord's, though somehow more vicious, and instead of dark hair, his was bright blond. His fingers dug into my jaw so hard, I thought he might tear it away.

"Release her, Sephtis," said a third voice.

But he did not loosen his hold. If anything, it tightened, and he bent over me, eyes boring into mine, irises red-tinged and unnerving.

"Why should I?" he asked, his voice so low it was as if he were posing the question to me.

A hand seemed to appear out of thin air and jerked Sephtis's free, and another elf came into view. This one looked the same as the first—dark-haired and beautiful. Only his eyes were different, a strange, mossy color, neither completely green nor completely brown.

"You were supposed to keep an eye on him, Lore," said the new elven lord, and I assumed he was talking to the first elf, the one who had taken my knife.

Sephtis glared.

"Here to spoil our fun, Silas?" he asked.

My stomach soured at Sephtis's idea of fun.

The blond jerked away and then fell into place between Lore and Silas. Two others had joined us since, one with amber-colored eyes and one who bore a deep scar on the left side of his face.

There were five of them in total. Five elven lords, four of whom were dark-haired, but they all looked the same, even the blond. The only variation was in their expressions, ranging from most severe to least. They stood at the end of my bed, blocking me in.

"Will anyone else be joining us?" I snapped, voice as frigid as my room.

"You could not handle any more of us, vicious thing," said Lore. "Careful what you wish for."

"I made no wish," I said vehemently. I knew the consequences of careless wishing and had seen it with my own eyes.

I wish you were dead! I had yelled at my sister, and then she was.

"She is a tiny thing," said Silas.

"A vicious thing," said Sephtis.

"She killed our brother," said the one with the scar.

"Your brother?" I asked, feeling the color drain from my face.

"Look, Talon! Her face is as pale as snow!" said Sephtis. He seemed the angriest and the scariest.

"You know of what we speak, human," said the one with amber eyes whose voice was quiet and calm.

"I did not kill an elf," I said.

"But you killed a toad," said Lore.

"Bashed him over the head with a rock," said Sephtis.

"You buried him at the edge of the Enchanted Forest," said Talon.

I swallowed a thickness that had gathered in my throat.

"I had no choice," I said, the words a fierce whisper. I knew they were futile. No one in Elk or the world beyond cared why I had done what I had done, only that there were consequences. "There was a curse."

"There is always a curse, always a choice," said Silas.

"You could have chosen to break our brother's curse rather than your town's curse," said Lore. "He would have made you his queen out of gratitude for your rescue."

"But alas, you bashed his brains instead, and so we must punish you," said Sephtis, a hungry glint in his red eyes.

"How was I to know he was anything but a toad?" I demanded.

"That is the folly of your human blood, to take everything as it appears and not as it is," said Silas.

"And is it the folly of elves to take everything as it is and not as it appears?"

"Foolish human," said Lore. "We have no flaws."

"Then how did your brother end up as a toad in a well?"

"He is no longer a toad in a well," said Talon. "He is dead in a hole."

All the elves spoke with a cold civility, save the one with amber eyes who had only spoken once since he arrived. They were not here because they loved their brother. This was about honor. It was the justice demanded by the Forest.

There was a beat of silence as the five elven lords exchanged looks.

"You shall spend six years as our seventh brother's prisoner," said Silas.

"I only count five of you," I said.

"Our seventh is a beast," said Sephtis, but I could not imagine anything more terrifying than him, who had cut me so easily and tasted my blood.

"He cannot be worse than all of you," I snapped, though dread seeped into my veins as I spoke those words. Somehow, I knew he was worse.

"I suppose you will find out," said Silas.

There was a beat of silence as I stared at the five, uncertain of what happened now. Would they march me through the forest to the doorstep of their seventh brother's kingdom?

"Where is your seventh brother?" I asked, considering how quickly I could reach for my ax, which still sat on the table near my bed. I could feel its presence burning my skin, I wanted it in hand so badly. "Why is he not here?"

"No one has seen the Thorn Prince, not in nearly ten years," said Lore.

"How can you be certain he is a beast?"

"Because we're all beasts," said Sephtis, a smirk on his face.

I reached for my ax.

The movement sent a shock of pain up my side. It squeezed my lungs and held on to my breath, making me dizzy. Still, I shot to my feet, unsteady on the lumpy bed, and lifted the ax over my head, angling for the elf closest to me, when a great wave of magic hit me square in the chest.

I fell, but instead of my knees striking the hard floor of my room, I hit lush carpet. Despite the softer landing, every injured part of my body screamed and a pained cry tore from deep in my throat.

It was too late to swallow, and still I slammed my mouth shut, grinding my teeth against the pain, though it was nothing compared to the sudden sense of dread that numbed my body as a cold, sensual voice dripped over my skin.

"Well, what have we here?"

Slowly, my gaze rose over shiny black boots and well-muscled legs clad in black leggings. They were so tight, they left nothing to the imagination. My eyes widened at the indecent outline of his cock, something that would normally be covered by a long tunic, except he was shirtless, the hard lines of his abs and powerful shoulders on display, obscured only by a ring and a white tooth which hung at the end of two silver chains.

I took him in—all of him—before meeting his gaze.

Black eyes stared back, and while it felt ridiculous to say, they were so dark, they felt almost endless like the well. A sudden fear seized me, an instinctive knowledge that if I drew too close, I might fall into those eyes.

This was the seventh brother—the beast.

He looked like his siblings, the dark-haired ones, but there was still something different about him, something harder and darker. His forehead was high, his cheekbones too, and his lips were full and colorless.

He was beautiful and cold, like winter in Elk.

My fingers closed around the handle of my ax, and I rose to my feet.

"Stay back!"

His lips curled into a wicked grin.

"Oh, vicious creature," he said. "Are you here to kill me?"

"If you give me a reason," I replied, tightening my hold.

"I could give you three."

"I do not need three," I said. "One will suffice."

He chuckled quietly, never losing that mischievous glint in his eyes.

"One then," he said, and his smile slowly faded. "Kill me… before I kill you."

His words hit harder than my fall down the well, and before I lifted my ax, he was behind me, his hand on my throat. I could feel his long nails pressing into my skin. He drew my head back to the point that I thought my neck would break.

Several sharp pricks stung my palm, and I hissed at the pain, dropping my ax. The handle had grown thorns. With my hands free, I reached for the beast's at my throat, but even as I sunk my own nails into his skin, he did not move.

"Vicious thing," he said, and I could feel his lips against my cheek. "Vicious fae."

"*Don't* call me that," I said between my teeth.

He chuckled, fingers pressing deeper.

"Which word? Vicious or fae?"

Being fae, no matter how little, had never served me. The villagers whispered that my blood had killed my mother and it had not saved my sister from the forest.

It had, though, ensured I would always be alone. I had no family, no friends, no lovers.

The prince's voice rumbled against my skin, and I felt it in my chest. He spoke slowly, his lips trailing along my jaw, and I hated the way it made me feel, too conscious of the emptiness between my thighs, of the heat roiling in my gut, fueled by the press of his cock against my ass.

I hated it, and yet I pressed into him harder. I almost wished he would hurt me so I could stop these awful feelings firing through my veins.

"You *know* which word," I seethed, my voice fierce but quiet. I could not speak any louder. I could barely breathe.

"But you are fae," he said.

"Not enough to tell," I said.

I was not even sure when my blood had come to mix with the fae I only knew it had been many great-grandfathers ago. No matter how many years passed, the people of Elk remembered, and the fae, they always *knew*.

"Enough for me to taste."

His free hand splayed across my hip, and my nails bit into him to keep from guiding him lower, to the heat between my legs.

"Tell me, she who does not wish to be fae, why have you come?"

"I didn't...not of my own accord," I said.

"Do you want to know what I think?"

I swallowed hard, and the pressure of his hand was heavy against my throat.

"I'd rather you let me go."

"You shouldn't lie to an elven prince," he said, and his hand began to gather the hem of my shift. My muscles tightened even more, screaming as I remained against him.

"What makes you think I'm lying?"

"Shall I give you three reasons?" he asked.

"One will suffice," I said again, though I could barely recall what he had said or what I had wanted to say, my mind so clouded with a lustful wish to feel him inside me.

Wish.

Great consequences came from careless wishes, even unspoken. One never knew who was listening, even to thoughts.

"Not once have you tried to run," he said.

For the first time, I jerked in his arms.

"Ah, ah, ah, vicious creature," he said, and suddenly he was in front of me, his hand never leaving my neck as he guided me back, pinning me against a wall. Every part of his body rested against mine, hard and aroused, and I was a willing prisoner to it, melting into something soft and supple.

I did not recognize myself.

"Answer my question. Bend to my will. Why have you come, sweet one?"

As he spoke, his lips touched my cheek.

"I told you—"

He pulled away, and I met his endless dark eyes.

"Not of your own accord but someone's. Whose?"

"If you cannot guess, then perhaps you have no right to know."

"No right?" he asked and inclined his head. "Bold words, vicious one, when you are in my kingdom, beneath my roof, within my arms."

I glared at him and jerked on his arm, his hand still around my neck.

"I would hardly call *this* in your arms."

He smirked and leaned in, his breath hot against my ear. "And yet you respond."

Then his lips touched my skin, and I held my breath, pressing my head into the wall as hard as I could.

"Hmm, you are sweet," he said, his tongue tasting. "I could eat you whole."

His free hand had gone to the hem of my nightgown again. His fingers slipped between my thighs, but he did not move to the place where I ached. I felt ashamed because he had to feel the heat radiating from me. I felt it everywhere.

"Are you wet for me, vicious creature?"

I kept my eyes shut, my fingers digging into his skin. I wanted to beg for his touch just as much as I wanted to bury an ax in his chest.

The beast lifted my leg and hitched it over his hip, leaning into me. His hard cock pressed into me, coaxing a harsh sound from deep in my throat. Our mouths opened against each other. For a brief second, his tongue darted out to taste mine, and then he chuckled. His laugh slithered over me, feeding both my anger and embarrassment.

I took that moment to charge, pushing him away so violently, he stumbled back enough for me to bolt. I snatched my ax from the floor and fled the room, but as soon as I was out the door, I found myself in a hallway that looked like a wooded lane. My feet now raced over cold ground, past several naked trees that seemed to bow over me. Where before I had been warm within the elf lord's room, here, the wind whipped me, each cold lash making me tremble.

There was a part of me that did not understand how I had seemed to be within the walls of a castle and was now suddenly running through the woods, but I also knew I had no time to question the magic of the Thorn Prince's kingdom.

I had to run as far away as possible before he caught me.

As I ran, the path grew narrow, as if the trees were creeping closer. Soon there was no path at all, only the leaf-ridden floor of a wooded forest. Above me, the trees groaned and reached for me, their great limbs coming down on me like clawed fingers. They scratched and split my skin, and I swiped at them with my ax, but some still managed to become tangled within my shift and tore the thin fabric. My sleeve hung off my shoulder, the neckline gaped, and the hem was in tatters. Still, I managed to free myself, escaping the vile wood as it let out into a field that looked more like an endless ocean, the night too dark to see what lay at my feet, but I could feel it.

The ground was tender and wet, and my feet sank in cold mud. I could barely stay upright. I slipped and my ankle twisted. The pain sent me to the ground, and I landed hard on my hands and knees when something sharp wrapped around my legs and squeezed. I screamed and rolled onto my back as thorned vines crawled up my legs, digging deep into my skin. They slithered up my body until they were wrapped around my wrists, holding them over my head, and suddenly, I was face-to-face with the beast.

The prince hovered over me, his face inches from mine, the pendants of his necklaces rested against my chest. Instead of thorns, his fingers dug into my wrists, and his ankles were tangled with mine.

"My brothers sent you," he said and rested his body against mine. "Are you a spy?"

"Do I look like a spy?" I spat.

His eyes dropped to my breasts, exposed. My nipples had pebbled, hard from the cold, hard from his gaze, which flashed as it returned to mine.

"You look like a distraction."

"Then perhaps you should let me go," I said.

"I cannot let you go," he said. "You must earn your right to be free."

"My *right?*" I asked, the words fierce. I lifted my head, drawing closer to him, lips nearly touching. "I was sent here against my will."

"You were sent here as my prisoner," he said. "Which will it be, vicious one? Six years with me or a chance to be free?"

I glared at him, breathing hard.

"If you knew, why didn't you lock me up from the start?"

He smirked. "Who said I keep my prisoners locked up?"

"Where do you keep them then?"

"Shouldn't you ask where I will keep you?"

I did not answer, and the longer he stared at me, the more I wished to disappear. Perhaps the ground would open up and swallow me whole so I would not have to face how I felt beneath him.

After a few seconds, he spoke.

"Guess my true name," he said.

I blinked. "What?"

"You have seven days to guess my true name, and I will set you free."

I took several deep breaths as I processed his proposal. I was not so eager to be free that I would blindly jump at the first offer. All deals with fae—especially elves—were traps.

"How many guesses do I have?"

"As many as you wish," he said.

"I do not speak in wishes," I said.

He raised a brow. "Don't you?"

I ground my teeth. "Say it another way."

He chuckled. "As many as you would like."

"Will you keep count?"

He smirked.

"Clever creature," he said. "Of course."

"I thought so."

I would have to be careful with my answers and keep them to a minimum.

"And if I fail?"

"Then you fail," he said. "And you will be my prisoner for six years, plus one year more for every wrong answer you give."

"And what are the consequences of guessing correctly?"

His smile turned wicked, his gaze shrewd, and I caught a glimpse of what lurked beneath his skin—perhaps the true beast.

"Speak my name and find out."

I stared at him, weighing my options, all with dire consequences.

Even if I did manage to guess the beast's name correctly, what sort of evil would I unleash?

And did it really matter if I was free?

"I'll guess your name," I said.

His answer was a grin.

CHAPTER THREE
The Beast

GESELA

he beast released my wrists, and I shoved my hands against his chest, but he vanished.

I sat up.

Where had he gone?

I tried to stand, but my ankle was swollen and bruised. I rolled onto my hands and knees and struggled to my feet, finding that I was now in what appeared to be the entrance of a castle, my eyes narrowing on a door.

I stumbled toward it and fell, moving too quickly for my injured ankle.

"Perhaps you should stay there," said the beast, and I looked up from the floor into his dark eyes. He stood guard at the door, looking far larger than he had before. "Your knees seem to like it."

"Fuck you."

"You will," he said. "Far sooner than you think if you leave my castle."

I felt the color drain from my face, and it seemed to spark joy in the beast's eyes. Until his gaze lowered. I was covered in mud, and now that I was inside and warm, it was drying on my skin.

"Bathe," he said. "You look and smell like a pig."

I glared, rising to my feet and crossing my arms over my chest. It seemed ridiculous to hide now, but his sudden cold demeanor reminded me how silly I had been this evening. I should have tried to kill him the moment I met his gaze. Instead, I'd let him touch me and it had done nothing but give him power over me.

My mouth twisted into a disgusted smile.

"Do I repulse you?" I asked, gleeful at the thought.

He arched a brow.

"Clearly not."

I kept his gaze, unwilling to let my eyes wander, knowing well enough what he meant. I could still feel the hard press of his cock against me.

Perhaps he wasn't the only one with power here.

I looked around the entryway, which was dark despite several lit candles waning away in corners, noticing that flowering vines covered the walls and draped from the ceiling. Behind me was a staircase covered in moss, the rails tangled in trailing vines, creating a path to a second floor that looked like the dark woods of the Enchanted Forest.

I was no longer surprised that I had found myself outside once I had left the beast's room. It seemed that his entire castle was a forest.

"Where do you suggest I bathe?" I asked.

"Before me," he said, and once again, my surroundings changed. Suddenly, I was in a large, cavernous room. Water wept from the rocky walls of a grotto into a dark pool overflowing into a small stream that disappeared into the darkness of the room.

I turned to face the beast, furious.

"I will not bathe in front of you," I said.

"If you will not bathe in front of me, then you will bathe in front of them," he said, inclining his head to the darkness of the room, which was lit by several pairs of red eyes. Awful, raspy laughs followed, and the creatures in the shadow came into the light.

The eyes belonged to several short goblins with long, sharp teeth and taloned fingers. Their hair was long and scraggly, more akin to the roots of an old tree. On their heads were pointed caps, red from blood, which they had let mat their hair and drip down their faces.

I swallowed a scream and scowled at him.

"I would rather die," I said.

"Suit yourself," said the beast with a lazy shrug of his shoulder, and then he vanished, leaving me to face the bloodied creatures. They scowled, red eyes alight and angry as they melded with the dark once more. For a brief moment, I thought they might leave me alone—until one launched a stone at my head.

I managed to dodge it, only to be hit square in the face by another.

Blood gushed from my nose, and I hid my face as more rocks pummeled my body.

"Fine! Fine, you miserable fuck!" I screamed. "I'll bathe in front of you!"

The attack stopped, and when I uncovered my head, I found the elven lord had returned. He stood near, a smug expression on his pretty face.

"I suppose I should have mentioned that the red caps throw stones," he said.

I glared as I rose to my feet and spit blood in his face.

"I hate you."

He did not wipe his face or approach me. Instead, he smiled, wicked and cruel.

"Oh, vicious thing, you do not know hate. Give me time."

I had never felt so murderous and wondered what the consequences were of killing two elven lords. My thoughts were interrupted when another rock flew from the dark. This time, the beast snatched it within his clawlike hand, lobbing it back. A loud crack followed, and one of the red caps fell facedown, blood pooling around its head. Seconds after, taloned hands tugged him back into the shadow while they muttered angry curses.

No more rocks were thrown.

The beast looked at me.

"Bathe. They will not bother you so long as I am here."

"Will they watch?"

"Likely," he said. "But do not worry. They will lust only for your blood, not your body."

I pressed my lips thin and then looked at the pool. It was slightly elevated, accessed only by a set of narrow steps. I considered refusing the bath altogether, but one glance down my front only made me want it more. The mud made it hard to tell just how injured I truly was—not just my ankle but my entire body. Not to mention the blood from my nose was drying on my face and chest.

I approached the pool, eyeing the water. Would a sprite surge from its depths and drown me? Did I really care? It had never occurred to me until now that I had little to fight for beyond myself. What freedom lay beyond these walls but loneliness?

I shrugged off what remained of my nightgown and took the steps slowly, and though I led with my uninjured ankle, keeping weight on the other was near unbearable. I started to kneel, thinking that I might be able to crawl over the edge of the pool, when the beast offered his hand, long nails like sharp blades. Tired and not wishing to injure myself further, I took it. He held my fingers and I slipped into the pool.

The water was not as deep as I had hoped, hitting mid-thigh.

I waded until I was at the center and then turned and held the beast's gaze as I settled into the pool. The water was surprisingly warm, and while it soothed, it also drew attention to how much I ached.

I took a breath, moaning as I exhaled.

"Did my brothers hurt you?" he asked.

He had not taken his eyes off me, and there was a harshness to his face. If I had to guess, he was asking because of the bruises blooming across my body.

"No. Your brothers were not the first unfortunate thing to befall me today…or perhaps that was yesterday."

I did not know the time and I did not explain further—not the curse of the well or even the toad, because none of it mattered. None of it was going to change my present or my future.

The beast did not ask.

"Is this what it means to be your prisoner?" I asked. "To never have a moment of privacy?"

"Do you wish to be stoned to death?"

"Do red caps lurk in every corner of your castle?"

He smirked but did not answer.

"I will give you a moment's peace once you are safely in your room."

"My room?"

"Your cell, your prison," he said. "Call it what you wish, but I assume you understand the importance of staying inside until daybreak?"

I glared.

Night itself was dangerous, but night in the Enchanted Forest was a death wish. When I was younger, foolish boys would dare each other to spend the night in the woods, never to be heard from again no matter how close they stayed to the border.

Sometimes the bodies were found in the daylight, beaten and broken or stripped to the bone. Others were not found at all, and I often wondered if they had been whisked away to another kingdom only to become slaves or concubines to some great fae ruler.

"And after daybreak?"

"You may go wherever you dare, but only when I have no use for you."

I ground my teeth. "What use?"

"Whatever I desire," he said. "You are my prisoner."

"And if I refuse?"

"You will always have a choice," he said.

I knew what he meant by choice. It was either allow him to watch me bathe or be stoned to death.

I studied him for a moment and then fell back into the water. I scrubbed my face and my hair, and when I was finished, I remained below the surface, letting the air escape my mouth until my lungs burned and the water felt heavy, like the walls of an iron coffin.

Hands clamped down on my arms, and I opened my eyes, taking a deep, gasping breath as I broke the surface. The beast glared down at me, eyes shining with acute anger.

"You do not get to leave this world of your own accord," he said, his gaze falling to my lips. "And if you manage it, I will follow you in death and haunt you for all of eternity."

I was confused by his fierce response but had no time to process his anger when he released me. I reached for him as I fell, but there was nothing to hold on to. He had already vanished. I landed on something soft—a bed, I realized as I sat up, still wet and naked.

I scanned the room. It was small, far narrower than it was wide. There was an uncovered window to the left and a hearth to the right, a fire crackling and popping within, making the room almost too warm. I slipped off the bed, and there was soft carpet at my feet. I paused for a moment and then bent to touch it with my hands. I had never felt anything like it. I had only ever known the feel of compacted dirt and the occasional handwoven rug.

If this was to be my cell, it was luxurious.

A tapping sound drew my attention. For one heart-stopping moment, I thought someone was at the window, but when I looked, it was only the trees rattling in the wind, and I could see nothing beyond the thick foliage and the deep night. There was a part of me that was unnerved by the obstruction. I'd have liked to look upon the beast's kingdom. At the same time, I was grateful and hopeful that it meant no one could peer in on me.

With that thought, I crossed to the door and tried the knob, ensuring it was locked, and then dragged a large wooden chest in front of it. I was aware of what the elven lord had not said—while I should not leave this room, he'd never said anything about someone coming in.

With the door barricaded, I returned to the bed and slipped beneath the covers and fell into a deep sleep.

CHAPTER FOUR
Mirror, Mirror

CASAMIR

 he creature in my castle is a seductress. She smells like sweet roses, and she clings to me like the cold despite the fire she's started in my blood. I want her. The need for her runs deep in my veins. It goes beyond soothing the swell of my cock.

In her presence, I can taste *freedom*.

"You will be the death of her."

"Did I summon you?" I asked, turning toward the jagged piece of mirror on my wall. It was one of seven pieces, the other six belonging to my brothers.

I could not see my reflection as I glared at him. He had made his visage dark, which was usual. When the mirror was clear, it meant anyone with another piece could spy. Though it was not as if I minded. My brothers would likely only catch me participating in various lascivious acts.

"You do not have to summon me. I am always watching."

"Charming," I said. "Will you linger while I pleasure myself too?"

"I have little choice. I am only a mirror."

"Suit yourself," I said, reaching for my erection, which strained against the fabric of my trousers. I had no shame, but before I had a chance to touch myself, the mirror spoke.

"Do you really think this mortal will learn your true name?"

I curled my fingers into a fist. "I would not have chosen her for the task if she did not show promise."

"You did not *choose*," the mirror drawled. "Your brothers *sent* her."

"It does not matter how she came to me. She is here. She is flesh and blood. She can set me free."

"*If* she falls in love with you."

"A small detail," I said.

"Small?" the mirror repeated with some surprise. "I would hardly call that detail small."

"I do not wish to speak on it," I said, my voice harsh, and my mood darkened, descending like shadow in the dying dusk.

I knew the mirror was right.

I needed her to love me, but I had waited nearly ten years for someone to come along with enough reason to learn my true name. This creature, she wished to be free, and if she wished hard enough, she might just set me free too.

"Do you truly believe they would send you a clever thing?"

"Perhaps you could tell me," I said. "Do you not exist in six other palaces and know all my brothers' secrets?"

"Five," he said, a reminder that one of my brothers was dead and that someone already had his piece of the enchanted mirror. It had once been whole and hung in our father's hall, but as he neared death, he broke it into seven pieces, one for each of his sons, and declared that whoever put it back together again would be king of the Enchanted Forest. "I only exist with five of your brothers now."

"Which of them managed to snatch Eero's piece?"

"None," said the mirror.

"None?" I asked, arching a brow. "Who has it now?"

"A pretty, petty thing."

"Hmm."

That will make things interesting for the others, I thought.

Especially Silas, who, of all my brothers, desired to be king most. Personally, I did not care for the crown, but I did not wish to give up my mirror either. He was a gateway, a portal to other parts of the Enchanted Forest.

That was the kind of power I wished to keep.

"You do not seem at all concerned," the mirror observed.

"I find it difficult to be concerned with anything beyond myself at this moment."

The mirror did not have expressions, but I could feel his disgust.

"You would think you would worry more about your life than your cock."

"I was talking about my life," I snapped. "But thank you for reminding me of my intention to fuck myself."

"To the image of your brother's murderer?" the mirror asked.

"Yes," I hissed.

I would have thanked her for it had I not wished to tangle her in my web.

Eero might be my brother, but blood meant nothing unless it was spilled in the Enchanted Forest, and at that point, it was currency.

Good fucking riddance, I thought, though it was not as if he would not be born again as all fae were. He'd likely crawl from the bell of a foxglove, as poisonous as ever.

Thinking of my brother darkened my mood.

"Show me the woman," I commanded, wishing to rekindle the desire that had inflamed my veins.

The mirror brightened, and now I looked on the vicious creature who had disturbed my night. She lay on her back, her arms splayed. She looked pale, even with the warmth of the fire igniting her limbs, though it did make her blond hair look ablaze.

I clenched my jaw, frustrated at how easily she slumbered, not at all caught in the throes of arousal like me.

Cruel creature.

It made me doubt she could love me at all, doubt that she could end this curse bestowed on me by the Glass Mountains.

"I need her to love me," I said.

"Love is learned," said the mirror. "Has it ever occurred to you that is the lesson the Glass Mountains hoped to teach you when they cursed you?"

I knew what the mountains were doing, but it was no lesson.

It was vengeance.

The Glass Mountains were a source of life within the Enchanted Forest, and they called the beings that sprang from their depths their *offspring*. What was born of them was immortal and moral.

I was immortal and immoral, born from the earth, and after I mixed my blood with one of their own, the Mountains cursed me to forget my true name unless it was spoken by my *one true love*.

That was nine years and three weeks ago.

I had one more week until I forgot my true name forever—until everyone forgot.

And if my name was forgotten, *I* was forgotten.

A name precedes you, and without one, you are nothing.

It was the truth of our world.

"A fool's errand," I said even as I stood before the mirror, aching and yearning for this creature in a way I had never before.

"For a foolish prince," said the mirror.

I might have reacted to his comment had the creature not rolled to her side. I was given a view of the dark bruises blooming across her back, reminding me that she had come to me injured.

My brothers were despicable creatures, but they would not have harmed her…physically at least.

My head became hot with rage.

"Show me who hurt her," I said, and the mirror rippled. My creature vanished and a man came into view. He was in bed, hovering over a woman, thrusting into her. She writhed beneath him, moaning in false pleasure.

I wondered why he had hurt my creature and if he had thought long it.

I drew nearer, pressing a clawed finger to the vision, anger gnashing my teeth.

"Fragile man," I growled. "I will break you."

The image went dark, and my reflection peered back at me, fierce and feral. The mirror laughed.

"Your lust is making you reckless."

"It is not reckless to make a mortal swallow his cock for hurting a woman," I said, and a slow grin spread across my face as I imagined the horror and pain that would contort the man's face. "It is…satisfying."

"You cannot curse anyone while you are cursed," said the mirror.

As if I had forgotten.

"I can be patient," I said.

I would take great pleasure in wounding the man who had wounded her—if she helped me end this cruel curse.

"You will be the death of her," the mirror said again.

"You are not a mirror of prophecy."

"I am a mirror of truth," he said.

I turned and crossed to my bed, and as I rested on the coverlet and took my aching length in hand, I thought of the creature and her rose-smelling hair and recalled how she fit against me. I pumped my hand faster, a little harder, until my head teemed with fantasies about how I would fuck her when she finally gave in.

"She will live. Long enough to speak my name," I said between clenched teeth just before I came.

I waited for sleep to take hold, but instead of my limbs growing heavy and my eyes sliding shut, my muscles grew tight, and my body filled with blood as if I had not found release at all.

"No." I sat up.

Vicious creature.

Vicious brothers.

They had sent me a siren.

CHAPTER FIVE
The Selkie

GESELA

 hen I woke up the next morning, my head ached and my mouth was dry. Blindly, I reached for the water I usually kept at my bedside, but instead of finding the handle of my mug, I touched something cold and slimy.

A scream tore from my throat, and I sat up to a chorus of snickers. My hand was covered in mucus, the table beside my bed crawling with slugs.

I was not home but in the palace of an elven prince, and there was a troupe of tiny pixies in my room. They hovered, wings vibrating. Some were naked while others wore tattered and dirty clothing.

I threw a pillow at them as I scrambled out of my bed, relieved my ankle bore little pain as I put pressure on my foot.

"If I get my hands on any of you, I will pluck your wings from your bodies and wear them as a crown!"

They laughed merrily, zipping close to my face as they scattered, flying out a crack in the window I had not noticed the night before. I glared after them and the door clicked open. My gaze shifted to the beast who filled the doorway.

For a moment, I was shocked that he was able to enter. I had pushed a chest in front of the doors last night, except now I found that it had been moved.

I gritted my teeth.

Those pixies would pay if I caught them in my room again.

The elven king looked cold and pale, his eyes severe and his mouth tight.

I could feel his disgust, and yet his gaze raked over my bare body.

"Picking fights?" he asked as his eyes met mine.

I started to respond when a short, stout brownie pushed her way into the room, grumbling as she went. Her ears were pointed and large, hanging off the sides of her face as if they were too heavy for her head. She wore a brown dress and a stained white apron.

I reached for the blanket on the bed and held it to myself.

The beast smirked.

"This is Naeve," he said. "She will help you prepare for the day."

"Prepare for the day?"

"You are welcome to remain as you are," he said, his eyes appraising. "Though I must admit, I quite like being the only one to see you like this."

"How do you know you are the only one?"

The beast narrowed his eyes.

"He isn't," said the brownie, who stood at my feet and ripped the blanket away. I rolled my fingers into fists and growled at her as she made her way around me, her eyes assessing, but in a different way than the elven prince, who had taken a seat across the room, reclining comfortably, obviously intent on watching me *prepare for the day*, whatever that meant.

Once Naeve had made several rounds at my feet, she walked to the wooden wardrobe and knocked twice. One of the doors flew open, and a small creature poked its head out.

Naeve spoke to it in a language I did not understand. It was fast and so harsh, I thought they might be fighting. The small creature turned its attention to me for a moment. It had large round eyes that were set close and deep and a long, crooked nose that stuck out over a wide mouth.

It blinked at me, eyes shining incandescently, and then disappeared into the wardrobe, slamming the door. I took that to mean whatever Naeve had asked was unceremoniously rejected, but the brownie was not deterred. She crossed to a mirrored vanity, climbing onto the cushioned seat and the tabletop. Then she turned and pointed at the bench.

"Sit!"

I hesitated, gaze shifting between the beast and the brownie. When I did not move, Naeve kicked a small bowl of powder off the vanity.

"Sit!"

The prince laughed.

"Forgive her," he said, and at first, I thought he was talking to me, but I noticed that he was looking at Naeve as he continued. "She is a bit dull."

Naeve snickered and I scowled.

"I can take care of myself."

"Are you saying you asked me to watch you bathe because you wanted me to and not because you feared the red caps?"

"I hate you," I seethed, holding his gaze as I sat for Naeve, wondering what more I had to fear from the brownie or the creatures in my wardrobe.

His grin was menacing, and I ground my teeth, keeping

them clenched as the brownie began to pull and twist strands of my hair. The beast watched, and for a brief moment, a harsh intensity returned to his face. I had no chance to study it or to think long on what had sparked it when he turned away, wandering toward the window from which the pixies had escaped.

"Must you remain?" I asked.

"Must you speak?" he returned.

"I suppose not, but then I would never utter your true name."

His jaw ticked. That was the only indication I had that my words affected him. He continued to stare out the window while I sat naked and Naeve plaited my hair. As soon as she finished, the doors to the wardrobe burst open, and a ball of fabric came flying toward me, landing on my head.

"Dress!" Naeve ordered.

I pulled the cloth off my head, a perpetual scowl on my face. I held up the fabric to find that the creatures in the closet had made a dress. The top was white and billowy, the skirt pale green, overlain with sheer white fabric. When I glance over at the prince, his back was still turned to me, so I stepped into the dress and reached behind to button up the back but found I could only clasp a few on my own.

I turned to look for Naeve, but she was gone.

Then I felt warm fingers take over, and I stiffened as the prince fastened my dress. Once he was finished, I turned to face him. He stared down at me and spoke, giving me no time to react to his intrusion.

"You are permitted to wander within my castle and my grounds, but go beyond the wall, and you may become another person's prisoner."

"Is there anyone worse than you?" I asked.

The beast lifted his hand and caressed the side of my face.

"Vicious creature, there is always something worse."

I held my breath beneath his touch, and when his hand fell away, the tension returned to my body.

"You will call me Casamir," he said. "It is my mortal name."

"I prefer beast," I said, suddenly aware of how much I had to crane my neck just to meet his gaze at this proximity.

His lips quirked and his hand snaked behind my neck and into my hair, fingers grazing my scalp. He had moved fast, and once he was close, my body warmed against his.

"Call me beast again," he said, his lips hovering over mine, "and I'll show you why I was given that name."

I could not help it. His threat provoked me, and a slow smile spread across my face.

"Beast," I whispered, and the prince's hand caught my throat. The black of his irises leaked into the whites of his eyes. He pushed me until I met the edge of the vanity, his hips pressed between my thighs.

I reached for his arm, but as I did, black tendrils rose from his skin and wrapped around my hands, becoming solid like the spindly branches of a bodark tree. They crawled over me, around my shoulders and down my back, wrapping around my waist. At the same time, another set of vines trailed up my legs, curling around my thighs, inching closer to the part of me that had ached for him last night. Even now, my body grew heavy and warm, wet for this cruel creature.

"Do not test me, vicious creature. I will swallow you whole."

I believed he could.

I wished he would.

We stared at each other for a long moment, and I felt like a spider caught in a web as the elven prince drew nearer. His free hand moved down the side of my body before gathering my skirt. I shivered as the fabric rose, exposing my leg, and when his hand landed high on my bare hip, my breath caught in my throat.

He never looked away from me, his eyes still drowning in black, his mouth hovering close to mine. I would be lying if I did not admit how desperately I wanted to know the feel of his lips against mine.

"Say my name," he said, the words a slow command. "My mortal name."

Silence spread between us, and his fingers were close to my heat, with the palm of his hand pressed flat against my ass. My heart beat fast in my chest like fluttering fairy wings, and my muscles grew taut. If I said his name, would he touch me instead of teasing me?

"What will you give me?" I asked.

He reared back only a fraction, as if realizing he had shown too much surprise. He studied me, eyes narrowed, before the corner of his lip curled.

"What do you desire?"

As if he thought he could guess, his fingers pressed harder into my skin.

"A number," I said.

His brows lowered, confused. "A number?"

"How many letters are in your true name?"

He stared and I could tell he was displeased with me. Had he hoped I might ask for his touch? I doubted he mourned that I hadn't, more that I had not fallen for his seduction.

"Tricky creature," he said, and this time, his fingers pressed against my throat, his lips grazing across my lower jaw to my ear where he whispered, "Seven."

As he pulled back, his fiery eyes met mine. He loosened his hold on my neck, and the blood that had built in my head rushed away. I was dizzy and far more desperate than before to feel him inside me.

"Are you lying?" I asked, breathless.

Seven brothers. Seven years. Seven letters.

"I cannot lie," he said, and I knew that was true.

I started at him and then his mouth.

"I am waiting, vicious creature."

I stared at him a moment longer, searching his endless eyes, tracing his high cheekbones and arrogant smile. I leaned up and I could feel his breath on my lips. I wanted to taste his mouth, suck his tongue like a sweet sugarplum. I wanted him to writhe against me.

"Casamir."

I hadn't had any idea how his name would sound when it escaped my mouth, but it was so wrapped up in my desperate emotions, it sounded like a plea. There was a part of me that hoped it would work like a spell and break his control.

But he did not shiver or swallow. He did not press into me or tighten his hold.

He did lean in, and he moved his hand from my neck before pressing his lips to my throat, speaking in a hushed tone.

"Come when I call, sweet one."

Then he vanished.

I remained against the vanity, mind scrambling to make sense of what had just transpired between me and the elven prince. My heart was still racing, and I could feel his phantom hands and the vines against my skin.

I should not have been surprised by his power. He had used it on my ax when thorns had sprouted from the handle and later when he tripped me as I fled into the enchanted night. But was that the power that made him a beast? Or was it something else entirely?

My gaze shifted as I caught movement from the window. The pixies I had chased from my room were gathered there, faces pressed against the glass.

I scowled and marched toward them, snatching the pillow from the floor I had thrown earlier and launching it at them. I knew it would do no good—they were on the other side of the glass—but it felt good to throw something.

The pillow landed with a soft plop and fell to the floor. The pixies giggled and flew off. I wondered what they had seen and who they might tell. Though it was more likely they just perceived me as another stupid mortal who had fallen for a pretty elven prince.

My gaze fell and I noticed that the broken window that had allowed the pixies entrance to my room was now mended, and while I'd have liked to feel a sense of gratitude toward the prince for the fix, dread filled my stomach like a bitter poison.

Elves did no favors.

What more did I owe the Prince of Thorns?

I left my room with some hesitation, uncertain of what I would find on the other side. I wanted to bring my ax, but the handle was still covered in thorns and impossible to hold. Even without a weapon, I did not wish to remain indoors. It was not in my nature, even when I resided in my cottage on the edge of the forest, even hating that whatever lurked between her branches watched. Worse, what would watch me within the beast's—*Casamir's*—realm?

My door opened to a stone hallway, the walls of which were covered in vines that flowered as I walked by.

Charming, I thought, except that the vines had thorns and they were red-tipped, as if each had pricked a person and drawn blood, and the flowers, which were white and pink and bell-shaped, were poisonous to the touch—a virtual death trap.

I followed them, careful not to knock into the wall. The hallway curved to the right, and I found myself on a portico lined with stone columns, wrapped in the same flowering vines. Beyond was a sprawling garden full of greenery and colorful flora. All around, rising jagged and sharp, were the tall and spindly spires of Casamir's castle, caging me like the bars of a cell.

Above, the sky was blue but heavy with white clouds that were so low, I felt as though I could reach and touch them.

It was truly beautiful here.

It had been a long while since I had looked upon anything and thought it was beautiful. It was a mark of how my life had changed, not because of Casamir or the five elven princes or even the toad in the well—all of that had been inevitable. My life had changed because I had come to know death at a young age, first when he took my mother and then when he took my sister and eventually my father.

Sometimes I would yell at him in the middle of the night.

You are selfish to have left me alone!

Ah, young one, he would reply. *It was not me who took your mother or your sister or your father. You killed your mother, you wished your sister dead, and your actions stole your father's last breath.*

He was not wrong, and when I questioned what I had done to deserve this loneliness, I remembered that I had made a terrible wish.

I hated that this place made me think of my family, and I ground my teeth against the feelings rising inside me, the strange cloudiness in my chest, the pinprick of tears in my eyes. I stepped out from the cover of the portico and into the garden.

A soft breeze caught my skirt, and it fluttered around me. I held on to handfuls of the flowy fabric to keep it from tangling in nearby brambles. As I wandered farther into the garden, it seemed to grow larger, full, taller, until it was all-consuming, and I could no longer see low-hanging clouds or even the pointed spires of Casamir's castle. The path I had followed had long disappeared, overgrown with foliage, though it still remained before me. I wondered if this was Casamir's magic or the magic of the Enchanted Forest? Were they one and the same?

I knew little about magic except that it was cruel.

As I continued, I was careful not to touch anything or look too long at a beautiful flower for fear it would hypnotize me and lead me to some cruel fate. I might not have anything to live for, but I did not wish to die here among the fae. The path I was on led straight to a murky pond. It was surrounded by tall blades of grass and flowering trees, the petals of which were scattered across the surface of the water, which was dark in color and crowded with star-shaped blossoms, but none of that drew my attention like the naked man sitting at the center of the pond on a rock.

He was a selkie, a shape-shifting fae. Their natural form was that of a seal, and it was a skin they could shed so they could walk on land as a human. The sealskin was valuable, as it was the only way the fae could return to their true form and their true home, the sea.

This selkie was far from home and careless to my presence, sitting with his hands slightly behind him, head turned toward the sky, allowing the sun to bathe his bare body in golden light. His hair was brown, tousled by the wind, and his skin was bronzed, reddening more as each second passed beneath its rays. His muscles were hard, and so was his cock, which he made no effort to conceal.

He spoke in a singsong voice, and the words made my skin prick with unease.

> *"There is nothing more sweet than a maiden's call for me;*
> *Body full of blood, a desperate heartbeat.*
> *Warmed with lust, she comes to me frantic for release*
> *And when that cloying death cry leaves her lips,*
> *She breathes no more for me."*

The words were a hypnotic spell, a weapon selkies used to lure their prey. I could feel it clouding my mind, and a strange lust tore straight down my chest like a knife, cutting me to the core. I fell to my knees, gnashing my teeth, digging frantically into the dirt and pressing the clay into my ears until the lyrics of the selkie's song were nothing more than a quiet mumble.

The lust dissipated and my body relaxed. I was disturbed by this creature's magic. I remained on my hands and knees feeling unsettled. For a split second, I had lost control of myself, and it had not been a choice. The realization shook my entire body, and I was struck by how this contrasted so violently with how I felt when I was near Casamir.

At least my reaction to him was genuine, no matter how much I hated it. I was attracted to Casamir, and that was all it took to desire him.

The selkie, though, was a predator.

My heart still pounded in my chest, frenzied from the fae's eerie song.

I gathered stones before rising to my feet, intending to use them as a weapon, but the selkie was no longer lounging on the rock. I scanned the pond for any sign of movement, but the water was still.

"Hmm, what do we have here?"

The voice came from behind me, and while it was muted, I could still make out the words. I twisted too fast and fell, a scream bubbling up from my throat. As soon as I landed, the selkie straddled me. He had round eyes that seemed to shift from blue to green like the waves of the sea. His hair was wet, weighed down and dripping.

"Who are you, young maiden?" he asked.

I lifted my knee, shoving it hard into his balls. The creature fell onto the ground, and I found myself astride him, lifting my rock-filled hands over my head, readying to strike him in the face until his teeth were broken and he choked on his own blood, but then I noticed the skin of a seal lying near and snatched it from the ground.

I stumbled back with the selkie's skin in hand, and when he saw that I had it, his eyes grew wide.

"No, please! Give it back!"

I grinned and held one of the rocks to it.

The selkie need not know it wasn't sharp.

"Is this important to you?"

"You know it is important, you terrible thing!" he shrieked, spittle flying from his mouth. He managed to rise to his hands and knees.

"You are right," I said. "You cannot return to your true form without it, can you? What a shame it would be if it was cut to ribbons."

"What do you want, terrible thing? I will give you anything!"

It was the promise I sought, but before I could speak, something hit my cheek. The impact felt like a sting. I pressed my palm to my face and drew it away to find blood. My eyes shifted to find something floating before me—a small creature with wings, a sprite.

It was dressed in the petals of a pink rose that was spattered with my blood.

The sprite charged at my face, and I swatted at it, but suddenly there was a great swarm of them, and all I could do was cover my face as they cut and kicked and bit.

I stumbled back and fell into the pond with the sealskin still clutched in my hand, unwilling to let it go even as someone attempted to yank it away.

The jerk brought me to the surface of the water, where I came face-to-face with the selkie again.

"Whatever you want," he repeated, another promise. "Just give it back."

"If you are lying to me, I will stalk you for the rest of your life. You will never bask in the sun. You will never step on land without fearing me. I will hunt you until I flay you alive and burn this skin before your eyes. Do you understand?"

The selkie glared at me for a moment, and then his lips spread into a wide grin.

"I like you," he said. "I give you my word, terrible creature. I will give you your greatest desire."

I released his skin, and he hugged it to his body. I instantly regretted letting my one weapon go, but he did not slither away into his swamp like I had expected.

"Clean your ears, terrible thing," he said. "And tell me what you desire."

I watched him, mistrusting.

"Do you doubt my word, thing?" he asked, irritation flaring in his eyes.

I held my nose as I dropped below the murky water, twisting my finger into my ears to dislodge the mud. I resurfaced as quickly as I could, thinking that the selkie would flee, but once again, he proved true to his word and remained where he was in the water.

"There now," he said. "All better?"

"I need your prince's true name," I said.

"He is not my prince," said the selkie. "And that is not your greatest desire."

"You said you would give me what I desire," I said. "I desire to know the prince's true name."

"I said I would give you your greatest desire," he said. "There is a difference."

We stared at each other. I wanted to accuse the selkie of lying, but I realized this was my error. I had not been careful enough in the wording of our bargain. Did the selkie know what I truly desired, or could he merely sense that I was lying? Terror filled me as I realized I had unintentionally given him power over me.

"What do you call the prince?" I asked.

"We call him many names," he said. "The Thorn Prince, Prince of Thorns, Dreadful King, Shadow King. Some call him by his mortal name, Casamir, but those who do are very few."

"Why few?"

He shrugged. "A name precedes you, and without one, you are nothing."

"Then why go by a name that is not his own?"

"All fae go by names that are not theirs," he said. "True names are for lovers. True names are for death."

"Why only lovers and death?"

"A true name is a gift to the lover and a token to death."

"How do I find a true name?"

"The prince must tell you," he said.

"The prince will not tell me," I said.

That would mean he willingly set me free, and I doubted his generosity unless it involved frustrating me and an abundance of thorns.

"He will tell you if he loves you."

"You have lived too long in this swamp of a pond if you think the prince will ever love me."

The selkie grinned, chuckling under his breath.

"I do not believe you, terrible thing."

"I lost my ability to love a long time ago," I said. "I do not want it back."

"Perhaps you don't," he said. "And yet you still wish to be loved."

The blood drained from my face.

"I have no *desire* to discuss this," I hissed. "I need Casamir's true name."

The selkie studied me for a moment and then offered, "The mountains may know."

"The mountains?"

"The elven lords are old. It is likely no one knows their true name, save that which came before them—the earth and the Glass Mountains."

I frowned.

"The Glass Mountains are outside Prince Casamir's realm."

"So they are," said the selkie.

"I cannot go beyond the wall," I said.

Though I had said otherwise, I believed there were far worse creatures outside the his realm.

"Even if I managed it, I could not return in a day. He would notice I was gone."

And then what? I wondered.

Would the Enchanted Forest reprimand me? Or perhaps Casamir's five brothers?

"Perhaps you should fly," the selkie suggested unhelpfully.

"I cannot fly."

"Come back tomorrow," said the selkie. "And I will give you wings."

I hesitated.

"What would you ask for in return?"

"For now? Your smile," he said. "But one day when you rule this castle, you will return me to the sea."

CHAPTER SIX
Pity a Fool

CASAMIR

 watched my creature leave the garden, her dress wet and clinging to her form like a second skin. There was a rage within me that the flowers and trees and the fairies and the selkie had seen her in such a state. My fingers curled into fists at my side.

"What are you sulking about?" Naeve demanded, hopping onto the bench beneath the window to peer out. When she saw my creature, she grinned wickedly, showing her crooked teeth. "Fancy her, eh?"

"I do not *fancy* her," I snapped, and yet I thought of how she must have gotten wet and knew the selkie had seen her. Had he seduced her with his horrible song?

"Is that why you begged her to speak your name?" Naeve asked.

The mirror choked, suppressing a laugh. I glared at the two.

"I *need* her to love me," I said again, just as I had last night, though I could not shake this feeling. It was sort of like dread, sort of like fear. What if she fell in love with someone else?

"And how will you make her love you?" asked Naeve. "She hates you."

I glowered. I knew that well enough, but perhaps with enough coaxing…

"Lust is not the same as love," said the mirror.

"I know the difference," I seethed.

The brownie raised a brow at me, and though the mirror had no expression, I knew it did the same.

"Who says she cannot lust for me and love me?"

Naeve exchanged a look with the mirror.

"Love is learned," said the mirror.

"You keep saying that, and yet no one has learned to love me," I said.

"And you have learned to love no one," said Naeve.

"She can learn to love me while she lusts," I said and turned back to the window, hating the disappointment that dropped into the pit of my stomach when I no longer saw my creature below.

"You will have to do more than fuck her if you want her to love you," said Naeve.

I spun to face her, no longer interested in the view.

"What do you know about love?"

The brownie glared back, a scowl on her face. "You expect true and devoted love from this woman, and yet you do not plan to give in return? What part about 'she hates you' do you not understand? You will have to woo her, and you have done a pitiful job of that thus far."

"She has been here for less than a day," I snapped.

"Precious time when you only have six days," said the brownie.

"Have you ever wooed anyone, Naeve?" I asked. She crossed her arms over her chest and lifted her brow at me. "And you, Mirror?"

His silence was telling.

"Then why would I listen to either of *you*?"

"The Mountains are trying to teach you a lesson," Naeve said.

I know! I wanted to scream so loud the Mountains would hear my rage, but I did not wish to give them the satisfaction of my frustration.

"What good is a lesson born from spite?"

"If you learn it, then it is revenge," said Naeve. "And you will know true love."

"True love," I snarled. "Who needs it?"

"You do, idiot," said Naeve, who jumped from her place on the bench and left my chamber. I had a feeling that if the mirror could leave, he would too.

"She is right, you know," said the mirror.

"No one asked you!"

"You posed the question. She answered it."

"It was hypothetical!" I yelled, throwing my hands in the air.

I started to pace. My body was tense, and I was frustrated. I had been frustrated since that creature had arrived in my room on her knees. This was her fault. I would not feel this way if she had never come. I would not have *hope*.

I hated hope.

I stopped pacing with my back to the mirror and began to ask, "How do I…"

I stopped abruptly.

This was ridiculous. I was an elven prince. Hundreds of women had fallen in love with me. Why was this one different?

"Were you about to ask me how to woo a woman?"

"*No*," I snapped, folding my arms over my chest. I hated the embarrassment I felt and how it warmed my cheeks.

"I am a mirror."

"I *know* you are a mirror," I said. His meaning was twofold. He had never wooed a woman, and he also knew the truth behind my question. Yet I could not bring myself to ask it. "I know you watch my brothers."

"Your brothers are no more knowledgeable about love than you are," he said.

"Lore is in love," I said.

"With a mortal who does not know he exists," said the mirror.

"Cardic is charming," I said.

"Yes, and he uses his charms to bed women."

"But do they fall in love with him?"

"They usually end up hating him," said the mirror.

I frowned as I considered my other brothers, but none of them had managed to fall in love. Not even our father had loved our mother. Their union was one of convenience, and while they produced heirs, they had other lovers. Had they loved them?

"Perhaps you should ask someone who is actually in love," the mirror suggested. "Like the mortal prince you imprisoned for stealing a rose from your garden."

"I doubt he will help me."

The prince, whose name I did not know, had come from a mortal kingdom. He had hoped to scale the Glass Mountains and return to his kingdom with a golden apple, which grew inside the mountains. On his way, he stopped, climbed my walls, and plucked a flower from my earth for his princess. I kept him captive even after he begged to be set free to return to his betrothed.

"There's no harm in asking."

"There is always harm in asking."

Besides, I did not fancy being vulnerable to the mortal prince.

"It seems to me there is more harm if you do not."

"I hate you," I said, though I knew the mirror—and even Naeve—were right. I needed this woman to fall in love with me, and I was running out of time.

Which was how I found myself in the depths of my castle in search of the prince who had stolen a rose for his beloved. When I found him, he was resting on the stone floor, one knee drawn up. His head was turned to the window, which was shaped like half a moon and barred. Just on the other side, flower fairies had gathered to look upon him, but when they beheld me, they scattered in a flurry of wings and loose petals.

The prince turned his head lazily to me.

He had not been long in this world, his face youthful and full. He was as I expected all mortal prince's to be: flamboyant and arrogant. He had all the belief that the title he held outside the Enchanted Forest meant something to those of us who lived within.

But here, he was nothing but fuel to feed spells and fill stomachs.

He wore purple velvet and a hat that crushed his golden curls, and in the hat was a long, red feather.

"My captor arrives," he said.

"I hope you are not making bargains," I said. "The fae can be cruel."

"No crueler than you," he said.

"There is always someone crueler," I said.

The prince was quiet, so I spoke.

"Will you not beg me to set you free again?"

The prince smiled. "No, because that is what you want."

"It is not what I want," I said, frustrated that this mortal would even venture to guess my desires.

"Then what do you want?" he asked.

My eyes narrowed on the young prince, and I felt my body

fill up with anger. He seemed to sense the danger, because he tensed.

"You are not to ask questions of me, mortal prince," I said. "I require your aid, and in exchange, I will grant your greatest desire."

"My greatest desire?" he repeated, his eyes gleaming.

"*Only* if your advice produces the results *I* desire," I added. I would set him free for nothing less.

"And what do you desire?" he asked.

I ground my teeth back and forth, not wishing to speak it aloud, but even as I stood here and thought about my true name, I had trouble recalling how it was spelled.

Seven letters, I reminded myself.

Your name knows no stranger.

Your name is the wail on the lips of a birthing mother.

Your name is the howl from the mouth of a grieving lover.

It is the cry that breaks the night when death is summoned.

"My desire is to make a maiden fall in love with me."

My nails cut into my palms as I waited for the prince to laugh, but all he said was, "She did not fall in love with you at first sight?"

"No," I gritted out.

She tried to bury an ax in my chest.

"Is that even real?" I asked.

"Of course it is," said the prince, who paused to think. "Perhaps she is not attracted to you."

"She *is* attracted to me," I snapped. I knew it. I could feel it in the air between us. The problem was that she also hated me.

The prince did not look so certain. I reached forward, wrapping my hands around the bars of his cell, and his eyes grew wide at the length of my claws.

"I asked you to tell me how to make her fall in love with me," I said. "Is your beloved princess not in love with you?"

"Of course she is," he said, as defensive as I felt.

"Then what made her love you?"

He thought for a moment and then said, "Have you told her she is beautiful?"

I blinked, slow.

"No."

"Well, is she beautiful?"

"Yes," I hissed.

She was more than beautiful, more beautiful than I cared to admit.

I thought of how she had looked at me upon her arrival, the shock that had come across her face, the fierceness that had taken over when she decided to fight me.

"Then you should tell her. All women want to hear they are beautiful."

I tried to imagine my creature melting into my arms at the sound of those words, but my mind only conjured an angry snarl.

"You are certain that will work?" I asked.

"If she does not fall in love with you immediately, it shall be a start."

My heart felt split in two. There was a side of it that rose with hope at the thought of having her love, and there was a side of it that felt completely ridiculous and would rather forget my name.

"If you are wrong," I warned, leaning closer so the prince could see my face between the bars of the cell. He paled and pressed against the stone wall, not as aloof as he appeared. "I shall cut the curls from your golden head."

With that, I left the prison to summon my creature.

CHAPTER SEVEN
The Fairy Ring

GESELA

 nce I returned to my room, I stripped off my wet clothes and opened the wardrobe only to have the door slam closed. I tried it again, and this time it wouldn't budge, as if it had been locked.

"Open this door!" I said as I pulled on the handle. "I need clothes!"

The door flew open, and I fell onto my back. A piece of cloth landed on my head. The door shut again, and I pulled the fabric off to find they had thrown a thin, sheer robe.

"This can hardly be considered clothes!" I yelled and shifted onto my knees, banging on the wardrobe, but there was no response from the creatures in the closet. I growled as I stood and slipped on the robe, laughing at its ridiculous coverage.

I crossed to the window and looked out, though the glass was mostly obscured by curling vines and golden-green trees. I could just make out the glistening peaks of the Glass Mountains, their jagged edges sitting on the horizon like ominous waves.

They were the mountains kings challenged suitors to scale, knowing no one ventured there and returned, and yet I was willing to go and learn the name of my captor—or at least attempt it—but dying out there was the same as dying here.

"I hate this place," I muttered, wrapping my arms around myself.

I turned to the bed and pulled back the covers, half-afraid I would find something slimy, courtesy of the pixies. While Casamir had fixed the broken window, I had no doubts they could find their way back in. But my sheets were clean, and I practically fell into the bed, curling onto my side.

For a few moments, I lay there, fighting tears stinging my eyes. At this point, I was not even certain what or who exactly I was crying for—my mother, my father, my sister, or myself.

Perhaps I only cried because everything in my life felt so unfair.

But the world did not care about fairness.

It rewarded those who already had, like Sheriff Roland, who believed he was entitled to anything and anyone as if it were his right by birth.

Casamir was no different, and I found myself at the mercy of both.

I buried my face in my pillow, eyes heavy, and drifted off to sleep, only to be woken suddenly by a loud knock at the door. Sitting up, I stared blankly at the door, heart hammering in my chest as the sound continued, rattling my bones. I felt as though I had just fallen asleep. My eyes were like jelly, and my body was damp with sweat.

"Yes?" I shouted groggily.

"Prince Casamir has summoned you," said the voice on the other side.

I did not recognize it as Naeve's raspy shout and did not respond. I groaned and fell back into bed, wondering what the prince would do if I did not come when he called.

Did I wish to find out?

I rose from the bed and knocked on the doors to the armoire. "Hello?" I called. "I need to dress for dinner!"

There was no response.

I tried the doors but they still seemed to be locked. My knocking went unanswered.

Growling, I turned, catching my reflection in the now-darkened window. I would not leave this room dressed only in this robe, and I certainly wouldn't attend dinner with Casamir like this, not after the encounters I'd had with him since I arrived at his palace. So I returned to bed.

It did not take long for my eyes to grow heavy again, and just as sleep was about to take me, the door to my room burst open.

Casamir stood in the doorway, his dark and regal presence filling the room like night.

He was stunning.

Like all elven princes, I reminded myself, but there was something about this one. I had not felt so attracted to the others.

He was different, though I did not know why or how. Perhaps it had something to do with his eyes, which were swallowed by pools of black, or his full lips, which were frustratingly pressed together. Whatever it was, my body *knew* when he was near and burned with a desire so keen, I found myself pressing my thighs together to suppress it.

"Did I not say come when I call?"

I narrowed my eyes. "Your creatures would not dress me."

"I do not care," he said, moving farther into the room until he stood at the foot of my bed menacingly, hands braced against the footboard. "Come as you are. Come when I call."

I glared at him and then shoved off my blankets and the bed, standing before him.

His eyes darkened as they roved over my body, veiled only in the shimmering, sheer robe his people had provided, and despite what he had said, I knew I would have seen something angry and possessive behind his eyes if I had shown up to dinner like this.

Without a word, he crossed to the wardrobe and beat on the door. When the fae answered, it was with a vicious expression until they saw Casamir, at which point they blanched.

"A gown for my guest. *Now*."

They slammed the door and returned in seconds with a neatly folded swath of sparkling blue fabric.

As the elven prince took it, he commanded,

"Give her what she asks for or you will live no longer behind these doors."

The threat shook their tiny spines, and as the door shut, Casamir gave me the dress.

"Change."

I took it and stared.

"Will you stand and watch?"

"Why do you ask such questions when I have watched you bathe and dress before?"

"These are the actions of a lover, which you are not."

"I could be your lover," he said.

The comment was delivered so softly, it stunned me into silence. For a moment, I could only stare, and when I recovered, I cleared my throat and attempted a sharp reply.

"I would have to like you."

"Who says there must be like? There is passion and pleasure in hate."

I was not sure why it mattered to me, but somehow, I did not wish to give him the satisfaction of watching me. Perhaps

I wanted it to feel like a punishment…like rejection. I turned from him and shed the robe, then stepped into the dress. As I slipped the sleeves on my shoulders, Casamir's hands were on the laces, pulling and tightening. I shivered as his fingers brushed against me.

The ease and intimacy of his actions burned my skin, and yet I did not dissuade him. I told myself it was because lacing my dress would be too difficult on my own and not because I had desired his touch from the moment he walked into the room.

"Do you help all your guests dress?" I asked, and while I managed to keep my voice light, I was surprised by how much jealousy wished to seep through.

"You are not a guest," he said.

I pondered asking him what he considered me—a prisoner, a curse, a thorn in his side—but kept quiet, and once he was finished tying the laces, I turned to face him. He offered his hand, and when I did not take it, his features grew hard.

"You have delayed my evening long enough," he said.

"What power you have given me," I said, amused.

He bared his teeth. "I am voracious," he said. "I shall feast tonight. Whether on food or on you, the choice is yours."

"I will hardly quell your appetite."

"Oh, sweet thing, I think you will."

The way he spoke was not lost on me, as if he and I were an inexorable truth.

I took his hand and let him lead me from my room, and as we passed into the hall that led to the portico, I could not help staying close to him to keep distance between me and the wall of thorned vines.

He glanced at me. "Afraid of my flowers?"

"Mistrusting," I corrected. "As with all things fae."

"But you are fae."

The urge to tell him to stop saying that clawed up my throat, but I did not speak, fearing if I did, he would torture me with those words.

We were quiet for only a beat, and then he spoke. "You spent time in my garden."

It was as if he were making an observation, and then I wondered if he had been watching me. Had he heard me speak with the selkie?

I glanced at him. "Is that a question?"

"Did you enjoy it?"

"Enjoy is not a word I would use to describe anything I have experienced here thus far."

I glanced at Casamir, noticing how his jaw popped as he ground his teeth.

"Why do I doubt you have enjoyed anything in your life thus far?"

I jerked my hand away from him and curled my fingers into fists as they hung at my sides.

We did not speak, and as we entered an unfamiliar part of Casamir's castle, I stayed one step behind, allowing him to lead. I hated how I now wished I had the warmth of his hand in mine. It was anchoring in this unfamiliar place, but I refused to reach for him and buried that want.

I needed no one.

Life had taught me that. Why else would it take away everyone who loved me?

We passed down a corridor, one side open to the night, and while I had watched it suspiciously before, I was suddenly distracted by the beauty of the vaulted ceiling, which was divided into sections by molding, detailed with vines and roses. The ceiling itself was painted blue, deep like the sky on a cold winter morning.

The hall opened into a dining room, which was dark, save

for a few burning candles. A long banquet table ran down the center of the room, packed with tall candelabras, bouquets of weeping flowers, and platters of food. The smell of roasted goose curled into my nose and made my stomach roar with hunger.

"Where is your court?" I asked as Casamir made his way to the head of the table, noting that we were alone.

"Here and there," he answered as he sat. "Perhaps we will join them after you have eaten."

A trickle of unease shook my spine. I did not fancy an evening spent with tricky fae.

"Sit."

He indicated a spot beside him that was already set for me. I did so, though hesitantly, eyeing the food.

"Help yourself," he said.

I didn't, though my stomach gurgled loudly.

"There are rumors about fae food," I said. "Is it true if I eat here, I will remain in your realm forever?"

"The only way you will remain is if you do not guess my name," he said.

I watched him and he watched me. I wondered what he was looking for, wondered what I was looking for in him. Perhaps some sort of sign that I believed him. But my hunger won out and I filled my plate. The elven prince offered wine, which he poured into a gold chalice.

"Will you not eat?" I asked.

In answer, the prince plucked an apple from the cornucopia of fruit and bit into the crisp flesh. I watched his mouth as he ate, unable to keep myself from thinking about how his lips had skated across my skin.

"Pleased?" he asked.

Hardly.

I turned to my own food and chose a round globe grape to

start. As I bit into the fruit, the juice burst from my mouth. I wiped it away with my fingers, sucking the stickiness from them.

When I glanced at Casamir, his mouth had hardened into a tight line, and his long nails had cut into the tender apple.

"Pleased?" I returned.

He narrowed his eyes and set the apple down. We stared at one another, and then I focused on my food, conscious that he was watching my every move. I felt his eyes on me—on my hands as I reached for another grape, on my mouth as I bit into it, on my tongue as it darted out to clean my lips.

"What progress have you made toward discovering my name?" he asked.

"None save what you gave this morning, seven letters."

"The selkie gave you no direction?"

I did not wish to discuss what the selkie had given me, so instead, I asked, "Is the selkie a prisoner too?"

"I suppose that depends on what you consider a prisoner."

"Anyone here against their will."

"Then I suppose he is a prisoner."

"What did he do to incur your wrath?"

"He lured one of my own into his trap, so I lured him into a trap, and now he lives in my pond, where he sings and seduces the vulnerable and convinces them to set him free."

I did not speak, recalling the selkie's words.

One day when you rule this castle, you will return me to the sea.

"Will you visit him again?" he asked, the words light and careful. I got the sense that he had to work to control his voice.

"Yes," I said. "Tomorrow."

A strange tension built between us, a push and pull. I think the elven prince wished to know if the selkie had succeeded in seducing me, but I remained quiet and let him seethe in his uncertainty. What care should he have over who had touched me?

I was not his.

"You are beautiful," he said after a long moment of silence.

I was in the middle of biting into another grape when he spoke, and I froze at his words and their stiff sound. It was as if he were forcing himself to speak them.

"Excuse me?"

"I said you look beautiful."

His brows were low, his features tense, and yet he continued to hold my gaze as he spoke.

"Why do you seem so angry about it?"

"I'm not," he snapped. "I told you you were beautiful. Be grateful."

"Fuck you."

I took the goblet and tossed the contents at Casamir; the red wine dripped down his face like blood.

He stood so suddenly, the table quivered, and I flinched, pressing myself into my chair, which seemed to stun him. His eyes, which had filled with black, returned to normal.

"Who hurt you?" he asked and remained standing, fingers curled, as if he might leave the moment I answered his question.

"What do you mean?"

"There are bruises on your back. Who hurt you?" he asked again. "I need a name."

I was quiet for a moment, uncertain of what to say. It was not that I wanted to protect Roland. It was more that I did not wish to share my life with this prince. Still, Roland had chosen me to break the curse of the well, and he had done so believing he could pose as my rescuer.

I could make this go away. Marry me.

Even if he had not meant it, disgust twisted in my stomach at the thought of wedding the sheriff, at the thought of spending the rest of my life beneath him, bearing his children and his expectation that I would be an obedient wife.

Stranger still that he thought I would be what he wanted.

"I fell down a well," I said.

"Is that how my brother died?"

"I wish it were that simple," I said. If it were, I would not feel so guilty for what I did.

"What did you do?" he asked, his words whispered in the space between us.

"He guided me from the well, and I thought he would leave once he was free, but instead, he raced back toward it. I fought him, and in the struggle…he died."

I left out the part where I bashed his brains in, though I had no doubt Casamir knew.

"I was told I had to kill the toad in the well. It never occurred to me I could do anything else."

"Who told you to kill him?"

When I did not speak, he prompted, "Was it the man who threw you down the well?"

I met his gaze, and neither of us spoke.

"I will learn his name," Casamir promised. "And when I speak it, I will curse him to die a terrible death."

"Why would you do that?" I asked, confused by his concern.

"Because he hurt you," the prince said simply. Then he extended his hand. "Come."

I hesitated, my hunger hardly sated. Still, I pressed my fingers into his, and he guided me from my seat toward another door on the opposite side of the dining room.

"Do you blame me?" I asked, unable to keep from doing so. "For your brother's death?"

"Yes," he said, and in the silence that followed, I felt guilt wash over me. "But you are asking the wrong question."

I eyed him. "What question should I ask?"

"If I care."

"Do your brothers care?"

"I imagine they do, or you would not be here."

He spoke apathetically, and rather than putting me at ease, it only made me angry. It would be easier to accept that I was a prisoner of someone who deeply loved the one they lost.

"Have you ever cared for anyone?"

I did not intend to sound so derisive, but I couldn't help it. If he could not stand up for those he loved, what did he stand for?

"I care for myself," he said. "I am all I need."

"Why am I not surprised?" I muttered.

If Casamir heard me, he did not speak. Instead, the doors before us opened to reveal his court and their unabashed revelry. The ballroom—at least I assumed that was where we were—looked more like a grove, ringed with trees, laden with glowing will-o'-the-wisps that cast a pale light on the crowd below. The number of fae in the room surprised me, considering I had seen so few through the day. But fae thrive beneath the stars, their antics fueled by the dark, and that was true of Casamir's court.

A cacophony of singing, deep laughter, and snickering jammed my ears, but the smell of fresh blossoms and sweet water was pleasant enough.

Fae of all types danced and drummed, dressed in the vibrant colors of new spring. My eyes moved from face to face, attempting to identify their kind, though my gaze caught on those who looked most like Casamir—tall, willowy elves who stared at me with contempt. They were all beautiful like him, cold like him, and they hated me...like him.

My heart had begun to race, and my hand tightened around Casamir's fingers.

"Do not fret, creature," he said and bent close, his breath hot against the shell of my ear. "No one will harm you...too much."

He pulled me into the fray without so much as a warning,

and my hands were taken by two fairies with iridescent wings, one very tall and one very short. They dragged me into their dancing ring.

"Casamir!" I bellowed as the fairies jarred me one way and then the other.

Just this morning, he had begged me to say his name, and I had done so in a heady whisper, lured by his touch, drunk on the power it gave me. Right now, I screamed it with rage. I wanted to kill him, but my murderous thoughts were soon overtaken as I tried to keep my feet beneath me. I did not believe for a second the fae would stop their merrymaking if I fell. They would pummel my body until my blood covered their feet.

The fae moved fast, coiling through the grove, hand in hand, while others danced around us. I craned my neck this way and that, searching for any sign of Casamir, but it was almost as if he remained just out of sight—a shadow in my peripheral, a literal thorn in my side.

"She is looking for the prince!" one of the fairies shouted.

"She is in love!" another said, cackling viciously.

"I am not in love!" I snapped bitterly.

I was angry, and when I got my hands on him, he would pay.

The fairies broke from their line, and the tall one took both my hands. We spun, the weight of our bodies fully in our heels, and I thought that if she let go, I might fly into the sky. Hopefully when I landed, it would be on the Glass Mountains, I thought.

But the fae did not let go, and she pulled me back into a line, skipping as she went, and soon I felt my body relax into something more malleable. There was something provocative about the grove, about the smell of woodsmoke and the sweat beading off my skin and the pace at which we moved. My body grew damp, and a fire kindled deep in my belly. My face felt warm and flushed, my breasts heavy as arousal tore through me, as fierce and as violent as it had the night I met Casamir.

I was not sure how long I danced, but I knew that my feet hurt, and by morning, they would be covered in blisters. Part of me wanted to stop, part of me wanted to keep going, and part of me wanted to fuck.

Someone pushed me from behind, and I stumbled forward, hands planting on the bare chest of a fae with curly hair and the feet of a goat. He wore a halo of leaves that sat just behind two black horns that curled out of his head. He spun me and another fae took my hands, then another and another, until strong arms enveloped me and I looked up to find Casamir.

His face was warm in the glow of the fire, but his eyes were all black. His hands pressed into my back, my body bowing against the hard contours of him. In his embrace, the sounds of the grove fell away and the air grew thicker, heavier. My eyes lowered with the weight of it.

His hand came up to my cheek, and his thumb brushed my lips.

"Creature," he whispered, inclining his head as if to kiss me, but before his lips could touch mine, my legs gave way and I fell into a darkness as deep as the well.

CHAPTER EIGHT
The Glass Mountains

GESELA

 ***woke up with a start and winced at the bright*** light streaming in from the window. Shielding my eyes, I sat up as last night's events reeled vividly through my mind. I did not know whether to be unashamed or embarrassed at how I had eventually played along, as fervent as the fae. It had not been wholly of my own will; the grove had its own magic, and it had seeped beneath my skin. I could still feel it clinging to my body.

I shoved off the blankets and discovered I was still dressed in last night's gown. At least Casamir had not undressed me, I thought. Though what would that have mattered? He had already seen me naked more than any man.

I moved to stand, and as I put weight on my feet, it felt as if they had been speared by a knife. I collapsed onto the bed again and lifted my foot to inspect my soles. They were red, swollen, and covered in blisters.

Fuck.

How was I supposed to meet the selkie today?

A growl of frustration left my mouth as I stood again. The pain was awful, and each step was like walking on needles. I should have guessed the consequences of dancing with the fae, should have known this would happen. I thought about how Casamir had thrown me into the fray, how he had remained out of sight until the very end.

I wondered now if he knew of my true plans with the selkie, if he had intentionally tried to sabotage me.

I held on to the bed until I came to the end of it and then hobbled across the floor, one slow step at a time, grinding my teeth until my jaw hurt.

I did not bother to change and slipped out the door, entering the hall, unable to use the wall for support as it was covered in poisonous flowers.

I made my way to the portico and sat, sliding down each step slowly. The relief it gave my feet was short-lived because soon I was standing again and making my way into Casamir's forest garden.

The dirt was no better on my feet, and I noticed that each footprint I made bore blood in the depressions, but still I continued. If anything, this horrible pain fueled my desire to make it to the Glass Mountains and learn Casamir's true name so I could be rid of this place.

Just when I felt as though I could not walk any farther, I saw the selkie ahead, perched on his rock, his curls a burnished crown beneath the sun.

I made my way to the bank of the pond and sat, shoving my throbbing feet into the cool mud.

The selkie raised his brow.

"Get caught in a fairy ring?"

My lip curled at his question. "Take me to the Glass Mountains," I said.

I saw no reason to make conversation. I had a bargain to win.

"I am afraid you will have to wait. Your escort grew hungry but will return."

I looked away from the selkie, over my shoulder, uneasy, and quickly looked back.

"Are you lying to me?"

"Are you accusing me of lying?" His eyes darkened, hinting at his fury.

"Who is this escort?"

"A trusted friend."

"There is no trust within these woods."

"He owes me a favor."

My shoulders tensed. I did not trust the selkie, and I would not trust him at all, even if his friend turned out to be real.

"Dip your feet into the water, terrible thing. It will soothe your soles…and your woes."

Again, I felt that dreadful sloshing in my stomach. I kept my feet in the mud and my knees pressed against my chest.

"How much do you know about Casamir?"

"So you are on a first-name basis?"

"He commanded it."

"And you listened?"

I glared at him. "You don't know anything about him, do you?"

The selkie narrowed his eyes.

"I know about him like we all know about him," he said. "But there is danger to speaking rumors as truth, especially in Fairyland."

Fairyland? Was that what they called this place?

"Then speak what you know as truth," I said.

His mouth was pressed into a hard line. "The prince is cursed like all his brothers. Some are cursed to despise, some are cursed to pine, but only one is cursed to die."

I considered the selkie's words and then asked, "Who cursed them?"

"Who didn't?" he countered, and his words made me angry, but I also knew that anything could become a curse if spoken close enough to magic.

"And you? What did you do to end up in the prince's pond?"

His jaw ticked, and I knew he did not like my prying question, but he answered.

"I lured a fair maiden to the edge of the sea, and she fell so deep in love with me, she died from longing. The fair maiden was a fairy queen, and when I left the safety of my sea, her people came for me. They stole my sealskin, and I wandered the land in search of it until I came to a cottage where a witch lived. I told her my woes, and she promised to help if I labored for her for seven years. So I did, and at the end, she offered a red-tipped thorn and said, 'Speak your wish to the thorn, and bury it beneath the full moon.'"

She gave no other instruction, and I did as she said.

"The next morning, I woke up beside my sealskin, which had grown from the ground. I had not felt such joy in seven years, but as I plucked it from the ground, the elven prince appeared—the one you call Casamir. 'Your sealskin belongs to me for it was made with my thorn,' he said. And I have lived in this pond since."

I remained silent following the selkie's story. It reminded me of the cruelty of the Enchanted Forest and renewed my wish to escape my own looming imprisonment, not that I lacked desperation.

"And if you were set free? What would you do?"

"Return to my home," he said. "Return to what is left."

I squeezed my knees tighter to my chest as I thought about what I would return home to—my empty cottage, the full well, the geese who wandered in and out of the Enchanted Forest.

There was nothing else, no one else.

"And what if there is nothing left?"

"Then I suppose I will die," he said.

A gurgling caw caught my attention, and I tilted my head to the sky, finding a large black bird circling overhead. He swooped down and landed near me, sweeping into a bow.

"Thing, meet Wolf the Raven."

"Wolf is an odd name for a bird."

"Thing is an odd name for a human."

"Thing is not my name," I said.

"Wolf is not my name," the raven said.

We stared at one another, and a smirk curled the corner of my lips.

"It is nice to meet you, Wolf."

The raven's eyes glittered. "It is nice to meet you, Thing."

"Wolf will take you to the Glass Mountains," said the selkie.

I looked from the selkie to Wolf. "How are you going to take me to the Glass Mountains?"

"You will climb on my back, and I will fly you there."

"But I am far too large to ride on your back."

"Drink from the selkie's pond, and you will become small."

I hesitated. "And when I return, will I drink again and return to normal?"

"What is normal?" asked the selkie.

I glared, and he answered, "Yes, you have my word."

His word was binding, so I knelt by the pond, dipped my hands into the water, and drank.

I stood to my full height and then felt the world grow larger and larger around me. The pond was now a vast ocean, the flora now a dark and deep forest, and the raven a monster. My feet did not hurt, and when I lifted my foot, I found that they had healed.

"Now then," said Wolf as he bowed. "Climb, Thing."

My fingers sank into his feathers, and I gripped them as I clambered onto his back.

"Hold tight!" he said, stretching his large wings and lifting off the ground.

The beat of his wings was loud, and the wind felt like a physical thing, cutting across my face as we ascended into the air and took off toward the mountains, which I could see in the distance now that I was above Casamir's castle. There wasn't much I feared, perhaps because I was not afraid of death, but seeing the mountains in all their splendor made me afraid.

They curtained the horizon, glittering in bright, blinding flashes of light. Their brilliance was almost too much to behold, but I squinted against the splendor, making out their sharp, needlelike peaks and harsh edges, realizing that without the sun, the mountains were nothing save slabs of cold rock.

Though that did nothing to lessen the dread boiling in the pit of my stomach.

I peeked at the world beneath my feet, which was thick with forest and cut through by streams, but my eyes held on the rounded green and gold roofs of what looked like a palace.

"Who lives below?" I asked the raven, though I was not certain he could hear me.

"That is the Kingdom of Nightshade. It is ruled by one of the seven."

"One of Casamir's brothers?"

"The third one, Prince Lore."

Lore. I remembered him, the one who had taken my knife.

What kingdom had the dead brother ruled? Who ruled it now?

"If there are seven princes, is there a king?"

"The Elder King is dead."

"And he left no heir?"

"He left seven."

"That is not what I mean. Why are there still seven princes? Why is there no king?"

"The king could not choose between his sons, so he declared upon his death that whoever reassembled the Magic Mirror shall be king of the Enchanted Forest. One piece to each brother and there has been no king since."

"That seems like a horrible way to choose a king," I said.

Though having met all seven princes, I was certain the king recognized that none of his sons would make suitable kings.

"Or perhaps it is a perfect way," said Wolf.

The raven continued to glide through the air until he soared over the Glass Mountains, and then he began to circle and descend.

I shielded my eyes as the sun reflected off the surface of the mountains and watched in wonder as we landed on a slope between crests that rose like great pillars and kissed the sky.

"Off, Thing," said Wolf, and I shifted my leg over his back and slid off the raven's back.

My feet slipped as I hit the ground, but I steadied myself before I could fall. Still, my legs felt fragile and shook with my weight after my flight through the sky.

"What do I do?" I asked Wolf.

"Knock," he said.

Gingerly, I bent and rapped my knuckles against the smooth surface of the mountain and was surprised by how the sound echoed around me, vibrating the air, but then silence fell like a shroud, pressing against my body like a heavy weight.

"Hello?" I called as I stood.

"Speak!" Wolf commanded. "The mountains are listening."

I watched the raven for a moment, hesitating, feeling silly only speaking to the wind.

"I've come to learn the true name of the Prince of Thorns," I said.

Wolf and I stood in the silence again, and as it blanketed us, I scanned the glistening slopes of the mountains as if someone or something might appear at any moment and eat me alive.

But then the mountain spoke, and it was as if its voice were inside my head. The sound resonated, rumbling throughout my body.

"What will you give me in exchange?" the mountain asked.

My heart beat harder in my chest.

"What do you want?"

The mountain paused and then spoke, "Bring me three hairs from the head of the Prince of Thorns, and I will tell you his true name."

Then the weight that had fallen on me when we landed dissipated. My body slumped, no longer on edge, and I could breathe once more.

I turned to the raven, expecting something more.

"Come, Thing. We must return."

Climbing onto the raven's back was harder with the slippery floor beneath me, and I yanked on his feathers as I mounted him. Wolf squawked in pain, but once I was seated, he took flight. I stared down at my hands, tangled with Wolf's feathers, reminding me of Casamir's thorns. My vision blurred, mind whirling with ways to secure three of Casamir's hairs.

Perhaps I could sneak into his room while he slept and pluck them from his head, but where did he sleep in his vast castle? I thought I had been there once, when I first arrived, but his castle was like an endless forest and felt impossible to navigate.

Though I should not care, I wondered what the mountains wanted with his hair. Worse, what if I gave it and received the wrong name?

I tried to recall the exact words I had used when I had told the mountains what I wanted but could not remember.

"Why would the mountains ask for Casamir's hair? And only three strands?"

"It is not for me to wonder," said Wolf, whose help, I realized, only extended to his wings, which I supposed was enough.

The selkie still lounged on the rock, and when we landed, he straightened.

"Well, do you have a name?" he asked in a bored tone.

"I have a task," I said. "But you knew that."

"Nothing in this world is free," said the selkie.

I looked at Wolf. "Thank you."

I was sincere, grateful that the bird had not tried to trick me or leave me on the mountains. Though, I was far more suspicious that he hadn't done anything at all.

He swept into a bow, one wing to his breast. "My pleasure, Lady Thing."

"I am not—"

But the raven sprang into the air and flew away before I could finish, and I was left with the selkie, who gestured to the water.

"Drink," he said. "And you will grow big again."

The pond was a vast ocean, and my feet sank into the mud as I neared the bank, but I scooped the water into my hands and sipped. As soon as it touched my tongue, my head spun and my world was righted once more.

My stomach revolted, and before I could stop myself, I bent and vomited into the grassy bank.

"Tsk, tsk, tsk," he said. "The fairies will not like that."

I spit, trying to remove as much of the sour taste from my mouth as possible, and wiped my mouth with the back of my head, glaring at the selkie.

"Why?"

"They are not fond of anyone who mucks up their space."

"What was I supposed to do? Swallow it?"

"That would have been better than what they will likely plan for you."

My stomach churned with dread at his words, but I turned and left the pond.

CHAPTER NINE
A Good Bargain

CASAMIR

 had seethed all night, my body simmering with rage and lust, both warring for a foothold inside me as I replayed my time with my creature. She had rejected my compliment and insulted my hospitality. All of that I might have punished had she not flinched when I stood.

It took the anger out of me as fast as it had swallowed my eyes.

"She expected me to hurt her," I said.

"You did hurt her," said the mirror. "You held her down with your thorns, and you let the red caps throw stones, and last night you let the fae dance with her until her feet bled."

I rose into a sitting position where I sprawled on my bed. "She fled," I said about the first. "As for the second, I gave her a choice, and the third…that was a mercy. She said she would visit the selkie again."

"Did you try talking to her about the selkie?" asked the mirror.

I crossed my arms over my chest. "*You* try talking to her. She's impossible!"

"She cannot be any worse than you."

"When I told her she was beautiful, she threw wine in my face," I said.

A garbled sound escaped the mirror.

I glared, and it turned into a choke, as if he were swallowing the laugh.

"How did you tell her?" he asked.

"What do you mean, how did I tell her? I said, 'You are beautiful.'"

"And...?" he prompted.

"She was confused," I admitted. "And then I told her she should be grateful for my compliment, and she was not."

There was tension in the silence that followed, and then the mirror said, "You are an idiot."

I slid off the bed and stalked toward him. "Careful, you glorified piece of rock."

"Do you think the creature is beautiful?" he asked.

"Of course I think she's beautiful," I snapped. "As if my raging erection wasn't evidence enough!"

"Then why don't you tell her again," he suggested. "And this time, mean it."

"I did mean it!"

"There is a time for these things," said the mirror. "Perhaps *after* she has softened toward you."

"You must be forgetting the part where I need her to fall in love with me."

"She will not fall in love with someone she does not know, and all you've managed to show her is how much of an ass you truly are."

"I am not an ass!"

I glared at the mirror, and he glared back—or rather, it *felt* like a glare—and after a moment, I let out a breath and fell against the bed.

"Okay, fine. I'm an ass."

I stared at my ceiling, which was covered in layers of fabric that draped around my bed like a heavy cloak in winter.

"Perhaps you could…take her on a picnic," the mirror suggested. "You could…take her to a favorite place and…*talk*."

A laugh tore from my throat. "That is a ridiculous idea. She will hardly speak to me at dinner. What makes you think she would follow me into the forest for a *chat*?"

"It was only one suggestion," said the mirror. "Maybe you could—"

"I'll ask the prince again," I said, interrupting him.

"You would give him another chance?"

I noted the surprise in his voice.

"Not without consequence," I said. "I have five days left. No more. I cannot afford to waste time!"

"Of course not," said the mirror. "You must be on your way. Hurry before it is too late."

His voice dripped with contempt, and if he had not made me so angry, perhaps I would have inquired after his tone.

Instead, I started to leave.

"Do you even know where she is?" the mirror asked.

I paused at the door and looked over my shoulder. From this distance, I could see my reflection.

"Likely in her room," I said. "She cannot walk."

When he said nothing, I turned fully toward him.

"Why?"

"No reason," he said airily. "But if I wished to woo a woman, my day would start and end with her."

I ground my teeth.

"What do you know? You are just a mirror!" I slammed the door behind me, but as I made my way to the dungeon, my steps faltered, the mirror's words worming their way into my brain.

Where is she?

Fucking mirror.

I abandoned my task for my creature's room. When I arrived, I knocked and gave her no time to answer before I entered, too impatient to know if she was there.

She wasn't.

The room was empty, the bed was made, and the sheer robe she'd worn the night before lay in a puddle at the foot of her bed. I crossed the room to pick it up. The thin material was almost as light as air, and when she'd stood from her bed dressed in only this, I had lost any hold I'd had on my anger and spent the entire evening and night attempting to quell my impossible arousal.

I should have taken her then. I could have. She would have bent to my will with just as much enthusiasm, and yet I could not bring myself to close the distance between us because I knew in the aftermath, she would hate me and I would despise myself.

I pressed the robe to my face and inhaled her sweet, rosy scent.

"What are you doing?" My creature's voice was sharp and demanding.

I turned, robe in hand, to look at her.

She was still dressed in last night's clothing, her hair windswept and wild, and her bright eyes narrowed. But her features lacked the tightness of anger. Perhaps she was too tired to hold on to those feelings, as a darkness gathered beneath her eyes.

She may have slept last night, but it certainly wasn't restful.

"Where have you been?" I asked.

A light ignited in her eyes, and it pulled at the corners of my mouth. There was her fury.

"I told you yesterday I would visit the selkie."

"You returned?" I blanched. "With those feet?"

"Of course with my feet," she snapped. "Whose would I have used?"

I dropped the robe and stalked toward her. "I warned you against returning."

She smiled wickedly. "Did you really think a fairy ring would keep me from learning your name?"

"Is that what you are doing?" I asked, stopping within an inch of her. She shifted, straightening her shoulders, curving her back. She was preparing to fight me, and I wondered if she knew it. I leaned in a centimeter more and demanded, "Did you bargain with the selkie?"

"So what if I did?" she asked.

I reached for her, my hand bracketing her neck where her pulse raced against my palm.

"Do not toy with me, vicious creature," I said, voice quiet. "Tell me truthfully, did you bargain with the selkie for my name?"

She must have seen something in my eyes that hinted at my anger, because I felt the fight leave her body.

"No," she whispered.

"And will you promise never to do so?"

"No."

I narrowed my eyes. "I can give you everything he could and more."

"There is nothing I want from you except freedom," she said, but as she spoke, her eyes fell to my lips.

I leaned closer, a whisper between our mouths. "Are you certain of that, creature?"

When she did not speak, I lost all control and crushed my mouth to hers. For a brief moment, she tensed, but as my tongue swept over her lips, she melted, her mouth moving just as hungrily as my own.

I could not decide where to put my hands. What would she want? I'd had no issue touching her before, but this felt precarious. The wrong move could end it too soon, and I wanted this for as long as possible. But it was she who fueled the fire when her arms wound around my neck to bring me closer. Her breasts pressed against my chest, her mouth opened for me, and her tongue caressed mine.

Fuck, she was sweet.

My hands went to her waist and then to her thighs, and I lifted her off her feet. Her legs encircled my waist, and I pressed my weight into her as her back met the door of her wardrobe. My cock was so hard and so heavy, and as it found friction between her thighs, I groaned and she gasped, her fingers tightening in my hair.

I sought purchase against the naked skin of her thighs, my palm resting against her wet heat, my fingers trailing the slickness gathered there.

"Sweet creature, say you are desperate for me."

"Do not speak," she begged. "I will hate you more."

She pulled on my hair and pressed her mouth harder to mine. I froze, reaching for her hands and pinning them against the door.

We glared at one another, breathing hard.

"Vicious creature," I said.

"Beast," she spat.

In retaliation, I ground into her, smiling wickedly when her head fell back against the door, exposing the creamy column of her neck to my mouth. I sucked on her skin until a cry tore from her throat.

"Deny yourself my pleasure, creature," I said, lips trailing her jaw. "It will only drive you mad."

I met her gaze but did not kiss her again. She glared back, her skin flushed, her lips swollen.

"Let. Go."

Her demand twisted throughout my body, frustrating every limb, but I obeyed and lowered her to the ground. I could not bring myself to give her distance, and she did not push me away. Instead, her eyes lowered to where my arousal strained against the front of my tunic before she stepped into me, her head tilted back to hold my stare.

"Give me a letter," she said, her breath caressing my lips. "And I will relieve you of this misery."

Her words made my body ache, and I twined my fingers into her hair, claws grazing her scalp. She barely winced. I wanted to refuse her, but I was desperate and lust-filled, and I did not think I could continue with this pounding in my head, heart, and cock.

"U," I said.

"Me?" she asked, a line appearing between her brows.

"U," I said again. "The letter."

There was a breath of silence before my hand tightened in her hair.

"On your knees," I said, and she lowered to one, then the other, gaze unwavering.

I lifted my tunic and reached into my pants to pull out my heavy cock, red in color from the amount of blood rushing to the head. I watched my creature as she looked at it. Her eyes widened, but she took it into her hands and licked me from base to tip. As her tongue and mouth closed over the crown, my hands returned to her hair, gathering it from her face so I could watch her taste me.

She kept her hand on me, a steady pressure that worked up

and down my shaft, and now and then, she would look up to watch my face as if she truly cared for my pleasure. I leaned into it, begging, hoping, *wishing*.

"Fuck."

The word slipped between my teeth as I lost myself in her soft, warm, and wet mouth. She was perfection at my feet, and I closed my eyes as my body tightened and a tingling feeling consumed me as I came, a raw sound escaping my mouth as she sucked me hard before letting me go. I took her face between my hands as I stared at her, flush and rosy and fucking beautiful.

"You are a sweet creature," I said, and she rose to her feet and pulled me against her, her mouth colliding with mine. I could taste my come in her mouth as her tongue thrust against mine.

I gripped her tight, but she pushed me away.

"A letter," she said. "For each time you wish to come by my hand."

I narrowed my eyes, a strange mix of emotions warring inside me. The futile hope I'd had that she might like me in some small way as she'd taken me into her mouth vanished.

"You presume much, creature."

"Tell me when your cock is in my mouth again," she said.

We were only inches apart, and I leaned closer to her, speaking in a half whisper.

"Do not act as if you are not wet for me, vicious creature," I said, a clawed finger trailing down her face. "I touched you. I *know* you."

She shoved against me, but I did not move.

"Leave!" she commanded, breathing hard, fists clenched.

I studied her, unable to keep my mind from imagining what it would be like to take her sweet center against my mouth. My once-softened cock hardened at the thought.

"As you desire," I said, but I paused at the door after restoring my appearance. When I looked over my shoulder at her, she was staring at the opposite wall, her profile tense and angry, and her mood only darkened as I spoke.

"Come when I call, sweet creature," I said. "Or I will come for you."

CHAPTER TEN
Three Strands of Hair

GESELA

 pressed my fingers to my lips in quiet disbe- lief of what I had done, what I had *wanted* to do to the elven prince. I had not expected him to kiss me, and when he did, I had been power-less to resist because I hadn't wanted to. This whole time, I'd been afraid that he would eat me whole, and here I'd desperately wanted it.

It was a means to an end, I told myself. Anything to make myself feel better about the fact that I had willingly taken the prince's cock into my mouth.

I could still taste him on my tongue.

I could still smell the warmth of his skin.

I could still feel the sharp tug of his hand in my hair.

And I would gladly take more.

Fuck me.

I knelt and plucked one dark hair after another from my

floor until I had three long, black strands sitting in my palm. Carefully, I twisted them around my finger and knocked on the doors of my wardrobe. Unlike last time, it opened a crack, though I could not see who answered.

"I need a pouch...a small one to keep something safe," I said.

The door shut quietly, and after a moment, the fae in the armoire produced a small square of fabric that closed with two golden ties. I took it, and before I could say anything, the door shut again. I slipped the hairs inside, pulling the strings tight, and shoved it between my breasts to keep it safe as I made my return to the selkie's pond.

My journey was easier now that my feet were healed, though my mind wandered to Casamir and the intimacy we had shared, and the more I thought about it, the more I ached. A desperation took root in the bottom of my stomach, and by the time the pond came into view, my mind had conjured images of me and the elven prince locked together and writhing.

I had to get out of here before I did something I regretted.

A feeling of unease shivered down my spine, just as it had when I had visited before. My steps slowed and the feeling continued, raising the hair on the nape of my neck. I turned my head slowly, peering into the flora around me, but saw nothing of note.

It is probably fairies playing tricks on you. I thought of the selkie's parting words, but my heart continued to race, and I felt an overwhelming sense of dread as I faced the pond.

"You've returned."

The voice startled me, and I whipped around to face the selkie, who stood in his human form. He was naked, his burnished body on display. I let my eyes descend over his hard muscles, unnerved by his erection, but I was seeking his weakness, the sealskin, which was not near.

"Can you call for Wolf?" I asked.

The selkie took a step toward me, and I took one back.

"So you have succeeded? You have three hairs from the prince's head?"

As he spoke, he continued his approach, as sly and stealthy as a jungle animal. I felt cornered as the back of my feet sank into the muddy bank of the pond.

His eyes narrowed on my neck. I did not know what he saw, but I could guess. Casamir had sucked my skin hard into his mouth.

"You bear his mark."

I covered my skin where it was most sensitive and narrowed my eyes.

"I did not tell you about the three hairs," I said.

And then the selkie launched himself at me. I barely had time to move before he crashed into me. I hit the water so hard, it stole my breath. As I sank beneath the surface, my chest was crushed under his weight. I struggled to be free even as my mouth filled with water and my lungs burned.

He held me down until I thought I would die and then dragged me to the surface.

"Where are they?" he demanded. Gripping me by my upper arms, he shook me. "Give them to me!"

I could not speak, too desperate for air.

The selkie dragged me up his rock at the center of his pond and held my legs down with his powerful thighs so I could not kick. I still fought, clawing at his hands, which drove into my pockets. When he did not find the hairs, he squeezed my breasts. I pulled his hair and jabbed at his eyes, but his hands clamped down on my wrists. Once he had them secure, he groped me and then ripped the bodice of my dress, smirking as he lifted the pouch.

"Foolish thing," he said, and his fingers closed over the bag as he forced his mouth on mine.

"No!" I screamed. "Wolf! Casamir!"

"Shut up!" the selkie said, and he placed his large hand over my nose and mouth, pressing down until I could not breathe. I dragged my nails down his arms, and I knew that I broke skin because I could feel it beneath my nails. Yet he did not loosen his hold, and just when my vision began to blur, a shadow passed over us from above. In the next second, Wolf swooped down and began to claw at the selkie's face with his feet and peck at his eyes with his sharp beak.

The selkie screamed as blood dripped down his face, and he dropped the pouch he had stolen from me. I raced to snatch it up and slipped off the rock, wading through the water as fast as I could.

"Drink, creature, drink!" Wolf commanded, but I could already feel myself growing smaller and smaller and the pond larger and larger. The bigger it grew, the farther away from shore I was and the more exhausted I became. And just when I thought I could go no farther, the raven swept me from the pond with his taloned feet.

I shook uncontrollably as a numbness took hold inside me. I felt nothing, not even the wind on my face.

"Are you all right, creature?" Wolf asked, but I did not answer because I didn't know what to say. I was not all right, but I had a purpose and I needed to see that through. I was too close to freedom.

I kept my eyes closed the entire flight, and when Wolf landed, he set me gently on the cold, glass surface of the same clearing and landed nearby. I rose dizzily into a sitting position, watching him.

"Why did you save me?" I asked.

"Because you will marry the prince," said Wolf. "And when you do, I shall be a wolf once more."

The selkie had said something similar. I had not believed

him then and I did not believe Wolf now, but I said nothing as I stood, untying the pouch and pulling out Casamir's dark hair. It was wet and stuck to my fingers, but I managed to count each strand to ensure all three were there.

"Mountains," I said. "I have brought you three strands of hair from the head of the Prince of Thorns."

After I spoke, the world seemed to go still and silent, the pressure of it pushing against my ears. Then the ground beneath me groaned and a hole opened up at my feet.

"Feed me, mortal."

"You promise to give me the prince's true name?" I asked.

The hole grew bigger, touching the tips of my toes, and I jumped back to keep from falling in.

"Feed me, mortal!"

My chest tightened, but I obeyed. I thought I had been careful in the way I'd worded my bargain with the mountains, but I could not remember the exact wording. Still, we had made a bargain, and I had no reason to believe the mountains would not honor it. I let Casamir's hair drop into the darkness below, and the hole closed with a snap, but then the ground began to shake. It was different from before—not the grumble of a voice but a tremor of anger.

"You think you can trick me, mortal?" the mountains roared in my head, making my ears ring. I fell to my knees and pressed my palms flat against them.

"It's not a trick!" I seethed. "The hair came from his head!"

"Liar!" the mountains bellowed. "Only one hair came from his head. The others did not, and now you must pay for your deceit!"

A smaller hole opened up before me, and the hands that were pressed against my ears were suddenly flush against the surface of the Glass Mountains.

"Only your flesh will suffice," said the mountains, and as

they spoke, my ring finger dropped into the opening of the mountain against my will. Just as before when it closed to swallow the hair, it closed to swallow my finger, slicing through skin and bone.

The pain was sudden and sharp, stealing my breath for only a beat before a scream tore from somewhere deep in my throat. I ripped my hand away and cradled it in the other, blood dripping through my fingers and striking the ground.

I looked at Wolf, who still watched nearby.

"Come, Lady Thing," he said and nothing more.

My face was hot with shame, made worse with the knowledge that someone had witnessed my failure. My eyes fell to my hand, and I wrapped it in the skirt of my dress before rising to my feet. The raven was gracious and bowed low so I could mount his back. While he flew, I did my best to keep the emotions mixing in my chest at a distance, but they raged, threatening and volatile.

When we were within view of the pond, I knew I was in trouble because Casamir waited at the edge of the water. He was a dark and foreboding figure, haloed in black thorns and shadow. In one hand, he held the selkie's sealskin. In the other, he held the selkie's severed head.

Wolf croaked, circling once before landing on the bank near Casamir's feet. I tipped my head up at him, a giant from where I stood, and slid off Wolf's back. As I took a drink from the pond and grew, the raven bowed to the prince, but Casamir did not seem at all concerned with the raven. His eyes did not move from mine.

"How did you know?" I asked after I had grown tall.

"You called and I came," he said.

Neither of us spoke for a moment, and then all of a sudden, I rested my head against his chest and burst into tears.

CHAPTER ELEVEN
A Daring Rescue

CASAMIR

 did not know what to do when my creature placed her head against my chest and began to cry, but her tears were like knives, tearing at my heart, feeding a desire to avenge her pain. I was not used to these feelings, mine or hers.

Bewildered, I looked at the raven, who circled his wings before him.

"What?" I mouthed.

The raven stretched his wings and repeated the movement.

I shrugged, confused.

"Comfort her, you idiot!" the raven said in a half whisper.

I let my magic recede and dropped the selkie's head to place my arm around her, but before I could, she pushed away.

"I hate this place," she said, glaring at me. I felt the full force of her fury as if she had slapped me. "I hate *you*."

"I told you not to return," I said. My body grew hot, my

hands tightening in the selkie's sealskin. She had no right to rage at me. She was here because she killed my brother, and she was here now because she had ignored my warning. "I told you he was dangerous."

"As if you are any better," she spat.

"Oh, vicious creature, you do not want me to *be* better. I am the only thing that can protect you here."

Her gaze fell to the sealskin in my hand, and then her eyes shifted to the selkie's head, which looked up at her from the ground.

Her eyes still glistened with unshed tears, like emeralds shining in the earth. I hated that I had missed the chance to take her into my arms. No doubt I would hear about it later from the mirror, who was likely watching this exchange with Naeve.

The raven was right. I was an idiot.

And now she hated me, though I supposed she'd never stopped.

I studied her, noticing the blood on her dress.

"Are you hurt?" I asked, uncertain if she had just brushed against the selkie's bloodied head, but then I noticed how she held her hand in her dress. I took a step forward, discarding the selkie's skin. "Let me see your hand."

"I'm fine," she said, taking a step back.

"Let me see it," I said, the words slow and deliberate. Something in my voice must have convinced her to obey because she lifted her bloodied hand to show her missing finger. "Where is it? Your finger?"

"The mountains took it," she said.

"The mountains have your blood?"

"I could not resist," she said.

"Because you bargained with them," I seethed. "Foolish creature! What did you trade?"

She was quiet.

"*Creature*," I warned, the word slipping between my teeth.

She did not look at me as she answered. "Three strands of your hair."

"Three strands?"

Her gaze met mine. "I only had one. The other two must have belonged to your mistress."

"Or a *brother*," I snapped.

Her mouth tightened. "This is your fault! I would not have traded anything if I had not wished to guess your true name!"

"No one told you to bargain with the mountains!"

"He did!" she said, pointing to the selkie's head.

"He wanted to kill me!" I yelled, kicking the head, sending it soaring into the surrounding woods. "I would have given you my name had you sucked my cock for four more days!"

It did not matter that I did not have the time. It did not matter that she must love me too.

"If I desired you the least bit, I might consider another trade, but as it is, you are the last person in this forsaken place I would ever fuck!"

"Do not be so certain, especially where your freedom is concerned."

"Do not degrade me for giving you pleasure."

"I am not degrading you," I said. I felt myself bending over her, but she was just as stubborn, rising on her toes to match my venom. "If you let me, I would *worship* you. Perhaps then you might know what it is to be grateful."

She slapped me and I reeled back, pressing a hand to my face to quell the sting, though it was covered in the selkie's blood.

Her eyes glistened as she stared back at me, and I could not figure out what I had said that had made her angrier.

"Do not make me feel worse for something I already regret."

I felt like she had cracked open my chest and laid everything inside me bare, and I hated it.

"If you had told me why you wanted my hair, I could have saved you a limb. The mountain does not know my name."

"I am beginning to think no one knows your name. Perhaps you have no name at all."

"I have many names," I said. "It is the consequence of living so long."

"A cruel existence," she seethed. "Perhaps you should die, and you would not have so many."

"Ah, but they do not end when you die," he said. "I have died many times and I will come back with more."

She paled at my statement, and I inched closer to her.

"Give me your hand," I said.

She hesitated but stretched her arm out, trembling.

I took her hand and placed her injured finger in my mouth. Just as I predicted, she tried to pull away, but I held her, sucking hard, and when I released her, her flesh and bone were restored.

Her eyes widened with amazement for one second and then darkened with horror.

"No! I did not ask this of you!"

"You did not," I affirmed.

"T-take it back!" she said, holding her hand aloft as if it did not belong to her.

"I will not," I said.

"I do not want to owe you for this. *Take it back!*"

"Did I ask for anything in exchange?"

"It does not matter that you didn't," she said. "Magic always requires a trade."

"Then let me worry about what it will want," I said and bent to pick up the sealskin. I stepped around her just as the selkie's head rolled out from the surrounding flora, pushed by a tearful winged fairy.

"Do not cry for such a creature," I said. "He touched what is mine."

I snatched the head from the ground by his golden hair.

When I turned to my creature again, she was staring at the selkie's head.

"What are you going to do with that?"

"I will plant it outside my window and watch what grows," I said.

She said nothing, and she did not ask me what I intended to do with the sealskin either, but if she had, I likely would have told her about my collection of skins, which ranged from animal to human. One never knew when they might need a different skin.

"Come, we must go," I said. "Dusk is approaching fast."

She raised a brow. "Are you afraid of the dark?"

"No," I said. "But you should be, even when I am near."

I spoke only once on our return and that was to instruct my creature to walk a step ahead of me so that I may watch her from all sides. When we came to the palace, I threw the selkie's head into the center of the courtyard and then looked at her.

"The mountains have your blood now," I said. "They will call to you, and when they do, you must resist."

"How will I know if they call?"

"It is likely you won't."

She narrowed her eyes. "You are *most* unhelpful."

I smiled, half-hearted, only amused by her frustration. "Do not leave your room tonight, no matter what calls."

Her throat constricted as she swallowed, and my eyes dropped to the mark I'd left on her skin. I reached across our distance and touched her there. I wanted to kiss her, to lick her, to suck her skin again, but she winced, so I let my hand fall away.

"Good night, creature," I said, and she fled.

I returned to my chamber and dodged a shoe as I entered.

"What the fuck was that for?" I asked, glaring at Naeve, who stood on the bench beneath the window, hopping on one leg as she tried to take off the other shoe.

"Because you are an idiot! A royal one!" she yelled.

"What did I do this time?" I demanded.

Her answer was to launch another shoe at me, and I brought my arm up in time to block my face.

"*You should be grateful?*" Naeve said, quoting me. "Could you be any less romantic?"

"That is not what I meant!"

I meant that she might understand how grateful I had been when she'd knelt before me and took a part of me into her mouth, and I was desperate to return the favor.

Naeve searched for something else to hurl at me.

"What else was I supposed to say?"

"Anything else! Anything *kind*!" she said. "If she is going to love you, she has to like you, and there is nothing about you that is remotely likable."

She plucked a pillow from behind her and pitched it at me.

"Stop throwing things!"

"You have five days! *Five*!"

"I can count!"

"Then make them count!"

"I'm *trying*!" I yelled. "Do you imagine this is somehow easy when I have had no love in my life?"

Naeve froze, the candlestick she'd chosen to throw at me next poised in her hand like a spear.

"Do you imagine I understand kindness when none has been given to me?" I continued. "Do you imagine it is easy to be anything other than what I am?"

"Easy? No, I do not imagine so, but change never promised to be, and if this is what you want, then you must do more than *try*."

I glared at her and then left my room, slamming the door

behind me, begrudgingly returning to the prince who lived in the depths of my castle. He lay on his thin bed beneath the window, one leg hanging off and scraping the floor. The strange hat he usually wore covered his face, and his hands lay folded atop his stomach.

"Your advice did not work," I said.

The prince startled and sat up, his hat falling into his lap.

"Wh-what do you mean?"

"I told her she was beautiful, and she did not fall in love with me."

"Well, how did you say it?"

"Why does everyone keep asking that? I just...*said* it!"

"Did you mean it?"

"Yes!"

"And she didn't fall in love with you?" He seemed confused.

"I ripped the head off a selkie today. Do you really want to toy with me?"

"Of course, she must be playing hard to get," said the prince quickly. "Perhaps you should save her from danger. She will be so grateful, she will realize her love for you instantly."

"I did. Today. I saved her today."

I'd killed the selkie for what he had done to her. She had seen me holding his head and his skin.

The prince opened his mouth and then closed it. After a moment, he said, "And was she witness to your prowess?"

"Well...no."

"That's it!" he said, snapping his fingers. "You must show her your skill, your bravery. She will melt at your feet!"

"If you are wrong, I shall take the feather from your cap."

"What about my curls?" he asked.

"What curls?" I asked, a wicked smile tugging at my lips as the prince paled and smoothed his hand over his shorn hair.

CHAPTER TWELVE
The Bell

GESELA

 hen I returned to my room, a metal tub full of steaming water waited. My body ached and my bones screamed, and the thought of sinking into the heat made me want to weep with relief.

I closed the door quietly and scanned the room for any signs of fae but saw none. Then I turned my attention to the water, attempting to assess if it had been enchanted. While I did, the door opened.

Naeve entered, grumbling. "What are you waiting for?" she asked. "Get in! You stink!"

I straightened. "Did you order the bath?" I asked.

"Who else?" she snapped.

"Thank you," I said.

The harsh lines carving the brownie's face softened at my gratitude, and she averted her eyes as if it made her uncomfortable.

"Hurry, hurry, before the water cools!"

I smiled at her embarrassment and reached behind me in an attempt to loosen the laces of my dress. Casamir had tied them, and they had grown tighter over the two days I'd stayed in this gown. Naeve pushed a stool toward me, climbed it, and took over. With deft fingers, she had the dress undone in seconds. It was stiff as I pushed it down.

Once I was naked, I stepped into the bath. I could not help the moan that escaped my mouth as I sank into the water. For the first time since I'd arrived here, I felt the tension leave my body.

I could not see Naeve, but I could hear her moving about, and I knew she was near when a scrub brush popped up over the edge of the tub. It was followed shortly after by her face as she climbed the chair.

"Lean over," she said.

I hesitated and considered telling her that I could scrub my own back but decided I'd rather keep her favor, so I did as she said. When she was finished, I leaned back in the bath and immersed myself in the water, enjoying the feel of it cradling my body. When I surfaced, she scrubbed my hair until I thought my scalp might bleed before she poured a fresh bucket of water over my head without warning and then stood, holding out a towel.

My bath was finished, and as I stood and the water dripped off me, Naeve said, "Our prince is an idiot."

My brows lowered. "What?"

"Take the towel," she said and then hopped off the chair.

I stepped out of the bath, watching the brownie as she pushed the stool back to the vanity.

Once it was in place, she turned and continued, "He is an idiot, and he is not a good person. He has few positive traits, save that he is handsome, but so are all elven princes, and he will likely never understand your needs because he has never had to think of anyone but himself, but that does not mean he will not try."

"What are you talking about, Naeve?" I asked, confused by her sudden speech.

"I am trying to help you fall in love with him," she said.

"What?" I asked on a breathless laugh.

"To be sure, he has not been kind by your standards," she said, as if she had not even heard me speak. "But by the fae, he has granted you every mercy."

"What *mercy*?" I asked. "I am his prisoner, and I must *earn* my freedom, and for what? Nothing but his pleasure."

"You must earn your freedom because he cannot earn his," she said. "Trust me, it is not a pleasure to watch both of you fail at this every day."

I stared at her, confused. "What are you talking about?"

"The prince is cursed by the Glass Mountains," she said. "And if you do not guess and speak his name in five days' time, he will forget it, and if a fae does not know their name, they fade away."

"Fade away?"

"Cease to exist," she said. "Never to return to the earthly plane."

I thought of my earlier conversation with Casamir.

I have died many times and I will come back with more.

Under the curse, I supposed the cycle would cease.

"Why should I care?"

"Because now your freedom is tied to his," she said. "And if you are not free before he forgets his name, then you never will be."

"And what does love have to do with this?" I asked.

"You can guess his name and even speak it, but you must also love him, or the curse cannot be broken."

I could not describe my shock, but the warmth that had

radiated off my skin from the bath suddenly chilled me to the bone.

"Then we shall never be free," I said.

"Let us hope that is not true," she said, and with that, she left me alone to process this blow.

You must also love him.

Casamir had completely failed to communicate that part of the deal, though why would he? He needed me and likely thought himself charming enough to sway me.

"Stupid, arrogant fae prince!" I seethed aloud.

I threw off the towel and crossed to the wardrobe, knocking as I spoke.

"I need clothes! Something...*modest*!"

The door opened, and I snatched the white gown the fae offered and slipped it on as I crossed to the mirror. It was a thin night rail that did little to hide my body from sight, especially the parts of me that were still wet from the bath. I laced the ties in the front, as silly as it seemed considering that Casamir had already seen all of me. It felt like a form of rebellion.

I turned from the mirror and wandered to the window where the day was fading into night, only a small sliver of golden light peeking through the thick foliage outside.

I thought about some of the things that had occurred over the last few days—the way Casamir touched me on our first meeting, the way he'd taken over lacing my gowns, the way he had kissed me in this room as if he were starved.

But as it turned out, he was just desperate for me to fall in love with him and break a curse. My hands fisted, my face hot with shame. I crossed my arms over my chest, frustrated that I had let him indulge in my body at all.

Never again, I thought as tears pricked my eyes.

I was so embarrassed. I felt so stupid. I wasn't even sure *why*. There was nothing wrong with indulging in pleasure. Except that…I think I might have hoped that this idiot elven prince was actually *interested* in me.

"Never again," I said aloud, and I watched as the golden light turned dark red. As the light faded, I swore I heard the sound of a bell. It was a soft chime I could feel in my heart, and it drew my attention like nothing ever had before.

I pressed my ear to the window, and it became clearer—a pretty peal of bells. All at once, I felt calm, the tension and anger that had tightened my insides releasing in an instant, and I could breathe again. I drew away from the window and left, the sound growing clearer without the walls of my room in the way. I followed the portico and escaped into the garden, guided by the echoing chime.

My feet were bare and the earth was cold, but the sound of the bells was warm, so I did not mind as I made my way through towering wood lilies and shoots of anemones, between trees hung so thick with brambles and thorns, their branches were hardly visible.

The chime did not grow any louder the farther I walked, and yet I followed, as if I might find the source. But when I came to a clearing where the ground was covered in flowering convolvuli, the sound abruptly stopped. When the bell ceased to sound, its hold on me fell away, leaving me cold and alone in the middle of the Thorn Prince's forest garden.

"Fuck," I muttered, turning in a circle at the center of the clearing, but I could no longer tell from which direction I came. Then I felt a tap on my shoulder and the color drain from my face as a familiar voice spoke.

"Do I know you?"

A knot formed in my throat, and I tried to swallow it, but I couldn't.

"Miss?"

I closed my eyes, torn between hope and horror.

I knew the voice, but I had not heard it in years.

"Darling?" Another voice joined the mix, and a sound escaped my mouth, so pained and so visceral, I could hardly hold myself up, bent beneath the anguish.

The voices were those of my dead parents.

"Darling," my mother said in her beautiful, breathy voice. It brought tears to my eyes to hear it, a long-ago echo I could never recall. "Look at my face, and you shall know that everything will be okay."

"Stop!" I said, choking on a sob that felt like a needle in my throat.

A cold hand touched my arm, and I tore away, squeezing my eyes shut tighter.

"Little one." My father's voice shook me to the core. "Listen to your mother."

"She is not my mother," I shouted, my voice raw and rough. "And you are not my father!"

"Ella."

The new voice broke me. It tore my heart out and left a gaping hole, and the blood that I saw at my feet was not my own but that of my sister.

"Do not be afraid," she said. "We are all together again."

I knew not to, but I did it anyway. I opened my eyes and beheld her. My sister, Winter. She was nothing but a corpse, a skeleton adorned in rotting flesh with an arrow lodged in her breast.

I reeled away and broke into a run, and my family followed, their shouts shrill and resonate in the wood.

"Ella! Come back!" my sister called.

"We have come to take you home," my mother said.

"Gesela! Stop running from your mother!" my father ordered in his gruff rasp.

"Go away!" I screamed and covered my ears. "Go away, go away, go away!"

I tripped, and when I hit the ground, I did not move. I felt as though my chest had been cracked open, the pain so great, I could barely breathe.

I sobbed, and my tears wet the earth beneath my head, and I only rose from where I lay when I felt something touch my cheek. I sat back and saw that it was a leaf. As I watched, the leaf sprouted a longer stem, and the stem sprouted a golden bloom, and the bloom opened to reveal a sleeping fairy. She was covered in gold. When she opened her eyes, she sat up and stretched and then smiled wickedly as she blew dust into my face.

"Fuck!" I heard Casamir curse, and the sound of his voice made my heart race in a way it never had before. I started to turn to him, but his voice cut through the air like a whip. "Close your eyes!"

His command was visceral, and I knew fairies well enough to trust him. I did as he had ordered, and a laugh sounded from the golden fairy, small and impish, though it quickly turned into a gurgled scream.

I covered my eyes with my hands, except that they were quickly ripped away.

"No, you must look! Look!" said a voice.

I could not see the source of the power that kept me from obeying Casamir, but I was not strong enough to resist. When I opened my eyes, I saw the Prince of Thorns holding the golden fairy within his clawed hand, teeth bared as if he were about to devour her.

"Casamir!"

I did not know what possessed me to speak his name, but I did not understand anything that was happening to me anyway.

When he looked at me, I suddenly understood what the fairy had done. Her magic was desire, and as soon as Casamir's gaze connected with mine, heat erupted between my legs and an unearthly groan escaped from my mouth.

"What. Did. I. Say?" He spoke between clenched teeth. His entire body had gone rigid, and I couldn't speak, noting his heavy erection.

The fairy had gotten him too.

"Fuck," he cursed as he tossed the fairy aside. She landed with a thud and did not move as he stormed toward me and dragged me to my feet.

I thought—hoped—he would kiss me. I was ready for it, desperate for it.

My fingers tangled into his shirt as I angled my head and opened my mouth, but he turned me away and drew my back to his chest, his hands on my hips.

An unearthly whine escaped my mouth as his arousal settled against my ass. I could not help grinding into him. I arched my back and reached behind me, hoping to secure my hand behind his neck, but his hand came down on my wrist, and then he trapped my arms beneath his own.

"*Don't*," Casamir gritted out.

"Please," I begged, panting, unable to think past the desperate need pulsing throughout my entire body. I had never been this aroused.

It was more than desperation.

If he did not fuck me, I would die.

"You hate me," he said, but he pulled me closer and held me tighter. It was the smallest reprieve, the tiniest stroke of friction. I wanted to weep. "You will hate yourself."

"It's not as if we can help it," I argued.

"I'd rather not fuck someone whose lust for me is only a spell."

"Yet you had no trouble when I sucked your cock."

"That was different. *This* is different."

"How?"

"Stop talking," he said. "This is harder when you *talk*."

"Why should I?" I challenged, frustrated. "I would have never guessed the Prince of Thorns was a man of honor."

"I am not," he said, his voice grating.

He lifted and carried me beneath the branches of a nearby tree where he sat with his back to the trunk and me before him, cradled between his legs. He kept me pressed against his front, his arms trapping mine as they encircled my waist. His erection was hard between us, and despite his resistance, even he could not keep from shifting against me.

"I can ease you," I said. "I have done so before."

"*Creature,*" he warned.

"I am only asking for you. Nothing more."

He did not respond. The longer I sat there untouched, the more distressed I felt. I rubbed my thighs together to create some kind of friction, desperate to end the throbbing at the apex of my thighs.

"Please, Casamir," I begged.

"Don't. Make. This. Harder," he said between his teeth, his fingers pressing hard into my skin.

"I will die," I moaned.

His face fell into the crook of my neck, and his lips brushed over my skin as his tongue darted out to taste me. I twisted toward him, and our mouths collided in a hot and vicious kiss. I let my legs fall open, frantic for his touch, hoping he would not resist, but he kept his hands planted firmly around me. I lifted my dress and broke the kiss, letting my head fall against his shoulder as I parted my own flesh, twisting my wrist to reach deeper inside me.

"Fuck." The curse slipped from his lips.

A moan broke past my lips, and I whispered to him what I never wanted to say aloud.

"I am so wet," I said as he watched me pleasure myself over my shoulder.

"Fuck me," he whispered as his lips danced across my shoulder and up the column of my neck, teeth scraping hungrily.

"I am trying," I said, shifting my legs over his so that I was far more exposed. "Don't you want to touch me?"

"That is a foolish fucking question," he said as his teeth nibbled at my ear, but it worked.

One of his hands broke away and tangled in my hair, and he jerked my head back so he could kiss my mouth, but his action only freed me enough to pleasure myself far easier than before. As I moved inside my heat, bliss threaded throughout my body, curling deep in my belly to the point that I could no longer contain my orgasm. I opened my mouth against Casamir's as I came. When I removed my hand and reached for him, he caught it and brought my fingers to his mouth, sucking each one clean. As he did, a laugh drew our attention.

The fairy Casamir had tossed to the ground had risen, and her wicked smile returned.

"No use resisting," she said, her voice as pure as the chimes that had led me here. "It would have come to this eventually."

Casamir went rigid behind me.

"What is she talking about?" I asked.

"I do not know, but if she does not shut up, I will pluck her head from her body."

The fairy giggled again. "I only gave you what you truly wanted. Your deepest desire. It is not every day I find two people who want each other. Consider yourself lucky."

Then she fluttered away, and silence stretched between us.

"Release me," I said.

He didn't listen, his body growing tense against mine.

"Casamir," I warned, and then my hands were free. I shifted onto my knees and faced him. His eyes were dark, our need screaming between us.

"I hate you," I said, even as I straddled him and his hands curved against my ass.

I had to say it because what I was about to do didn't make sense.

But I wanted this.

I wanted to be wanted.

A small smile curved his lips.

"The feeling's mutual, creature."

As my mouth collided with his, Casamir tore my dress in two, each piece falling off my shoulders and pooling around my waist. I didn't care, couldn't care. My need for release had gone beyond anything rational, and I was consumed by him—by his mouth and his touch, both of which were now on my breasts.

"Is it true?" Casamir asked. "Is it true that you desire me?"

I was quiet.

"Answer the fucking question."

His hands tightened on me, his lips pressed to my neck.

"Yes," I breathed. "And you?"

The sound he made was something between a growl and a sigh.

"I knew you wanted to fuck me," he said.

"Beast," I said, pushing against him. "Answer me!"

"Yes," he growled and kissed me hard on the mouth, his hand knotted in my hair.

When he pulled away, he spoke. "You will call me Casamir if you want my cock. Do you understand?"

I parted my lips and offered a small, teasing smile. This prince was about to discover he had no control.

"Casamir," I breathed his name, my lips hovering over his.

He kissed me again, hands digging into my body as he shifted and pressed me to the ground. He sat back on his heels, eyes full of black.

"You are beautiful," he said, and this time when he spoke, I knew he meant it.

Then he shed his clothes, and his cock was thick and full. He settled between my hips, only wearing the silver chains, which were cold as they rested against my skin. I sighed with relief at the feel of him against me, widening my legs so that his crown rested within my heat.

He paused for a moment and brushed my hair from my face. The movement was strangely gentle, and then he spoke, voice warm and low. "I will give you everything," he said. "But right now—"

"You have never been charming," I said, interrupting him. "Do not waste my time with it now."

He smiled shrewdly and then pushed inside me in one fluid movement. I hadn't known how much I needed this until now. We both groaned, and I let my head fall back against the ground as his fingers wrapped around the column of my neck, though he did not press. As much as I hated to surrender to this creature, lying beneath him right now, it only seemed right.

"Choke me," I said.

He did not need encouragement, and I had expected this because since our first encounter, he had had an obsession with my neck. As he gently squeezed and thrust inside me, I thought I might die from the rush of pleasure that blossomed through-out my body, only growing in intensity as he continued to press on either side of my neck.

I grasped his forearm and tried to take a breath when my chest started to burn. He loomed over me, watching my face, and then he bent to kiss my mouth before releasing me. I took a deep, guttural breath, light-headed but so fucking aroused I could barely hold on to my orgasm. I did not want this to end because beneath Casamir's heated gaze, I felt like *someone*.

"So fucking beautiful, so fucking wet," he said, panting, but he whispered the words, as if he were only speaking to himself. Then his hand returned to my neck and his pace shifted into something far more visceral and carnal. I loved it and wanted it more than I had ever wanted anything, even my freedom.

When he released me, I came, but he continued to move, chasing his own release.

"Come inside me," I said.

"Fuck you," he breathed, but he planted his arms on either side of my head and leaned close, and I reveled in the crush of his body against mine. Perspiration gathered on his brow, and I held on to him, fingers pressing into his skin until he kissed me, coming with his mouth against mine.

I wrapped my legs around him to keep him inside me, expecting him to soften, expecting to find myself sated, but as the prince pulled back and met my gaze, the fire that had spurred us on from the start reignited.

"What kind of magic is this?" I moaned as I arched against him.

"This is not magic," he said and bent to press a kiss to my neck, then my jaw. It was a sweet gesture, and it sent a strange feeling of comfort throughout my body, even as the heat from our coupling raged inside me. "This is *need*."

If this was need, I had never known it before, but I was certain I could not live without it, and I had sense enough to feel the dread of that thought before I was consumed once more by passion for the elven prince whose name I did not know.

CHAPTER THIRTEEN
Enchantment

GESELA

 was only half-awake, but there was a part of me that was aware of the heat and hardness pressed against my back and how heavy Casamir's arms were around me. The longer I lay there, the more I became aware of my body and the places where I ached. Despite how exhausted I felt, a fire still raged beneath my skin, desperate to take this elven prince inside me once again.

I had to be enchanted, I told myself, but even I knew that was not true. If either of us were still under the fairy's spell, we would not have fallen asleep. We would have continued to come together beneath this cursed sky.

What was wrong with me?

Casamir was my jailor. He was a beast.

He was fae and he lived within a place that had taken so much from me.

I could not do this. I could not let this happen again no matter how much I wanted him.

Desperately.

Casamir stirred, and as he moved, I sat up, my back to him. It seemed wrong to face him, especially in the aftermath of what we had done, though I wanted to. We were not lovers, and I had no tender feelings toward him.

I couldn't, though that thought made my chest ache.

I felt his eyes on me, and after a moment, he spoke.

"Are you well?"

The question straightened my spine.

It was the last thing I expected him to say. I thought he would taunt me, remind me of how he had known I wanted him.

I swallowed and turned my head to the side to answer. I still could not look at him.

"I...don't know."

"Did I hurt you?"

"No," I answered quickly. "No, you didn't."

We were silent after that, and I remained where I was, even as Casamir stood. I was not certain what he was doing, but after a moment, he walked into view, half-dressed, his tunic in hand. My eyes trailed up his front, and I met his dark gaze.

"Will you come with me?" he asked.

Perhaps it was because he had asked and not commanded, but I placed my hand in his without question, and when his fingers closed around mine, warmth blossomed throughout my body at the thought of everything these hands had done to me.

He helped me to my feet and trailed a finger across my cheek and then over a spot on my shoulder, frowning.

"You lied," he said.

I lowered my brows. "What do you mean?"

But when I looked at the place he traced on my skin, I saw what he meant. I was scratched and bruised.

But so was he.

I met his gaze.

"It's…not as if you could help it," I said.

Still he frowned, but his fingers tightened, and he tugged me along through a curtain of trees and down a sloping hill. At the bottom was a small body of water that was fed by a trickling waterfall. Here, I could see nothing beyond the thick wood.

Casamir dropped his tunic to the mossy ground, and the rest of his clothes followed.

"I thought you might want to bathe," he said.

I stared at him for a few seconds before my gaze shifted to the shimmering pool. It was beautiful and felt isolated, though I did not trust it was private.

"It's safe," Casamir said, and when I met his gaze, he added, "I promise."

From a fae, those words bore the weight of a blood oath. Despite what he had promised, I could not help thinking about how the selkie had attacked me, and though he was dead, the memories had me hesitating at the edge of the water.

I felt Casamir approach, and he touched my side with the tips of his nails.

"Do you trust me?" he asked, his mouth close to my ear.

I took a breath, turning toward him slightly.

"This second, yes, but I can promise nothing beyond this moment."

He pressed a kiss to my shoulder, and his hand flattened against the small of my back as he guided me into the lake. I stood for a few moments in the water, thigh-deep, and when nothing happened, I dove beneath the water to put distance between us. When I broke the surface, I faced him.

He had not moved, and I could not place the expression on his face. It was dark and sensual. It made me feel desired and it also scared me.

"Why did you leave the palace?" he asked.

"I heard a bell," I said, and even now as I thought about the sound, the beauty of it brought tears to my eyes. "And I could not help but follow."

"Where did it lead?"

"To my dead family," I said.

His jaw tightened and I expected him to ask about them, but he didn't.

"The bell was the mountains' hold over you," he said. "Your family…that was the fairies."

I did not ask why because I knew. Casamir had warned me about the mountains, and the selkie had warned me about the fairies and their retribution.

"Naeve tells me you are cursed," I said.

Casamir did not react.

"What did you do?"

He waded farther into the lake, and I tracked him as he moved, but he did not speak until he dipped below the water and resurfaced, his dark hair plastered to his face.

"I slept with a daughter of the Mountains," he said. "And she fell hopelessly in love with me, and because I did not return her love, the Mountains cursed me to forget my true name."

"Unless it's spoken with love," I said. "Isn't that right?"

He only stared at me.

"Is that what you hoped for from me?"

The hollows of his cheeks deepened as he ground his teeth.

"I do not hope for anything," he said.

We circled one another.

"I cannot believe that no one has fallen in love with you."

"Many have," he said. "But none are clever enough to guess my name."

"And if I do not guess, you will cease to exist?"

"Eventually," he said, and then he smiled, reaching to draw

126

a piece of my hair behind my ear. "Something for you to look forward to."

I wanted to argue, to tell him I would never feel that way, but the words were stuck in my throat, and I swallowed hard.

We did not speak after that, and once we had finished swimming in the lake, we came to shore.

"Put this on," Casamir said, offering his tunic. It was a reminder of how I had come here and how I was leaving, my nightdress torn in two, a mark of the desperation we had felt to be inside each other.

A rush of warmth burned my skin.

I took his tunic and slipped it over my head. There was an element of regret as his smell surrounded me, and it pulled at memories from long ago when I would climb to the roof of my parent's cottage with my sister and watch as the sun rose, the morning light catching on the dewdrops, making our little hollow glimmer.

I used to think it was magic, but now I knew otherwise.

Magic was the darkness that existed between the trees, the place where light did not shine, and it had taken everything.

"Are you so regretful?"

I opened my eyes and looked up at Casamir, whose features were harsh but not angry. I could not tell exactly how he felt, but there was a tightness to his mouth and eyes that made me think that he was struggling, but with what, I did not know.

"It is not as if we can help what happened," I said and looked away before I could see his reaction. I was too afraid to know what he was thinking or how he really felt. What if he regretted me?

"Will you not look at me?" he asked.

So I did. We glared at one another, a tension building between us that I could not exactly place, but it was hurt and angry and strange, and even with all those emotions, I still felt a keen desire for him.

"How much do you hate me now?" he asked.

I ground my teeth and lowered my brows. All I could manage to say was, "I don't hate you...not for this."

I did not think that would make him angrier, and yet his eyes darkened and his jaw ticked, and this time, he looked away.

"Come."

We left and I remained a step behind him as he led me from the clearing in the woods where our madness had come to a head. He was shirtless and the muscles in his shoulders rippled with each tiny movement. His back was scored with red lines from my fingernails. I liked that I had marked him in some way, but the fact that others would see it and *know* embarrassed me, though I wasn't sure why I cared.

Perhaps it was because I was supposed to hate him.

I was supposed to hate him and...I didn't.

Why don't I hate him?

It was not as if he'd done anything to deserve my favor, but there had been a few strange and tender moments last night that had made me feel something beyond the cold anger that had seethed inside me for years. For once, I had not been invisible or forgotten or alone.

Casamir paused and held out his hand to halt me. The sudden stop made my heart race, and I looked at him as he spoke.

"Stay here," he said. "I'll only be gone a moment."

Anything could happen in a moment within his woods, but I stayed where I'd stopped and did not move a single muscle as he vanished into the surrounding trees, returning a moment later as he had said with a red apple in hand.

"Here," he said, holding it out to me. "It's safe to eat. I promise."

Promise.

I liked that word coming from his lips, and I wanted to hear it more. I should have said so, but the strain between us had only grown since we had begun our journey back, so I held on to those words.

I took the apple but only stared at him.

"What's this for?"

He shrugged and looked a little uncomfortable. "I thought… you might be hungry."

I laughed. I couldn't help it. His actions were so contrary to what I had expected. But he remained very serious, so I pressed my lips together to keep quiet and then cleared my throat.

"Thank you," I said, and I took a bite from the apple, which was crisp and sweet, noting that Casamir watched my mouth as I ate.

He seemed to realize he was staring and then turned away.

"We should get back."

We did not speak for the rest of the walk, and when the castle came into view, I felt a sense of dread. I did not know where it came from or what spurred it until Casamir paused and faced me. Suddenly, I realized I did not know how to move beyond this point. There was no going back to whatever had existed between us before, and while that had not been easy, it was better than this strange longing inside me now.

"I," he began but did not continue.

"What?" I prompted.

He took a moment to speak, but as he did, his tone became more biting.

"Another letter from my true name." I could not help feeling disgusted by his words, and still he continued. "Did you not set the rules for our encounters? A letter for each time I come by your hand?"

I was so shocked by his words, I couldn't think, could do nothing but strike him. My hand stung, and his cheek was red.

"How dare you."

He did not flinch, did not even press his hand to the mark on his face to soothe the pain.

"I only thought I should give you something you wouldn't regret."

"When it comes to you, Casamir, I regret *everything*."

I turned from him and fled.

The sooner I learned his true name, the better.

I had to get out of here.

CHAPTER FOURTEEN
Rule of Three

CASAMIR

 watched my creature retreat with all the fury of a storm. I did not understand her. Perhaps I did not want to. I had given her what she wanted, offered her a letter from my name so that her shame might not feel so heavy, and instead of expressing gratitude, she had struck me.

It is because you are an idiot.

The mirror's voice echoed in my mind, and I ground my teeth against his words.

"She clearly regretted our time together," I said aloud.

Did you ask her what she regrets?

"She said it!"

Only after you offered a letter. Perhaps she was not so regretful but more embarrassed.

"They are the same."

They are not the same.

"You expect me to rejoice that my creature was embarrassed about our time together?"

Perhaps it has nothing to do with you, said the mirror, who paused and then added, *Idiot*.

I pressed my hand to my face, but the memory of her lived beneath my skin and all over my body. I knew I would never be rid of this hold she had on me. It was just as strong as the Mountains that had cursed me, and I did not know why, but I felt it with more certainty than I had anything else in my long life. It felt silly to think such a thing, especially in the aftermath of what we had done, but I had had sex with many, many people, and I had never felt this way before.

Perhaps this was the Mountains' attempt to curse me further. Had they taken her flesh only to make me crave it?

You have always craved it. You have always craved her. You only expected that your appetite would ebb once you had a taste, but it has only made you ravenous.

I left the garden outside my palace and went to visit the mortal prince, who was standing on the bench beneath his window, hands wrapped around the bars.

"I will give you anything you desire if you tell my father where I am being held prisoner," he was saying.

"Careful of offering desires," I said. "That is a good way to end up giving away your firstborn."

The prince froze and turned toward me, his eyes wide with fear.

"Don't...don't kill me."

"I will not kill you," I said. "But I will settle for stripping you of what you hold most dear."

"You mean my hair and the red feather in my hat?"

"I have not yet taken the feather in your hat," I said. "But I will take it now."

The mortal was wearing his hat over his shorn hair, and the

feather vanished from it with a pop. He did not take it off to check that it was gone.

"So you saved her from danger, and she still does not love you?"

I knew she did not love me, but there were moments when she looked at me differently since last night, and I did not know what they meant or if they were even real.

"When you rescued your princess, what happened?"

The prince shrugged. "She was grateful."

"And?"

"And?" he repeated, confused.

"What else happened?"

"We returned to her kingdom where her father declared that we would wed," he said. Then he asked, "Did you rescue your princess?"

"I did," I said.

"And what happened?"

"I fucked her in the woods all night long."

The prince gasped and his eyes widened. "You... Are you married?"

"Do I *look* married?"

"Well, not exactly, but you cannot...*fuck*...a lady until you have married her. You will ruin her!"

I raised a brow. "Have you never had sex?"

"Not with a lady. I am *honorable*."

The prince might be many things, but honorable certainly wasn't one.

I frowned. "How is sex not honorable?"

The prince hesitated. "I...I don't know."

"Then why do you speak on things you do not know?"

The mortal was quiet and then he asked, "Do you love this woman? The one you fucked in the woods?"

I did not know what to say.

"You must," said the prince more to himself than to me. "Or you would not want her to love you."

"Do not presume to know how I feel, mortal," I hissed. "I *need* her to love me."

I needed her to speak my true name.

"At some point, if you do not love her, someone else will."

"What do you know about love?" I countered. "All your advice has only made my creature hate me more."

"What worked for my princess may not work for yours. Have you tried asking her what she wants?"

She wanted freedom, and that was beyond what I could give even if I wanted to. Magic was binding. She was the only person who could free herself now, and her choices were to speak my name or live out the next six years while I descended into madness and eventually ceased to exist.

"What if she does not tell me?"

"Then I suppose you will take something else from me."

CHAPTER FIFTEEN
A Riddle

GESELA

he prince of thorns is an idiot, *I thought as I* sprawled on my bed, staring up at the bland ceiling.

I wanted to hate him.

I was definitely angry with him, especially at how we had parted this morning. After everything we had shared, he'd thought to diminish it by offering a letter from his true name.

An *I*.

I already had a *U*.

I should feel excited. It was two steps closer to guessing Casamir's true name, and all I needed were five more letters, but I could only think of last night. It wasn't even the most passionate parts that clung to my memories now. It was the moments when the cruel elven prince had gently kissed my forehead and asked if I was okay, when he had offered his shirt and then the apple, when he had expressed concern over my wellness and feared he had hurt me.

He had made me *feel* things…not just desire but *desired*.

He had done all that and then ruined it with a stupid letter. *Why is he an idiot?* I fumed.

I tried not to think about him but failed.

I had already softened toward him, had already felt the long-forgotten rise of hope inside me, and now that it was awakened, I could do nothing but wallow in misery and try to convince myself that nothing that had happened last night was real.

Except that every time I looked in the mirror, I saw reminders of his touch—bruises and swollen skin—and I could recall every action that had led to each blemish.

Those thoughts drove me from my room and motivated me to search the castle for any clues that might lead to Casamir's true name—if they existed. I only hoped I could avoid the elven prince as I roamed his corridors, but as I did, I noted how this place was far from personal.

If I had wandered here on my own, I would have assumed the castle was abandoned with its moss-covered walls and flowering vines crawling from floor to ceiling. There were no portraits, not even of himself, and instead of soft carpet, there was an array of ground cover—vines, shrubs, mosses—at my feet. One fed into the other as I turned down each winding hall, pausing to look out windows that were either draped with vines or obscured with thick branches from trees that had grown into the facade of the castle.

There was no doubt about its beauty, though I wondered if all elves lived this way.

I came to the end of a hall where a set of stairs rose into darkness. I looked about before I took them, slow and steady as they wound upward and opened into a large bedchamber. While the colors in the room were dark and grounding, there were four floor-to-ceiling windows that made the room bright and full of light.

A large four-poster bed sat against one wall, each post richly carved, and the curtains that hung to veil the bed were open and dark green in color. A broken mirror hung between two of the large windows.

I realized I had been here before, that this was where Casamir's five brothers had sent me at the start of my punishment. I remembered the soft carpet at my feet and the hearth and fireplace nearby.

Unlike the other rooms, the plant life was contained to a corner where several shelves were lined with flowers, vines, and weeping greenery. It was strange, considering the whole castle was overgrown in flora.

"You must be the mortal our prince is obsessed with."

I gasped and turned to see who was speaking, but no one was there.

"Who's there?" I asked.

"Over here," said the voice, which sounded like it came from the windows.

I crossed to look behind the heavy curtains.

"No, no. The mirror," said the voice.

My brows lowered as I stepped in front of the broken shard of glass, but I saw nothing, not even my reflection. I started to peek behind it, thinking that perhaps a fae was playing a trick.

"What are you doing?"

I gasped and released the mirror. It clanked lightly against the wall.

"I thought you might be fae," I said.

"I told you I was a mirror."

"Have you always been a mirror?"

"Yes. What kind of question is that?"

"I thought you might have been cursed."

"I am not cursed. I am enchanted."

"What is the difference?"

"Perspective, I suppose."

I stood, silent for a moment, before the mirror.

"You are the Magic Mirror," I said, recalling my conversation with Wolf about how Casamir's father had deemed the next king would be chosen.

"So you have heard of me," he said, his voice filling with pride.

"I do not know much, I am afraid. Only that you are not whole."

"There is not much to know beyond that," he said.

I turned to look around the room. "So this must be Casamir's chamber?"

Though I had been here before, I had not taken the time to observe. I had been too consumed by the elven lord in front of me to focus on anything other than him and survival.

"Have you come in search of him?" he said.

"No," I said. "I would rather not see him today or tomorrow, perhaps not ever again."

"That does not bode well for him," said the mirror.

I glanced at the mirror. "You know about the curse?"

"*You* know about the curse?" he asked.

I stared at the mirror, and I think he stared back. We were both silent.

"If you have not come for Casamir, then why are you here?"

"I came in search of his true name," I said.

"Ah," said the mirror. "You will not find answers here."

"Where will I find them?"

I imagined that the mirror shrugged as he answered, "Here and there."

I ground my teeth, frustrated. I walked to the end of Casamir's bed, and all I could think, all I could imagine, was us, tangled together in a sea of dark silk. If we had sex again, would it be different? Would he be gentler, sweeter, far more protective?

It all made me too angry. I should not even be thinking about a next time. I should be focused on my goal of getting out of here.

I ground my teeth and turned to look at the mirror, leaning against the end of Casamir's bed.

"Do you always watch him?" I asked.

"I have no choice," he said. "I am a mirror."

"Does he…" I started. "Does he have…visitors?"

"He does not," said the mirror.

I hated the relief that unfurled in my body, hated that I had asked at all.

"Why does he keep these plants when his whole castle is a garden?" I asked.

"He loves them," said the mirror. "That is why the castle is a garden."

My brows lowered and I crossed again to the corner where all his plants were on display. Suddenly I saw his home in a new light. I had thought there was nothing personal about it, but the whole thing…it was a reflection of what he loved.

Something warm filled my chest.

"Why does he love plants?"

"I imagine it is because with plants, he can be who he truly is without consequence."

"And who is Casamir?" I asked. "Truly?"

"I think you know," said the mirror. "The question is, are you willing to see it?"

I pursed my lips and crossed my arms, feeling strangely exposed.

"Where is he?"

"I can show you," said the mirror. "Though you may not wish to know."

I waited and watched as the mirror's surface warped and changed, and I saw Casamir waist-deep in water. He was washing a spray of blood and gold dust from his body. I did not think I needed to know what he had killed. I could guess. The fae who had drawn me into their trap last night, the fae who had blown into my face and made me ache for him.

His features were hard, and there was a part of me that wanted to trace away the tension between his brows and his mouth. I followed his hands, trailing over the hard muscles of his shoulders and arms, his chest and stomach, before he disappeared below the surface of the lake.

When he rose again, he waded to the shore. As his body was slowly revealed to me, I could not help but ache for him again, and as much as I wanted this to be magic, I knew it wasn't.

I took a deep breath and turned from the mirror.

"How do I find his true name?"

I had to find it. I had to speak it.

"You don't," he said. "It will find you."

"How? How when no one knows it?"

"Everyone knows his name. It knows no stranger. It is the wail on the lips of a birthing mother, the howl from the mouth of a grieving lover. It is the cry that breaks the night when death is summoned and the scream that echoes at daybreak when truth makes you ache."

"I am not looking to solve a riddle," I said, frustrated by his words but also processing them, feeling them. "I need a name."

"You know his name," said the mirror. "You have felt it."

I considered what he had said and could acknowledge that I knew what it was to watch death arrive and steal away life. I knew what it was to wish through the night that it wasn't true. I knew what it was to have my heart broken each morning at daybreak.

"I know grief, that is true," I said. "But grief is not a name."

"Anything can be a name," said the mirror. "But you are right. Grief is not Casamir's true name."

We were silent for a moment, and then the mirror said, "Think on it, creature. You have four days."

CHAPTER SIXTEEN
Love Me, Leave Me

CASAMIR

 waited for my creature to come as I had called, just outside the entrance to the dining room dressed in my finest robes. I felt ridiculous and uncomfortable and the anticipation was driving me mad. It ate within my chest like a seething parasite. Why did I feel this way? I had seen her before, a hundred times, but this time was different because I had been inside her. I had given her pleasure and she had writhed beneath me, and I wanted that again even if she did not.

I was not prepared for her when she came into view. She had always been beautiful, but tonight she was exquisite. She wore a fitted gown, as thin as fairy wings. The colors changed as she moved, from pink to gold.

The elves in her wardrobe had done well, the best since she had arrived.

She stopped in front of me, and we stared at each other in a strange and uncomfortable silence.

"You look beautiful," I said, and I hoped she could tell how much I meant it.

Her chest rose as she took a deep breath. "Thank you."

I held out my hand for her. It took her a moment to accept, and when she did, I pulled her to me. Her eyes widened, and one of her hands pressed flat against my chest but she did not push me away.

I held her gaze and brushed a finger along her cheek.

"I want you," I said, and the truth of it echoed in my bones.

"A letter," she said, her voice quiet and her eyes lowered to my lips. "And you can have me."

Anger twisted through me like a knife.

I wanted her to want me too. I wanted her to want me without expectation, though there was a part of me that knew I had done this when I had given her a letter this morning.

"A letter," I said. "And you will serve me dinner. Naked."

She pushed away from me.

"Fuck you."

"I'd really rather not talk about fucking," I said, scowling.

The mood between us changed rapidly, and a thick tension descended. I hated the feel of it, making me feel overdressed and on edge.

"You are despicable," she said.

"Then be free of me sooner and accept the fucking offer."

"I thought you didn't want to talk about fucking," she spat.

We glared at each other, and then she lifted her head, chin jutting out, eyes flashing confidently. "Two letters."

"Fine," I said and turned from her, stalking into the dining room where I took a seat at the head of the table.

"Undress," I ordered.

"The letters," she said.

"A," I said. "The other after you are naked."

"I hate you," she said.

"The feeling is mutual, mortal."

"Fu—"

I stood, the chair scraping against the floor as I did, silencing her. My hand came down flat on the table, the sound echoing in the dining room.

"*What did I say?*"

She glared, her eyes gleaming, and with her silence, I sat. She reached behind her and managed to loosen the ties of her dress. I would have liked to help, would have liked to feel her skin against my fingertips as her dress pooled to the floor, but I knew she did not want that. Still, it was a pleasure to watch her. She was glorious. I shifted uncomfortably, my arousal growing long and hard.

"Why are you angry?" she asked.

"You make me angry. You make me insane," I said.

"You asked for this."

"*You* asked for this!" I said. "Words in this world are binding, vicious creature, or have you learned nothing living in its shadow?"

Her fists clenched.

"Give me the second letter, bastard."

"S," I said. "Are you pleased?"

"I will never be pleased by you."

"We both know differently, creature."

"That was *not* a choice."

"But it was a desire, was it not? No matter how much you wish it wasn't."

She was silent as she crossed to the table where the food had been piled among glittering candles, choosing to ladle soup from a silver tureen.

As she worked, she glanced at me.

"What happened to your nails?"

I fisted my hand so she could not see them, though it was too late.

"I cut them," I said. Because they had hurt her, because I could not pleasure her with claws.

The choice seemed silly now in the face of her hate.

She said nothing, and once the bowl was full, she crossed to me, spit in it, and placed it on the table in front of me.

I could feel her eyes on me as I stared at it, quiet and still, before swiping it off the table and reaching for my creature's wrist. I stood and pulled her to me, trapping her against the table. As I settled my hips against hers, she gasped. I twined my fingers into her hair and pulled her head back.

"Not a choice?" I whispered as I trailed my lips over her taut neck. "Are you certain, creature?"

Her hands tightened in my shirt.

I reached for the closest bottle of wine, uncorked it, took a drink, and kissed her with the liquid in my mouth, feeding it to her as I tasted her. It spilled from our mouths as our lips and tongues moved desperately together.

She did not push me away, so I guided her onto the edge of the table, and when her thighs parted around me, I pulled away.

"Do you want this?" I asked.

"What is this?" she asked.

I smirked and spoke, my lips hovering over hers. "My mouth. My tongue. My fingers. *Me*."

She stared at me, and when she did not answer, I began to pull away, but her hands fisted in my shirt, halting me.

"No," she said.

"No?" I asked.

"I mean yes," she said, breathless. "Yes. I want this."

I had never felt such relief, and I kissed her for it before pulling back again to look at her.

"Fucking beautiful," I said, appreciating how she was spread before me, legs parted, her breasts heavy, her eyes hooded. "I will show you what it would be like if you were to stay with me forever. The pleasure I will give you. The care I will take. You will beg for it. You will love it."

You will love me, I thought. I hoped.

I took the wine, and she gasped as I poured it over her body. Trails of deep red beaded down her skin, over her breasts and down her stomach, pooling in her navel and over the dark curls between her thighs. When I was finished, I bent and licked the bittersweet liquid from her. I started with her pillowy breasts, taking each into my mouth and sucking her nipples into harder peaks. Her back arched, her body curving toward mine, and her fingers glided through my hair, nails scraping my scalp.

I moved down her stomach, kissing and letting my tongue swirl and taste, sucking parts of her skin into my mouth until her breath caught. I had no motive save her pleasure, knowing she had chosen this without the influence of a fairy.

Tomorrow, she could not run from this.

I came to her hips and kissed each before letting my lips feather across her thighs. Her breaths were short and shallow, and she squirmed beneath me. I let my tongue touch her heat and she groaned, offering a keen whimper as I pulled away. I met her gaze as she reached for me, guiding my head between her legs.

"Touch me. Casamir, *please*."

"Remember that you begged," I said, and then I let myself have her. I licked her slowly. I licked every fold. She tasted so good, she tasted so sweet, and I buried my face in her, chasing her as she wiggled beneath me. I moved to her clit, which was swollen and full, heated against my tongue. I licked it and sucked it, and as I touched her there, I let my fingers slide inside her.

She gave a guttural cry and lifted off the table. I pressed my hand down on her stomach to keep her in place, looking up from my place between her thighs, watching as her head rolled back against the table, her hands squeezing her breasts.

Fuck me. She was glorious.

My lust was so acute, my cock hard to the point of aching. I wanted to be inside her again, I wanted to feel her come around me, but I would settle for this tonight. If she wanted more, she would have to come to me.

My creature's heels dug into my shoulders, her knees fell open, and she moved against my mouth, grinding harder, writhing. When she came, it was decadent and delicious, and I kept my mouth against her until she went slack. Then I climbed up her body and kissed her, my tongue stroking hers until I could no longer taste her.

Her hands tangled in my hair and dug into my scalp. Her legs wrapped around my waist, sealing our bodies together, and then she tore her mouth from mine.

"I need you inside me," she said.

"Do you need me?" I asked, breathless. "Or do you want me?"

"Does it matter?" she asked. "I have asked. I have begged."

"Want or need, vicious thing?"

She pushed against my chest, and I straightened, staring down at her as she sat there, marked and rosy by my mouth.

"Do you not want me?" she asked.

"That is a foolish question," I said.

I was desperate for her.

Her eyes lowered to my erection, which strained against the fabric of my trousers, and darkened. Her foot caressed me there, teasing.

"Then take me," she said. "I am offering."

"You will regret it," I said. "As you regretted last night."

Her eyes hardened, and as much as I hated to deny her, I

did not trust that she wanted me. She was caught in a haze of pleasure, and in this state, she would welcome me even if she did not truly want me, and that would bring her no closer to loving me.

She pushed off the table and leaned forward on the tips of her toes, her face close to mine.

"Coward," she said, letting the word slip between her teeth.

Then she snatched her dress from the floor and fled.

CHAPTER SEVENTEEN
Sweet Poison

GESELA

 raced to my room, stumbling, blinded by tears I refused to shed for that...*pathetic* excuse of a *man* who was not a man at all but a horrible, conniving, vicious elf. When I was safely in my room, I leaned against the door and closed my eyes, waiting until my heart rate eased, until the heat in my face lessened, until I had swallowed enough that the tears no longer threatened to release.

What did he *want* from me?

I had done everything he had asked.

He said "Beg," so I begged.

I should rejoice that he had stopped, because what had I been thinking? I had been so caught up in the pleasure of his mouth, his touch, I was willing to compromise myself further, and this time I would not have an excuse for enjoying him because I had been under no enchantment.

But instead, I only felt ashamed, ridiculous, rejected, because in the end...I had truly wanted him.

How could I want him?

He was an elven prince, and I was his captive.

I pushed away from the door and threw the gown I had worn to dinner into the corner of the room. I wasn't even sure why I had bothered to dress. I should have worn the sheer robe the elves in the wardrobe had crafted. It would have been more fitting for what Casamir had planned.

That thought made me angrier.

He had humiliated me, and in exchange for what? A few letters—*U, I, A, S*—four of seven that were completely useless.

The more I thought about it, the angrier I grew. I snatched my robe off the end of my bed and slipped it on as I reached for my ax. The handle was still full of thorns, but I did not care that they pricked my hand as I ventured out of my room and made my way to Casamir's bedroom in the dark.

I held my ax aloft, the stab of each thorn in my hand sharp, my hand already sticky with blood. I was unsure of what might come my way in the night, but I was so full of rage, I was willing to fight just about anything. Perhaps the fae knew not to tempt me, because I made it to Casamir's room with no trouble.

Despite how determined I was, I hesitated, standing outside his door. I felt a deep sense of dread...a knowledge that once I entered here, I would not come out, and yet I wished to end this. To end him.

I touched the handle of his door and turned it carefully. I slipped into his room and approached his bedside, parting the curtains slightly to look at him. A slice of moonlight cut across his bare chest.

"Have you come to kill me?" he asked.

I did not answer but climbed onto his bed. It was tall and I felt clumsy as I struggled to keep hold of my ax, each sharp

point digging farther into my skin. He did not move as I straddled him, just looked at me with those gleaming eyes.

I held my ax close to my chest. He did not try to take it, but he did frown as he observed the blood seeping between my fingers.

"You are wounded."

I lifted my weapon over my head and held it there. I wanted to hurt him, but I also wanted to fuck him.

"If you are going to do it, aim for my head," he said.

"Which one?" I asked. "The one I am looking at or the one between my thighs?"

"If you cut off the one between your thighs, you likely will not get what you came for."

I lowered the ax a little. "I want to hate you."

"I know," he said, his voice quiet, and as he rose to me, he wrapped his hand around my wrist and his mouth collided with mine.

I lowered the ax, letting it fall to the floor. He gripped my face, fingers digging into my scalp. I held on to his forearms, unsure what I intended, only knowing that now I could not think beyond the pleasure of his mouth moving against mine, demanding my complete submission. I was ready for it. I opened to it, and when his tongue moved past my lips to coil with mine, I sighed into his mouth and my body relaxed into his. My arms slipped around his neck, and I crushed myself to him, relishing the feel of his arousal against me as I shifted closer, addicted to the way he made me feel—completely lost and not of this world.

Casamir broke away and his hands tightened in my hair. As he pulled my head back, he growled against my throat.

"You are poison, sweet creature. I want you in my blood."

Then he sucked my skin into his mouth until a cry broke from my lips, and once it had, he pushed me onto my back and sat on his heels, staring down at me.

"Thank fuck for wicked fairies," he said as his eyes skimmed over my body, veiled by the sheer robe. The longer he looked and did not touch, the more impatient I became, warmed and writhing.

I reached for the tie at my waist, but Casamir stopped me.

"Let me," he said.

I held his gaze. "You have seen me like this before."

"And it will never be enough."

I stared, unable to fully comprehend his tone, but he spoke as if he were reciting an oath, sincere but forlorn, and it shifted something inside me.

I let my hands fall away and gripped the blankets beneath me as he pulled the tie and parted my robe. And though it hid nothing, he acted as if he had unveiled the most precious gems in the world.

He bent and pressed a kiss to my stomach, his eyes meeting mine for only a moment, burning like coals in the darkness.

Then he kissed me again and again, trailing down to my thighs. I fisted the blankets and arched my back. I would have rubbed my thighs together just for the sake of friction, but Casamir was between them, teasing me with featherlight kisses.

He smiled at my desperate writhing.

"Casamir," I said, my chest so tight with anticipation, I could barely take in air.

"Yes, sweet creature?"

His voice rumbled against my skin.

"This is torture."

"Ah," he said, lips grazing the bottom of my stomach. "But is it good?"

"It could be better," I said.

"Is that so?" he whispered. "How?"

"Touch me."

"I am touching you."

I gave a guttural cry and reached for his head, but he pushed me flat against the bed with one hand and used the other to spread me apart. But all he did was stare.

"Forgive me, sweet creature," he said. "You must be starved."

Then he licked me, circling my clit, and I thought I might die from the rush of it, from the sheer pleasure that twisted low in my stomach and threaded throughout my body.

"Fuck." I lowered toward him, spreading my legs farther, and he took the invitation, slipping a finger inside me, then two. "Yes."

It did not matter that he had just done this earlier; it felt even better now. His touch and tongue were different, far more intense. I felt all of him and everything, as if my body were one exposed nerve, every part of me pulsating around him.

I never expected this strange fae to become the center of my universe, but I would lie beneath him forever if I could feel like this every second of every day.

Here, where there was no pain and no loss.

Here, where I was not alone.

I reached for his head, grinding into him, and a sound I had never made came from deep in my throat as he chased my pleasure. The pressure built and built, and I could no longer contain the sounds escaping my mouth.

"Yes, yes, yes," I whispered until my words broke on a sob, and I came against his mouth so hard my body shook. As Casamir pulled away and pressed kisses to my lower stomach and up and over my chest, he was breathless, and still, he kissed me, desperate, as if he had gone too long without me.

His body was warm and damp against mine. I reached between us and wrapped my fingers around his cock. He was hard and soft at the same time, and he groaned against my mouth as I touched him.

When he pulled away, he must have understood the desire in

my eyes because he drew his finger over my lips and answered, "Only if you wish it."

I would correct him and tell him I never wish for anything, but this, I wished for.

We traded positions, and as he stretched before me, I stared, eyes roving the planes of his chest and the swell of his arousal, which pressed against his stomach. He was beautiful and it made my heart ache.

I met his gaze.

"You were made for this," I said.

He smiled and asked, "Made for what, sweet creature?"

Pleasure, I wanted to say. *Sex.*

But instead, I answered, "Heartbreak."

He remained still, but there was an edge to his expression that told me he did not disagree. If he was going to speak, I did not know, because I kissed him, pressing my lips to his stomach as he had done to mine.

He held himself up but reclined, moving my hair over my shoulder. I could feel his cock between my breasts as I moved down his body, and when the crown touched my chin, I shifted and closed my mouth over the tip.

Casamir took a breath, and I looked up at him as I released him and licked him from root to tip before taking him into my mouth again. He braced his hands behind him, his head falling back, neck exposed as I worked.

His breath came heavier and he moaned louder. His fingers threaded through my hair, but they did not tighten.

"Fuck," he said, his voice airy. "You are a sweet thing."

Come beaded thickly from the tip of his cock, and it tasted salty on my tongue. I thought of all the times he had come inside me last night, how I had demanded it and wanted it again.

I did not know what he was feeling as I touched him and

sucked him, but I felt the power of having him in my hands and mouth—I controlled his very breath, and right now it was ragged.

It made me ache for him, and when I released him, I climbed up his body and pressed my mouth hard to his before rolling so that I was beneath him.

He rested between my legs, fingers brushing strands of my hair from my face.

"Are you sure about this?" he asked, studying my face, searching for something beyond the confirmation I spoke.

He wanted to know that I would not have regret.

"I came," I said. "And you did not have to call."

He stared, then his eyes dropped to my lips, and he kissed me softly and lushly, letting his hips press into me before he rose onto all fours. As he shifted closer, I widened and lifted my hips. He drew the head of his cock along my entrance and slid inside.

I took a breath as he settled all the way in, and instead of moving, he lay against me.

"Last night," he began, and I silenced him, fingers pressed to his mouth.

I did not wish him to speak ill of last night. I did not wish for him to regret it.

Last night was our beginning, and I did not wish to look at it with anything less than fondness, magic fueling our passion or not.

When I was sure he would be silent, I drew away. We stared at each other for a moment longer before Casamir's lips fell to mine and he began to move. I moaned at the feel of him inside me, and his tongue dipped into my mouth, twisting with my own. He still tasted like me, and a powerful and warm feeling blossomed in my chest. I opened wider for him, lifted my hips higher to meet his thrusts.

Casamir pulled back, bracing his arms on either side of my head, and watched me with an intensity that made me feel raw and exposed, as though he could see my heart and how it beat hard for him.

He shifted to reach for my leg, which he cradled in the crook of his arm. A sound escaped my mouth at the pleasure of this new position, and I pressed my head into my pillow as wave after wave of pleasure rocked my body. Casamir bent to kiss my neck and take the skin into his mouth, sucking hard.

I moaned, my fingers tangling in his hair, bracing behind his neck.

"Yes," I whispered. "More."

"More of what, sweet creature?" he asked.

I did not know, to be truthful, but I lifted my other leg and dug my heel into his ass, and my body moved against his, driving apart and ramming together, and there was nothing beyond this to focus on or to feel.

I pressed my palms against the headboard to keep my head from hitting it. Casamir seemed to notice because he placed his hands atop my head, and then he kissed me, moving harder, faster, deeper. Our bodies became damp and the air smelled thick with our sex, each of us on the cusp of erupting.

I felt my release in my bones and Casamir followed after, his arms shaking as he lowered himself to kiss me, his tongue stroking my mouth with a soft passion I felt deep in my gut. When he pulled away, I questioned who this man was who had made love to me so tenderly.

It left me feeling strange—changed.

There was a part of me that wanted to run from it, but I was still beneath Casamir and he had yet to leave my body. I could not deny that I liked it here.

He brushed my lips with the tip of his finger.

"Are you okay?" he asked, his voice a quiet whisper.

"Yes," I said, though my body still shook. "More than."

He offered a ghost of a smile, as if he did not trust my words.

"Are you okay?" I asked in return.

He smiled a little more.

"Yes," he said. "More than."

He bent to kiss me, and I closed my eyes, expecting to feel his mouth on mine, but instead, he pressed his lips to my forehead and rolled off. I instantly felt cold without him and wanted to turn into his heat, but he left the bed entirely, stepping outside the curtains.

I considered asking him what he was doing, but I could hear water dripping into a basin and could guess. He returned only a few seconds later with a cloth in hand. He said nothing as he handed it to me and closed the curtains as I cleaned myself—first focusing on the blood that had since dried on my hands from the ax, then the rest.

"I'm...finished," I said, feeling awkward when Casamir appeared and held out his hand to take the cloth. I hesitated.

"We have become too familiar with one another for this to be embarrassing."

He might be right, but that did not keep the warmth from my cheeks as I handed over the cloth.

When he returned, he placed one knee on the bed but did not return to my side.

"Do you wish to leave?" he asked, his expression neutral, though I sensed that he was working hard to remain in control of his emotions, unwilling to show disappointment if I said yes. But I had no intention of leaving. I was still cold, and I wanted his warmth.

"No," I whispered.

Casamir released a breath and then pulled the blankets back so we could crawl beneath them. I waited for him to lie down before I rested beside him, curling against his warmth. I let my hand rest on his chest, and beneath my palm, I could feel his heart beating fast. I closed my eyes, and in the quiet, the steady thrum lulled me into a quiet sense of calm. But as my body relaxed, Casamir spoke.

"What happened to your family?" he asked.

I opened my eyes and stared into the dark. It was a question that made my heart clench, as if he had taken it into his hand and squeezed.

"They died," I said.

Thinking about it made me sick and sad. I was the reason they were gone, the reason I was alone. My blood had killed my mother, I had wished for my sister's death, and my father had died of heartbreak from her loss.

"Your sister died too? Or was she murdered?"

I curled my fingers on his chest, and he covered it with his.

"Tell me," he said. "Please."

It took me a moment to speak because I suddenly felt like my tongue was swollen.

"When I was younger, I would dance with the fairies on the edge of the forest. Small ones with butterfly wings. I loved them and they never harmed me. When my sister found out, she chased them away. I was so angry, I wished she were dead, and she transformed into a deer right before my eyes and raced into the forest."

I paused and swallowed the thickness in my throat.

"I searched for her in the forest for years, and on the final day of the seventh year, I found her, resting beneath a tree, but when I started to go to her, an arrow flew from the trees and hit her.

I will never forget how her eyes widened, and as she fell, she became human again. There was so much blood, and I couldn't stop it, so I just held her and told her how sorry I was…how much I wished I could undo what I had done. Then, as if the forest had not punished us enough, I noticed something slithering and saw that roots were shifting beneath us, wrapping around my sister. I screamed and clawed at the wood, but the tree took her."

This time, I could not keep the tears from sliding down my cheeks. I took a shuddering breath and whispered, "I have never wished for anything since."

There was a beat of silence as Casamir's hands tightened around me.

"Your sister is not dead," he said.

I pushed away from him and sat up. "Do *not*."

Casamir rose with me and reached for my hands. I tried to pull away, but he kept them close to his chest.

"She is healing, not dead," he said quickly. "*Trust* me."

I stared at him, searching his eyes for the truth, but he looked so serious and so sincere, it took the breath out of me.

"What are you saying?"

"If the tree took her as you said, then she is healing. It is not quick. She could be within its roots for years, a hundred even, but it is likely that her heart still beats."

I scrambled from the bed.

"*Creature*," Casamir hissed. "Where are you going?"

"To my sister!" I said, searching for my clothes, but recalling I had come only in a robe, I ran for the door.

Casamir caught me about the waist.

"It is too dangerous tonight."

"Let me go!" I snapped, clawing at his hands, but he would not let me go.

"Not in the dark," he said, his mouth against my ear. "Please, sweet creature."

"But she is *alive*!" My voice broke. I was no longer alone.

"And she is likely still in the tree, where she will be tomorrow."

His words stole my fight, and I sagged against him. His arms were tight around me, and his head still rested in the crook of my neck.

"I will take you tomorrow. I will take you as soon as day breaks. I promise. I swear it."

After a moment, I turned to face him.

"Why promise?" I asked. "Why swear?"

He seemed confused. "Because…it is what you want."

My chest felt warm and open, and I felt as if my heart were beating in my whole body. I gripped his face and pulled him to me. As our lips collided, we staggered and Casamir's hands fell to my ass, gripping me tight, his arousal hard between us.

"Down," I commanded, and we knelt to the floor. I guided him to his back and straddled him, grinding over his cock. I bent to kiss him again, letting my tongue collide with his. Casamir's fingers pressed into me as I chased friction we both sought, and when that wasn't enough, I guided him inside me, hips grinding into hips, hands planted against his chest. When I grew too tired, he sat up and gripped me, helping me move, our foreheads resting together, our bodies warm and wet. As the pressure built between us, Casamir kissed me, lavishing my mouth with his tongue, and I came, collapsing against him. He held me as he settled onto his back, and we lay there until our breaths evened.

"N."

I winced at the letter, and Casamir stiffened, expecting me to tear away from him. But instead, I remained where I was, body heavy against his.

"I did not mean it," I said.

"You did," he said. "At least when you first spoke the words, but I did not offer it because of the bargain. Think of it as a gift, another letter closer to freedom."

"Is that what you want?" I asked, feeling the slightest twinge of pain at the thought that he would want me gone.

"Isn't that what you want?" he countered.

I thought about it, uncertain now, and after a moment, I spoke. "I want a choice. To stay or go."

Wasn't that freedom? A choice.

"Which would you choose?"

"I cannot say," I said, my words slow and sleepy. "I am not free."

Casamir stared, and I wondered what he was thinking, what was moving behind his dark eyes, but he rose to sit. With my legs wrapped around his waist and my arms around his neck, he stood and carried me to bed. As I lay beside him, my mind reeled with thoughts of what it would be like to do this for the rest of my life, and I did not hate it.

CHAPTER EIGHTEEN
The Old Willow

GESELA

 ake, sweet creature," said a voice, quiet and warm.

Groggily, I opened my eyes to find Casamir standing over me, fully dressed. A golden-orange light burned behind him. The sun was rising.

"It is daybreak," he said. "And I have promised to take you to your sister."

Those words woke me immediately, and I rose and swung my legs over the bed. I was naked and suddenly beneath Casamir's appraising gaze. His eyes roved and my skin warmed, the bottom of my stomach igniting with a desire so keen, I shifted closer to the edge and parted my legs.

Casamir's gaze held there, and his tongue slid across his bottom lip.

"Oh, sweet creature," he rasped. "This morning is not for temptation, for I have made promises."

He touched my chin and tipped my head back while his other hand fisted my hair and he ravaged my mouth. He pulled away with a groan and rested his forehead against mine.

"Get dressed," he said, stepping back to hand me a pile of clothes.

I was surprised when he did not watch and instead crossed the room toward his plants as I changed into a pair of leggings and a long dress with high slits for riding.

"Rested?" a voice asked.

I snapped my head toward the mirror, and my mouth fell open, but I could not respond. I had forgotten about him.

"I—"

"Ignore him," said Casamir, his back still to me.

"How do you ignore him?" I asked. "He's *there*."

He had *seen* everything. *Heard* everything.

My cheeks flushed at the thought.

"Trust me, the more he speaks, the easier it is."

"Do not worry, creature," the mirror said. "I am used to the prince's lovemaking."

"Oh really?" I asked, my embarrassment overtaken by a sudden shock of jealousy.

"Do not say it like that, you foolish thing," Casamir said.

"How should he say it then?" I asked.

"Yes, how should I say it?" the mirror echoed.

Casamir continued to inspect his plants, oblivious to the anger boiling my blood.

"To say I have made love to anyone but you is a fallacy," he said. "And I have spent the better part of ten years pleasuring only myself. If the mirror has been watching anyone fuck, it must be one of my brothers."

"Would he not know the difference?" I countered.

"Well, he is only a mirror," he said, and then he turned to me, his expression serious, growing far more severe the longer he stared. After a second, he crossed to me and reached for the remaining piece of clothing that lay on the bed—a cloak that he draped around my shoulders and clasped at the front. He let his fingers glide down the edges of each side until his fingers twined with mine.

"Beautiful," he said.

My gaze fell to his lips, and I leaned closer, just grazing his mouth with my own when the mirror spoke.

"That was well done, Prince," he said.

We both glared.

"You know you do not *have* to speak," Casamir said.

"I only wish to offer a compliment," the mirror said. "You have improved since last time."

My brows lowered, and before I could speak, Casamir took my hand and dragged me to the door.

"It is time to go."

He did not let go of my hand until we came to the courtyard where a white horse grazed. His coat shined beneath the sun, so bright it was almost blinding.

"I did not know you had horses," I said. I had seen no stables since I had arrived.

"I don't," he said. "Balthazar is wild, but he has agreed to help us today."

"You do not keep animals, but you keep humans?"

"Animals are pure of heart," he said. "Humans are not."

I did not disagree. I pet Balthazar's nose.

"Have you ridden before?" he asked.

"Of course," I said, and he stepped back as I mounted Balthazar. He followed and settled behind me, arms circling my waist, hands smoothing down my arms to my hands.

"Do you know the way?" he asked.

"I know the tree. I go there every day," I said, then corrected myself. "I used to. It is an old willow by the wide river."

"Hold on," he said. Our fingers tightened into Balthazar's mane, and the horse bolted into the Enchanted Forest. I could not tell if Casamir guided the steed or if he knew the way, but he carried us deeper into the woods on a smooth and even gait, dodging limbs and bramble walls. Soon we came to a river, which Balthazar followed until it forked, at which point he made a hard left, right into the river.

The water splashed us, and I gasped at how frigid it was. Casamir chuckled near my ear but said nothing as Balthazar waded through to the bank and continued galloping through the forest, always within sight of the river, which curved like a snake around tall trees and between hills. There came a moment when the surroundings looked familiar and I realized I knew this place.

My heart rose into my throat as the willow came into view, its long, slender branches sweeping the ground like a cascading waterfall.

Balthazar slowed to a stop and Casamir dismounted. I followed, and once my feet touched the ground, I raced to the tree. The ground was disturbed by an elaborate root system, making it difficult to stand beneath its eaves, and yet I managed to walk the perimeter until I found the spot where Winter had once lain. But there was no sign that anyone had risen from these roots.

I felt panicked as I fell to the ground and tried to pry the roots apart, but they would not give.

Then Casamir's hands covered mine and I stilled, meeting his dark gaze.

"Feel her," he said and pressed my palms flat to the roots.

"I *can't*," I said, my voice too high, my head too light.

"Breathe, sweet creature," he said. "Your sister is not far away."

My chest rose and fell rapidly for a few seconds longer before I closed my eyes and took a deep breath, focusing on the

warmth of Casamir's hands atop mine and the roughness of the willow's roots beneath my palms.

Then I felt it—a faint pulse against my skin.

A heartbeat.

I opened my eyes.

"She's *alive*."

I met Casamir's gaze, and I could not quite place the expression on his face. It was caught somewhere between kind and compassionate, and I was not prepared for how it would complement his beauty.

"I told you," he said.

My brows lowered. "But…how long until she's healed? It has been ten years."

"The willow does not often heal mortals," he said. "She likely only did because each of you have some fae blood."

For the first time in my life, I was grateful for that little bit of blood.

"She may rise in a day or ten. She may rise long after you and I are dead and the world no longer looks the same."

Tears welled in my eyes at the thought of being without her for any length of time beyond today, now that I knew her heart beat.

"How will I know? She cannot rise alone."

"She will not be alone," said Casamir. "The fae will help her. By then, she will be fully one of them…one of us."

My gaze snapped to him, but he did not look at me, as if he did not wish to know my reaction to this news.

He rose abruptly and left me beneath the willow.

I lingered a moment longer and pressed a kiss to the willow roots, whispering, "I love you. I'll come for you. I *promise*."

When I left the eaves of the tree, Casamir stood at the center of the meadow, Balthazar waiting nearby. To an untrained eye, he looked menacing and dangerous, but I knew the truth.

I started toward him but stopped a few feet short of reaching him.

"Why did you do this for me?" I asked.

"Because it was what you wanted," he answered.

I shifted on my feet, swallowing hard.

"And what do you want?"

I thought he would reply quickly, but he waited a moment, and when he answered, he spoke slowly, almost uncertain. "I would like to keep my name."

"Why is your name so important?"

"It reminds me of who I was and who I have become," he said.

"And you cannot remember all that if you choose a new one?"

He nearly flinched, and I wondered what tumbled around inside his head as I spoke. I stepped closer, careful, as if I were approaching a predator. I stopped inches from him, our heads inclined, the tension between us thickening, a weight I could barely breathe beneath.

"Is it the name you truly want?" I whispered, my eyes lowered to his lips.

"There is nothing else to desire beyond a true name," he said. "Yours or mine."

His words confused me. "Not even love?"

Casamir's brows lowered. "Are you taunting me?"

"No," I said.

He stared at me and then let his finger trail softly over my cheek, warming my skin.

"Could you love me?" he whispered.

The question stole my breath and burned my lungs in the silence that followed.

I wanted to answer, to whisper yes into the space between us, but I was afraid.

What if I confessed but he could not love me in return?

Did it even matter if I was content to spend my days with him?

His features grew cold and distant, and he took a step back. The tension that had built around us burst, leaving my limbs weak.

"We should return," he said and crossed to Balthazar.

He waited for me to mount before joining me, and he rode without holding me or the horse. And while I would usually be hyperaware of his presence, I was now hyperaware of his absence and found that I hated it far more than I had ever hated the Prince of Thorns.

CHAPTER NINETEEN
What is Love?

CASAMIR

 ould you love me?

What a *stupid* question, I seethed as we returned to the castle. Of course the creature never could, never would love me.

Despite being desperate to touch her, I curled my fingers into fists, refusing. I could not let myself fall deeper into this well—into the hope that she might find me somehow enough.

I thought I would feel some sort of relief when the castle came into view, but I would find no such reprieve. Instead, this feeling of distance created turmoil in my chest.

Balthazar halted, and I dismounted, only to turn and help my creature dismount, my hands closing around her waist.

Once she was safely on the ground, she turned to me.

"G," she said.

My brows lowered. "What?"

"A letter from my name," she said, and then her eyes fell from mine as she added, "You will never know how grateful I am to know my sister lives."

Without another word, she whirled and left the garden. I stared after her, even when I could no longer see her, my mind a chaotic mix of emotions I did not understand, and the longer I felt them—the confusion and strange affection for this mortal woman—the more frustrated I grew. And so I found myself again outside the mortal prince's cell.

"What is love?" I demanded.

I was not certain what he had been doing before I arrived, but he had his face pressed between the bars of his small window so hard that when he turned to me, I could see their impression on his face.

His eyes widened. "Wh-what?"

"Love," I said. "What is it? What does it *feel* like?"

His mouth opened and closed, and then he cleared his throat.

"Well, it is a feeling," he answered. "It…uh…it feels *nice*."

"Nice?" I repeated with a click of my tongue.

"Yes, you know…*good*," he said, rubbing his palms on his clothes as if he were sweating profusely, though it was cool in his cell. "It's good."

I drew my bottom lip between my teeth, nodding.

"Tell me your greatest desire," I said.

He stared. "Is this a trick?"

"It is not," I said, and when the prince did not speak, I added, "You have my word."

Though that promise felt like glass between my teeth.

"My greatest desire is not so simple," he said. "While it is to be free, if I do not return to my kingdom with a golden apple from a tree that grows in the depths of the Glass Mountains, I cannot marry my beloved."

It was the most articulate he had been since I began seeking his help.

I raised a brow. "Must you marry her?"

The prince balked. "Of course! If I do not marry her, she will marry someone else."

"Then she must not love you."

"She loves me," he said. "But she is a princess, and all princesses must marry."

"Who says?"

The prince hesitated and then answered, "Her father."

"And if her father is dead?"

"If he is dead and no one has married the princess, then there is no king."

"So you wish to be king?" I asked.

The prince said nothing, and I knew I had hit at the root of his desire.

"So all this advice you have offered…?"

"I did not lie," said the prince defensively. "You asked how to make a maiden fall in love with you, not how to fall in love with *her*."

My face felt hot with frustration, but the prince was not wrong.

"So…has she fallen for you yet?" he asked.

"Would you be here if she had?"

The prince paled, but he was not deterred. "But you have fallen for her?"

"That is what I am trying to figure out," I gritted out.

"Well, how do you feel?" he asked.

"Insane," I said.

"I think you were insane before her," said the prince.

I glared.

"I cannot describe it," I said after a moment. "I only know that I do not wish to know the world without her."

The prince hummed softly and then replied, "Well, if you are not in love, then that is a promising start."

I met his gaze and scowled. "You are most unhelpful."

I vanished, returning to my room. Naeve, who had been making my bed, yelped as I landed on the mattress. I ignored her, reached for a pillow, covered my face, and screamed.

"Feeling better?" the mirror asked when I was finished.

"No," I said, the pillow muffling my snappy response.

Naeve yanked it off my face and then hit me with it. I scowled at her, and she hit me again.

"Why are you here? You should be wooing your creature! You have only three days to make her love you!"

"I have done all I could!" I said, sitting up.

"You mean you have fucked her?" asked Naeve.

"I did more than fuck, you naughty little sprite!"

"And you think that is enough?"

"I cannot *make* her love me, you idiot! Love is a choice, and she has not chosen me."

There was silence, and then I heard Naeve's sharp inhale.

"Well, we have finally made progress."

I stared at her, confused.

"What are you talking about?"

"If love is a choice, then you can choose it too," she said.

"She is supposed to fall in love with me, Naeve, or have you forgotten?"

She shook her head. "You have one day to live however you desire before you forget yourself forever. How do you wish to spend it?"

I was silent.

"How?" she demanded.

I growled, my teeth clenched together as I answered, "With her, you frustrating thing! I would spend it with her!"

As those words left me, I suddenly felt exhausted.

"She makes me feel like it won't matter if I have a name or not. So long as I know her, I will know myself."

A choked cry erupted in the silence, and I looked toward the mirror.

"Are you…crying?" I asked.

"Of course not," he said, voice quivering. "I am only a mirror."

I rolled my eyes.

"Perhaps instead of worrying over whether she loves you, you can spend these last few days loving her."

"What if she doesn't want it?" I asked.

"She seemed accepting from my vantage point," said the mirror.

I scowled. "Could you…*not* for once in your life?"

"It is not as if I have a choice. I am only…"

"If you say 'only a mirror' one more time," I warned, the words slipping through my teeth.

"Focus!" Naeve snapped. She lifted her hand as if she were going to slap me, and I bared my teeth. "Don't let this woman forget you, Casamir, even when you do not know your name."

I looked at her and then at my hands. "What should I do then?"

"May I once again suggest a picnic," said the mirror.

CHAPTER TWENTY
A Pleasant Picnic

GESELA

, *I, A, S, N.*

I lay on my bed, staring at the ceiling again, considering how the letters of Casamir's true name fit together and which ones I might be missing, I found myself wondering what would happen when I learned his name, when I spoke it and managed to free myself. Did I have to leave? Did I have to return to my lonely cottage on the edge of the Enchanted Forest? If I stayed and Casamir did not know himself, would he still know me?

The thought hurt more than I liked to admit.

Of course, all this would be remedied if I loved him.

But what was love? True, I had loved my mother, my sister, my father. I had loved them and hurt them.

I did not want my love to hurt Casamir, not when he took away so much of my pain.

A knock sounded at my door, and I let out a breath, blinking rapidly to clear my eyes, which had blurred with tears.

I sat up and stared at the door, mistrusting who might be on the other side.

The knock sounded again, and I rolled onto my knees and reached for my ax, which had been returned to my bedside table, likely by Naeve. Its handle was no longer riddled with thorns but smooth—Casamir's magic, if I had to guess.

"Come in," I said.

The door opened, and Casamir entered.

I was startled to see him, given his cold departure, but as he closed the door, a slow smile spread across his face.

"Preparing for battle, creature?" he asked.

I held the ax to my chest.

"That depends," I said. "Have you come to declare war?"

"I was thinking something a little less bloody."

I raised a brow, and his features became a little more serious.

"Perhaps a picnic?"

I pressed my lips together, attempting not to smile at the thought of the Prince of Thorns on a pleasant picnic.

"Do you even like picnics?" I asked.

"I like anything with you," he said.

I stared and swallowed.

"Well?" he prompted.

"Yes," I said. "I'll go on a picnic with you."

He smiled, full and real, and as if he could not be any more beautiful, he suddenly was. He stole my breath.

"I will meet you in the courtyard," he said.

I nodded, and when he left my room, I let out a long breath and collapsed against the bed.

What was happening to me that I desired his presence so much? This was more than wanting his body in mine.

I had sought him out.

I had wanted him.

And lying here alone had only made me wish for him more.

I rolled off the bed and knocked on the wardrobe door.

"I need something to wear to a picnic," I said.

The door opened, and I expected the elves to toss something at me as they always did, but instead, six pairs of eyes stared back, assessing. After a brief moment, the door closed quietly. I was surprised by their discreet action and continued to be when they opened the door a few seconds later to dangle another white dress before me.

I took it and held it to my chest.

"Thank you," I said and then turned from them to slip into the airy gown. It was off the shoulder with a laced front, which I tied loosely. The fabric was nearly see-through, as the fairies were keen to craft. I slipped on a pair of flat shoes and checked the mirror. My hair was wild and wispy from our earlier ride to the willow tree, and I smoothed it into a braid before I left for the courtyard, unable to calm the strange fluttering in my stomach.

It did not lessen, even when I found Casamir waiting for me. If anything, it burned hotter, filling my veins and flushing my skin. He wore black trousers and a loose white shirt, the collar of which was open, exposing the long column of his neck and chest, his creamy skin marked by my mouth.

His eyes darkened as he took me in, and I shivered beneath his gaze.

"Are you ready, sweet creature?"

"Yes," I said, voice quiet.

He held out his hand, and as I took it, he drew me to him, his arm snaking around my waist.

"You are beautiful," he murmured.

I smiled up at him. "You are getting very good at giving that compliment."

His fingers touched beneath my chin. "It is easy to say when it is the truth."

I felt as though I couldn't breathe and let my gaze fall to his chest, fingers tracing his skin.

"I thought we were going on a picnic," I said.

"We are."

"You have no basket," I said. "No blanket."

He chuckled, and the sound drew my attention again. His eyes gleamed with mirth, and I loved it. I wanted to see that expression in his face every day.

"Come, sweet creature."

Casamir did not release my hand as he led me into his garden. As we passed clusters of blooming flowers, sprites rose from the petals, flying in swarms ahead of us. As before, the garden grew thicker and fuller the farther we walked, and despite being with Casamir, I could not help feeling on edge. The garden seemed to open up and fall away until we stood at the center of a clearing where the ground was covered in small white flowers. Trees with crooked and twisting trunks framed the space, but it was beneath the tallest one that our picnic was splayed on a white quilt. Amid bouquets of small, pink flowers and pillar candles were bottles of wine, plates of meat and cheese, and sweet treats.

"Is it to your liking?" he asked.

"More than," I said, smiling.

I had never seen a more beautiful picnic, but then I had never been on one.

He held my hand until we were seated and poured wine into elegant glasses. I watched as Casamir reclined on the blanket, looking relaxed and far too beautiful. I sipped my wine, which tasted like raspberries, both sweet and tart. Now that we were here, I felt so uncertain and so confused.

"I never thought any part of the Enchanted Forest could be beautiful," I said.

"It is all beautiful," he said. "But that does not make it any less dangerous."

I offered a small, almost sad smile. "If I didn't know better, I would think you were talking about yourself."

"You think I am beautiful?" he asked, amused.

"Of course," I said.

His stare captured and held mine, too intense to release.

I took a breath. "What are we doing?"

"Having a picnic," he said.

"No, Casamir. What are *we* doing? I don't understand this...*us*."

He frowned and then rose, setting his glass aside. He leaned toward me and drew my hair behind my ear, fingers lingering along my jaw.

"Do you need to?" he asked.

"I think I should," I said. "Before I make a mistake."

"What mistake could you possibly make?"

His mouth hovered over mine, his breath caressing my lips as he waited for my reply, but it never came. Instead, I let my tongue slip into his mouth and gave in to his kiss, which deepened with a slow caress.

Casamir tugged on the ties of my dress, and I helped him pull the neckline down, slipping my arms from the sleeves. It pooled around my waist. Bared to him, I swung my leg over his and he jerked me forward, hands beneath my knees, until I settled against his arousal. I groaned at how he fit against me. Just the promise that he would soon be inside me was pleasure, and for a brief moment, I considered how I had ever lived without this—without him.

Casamir kissed me as he squeezed my breasts and then took each one into his mouth. I gasped, raking my fingers through his hair, pulling on his long strands until he released me and brought his mouth to mine.

"Tell me what part of this is a mistake," he said, and his

hands swept beneath my dress, over my thighs and hips before
he gripped my ass, his fingers digging into me as he moved me
against him, his arousal creating a delicious friction between
my thighs. All the while, Casamir's mouth explored my jaw
and neck, my collarbone and my breasts. He was everywhere
all at once, and somehow I still wanted more. Then he shifted
and rolled me onto my back. He gave me no time to adjust
as he moved down my body, leaving a path of fire in his wake
as he descended to the apex of my thighs and kissed there,
his mouth closing over my clit, his tongue dancing in gentle
circles, his fingers parting my flesh, curling inside me. When
I came and lay boneless and breathless, Casamir pulled my
dress off and then stripped himself of his clothes. Everything
inside me felt like liquid fire as I watched him, lean and hard,
return to me.

He settled between my legs. I expected him to kiss me, but
all he did was stare, his heavy arousal growing harder, pressing
into the bottom of my stomach.

"What's wrong?" I asked.

"Nothing," he said. "I am just trying to memorize you."

"Are you saying you will forget me?" I asked, my tone light,
teasing, but he frowned and I felt the dread blossoming inside me.

"I don't know."

I studied him and then took his face between my hands.

"I wish that I could have at least given you freedom," he
said. "I do not wish for you to watch me fade away." There was
something in his dark and deep eyes I had never seen before—a
hint of fear—and it felt like it was more for me than for him.

My heart stuttered in my chest.

"You won't," I swore. "I will remind you of who you are."

"Every day?" he asked.

"Until you remember."

"I will never remember."

"Will you remember me?" I asked, voice trembling slightly, unable to keep my fear at bay.

"I never wish to forget you."

We stared at each other in silence for a moment, and then I brought him to me and kissed him, reaching between us to position him against my heat. In one thrust, he was inside me.

There was a slow and sweet rhythm to the way we began. I felt every ridge of him as he moved, and our breaths came quietly, quickening as his pace increased. I began to move with him, and then we were suddenly completely different and desperate.

His hand went to my neck, but he did not squeeze. I waited, and then ordered it. He kissed me instead, and when he broke away, I felt his fingers press on either side of my neck and relished in the pressure building in my head. When he released me, the pleasure nearly shattered me.

I gave a guttural cry and lifted my head toward his. Our lips crashed in a messy kiss as I gripped his forearms for some semblance of control. But I was already lost, and when I came, he followed shortly after, my muscles clenching around him, eager for every drop of come he possessed.

We lay on the quilt afterward, and Casamir fed me grapes and plums. They were sweet and ripe, and after I finished, he would kiss me, tongue swirling, lapping at the sugar on my skin.

There came a point when he hooked my leg over his and spread me wide and entered me as he lay on his side behind me. I arched against him, my hand anchoring behind his head so I could bring his mouth to mine until I could hold on no longer and instead braced myself against the ground as he thrust inside me. My eyes watered from the bliss of it, and he kept going until I felt like I could no longer handle the ecstasy of it and I burst open.

As I came down from the high, I felt raw and exposed, and I wondered if Casamir could see how I felt—how much I *wished* to have this for the rest of my life.

He placed a kiss in the hollow of my neck and spoke near my ear.

"I would give you a letter," he said. "But I fear I cannot recall my name."

I frowned and lifted my head to look at him. "It isn't time to forget."

He smiled faintly.

"Perhaps I have miscounted the days," he said in a sleepy voice, and as he fell into an untroubled sleep, I lay awake, desperate for his name.

CHAPTER TWENTY-ONE
The Riddle

GESELA

 e left the clearing and returned to the castle where I followed Casamir to his room. For a few more hours, I was able to forget my fear of losing him. When he was in front of me, touching me, making love to me, it was hard to imagine he would ever forget me, but I knew the evil of magic. It had hurt me before and it would again.

Casamir slept beside me, his warmth a welcome weight, and though I was exhausted, I could not stop my mind from reeling, turning over the mirror's riddle in an attempt to make sense of the words.

> *His name knows no stranger.*
> *It is the wail on the lips of a birthing mother,*
> *the howl from the mouth of a grieving lover.*
> *It is the cry that breaks the night when death is summoned*
> *and the scream that echoes at daybreak when truth makes you ache.*

You know his name. You have felt it.

I turned my head and stared at his profile and tried to imagine returning to my solitary life, knowing that his memory would always live beneath my skin. I would never be able to let him go. He would drive me mad, and he would not even know it because he would not know me.

Despite being tired, I left the bed and slipped into the white dress the elves had made me for the picnic. Dawn was just breaking, and a pure golden light warmed the curtains covering the windows. I crossed to the corner of the room where Casamir's plants thrived.

"Will he remember why he loved them?" I asked as I took a velvet leaf between my fingers.

"He will remember nothing about himself," said the mirror. "That is the power of losing one's name."

My chest felt tight, and I swallowed something hard in my throat.

"And if I were to give him my name?" I asked and then looked at the mirror. This time, I saw my reflection, haunted and pale.

"Well then, that would be power too."

I left Casamir to sleep and wandered into the garden, hoping to clear my head. I needed time to think, to cycle through the letters I had and the words I knew. Now that I was faced with losing Casamir, I felt a bone-deep sorrow.

It hurt and ached.

I had been alone so long, I never thought I would desire anyone, but here I was, wishing for an elven prince to love me.

I halted in my steps.

Surely that was not what I had meant.

I wanted Casamir to remember me, not *love* me.

A sudden and intense rush of dizziness overtook me, and I shook, unable to breathe as I came to terms with the truth of my feelings. I wanted Casamir to love me because I loved him, but I needed his name.

What was his *name*?

The more frustrated I grew, the less hold I had on my emotions. I felt frantic and my chest tightened, and my heart felt as though it was beating all over my body. I bent at the waist and tried to take in air, repeating the letters of Casamir's name.

U, I, A, S, N.

I said them over and over until I could breathe again.

Slowly, my thoughts turned to the mirror's riddle, and I recalled the times when I had wailed and howled and cried at my family's deaths. My grief had spanned mornings, and all I had ever felt was agony. All I had felt was—

Anguish.

My heart rose. That had to be Casamir's true name.

My body danced with delight, vibrating with excitement. I whirled, intending to race to him and speak it against his lips as I confessed my love, but as I turned, I came face-to-face with a man.

"Well, hello," he said, and while he tried to sound pleasant, I immediately felt on edge.

I got the sense by the way he approached, as if I were a wild animal, hands outstretched, palms flat, that he had been trying to sneak up on me.

He wore a purple hat and strange purple clothes that seemed to be missing buttons down the front, for his shirt hung open, exposing his chest and stomach.

"Who are you?" I asked, my pulse racing. He tried to circle me, but I followed, wishing I had my ax. I would show him what to fear then.

"I am a prince. A mortal one," he added, as if I could not tell. No fae would wear such clothing. No fae would approach me as if I were the threat. "My name is Flynn."

He paused to bow and added, "At your service."

"I do not need your service," I said.

He watched me, blue eyes sparkling.

"Are you the maiden the prince is in love with?"

I wanted to ask how he knew about me, but I was stunned by his words.

Had he said the prince was in love with me?

I opened my mouth and then closed it, finally deciding to ask, "Why are you here?"

"The same reason you are here, I imagine. We are captives, are we not?"

I did not speak and instead took a step away.

"Do not be afraid," he said, inching closer. "I will not hurt you. I am here to rescue you."

"I do not need rescuing," I said.

"It looks to me like you do," he said.

Casamir's name was poised on my tongue. I knew if I called, he would come, but before I could speak, something tight wrapped around my wrists and mouth—vines.

Something struck me from behind, and I fell to my knees. When I looked up, a cluster of pixies flew from behind me, hovering near Prince Flynn. They were the ones who had left slugs in my room on my first night in Casamir's castle.

Each held out a hand, and he popped a button from the cuff of his sleeves. The pixies took them in hand, the buttons as big as them, and they dragged them away, wings beating furiously.

It was their magic that restrained me, their magic he had bargained for. Two remained, each sitting on one of his shoulders.

"The pixies tell me you have been to the Glass Mountains."

Fucking fae. Casamir would not have the pleasure of tearing them to pieces because I would tear them limb from limb.

"You will take me there," he said. "And once I have obtained a golden apple from the Mountains, you will come to my kingdom and aid me in conquering the Prince of Thorns. Do you understand?"

I glared, and then he produced my ax from behind his back, and my eyes widened. Another bargain made with the pixies, no doubt.

"If you try anything, I will not hesitate to bury this blade in your head. It's what you deserve, after all, for fucking a fae prince. Up!"

I rose to my feet on shaking legs, and the mortal prince put his hand on my forearm.

"The pixies say there is a pond you depart from, and from there you call a wolf."

I tried not to react to what the pixies had told the mortal, knowing he had to have made a desperate bargain. What had the prince given up for this aid? More than buttons, I imagined.

"I shall know if you lead me astray," said the prince as he pushed me ahead. "Walk."

I led the way as I considered my next move. It was as if the pixies knew I was considering my escape, because the vines tightened on my wrists and around my mouth, but they could not stop my thoughts, which wished for Casamir, for Anguish, for my elven prince to wake and realize I was gone.

All the while, Prince Flynn kept busy, rattling away about his time in the dungeons of Casamir's palace.

"And did you know he came to me for love advice?" he was saying. "And each time he took something from me. First my hair, and then the feather in my hat, as if the hair could not grow back, as if I could not obtain another feather. The fae, they are foolish!"

His words made me cringe. Even if he managed to obtain a golden apple from the Glass Mountains, I knew he would come to regret those words, though I wondered why Casamir had asked for his hair and the feather in his hat. I knew the Prince of Thorns, and he did not ask for anything without reason.

"For a harlot, you are a picky thing."

I jerked in his hold at his horrible words, and he wrenched me against him, placing the sharp blade of my ax against my neck.

"Ah, ah, ah," he said. "Remember what I said?"

"Fuck you," I tried to say, but the vines tightened to the point that my jaw ached.

The mortal prince laughed and then pushed me forward.

"Do as you're told, and the pixies might let you survive this."

The walk to the selkie's pond seemed to take forever, but when we arrived, I turned to face the prince.

"Well? What now?" he asked.

I stayed silent. It was not as if I could speak with the vines wrapped so tight around my mouth. He seemed to realize this and chuckled.

"Oh, of course," he said and lifted the ax. "Allow me to help."

When I started to move away, his hand braced my head.

"Careful," he whispered. "I wouldn't want to cut you."

He touched the blade of the ax to the vine and pressed. They snapped, and I felt the distinct burn of a cut on my skin.

I hissed and the prince chuckled.

"I told you not to move."

I considered kneeing him in the groin, but he still had the ax aimed at my chest, and without my hands free to grab it, I worried it would end up buried inside me.

"Now what, harlot?" he asked.

I ground my teeth.

"Drink the water," I said. "And I'll call for Wolf."

"Drink the water?"

"You must drink the water to grow small enough to ride Wolf," I said. "Do you want your apple or not?"

He looked from one shoulder to the other where the pixies

still sat, and once they had confirmed what I said, Prince Flynn grabbed me and directed me to the water. He kicked my feet out from under me, and I fell hard, mud splattering my entire body.

"You drink," he commanded. "And then I will."

I could not wait to gouge out his eyes, and I would do it with my thumbs and revel in the feel of it beneath my nails. I bent, hand still tied behind my back, and slurped the muddy water into my mouth. As I did, I felt the familiar dizziness that came with growing small. I ended up in a pool of water my knee had created on the bank of the pond and waded from it onto the soft ground.

"Well, would you look at that," he said, and I watched as he hurriedly scooped water into his cupped hands and drank.

When I called Wolf, I shouted his name and hoped that the wind would carry my summons to the castle as well, but the longer we waited, the more anxious I became. Would Casamir catch up with us soon? Would he realize I was gone and think I ran away? Would he even remember me if he truly had miscounted the days?

I chewed the inside of my cheek.

"You had better not be lying," the prince threatened as a shadow passed over our heads.

When I looked up, Wolf was circling.

"What is that?" the prince demanded.

"Wolf," I said.

"That is not a wolf!"

"I did not say Wolf was a wolf," I replied.

The raven landed and bowed his head.

"Lady Thing," he said. His beady eyes narrowed at me, noticing that my hands were tied behind my back and blood dripped down my face from the slice of my ax. "How may I assist?"

"This is Prince Flynn of the Kingdom of…" I paused and

looked at the prince. I did not know from where he came, but I wanted to know, because later, when I had plucked his eyes from his head, I would return them to his father in a glass coffin, so that his whole kingdom would know what happened when he crossed me.

Prince Flynn hesitated and then spoke. "The Kingdom of Rook."

"Rook," I repeated. "He wishes to be taken to the Glass Mountains to obtain a golden apple."

"She must go too," Flynn added quickly. "You must take us both."

The raven looked from the prince to me.

"Of course," he said. "But, Lady Thing, you cannot ride with your hands tied. Allow me."

The prince raised the ax to threaten Wolf, but he moved quickly and snapped the vines around my wrists, then he shifted and plucked the prince up by the scruff of his neck and launched into the sky. The ax fell from his hand and landed at my feet, and I was hit hard by the violent splash of mud and water.

The mortal's arms flailed and despite how tiny he had become, I could still hear his desperate screams as the raven continued higher and higher until they were nothing more than a tiny, black dot in the sky.

"I command you to let me go!" he said, and when that did not work, he dissolved into tears. "Please, let me go! Let me go! I will give you anything, anything!"

Wolf obeyed and let the tiny prince drop, but before he could hit the ground, a large hawk shot from the trees and snatched him up, gobbling him whole.

I stood, staring blankly at the sky where he had been, before I knelt and drank from the pond, head spinning as I grew. When I came to my full height, something zoomed past my face—the two pixies who had helped the prince capture me. They came so close, I could feel the vibration of their wings and hear their shrill laughs.

I reached out and managed to capture one in my palm, its joyful cackle turning into a terrified scream as I squeezed. The pixie cracked and burst, and when I opened my hand, its bloody and broken body lay at the center of my hand, wings contorted, legs twitching.

A high-pitched scream sounded, and I looked up in time to see the other pixie racing toward me, but before it could land a blow to my face, I slapped it, and it landed some distance away in the grass and did not rise again.

I washed my hands free of the blood and bone in the water and reached for my ax when I noticed black thorns and solid shadows trailing across the ground. As I straightened and turned, I found Casamir before me, his magic surrounding us like a wall, a comfort I never thought I would want but desired now forever.

He took me by the shoulders and brought me close, his eyes as black as the night sky, gleaming like the stars.

"Casamir," I breathed.

I wrapped my arms around him, though he looked vicious and bloody. If I had to guess, the other pixies who had helped the prince capture me had met their ends at his hands.

"You are hurt," he said.

"It is only a scratch," I said, pulling back to look at him. "The prince is dead."

Casamir bared his teeth.

"I am sorry. I did not know—" he began.

"It's all right, Casamir," I said and pressed my fingers to his lips. "It does not matter. I am well and I know your name. Your true name."

The harshness etched on his face did not ease.

"My name?"

My brows lowered. "Aren't you pleased?"

I thought he would be. Wasn't this what he wanted?

It was what he had said when I'd asked him what he wanted most.

My name. My true name.

"I lied," he said. "When you asked what I wanted most. I want you. I know myself when I am with you."

"Casamir," I said and drew a stray piece of his hair behind his ear, then I smiled before whispering, "My name is Gesela."

His eyes widened, and I leaned in, whispering his name before my mouth met his.

CHAPTER TWENTY-TWO

Happily Ever After

GESELA

 t was almost noon, and the sun burned high in the sky as I road into the town of Elk on Balthazar's back, dressed in a gown of thorn and shadow. On my head, I wore a crown of twigs and iridescent wings, a gift from Casamir. They'd come from the backs of the pixies who had aided the mortal prince in abducting me. I wore it proudly, a mark of my status as his future wife.

The thought made my chest feel warm, and as it spread through my limbs, I sat up taller.

"Gesela," Casamir had murmured as we lay together in bed once we returned home from the selkie's pond, once we had washed ourselves of the mud and blood. "Princess of the Kingdom of Thorn."

I shivered at the sound of my name on his lips, at the title he would bestow on me.

I looked down at him, tracing his mouth. "But that is my true name," I said. "Only you can call me by my true name."

Only he and death.

He smiled. "True," he said. "What would you like to be called by everyone else?"

My grin matched his. "Princess would suffice," I said, pausing. "Princess...Ella. It is what my sister would call me."

I only hoped that one day soon, she would emerge from the roots of the willow tree where she had lain and healed to hear her call me that again.

"Princess Ella it is," Casamir said.

I laughed quietly, shaking my head.

Casamir raised a brow. "What is it?"

"The selkie was right," I said. "And so was Wolf. They both said I would come to rule at your side."

The elven prince did not speak. He only stared, and I bent, my lips close to his.

"How does one turn a raven into a wolf?" I asked.

"Hmm," he said, his arms tightening around me. "I suppose you could make a wish and I could grant it."

"Wishes come with great consequences," I replied.

"And if the consequence means remaining at my side for the rest of our eternal life?"

"That is not a consequence," I said. "That is a gift."

We kissed and descended into our own heated madness.

Later I would ask, "Why did you demand the hair upon the prince's head and the feather in his hat?"

"The prince was too blind to see what he had before him—his golden curls might have become golden apples, his red feather a key to his cell, the buttons he traded to the pixies, feed to summon a horse. He had all the tools he needed to escape me, but he chose to use them incorrectly."

We spent the rest of the evening together in bed, and the

next morning, Casamir granted my wish, which saw Wolf the raven return to his true form as a great, white wolf.

In his true form, Wolf bowed and spoke.

"I am in your debt, Lady Thing," he said. "I will come when you call."

And as he disappeared into the surrounding wood, I mounted Balthazar who Casamir had also summoned from the Enchanted Forest.

"Are you certain you wish to return to your village?" Casamir asked before I departed.

"It is not my village," I said. "But yes, they must know what they have done to me."

I wanted them to look upon me and fear me, to know that their actions had created something far worse than a curse.

Now, as I passed cottages and shops, I smiled. The townspeople left their cottages to watch, and I heard their whispers.

I thought she was dead.

She has been ravished by fae.

Look at her dress! How indecent!

It was true the dress was indecent, exposing wide strips of skin, the thorned vines only covering my thighs and my breasts, but I loved it because it was a gift from Casamir.

I halted by the well just as bells rang in the late morning, disturbing the quiet. They were not nearly as beautiful as the ones that had drawn me into the forest, as if they were cracked, the sound harsh and jarring.

The doors to the chapel swung open, and more people spilled out onto the steps, among them many council members and the mayor of Elk, all of whom had voted to send me down the well.

In some ways, I had them to thank for my life's turn of events.

Their merrymaking silenced once they spotted me.

Behind them, Roland appeared dressed in powder blue and Elsie all in white, her straw-blond hair threaded through with white chrysanthemums.

I was not so surprised to see that the two had chosen each other. After they had led me to the well, they deserved each other.

They halted atop the steps, both pale as the snow still piled around the town.

"Gesela," Elsie said, breathless. "We—we thought you were dead."

"What a surprise it must be," I said, "to discover I am not."

Roland and Elsie exchanged a look.

"We went to your house, searched the whole thing," said Roland, who attempted a hard and indifferent expression but could not hide the haunted look in his eyes. "You were nowhere to be found."

"I imagine you did not expect to find me at all," I said. "Which must be why all my things have gone missing."

There was silence.

I looked at those gathered, their faces much the same as the day I left, a mix of pity and fear and discontent.

"What will you all do to atone?" I asked.

"Atone?" Roland seethed. "You cannot blame us for thinking you were dead! You fell down the well!"

"I can blame you all I want," I said. "There is no part of this that isn't your fault, Roland."

He shivered as I spoke his name, and I rested my hands atop one another as I sat, elevated above them all, on Balthazar.

"I shall ask you again. How will you atone?"

The mortal ground his teeth and released Elsie's hand. Taking a step down, he drew his sword.

The gathered crowd gasped, and Elsie reached for his arm. "No, Ro!"

I did not move as he bellowed. "You are a wicked spirit come to haunt us!"

His dramatic display brought a smirk to my lips.

"You dare draw your blade against me?"

"Do you think you are someone? Now that you have survived the wood?"

Whispers erupted, and Roland silenced them with a shout.

"Be gone, beast!" he hissed.

"She is not a beast," said Casamir's voice. "But I surely am."

The thorn and shadow of my dress began to move, sliding over my skin.

"What witchcraft is this?" Roland demanded as Casamir took form behind me, his arm banded around my breasts, hiding my nakedness now that I no longer wore his gown of thorns.

The crowd gasped in earnest now, shocked by the sight of him.

"An elven prince!" someone shouted. A few people screamed and some fainted at the sight of him, which I was certain he enjoyed.

"Silence!" Roland cried. "Gesela, what is the meaning of this?"

I felt Casamir stiffen at the sound of my name on the sheriff's lips.

"Forgive me," I said to Roland and placed a hand on Casamir's thigh to comfort him. "For I have yet to introduce you. Roland, meet my future husband, the Prince of Thorns, the seventh son, brother of the sixth, who you ordered me to kill."

"Husband?" he whispered.

A stunned silence followed.

"Yes," I said. "You asked who I was now that I had survived the forest? Here is your answer. I am Ella, lady of thorns and keeper of wings, wife of the seventh brother, and I have come to wish you only *Anguish*."

At the sound of Casamir's true name, a shattering sound filled the air, and then shards of gleaming glass rained down from the sky and speared Roland through the head, along with the mayor and every terrible townsperson who had treated me with contempt. Despite Elsie's participation, she remained unharmed, staring in horror as her new husband bled at her feet, her dress spattered with this blood.

Amid the pure clink of the glass and the screams of the villagers, I turned to my elven prince.

"I love you, Anguish of Thorn."

He pressed a hand to the side of my face, aligning our lips. "I love you, Gesela of my heart."

We kissed amid the carnage, but we did not feel the sting of the glass, for Balthazar had already begun the journey home, through the Enchanted Forest, past my sister's willow, to our castle of thorns.

AND THEY LIVED HAPPILY EVER AFTER.

THE END

Author's Note

Y'all know how I like my author's notes.

First, I know initially I called *Mountains Made of Glass* a *Grimm Retelling,* but it's really a fairy tale retelling as I do not just take inspiration from Grimm fairy tales. In this author's note and my references, you'll see I drew from Hans Christian Anderson and Irish fairy tales too.

I have wanted to write a fairy tale retelling for a long time because I feel like they are a great mix of fantasy and horror. They are also ridiculous and romantic. There is no explanation for any of the magic or even the curses. Things just exist in the world, and everyone in the stories accepts it.

I read a lot of fairy tales and many translations. Because of that, not everything taken from each tale is the same across stories, not even the title. I will list the translations I used at the end of this author's note, but I am also going to go into a lot of detail so maybe you can see how I use various elements of existing stories to create a new one.

First, let's talk about the title of this novella. The Glass Mountains are actually referenced in more than one fairy tale, but the details I used in MMOG came from "The Seven Ravens." The other element I took from this particular fairy tale was the use of Wolf (the raven) who flew Gesela to the mountains and the sacrifice of a limb. In "The Seven Ravens," the main character, a young girl, goes in search of her seven brothers, who were turned into ravens at her birth. To enter the mountains and find them, she must sacrifice her pinkie finger. I had Gesela sacrifice her ring finger, which seemed fitting as a reference to marriage.

The fairy tale that really started all this, however, is called "The Devil and the Three Golden Hairs." Just by the title, you probably already know where I got the idea that Gesela had to sacrifice three of Casamir's hairs to learn his true name, but what you may not know is that the start of this story comes directly from this tale. In "The Devil and the Three Golden Hairs," a man is sent on an impossible task—he must obtain three hairs from the devil's head (also, who knew the devil was a blond?). On his way, the man encounters three towns, and each one gives him a riddle or task to solve (note the use of numbers here, too, three golden hairs, three towns). In one town, the well has gone dry, and we learn it is because a toad lives under a stone at the bottom, and if it is killed, the water will return. This was the foundation of my story, and I thought, what happens if the toad is a prince? An *elven* prince (because I have always loved elves since Tolkien). What happens if all these curses that are broken have greater consequences?

The story grew from there.

In the same story, in another town, a fig tree is rotting and no longer bears fruit. We learn a mouse is gnawing at the roots. I reference this as Gesela is explaining what happens when curses are broken. Instead of figs, though, the tree bears golden fruit, which is a symbolic reference to many Grimm fairy tales (and many other myths, including Greek Mythology).

Beyond this, there are many small elements that are pulled from various stories. The first and most obvious would be most of the town names, which you can see on the map at the start of the book (Briar, Rose, Cinder), and any name given to a side character: Roland, Flynn, Elsie. These are all names used for characters in Grimm fairy tales. I also use common animals or flowers throughout the book as symbolic nods to stories, such as the goose Gesela had slaughtered at the start of the book. Geese appear often in Grimm fairy tales ("The Golden Goose," "The Goose Girl"). The idea of using numbers—seven brothers, seven letters, ten years—comes straight from a variety of Grimm retellings. Everything in these stories is either executed in a very short amount of time (like falling in love) or a ridiculous amount of time. I also use hair. You see this, of course, with Casamir's three hairs and the prince's golden curls. Many academic articles have been written about the role of hair in fairy tales, and I highly encourage you to read a few because the symbolism of hair is very interesting and at times, unexpected—particularly for me how it relates to beauty, sensuality, and sexuality.

It probably goes without saying that the idea of the true name is a reference to "Rumpelstiltskin," and at one point, Casamir warns that bargains with the fae can lead to sacrificing a newborn. The Magic Mirror is a reference to "Snow White," but so is Gesela's sister, Winter, who will eventually rise from the dead. Prince Flynn is an archetype of the typical Prince Charming who appears in all Grimm fairy tales. All this character ever does is rescue beautiful maidens from danger and then lives happily ever after, so I thought it would be hilarious to play on that, funnier when he gives terrible love advice because all he ever knows is that if you tell a woman she's pretty and save her, she has to marry you.

There are several situations in Grimm fairy tales when people are turned into animals. In "Little Brother and Little Sister," a spring speaks to the sister, informing her that if she drinks from it, she will turn into a fawn. The brother drinks instead and turns into a fawn, and through several fairy tales, witches turn various people into bears, ravens, geese, doves—the list goes on.

When Casamir tells Gesela that he will bury the selkie's head in his garden and see what grows, this is a reference to Hans Christian Anderson's "The Rose Elf," where a grieving woman places her dead lover's head in a pot and plants a jasmine bough on top. The use of the bell that leads Gesela into the woods comes from Anderson's "The Bell," which is literally a story about a bell that everyone can hear and no one can find. The ending is boring, about the glory of God, but I preferred Gesela finding her dead family instead, which is a reference to an Irish fairy tale called "The Ride with the Fairies."

The selkie did not come from a Grimm fairy tale, though they do have a story about a nixie, and I felt like if nixies existed in Grimm fairy tales, then a selkie would be just as plausible. I did not reference any particular story to bring in the selkie, but a good one to read is "The Selkie Wife," and before you ask why I didn't just choose a nixie, I'm not sure. I just felt like the sealskin worked really well as a plot device here. I also referenced two curses in the first chapter, boils and a harvest destroyed by locusts, which are biblical references. I did this because some translations of Grimm fairy tales are extremely religious and Hans Christian Anderson was *very* religious so it's a nod to the influence of Christianity.

There are several other elements I added to the story that were my own creation but I felt sounded plausible within a fairy tale world. Some include drinking from the pond and growing larger or smaller, the sealskin that sprouted from the thorn, the tears that made the flower grow and bloom with a fairy inside, the ax growing thorns, the willow healing Winter. These are just some I can think of off the top of my head.

Even given all this, there are likely more references I haven't touched on, but such is the nature of a retelling.

A final note: the Grimm Brothers are often credited with collecting existing fairy tales, while Hans Christian Anderson is noted for creating his own. I find they follow a similar tone and pattern.

I truly hope you enjoyed this tale, and before you ask, I plan on writing six more of these, one for each brother. Even the dead one.

Much love,
Scarlett

APPLES
DIPPED IN
GOLD

The Seven Brothers & Their Seven Kingdoms

The Seventh, Casamir: The Kingdom of Thorn
The Third, Lore: The Kingdom of Nightshade
The First, Silas: The Kingdom of Havelock
The Sixth, Eero: The Kingdom of Foxglove
The Fourth, Talon: The Kingdom of Hellebore
The Second, Cardic: The Kingdom of Larkspur
The Fifth, Sephtis: The Kingdom of Willowin

CHAPTER ONE
Three Wicked Brothers

SAMARA

 ***stood at the center of Daft Moor staring into*** the endless night, made darker by the thick tree line of the Enchanted Forest. It grew so tall, it blocked out the moon and stars. The ground beneath my feet was soggy and cold as ice, the frosty air smelled rich and sweet, and blood stained my hands. It felt thick and seeped between my fingers to the ground, splashing my bare toes like raindrops. I refused to look at the pool of crimson gathering at my feet. I did not want to face what I had done. Knowing was enough.

The blood was not my own.

It belonged to a fae I had once almost loved but had betrayed on this very moor.

My heart ruptured with guilt, carving a painful path from my chest to my throat.

The ache woke me, and when I opened my eyes to the dark, a fresh wave of grief roared to life. I was used to the feeling. I had dreamed the same dream for the last seven years, coaxed into slumber by a haunting voice whispering my name.

Samara, it sang. *Samara, my love, come to me. Flee with me. I can set you free.*

But those words were nothing more than a broken promise, and each morning when I woke to the same heavy darkness, I was left alone to face my punishment for the wrong I had committed before the Enchanted Forest.

I sat up slowly, my lower back aching as I threw my legs over the side of my bed, though calling the pallet I had built up in the corner of the kitchen "a bed" was quite an exaggeration. Still, it was better than sleeping on the floor where the rats could reach me.

I shivered at the thought and looked down at my hands, which were also sore. I spent yesterday bent at the waist for hours, cutting into packed layers of peat. I had been working little by little each day, hoping to harvest enough for the coming winter, though it promised to be long and harsh. I might have harvested more had my three burly brothers helped, but it was not a task that fell to them. No task fell to them.

That thought brought a wave of guilt. I knew I was being unfair. My brothers—Jackal, Michal, and Hans—might not help with the house or the animals or harvest peat, but they did hunt, and they were the greatest hunters in all of Gnat. Only they managed to enter the Enchanted Forest and return with spoils—spoils that kept the entire village fed.

They were heroes, and I was nothing more than what *they* made me, because I could be nothing else with the blood of the fae on my hands.

"Your fingers look as if they have been dipped in blood," my brothers had said upon first seeing my hand. "You will be marked for shame by the villagers and death by the fae, but if you will listen to us always, we will keep you safe."

I believed them at first and had been scared enough to listen, but as the days passed, one after the other harder than the last, death did not seem so dreadful.

In fact, I had begun to think favorably of it. There was something beautiful about ceasing to exist—something that sounded a lot like…rest.

Shame burned my cheeks. I should not think of resting while so many suffered around me, and now, as winter drew near, it was imperative everyone pulled their weight, especially me, who had the responsibility of ensuring the three greatest hunters of Gnat were well rested and well fed.

It was that obligation that drew me from bed.

There was a chill in the air that made my flesh prickle. Still, I crossed to a table in the corner and poured icy water into a bowl and splashed my face. The cold shock roused me, and I dressed in warm layers before kneeling before the fireplace where embers glowed beneath white ash. I raked everything into a pile and reached for the bucket I kept near the fire that was supposed to be full of kindling, except it was empty.

Strange.

I knew I had gathered branches and bits of bark before dusk to keep from having to do it this morning.

Anger twisted in my gut. One of my brothers must have taken it.

"Ladies do not get angry," I heard my mother say. *"It is unbecoming."*

My teeth ached as I fought to quell what felt like violence in my veins and rationalized their behavior.

Perhaps one of them had grown too cold in the night, used all their kindling—which I had also refilled—and came for more. After all, if they did not sleep, they could not hunt, and if they did not hunt, we would not eat, and if we did not eat, we would all die.

I sighed and tossed the rake aside. It clattered to the ground as I swiped the bucket from the floor and ventured into the semidarkness. The cold felt like a fist pushing on my chest. It hurt to breathe, but it was a familiar feeling.

As I stepped out onto the frozen ground, I thought I could smell snow coming. There was a sharpness to the cold—like knives poised against my skin.

I made my way across the yard to the wood I kept piled near the barn. As I gathered juniper, pine, and a few large pieces of oak, a slim black cat hopped onto the heap, stretching and purring, eager for attention.

"Good morning, Mouse," I said, scratching behind her ear. "Have you roused Rooster?"

Rooster was a stallion and older than Jackal, my eldest brother, who was two and thirty. Mouse gave a high-pitched mewl. It was her way of saying no.

"You had better wake him. The boys will be impatient to leave today. The snow is coming."

Mouse's response was a growl. I knew why she protested. Rooster was tired, but it could not be helped. Even the old worked in Gnat, human and animal alike.

"I know he needs rest. If it were up to me, I would not send him into the forest at all."

Rooster accompanied my brothers on their hunt, and since we only had one stallion, they took turns riding him. Rooster was not fond of the woods and moved slowly. My brothers took this as being disobedient and whipped him to keep him moving. I hated it, but when I had voiced my anger, Jackal threatened to whip me. Rooster, sweet Rooster, had stepped between us, and his defiance had angered Jackal, but the threat of a strike from the powerful stallion kept him at bay.

"Strike me and I will put an arrow through your leg. I do not care if you are the only horse in all of Gnat," Jackal had threatened through clenched teeth. Then he looked at me. "And you. You will pay for his disobedience. Do you spend all your evenings in the barn whining about how terrible we are? No wonder he defies us. Well, I will show you cruel, you ungrateful git."

I spent the night in the barn after Jackal's threat, too afraid of what he might do in the night, but that had only delayed the inevitable. The next morning, he woke me by dousing me in ice-cold water and threw a dull knife at my feet.

"You will go to the moor and dig peat for our fires."

Still soaked, I had ventured into the bog. My fingers were so frozen, I could hardly hold the knife.

I would have never guessed that day, born in so much misery, would lead to an even worse day—the day I would eventually betray the fae man I loved.

You really are a silly git, I told myself. *You cannot love a man you have never really seen.*

But I knew by the way my chest ached, I had.

Thankfully, I was roused from the pain by a sharp cry from Mouse, a familiar sound that usually signaled the approach of one of my brothers. My heart raced as I whirled to see which of the three were approaching, except no one was there.

Still Mouse continued to hiss, showing her sharp teeth. The hair on her back stood on end.

I studied the tree line just beyond the rotting wooden fence that lined our property. The trees there were like giants— ancient and menacing. Thick fog poured from the darkness between the trunks, snaking through the air toward me like beckoning fingers. Though I saw nothing else, that did not mean no one was there. The fae usually moved about the world invisible to mortals. It was when they chose to show themselves

that trouble followed, and while there was a part of me that wished I had never met the nameless, faceless fae, there was also a part of me that wondered—that wished, though those were dangerous things—that it was he who watched me so closely.

I shook my head to dismiss the thoughts and then reached for Mouse, who I held against my breast.

"Nothing to worry over, sweetling," I said, placing her on the ground. "Now go and rouse Rooster."

Mouse cut me a sharp look before stretching and wandering off to the barn.

I finished gathering the wood and returned to the cottage. With the kindling restocked and the fire lit and warming the house, I started breakfast, frying ham and potatoes, boiling eggs, and porridge. With everything prepared and warming, I headed upstairs to perform my most dreaded task—waking my brothers.

It did not matter that the three expected me every morning. I was always faced with some kind of threat. If they did not curse at me, they threw whatever was in reach. I'd already tried keeping their tables clear, except that night, each brother had brought every breakable thing to their bedside and threw it at me when I opened the door the next morning.

I decided then my attempts to make my life a little more bearable weren't worth the consequences. So my brothers did what they wanted to me, and so long as Mouse and Rooster were safe, I thought I could take it.

I topped the steps and approached the first door on the right. The room belonged to my youngest brother, Hans. He was the quietest of the three, and while that meant he did not subject me to quite as many insults, his preferred method of torture was what he called *tricks*.

The door creaked as it opened, and it was dark. The embers in his fireplace were nearly snuffed out. I glanced at the bed and could not see Hans, though that was usual. He liked to bury himself beneath the covers. That was probably best. It would be easier to revive the fire with him asleep.

I crossed to the hearth and kneeled, repeating the same process I'd gone through downstairs, except this time, the bucket of kindling was full. With the fire blazing, I started to rise when someone shoved me.

I flailed and caught myself, palms pressed flat against the hot stone of the hearth. The pain was instant and sharp. I yelped and pushed away, landing on my ass. For a few seconds, I could do nothing but sit in quiet shock, palms red and throbbing.

Behind me, Hans broke into peals of laughter.

"You should have known better than to assume I was asleep!"

My eyes watered, partly from the pain but also from embarrassment. I shoved those feelings down, because they had no place here. No one survived this life feeling sorry for themselves. Besides, Hans was right—I should have known.

I rose to my feet, pushing up from the cold stone floor, wincing at the pain. The palms of my hands felt taut, as if I suddenly didn't have enough skin.

I would have left without a word, but I thought the consequences might be worse if I did, so I spoke.

"It is good you are awake," I said, meeting his blue eyes. They were most like mine but untouched by burden or fear. "Breakfast will be ready soon."

His face turned pink, the color settling most in his cheeks.

"Aren't you going to laugh at my trick?" he asked.

I stared at him for a few seconds, knowing he wasn't joking, and then opened my mouth and laughed—or tried to. It was a hollow, joyless sound, but I had never truly laughed around my brother, so Hans would not know the difference.

Hans joined, laughing so loud, I could barely hear myself, and then he stopped abruptly, a cold mask descending over his face.

"Get the fuck out of my room," he said.

I left and moved to the next, which belonged to my middle brother, Michal. When I opened the door, I found a naked woman with long blond hair straddling him. They moved together, moaning. It was not the first time I'd gone to wake up my brother and found him like this, but it was the first time I'd seen Llywelyn, the chaplain's daughter, in his bed.

I walked farther into the room to tend to the fire. Llywelyn shrieked when she noticed me and reached for the blankets to cover her chest.

"What are you doing, you ugly little wench?" she snapped.

"Ignore her," Michal grunted.

"Ignore her? How am I supposed to ignore her? She is right there!"

"Think of her as a maid," he said.

"But she isn't a maid. She is your sister! What if she tells my father?"

"She will keep our secrets, or she will find herself in a grave."

Llywelyn giggled at Michal's threat, but it was not the first time he had made it. Truthfully, I did not care what my brothers did outside of hunting, and I only cared that they hunted so I could be alone.

When I was finished, I stood and turned to them. They were still kissing and rocking against each other. Michal's bed frame squeaked with each movement.

"Breakfast is soon," I said, adding as I headed for the door, "The church bells will ring in less than an hour."

I left Michal's room and made my way to my eldest brother's door, my heart pounding hard in my chest. Despite being used to Jackal's cruelty, my body always warned me away. But I knew if I ran, things would only be worse, so I entered his room.

It was dark, save for the hearth, where dying embers burned. I crossed to the window and opened the curtains to let in the dreary morning light. Sometimes that was enough to rouse him, but not today. He remained on his side, eyes closed, dark hair mussed from sleep.

"Jackal," I whispered, afraid to startle him. "Jackal."

I spoke his name louder, noticing his eyes fluttering.

"It's time to wake up. Breakfast will be—"

Jackel's eyes flew open, and I stumbled back as he sat up and reached for the pitcher by his bed and threw it. I could feel it brush the edge of my clothes before it slammed against the wall. Pieces of ceramic and water exploded everywhere.

"You fucking ratbag!" he seethed.

His eyes were dark with rage. I had given up trying to figure out what had angered him. Sometimes, he just woke up like this.

"Get me another pitcher!" he ordered. "And clean this up!"

I obeyed, leaving to retrieve a new pitcher, though the only other one I had was my own. I filled it with water, gathered rags and a broom, and headed back upstairs.

Jackal waited, standing in his nightshirt. I started past him, intending to place the pitcher on his table again, but he stopped me.

"Give me the pitcher," he said.

So I did.

Then he poured the contents over my head.

"More water, wench," he said, shoving the pitcher into my hands.

There was nothing else to do but obey.

When I returned a second time, Jackal was dressed. He wore a dark woolen tunic over trousers and high boots. He looked like our father, with his proud, chiseled face and dark shorn hair. I hated it because my father had loved me, and Jackal did not.

He let me pass and return the pitcher to his bedside table. While he washed his face, I hurried to clear a path so that Jackal could leave his room without his boots getting wet or pieces of ceramic in his soles.

I worked fast and was finished by the time he turned and strolled out of his room, following at a distance as he headed to the kitchen. I would have to finish cleaning later. For now, I had to serve the hunters breakfast.

When I entered the kitchen, my brothers and a now-clothed Llywelyn sat around the long banquet table. It was far grander than any other piece of furniture in our cottage, because my father had made it, though over the years, the wood had worn, and if they weren't careful, they would end up with splinters in their fingers.

I worked in silence as I filled plates of food and tankards of beer for the boys and Llywelyn, who sat in Michal's lap.

"It is so dangerous to hunt in the Enchanted Forest!" said Llywelyn. "How do you manage to come out alive?"

It was the answer everyone in Gnat wanted. There were rumors, of course, that my brothers had been kissed by the fae or graced by witches, but I suspected something far more nefarious.

The fae were not kind, and neither were witches. Whatever gave my brothers the power to enter the forest unharmed was closer to a curse than anything.

"It is a skill," said Michal.

"I should like to watch you hunt," she said.

"No," Jackal snapped.

Llywelyn glared at him but was not deterred by my brother's rudeness.

"What will you hunt today?" she asked.

"Whatever crosses our path," Michal answered.

"I hope you will find a stag," she said, and then in a low, sultry voice, she added, "It would keep me fed for a whole month."

"I will keep you fed," said Michal. "I will fill you up."

She giggled and leaned close as if to kiss him, but before their lips could touch, Hans spoke.

"Funny," he said. "I heard you say the same thing to the sheriff's daughter last week and the mayor's daughter the week before."

Both Michal and Llywelyn glared at him, but Llywelyn did not seem to care that Michal had more than one lover. She turned her attention to him, looping her arms around his neck.

"Perhaps you have promised them something, but you have promised me more."

A heavy silence followed her statement, and after a few seconds, Jackal stopped eating and set his fork and knife on the tabletop, his stare trained on the two lovers.

"Promises are dangerous," Jackal said. "You did not promise, did you, Michal?"

"N-no," Michal stammered. "Of course not."

"And why should he not promise?" Llywelyn demanded. "I have been a good lover. I have been a loyal lover."

"You are engaged to the sheriff's son," said Hans. "You are anything but loyal."

Llywelyn had nothing to say.

Jackal rose to his feet.

"Promises are binding, but they can be broken," said Jackal. "Lies do the breaking, Llywelyn. There are always consequences for lies."

Llywelyn straightened beneath my brother's threat but said nothing. Jackal left the kitchen. Hans followed, and so did Michal, who shoved Llywelyn aside and stumbled after them, not sparing her a single glance. She sat, stunned, mouth open and eyes wide, realizing suddenly that she had chosen the wrong brother to seduce.

I grabbed my cloak and trailed behind my brothers, stopping at the door. Jackal had mounted Rooster, and Hans had hopped in the wood cart tethered to his harness. Since Michal was the last to join, he walked behind them as they made their way into the forest.

I watched them go and Llywelyn approached, pausing to look at me.

"Why do you stay here?" she asked. "You could leave while they are away."

Her question felt like a trap, a way to trick me into saying something she could offer to my eldest brother.

"I belong here," I answered.

Llywelyn gave a breathless laugh. "I thought there were consequences to lies, Samara."

I looked at the woman, fair even in the pale morning light. It might be a lie, but for me, the truth always had greater consequences. It was something she would never understand.

"The church bells are ringing," I said, and as the words left my mouth, a silver sound echoed in the faraway distance.

Llewelyn's eyes grew wide and her cheeks red. "You cruel wench! You were supposed to warn me!"

She shoved past me, my shoulder slamming into the frame of the door as she sprinted across the frozen ground, down the winding road, and into the town of Gnat.

CHAPTER TWO
A Handsome Prince

 watched my brothers until they were consumed by the forest, and for a brief moment, I found myself hoping they never returned, but my guilt was so great, I spoke aloud to whoever might have heard my thoughts.

"Forgive me. I know not what I think," I said.

It would be better if I disappeared. I had nothing to offer Gnat, save what I did for my brothers, but there were a number of women, as Michal so often demonstrated, willing to fill my role, and they would do so happily.

Even knowing that, I did not leave. I couldn't. Llywelyn was wrong. This house belonged to my parents. My father had built it, and my mother had made it beautiful with her paintings. They were buried in this ground. I could not leave them, and I could not leave Mouse or Rooster. They were my best friends, and I would never abandon them to the cruelty of my brothers no matter how often I dreamed of a different life—or none at all.

I closed the door and headed back to the kitchen where I gathered the dishes, sliding scraps into a bucket. I'd have to bury them later, since I could not be sure that Hans hadn't poisoned what remained. I had only made that mistake once— tossing leftovers out the back, thinking that the birds or the deer might eat them, but the next morning, I'd found three dead wolves.

Hans had laughed—and then laughed harder when I'd had to bury them.

Once the dishes were washed, I moved upstairs to finish cleaning Jackal's floor.

I lowered to my hands and knees, prying pieces of ceramic from between the cracks of the wooden floor with a knife. I suspected my brother had crushed them into the seams when I'd gone downstairs for another pitcher, and I knew if he found so much as a sliver of porcelain remaining, he'd break everything in the house in retaliation.

So I was careful, but the pieces were sharp and cut into my fingers. I did not mind the pain so much as the blood, because it reminded me of my dream, and my dream reminded me of the fae, and the fae reminded me that I had once been in love.

Foolishly in love.

And when I thought about love, I thought of everything that came with it and what I would never have—passion, protection, trust. I'd longed for someone to touch me because they desired me, and I'd wished for it only once. In the aftermath of that wish, whatever magic hung heavy in the air forced me to cut off the only hand that had offered me any kindness.

When I was certain there was not a single shard of ceramic left, I scrubbed Jackal's floor on my hands and knees and moved on to Michal's and Hans's rooms, then the staircase and the small living room, where I had to pause because the floor was covered in what appeared to be black soot—ashes from the fireplace.

Another one of Hans's cruel jokes.

My face was suddenly flooded with heat, and my fingers curled into my palms. I was used to this feeling—this deep and painful anger—but this time, it frightened me because I couldn't shove it down. Instead, I let it erupt and used it as I dragged the ash-covered rug outside and heaved it over the rotting wooden fence. I swiped a log from the ground and began to beat the rug.

Plumes of dust blinded and choked me, and my fingers slipped on the loose bark, but I couldn't stop, and I didn't until the fence collapsed.

My chest ached with each panting breath as I staggered back, dropping the log at my feet. I screamed until my anger was gone and I had no strength left to stand. I fell to my knees, my throat raw, tears burning my eyes. The rage that had fed me turned to panic.

"No, no, no."

I got to my feet and moved the rug, which had fallen into the mud. It was ruined, and so was the fence. Two posts were broken, and the rotting rails that ran between them were shattered.

If my brothers came home and saw the fence broken, the punishment would be severe—likely a beating with the very log I used to destroy it.

How could I be so stupid!

I looked toward the Enchanted Forest, wondering how long until my brothers returned. Could I repair the fence in time? My eyes shifted to the pile of wood by the barn. Or could I hide it?

Something furry brushed my ankle.

"You wouldn't happen to know where I could find some wood, Mouse?"

She paused, looked up at me, and meowed, then took off, trotting toward the side of the house. I followed as she rounded the corner and found her sitting beside a pile of wood, but it was not wood for the fence. It was the kindling I'd gathered for the fire, and it lay beneath my eldest brother's window.

I thought I'd been pushed to my breaking point already, except now I knew otherwise.

This was my breaking point.

But it didn't feel like I had expected. It was not the anger that had stolen my sanity moments ago. This wasn't even emotion—it was a lack of it. I was no longer worried about what would happen if my brothers returned to find the fence broken or the rug destroyed, because neither of those things mattered, especially because I would not be here for them to punish.

I turned and walked down the sloping hill behind our cottage. At the very bottom, two rounded rocks marked where my mother and father lay. I continued past them, knowing if I stopped, I would succumb to the guilt that had kept me obedient.

I followed a worn and familiar trail through the woods. These were not the same ominous trees and dark pines of the Enchanted Forest. There was a creek at the bottom, and I followed it as it twisted and turned through more rolling hills, all covered in decaying leaves and pine needles. I walked until my calves hurt and my feet ached. I could tell when I was near my destination because the sky seemed to open up before me, and as I came to the cliff's edge, it was truly endless. The clouds hung heavy and low, casting large shadows over the rocky valley below. That was my destination, where the earth would cradle my body, eat my flesh, and consume my bones.

I thought that sounded beautiful. Peaceful even.

I desired anything but what lay behind me.

Sand and stones tumbled over the cliff as I inched closer, until the tips of my toes hung over the edge. A wave of dizziness rushed to my head, and my legs shook. I should have closed my eyes, but I didn't. Instead, I spread my arms wide, letting the cold wind wash over me, and as I did, it began to snow.

"Are you going to kill yourself?"

The sudden sound of a strange voice drew my attention. I turned my head to find a man standing near. He was handsome with large blue eyes and dark hair, but he was almost too pretty. His skin was unmarred by sun or scars, and his lips were full and pillowy, not cracked and dry. He wore a heavy wool cloak, and though it concealed what he wore beneath, I suspected his sleeves were threaded with gold. He held a hat against his chest. A long red feather was stuck in the band.

I looked away and answered, "I have not decided."

"It would be a shame," he said.

I thought I could feel him draw nearer.

"You are too beautiful to die."

"That is a foolish thing to say," I said. "Death does not care about beauty."

If he had, he would not have taken my mother or my father. He would have taken my brothers.

"Every man cares about beauty," he replied.

"You believe death is a man?"

"Do you think a woman can take a life?" he returned.

"Yes," I said, meeting his gaze. "At the very least, I could take my own."

"Why do I get the feeling you would just to prove me wrong?"

"You are vain, my lord," I said. "This is not about you at all. Now if you would kindly leave me to my death."

"I couldn't possibly leave now that I know your intentions."

"Why not? Do you want to watch?"

"No, I hope to change your mind."

"You won't," I said. "I have decided."

"Truly?"

"Yes."

"Then why haven't you jumped?"

"Because you have interrupted my concentration."

"Ending your life doesn't sound like something that needs concentration."

"So you have tried before?"

"Well, no."

"Then how would you know?"

"By deduction," he replied. "Hard things require concentration. Jumping off a cliff isn't hard."

"I suppose that depends on your definition of hard. The ground is quite solid."

The man chuckled, and there was a glint in his eyes I had never seen in anyone else's, but that was because this man was not burdened with the worry of surviving. He probably carried a silver spoon in his pocket, and while he had likely used it all his life, it had not given him a silver tongue.

"You are quite clever," he said.

"Too clever to die?" I asked.

"No one is too clever to die," the man replied.

"Once again, you speak for death," I said. "Worse, you believe he values beauty over genius."

"Beauty is genius," said the man. "Surely, it sways you."

"Sways? No," I said. "I have met many beautiful, terrible people."

"I suppose I have too," he said and then paused. "So what is it, then, that you value?"

"Kindness," I said.

I expected the lord to laugh, but he didn't, and when I looked at him, his eyes had changed.

"Has anyone ever been kind to you?"

I looked away. I could not face his pity.

"A long time ago."

"Have I been kind to you?"

"I hardly know you," I said.

"Would you give me time to show you I can be kind?"

"We will not see each other again beyond this moment," I said.

"Because you intend to die?"

"Yes," I said. "But even if I lived."

He paused for a moment, inching closer. I considered what I would do if he reached for me. Would I jump to spite him, or let him pull me close?

"Would you be treated poorly if I saw you again?"

I did not answer.

"What if I took you from this place?"

I was surprised by the sound that came out of my mouth—a guttural laugh.

"I could not leave even if I wanted to."

"Why not?"

"Because—" I started, but when I could think of no reason, I paused. "Just because."

"I would keep you safe," he said.

"I do not even know that word," I said. "And I do not know you."

He held my gaze with those beautiful blue eyes. They were startling, and while I had never seen the eyes of the fae I had yearned for the last seven years, they reminded me that I had once dreamed of meeting his gaze and discovering his eyes were the same icy shade.

The man extended his hand.

I did not take it, but he waited.

Finally, I relented, startled by how soft his fingers were, and I immediately felt flushed, aware of how rough my own were.

"I am Prince Henry from the Kingdom of Rook," he said and pressed his lips to my red and swollen knuckles. Then he lifted his gaze to mine and smiled. "Now we are not strangers."

"Your name does not make us anything more than acquaintances," I said.

"Usually when one offers a name, the courteous thing to do is give yours," he said.

"You must do this often then," I said.

"Meet strange girls in the woods who want to end their life? No," he said. "I must admit, this is a first for me."

I tried not to smile at him.

I didn't *want* to smile at him.

"Samara," I said.

"Samara," he repeated, grinning. "Was that so hard?"

"Terribly," I replied.

"Samara," he said again. "Let me take you away from this horrible place."

I shook my head. "And trade my situation for what? Something far worse? Never."

"I do not think becoming my wife would be worse."

"Your *wife*?"

"Marry me," he said.

"You are delusional," I said.

"I am not."

"You just met me. I'm a strange girl in the woods, remember?"

"Yes, and you are very enchanting."

"Did you eat mushrooms?"

He opened his mouth but hesitated. "That's not the point. The point is I would like to offer you a better life."

"There are other ways to do that than marriage."

"If you will not marry me, then come away with me to

Rook. I can give you a better life, and perhaps, after some time, you will agree to be my wife."

"Why? Why would you want to rescue me?"

"Because despite what you believe, there are kind people in the world, Samara."

I stared at this man—this strange man who had found me in the woods.

"You will have to ask my brothers," I said. "It will not be easy."

"Am I correct that it isn't because they love you dearly?"

"If that were the case, you would not have convinced me with so little effort."

"You call that little effort?" he asked, though his eyes sparkled with mirth. "I practically had to beg."

"I'm sure it must have been difficult for you to be told no," I said. "First time?"

He chuckled. "Unfortunately no," he said and then grew a little more serious. "I know you must think poorly of me given my title, but I intend to show you we are not all so terrible."

"It is just like a prince to presume to know my mind," I said, but the statement had no power behind it, because the prince was right—I did not have a high opinion of him or any who ruled by right of blood.

Henry smiled. "Do not worry about your brothers," he said, tugging on my hand. "I will make them an offer they cannot refuse."

I allowed him to lead me away from the cliff, down the balding path and into the woods where a beautiful horse waited. I had never seen one with such a coat and mane—white with black spots.

"Oh, he is beautiful," I said.

"Thank you," Henry replied, taking the reins. "Her name is River."

"Oh," I said, blushing. "I'm sorry."

"Do not worry. She is not offended," he said. "Come, I will help you up."

"I do not need help," I said.

I knew how to ride a horse.

I put my left foot in the stirrup and held the pommel as I swung my right foot over, sinking into the saddle with ease. When I met the prince's gaze, his cheeks were tinged with pink.

"You," he said and then cleared his throat. "You do not want to sit sidesaddle?"

"No. Why would I?"

He rubbed the back of his head. The redness had spread to his ears.

"Well, you are in a gown," he said. "And riding astride shows your…legs."

"My legs?" I looked down, seeing that my dress had ridden up to the tops of my knees. I hadn't noticed it because I was used to it, but suddenly I realized why the prince was so embarrassed.

"Haven't you ever seen a woman's legs before?" I asked.

"Well, yes, but—"

"But mine make you nervous?"

"Not nervous," he said.

"So they offend you?"

"No, of course not," he stammered. "They are very nice legs. You…have very nice legs."

I stared at him, smirking.

"Forget I said anything at all," he said, putting on his hat.

"I will never," I said, as he mounted River, but my amusement died as soon as he was seated behind me.

I had never been so close to a man before, never felt another body against my own like this. He was warm, and as he reached past me to take the reins, I felt like I could sense his strength in the hard muscles of his chest and arms. It was the first time

I found myself thinking about what was beneath the finery of his clothing.

Suddenly, I was the one blushing.

"Ready?" he asked.

I went rigid when I felt his breath on my ear, and all I could do was nod, humiliated by my sinful thoughts.

He chuckled as he tugged on the reins. I didn't dare ask him what was so funny, because I knew that if he tried to guess my thoughts this time, he would finally be right.

I did not speak beyond offering the prince directions to the cottage, too focused on every part of my body that touched him. It was an odd feeling, to be so close to a stranger. I found myself studying his hands as he held the reins before me. They were…normal. Not overly large but graceful. His nails were trimmed short and clean, and he had no cuts or scars.

A strange disappointment blossomed in my stomach.

"Do you have a sword?" I asked.

"Why? Already planning my demise?" he asked.

"I just wondered if you used it," I said.

"When the occasion calls for it," he said. "Why?"

"Because…your hands are soft."

"You think my hands are soft?"

"It isn't a thought," I said. "I know."

The prince was quiet for a moment.

"You have a strange way of making me feel very insecure," he said.

"It was only an observation," I said.

He lifted his hand, and I could not help but flinch. He quickly lowered it again.

"I won't hurt you," he said, his voice gentle, yet I did not believe him.

"So you say."

"I will prove it in time," he said.

There was a part of me that wanted to hope he was honorable and would keep his word, but I had already let myself hope once, and it had only led to disappointment.

"You may not want to after you meet my brothers."

We were silent after that, and I found myself worrying over what my brothers would say when they arrived home to find a handsome prince asking for my hand in marriage. I was certain they would not expect it, because they did not think it possible that anyone could ever want me. I was not even sure this was real. Maybe it was just one of Hans's cruel pranks.

Why would a prince of Rook be wandering through the woods in Gnat alone? The longer I thought, the more suspicious I grew, and my body responded in kind. I straightened my back and leaned forward, attempting to put as much distance between me and the prince as I could, though the horse did not allow for much, and the prince only tightened his hold around my waist.

"Do not be afraid," he said.

"I don't know how," I said.

"You do not know how?" he repeated.

"I have only ever been afraid," I said.

Again Henry did not speak, and I was certain he did not know what to do with me.

Once we came to the creek, the prince led River along the bank, up and down every hill, past my mother's and father's graves, to the doorstep of my weathered cottage where my three brothers waited. They each carried a weapon—Hans an axe, Michal a bow, and Jackal a sword.

"What is the meaning of this?" asked Michal.

The prince dismounted and then held his hand out for me. I did not take it and instead slipped off River's back and put distance between him, myself, and my brothers.

"Good sirs," he said, taking off his feathered hat and holding it to his breast. "I am Prince Henry of the Kingdom of Rook. I happened upon your sister in the wood, and I would like to have her to wife. What say you?"

There was a long pause, and Hans was the first to laugh, followed by Michal, but what scared me the most was that Jackal had yet to speak or even blink.

"You want to marry our sister?" Hans asked, still laughing. "You'd be better off marrying a pig!"

"Aye," said Michal. "And a pig is prettier."

"I am certain we are not speaking of the same woman," said the prince, whose voice was stern.

"He has been bespelled!" said Michal.

"Enchanted, I assure you," said the prince.

"Prince," said Hans. "You have looked upon the fae, and they have given you false eyes!"

"I have gazed upon no fae," said the prince. "I have only the assurance that I have met my future wife, your sister. I will ask once again for her hand in marriage."

There was a quiet pause after the prince finished speaking.

Michal shook his head in disbelief. "Are you hearing this, Jackal?"

It wasn't until I heard my eldest brother's name that I looked up, catching his cold stare before he turned his attention to the prince, angling his head so that he appeared curious.

"Tell me, Prince," said Jackal. "What do you want in a wife?"

The prince hesitated. "I suppose I have not given it much thought."

"How can you want my sister to wife if you don't even know what you want?"

"Because I can see her," replied the prince.

"So this is about fucking," said Michal. "If that is the case, there is the barn."

"Are you suggesting I am dishonorable?"

"No, Prince, but you are a man," said Michal.

"A man, perhaps, but I would never dishonor a woman in such a way, especially one I intend to marry. Now, I will ask for your blessing a final time. Allow me your sister's hand in marriage, and you will be rewarded handsomely."

There was silence.

"Handsomely, you say?" asked Jackal. "What have you to offer in exchange for our dear, dear sister?"

"I will bring you three treasures from my father's vault. A golden ring, a singing lark, and an enchanted rose."

"What use would we, three starving hunters, have for a ring, a bird, and a rose?"

"Then I shall bring you gold and silver," Henry said. "And everything else I have named shall go to your sister."

"Bring us gold and silver," said Jackal. "And you can have our sister as a wife."

"Do I have your word?"

"You have my word," said Jackal. "We shall wait for your arrival at sunrise—and not a moment past or our agreement is forfeit."

The prince turned to me, and my eyes widened.

"I will think of nothing but you until we are reunited at dawn."

He glanced at my brothers before he secured his hat, mounted his horse, and rode off, feather bouncing as he went.

"Do you think he'll be back?" asked Hans.

Michal scoffed. "Not a chance. He will return to his golden castle on his golden hill and forget she ever existed."

It was something I did not doubt.

Jackal shoved past Michal and Hans as he came for me. I stumbled back and fell to the ground at his approach.

"What do you think you are doing?" he snarled, looming over me with hate-filled eyes.

"N-nothing," I said. "I didn't do anything!"

He grabbed me by my hair and dragged me to my feet, but

I had grown so used to the feeling, I didn't even cry out. I just followed as he pulled.

"Did you seduce him?" he demanded.

"No! I would never!"

I didn't know how.

"Liar!" he accused. "You fucked him, didn't you?"

"I swear I didn't!" I said. "I swear upon the graves of our parents!"

His grip tightened, and he leaned closer to me, his eyes full of such hate, I could feel the heat of it burning me from the inside out.

"If I so much as sense a baby in your belly, I will slice you open and tear it out," he said, and then he shoved his knee into my stomach, and I felt a burst of pain and nausea all at once.

He released me, and I fell to the ground, curling into myself as he landed another blow to my stomach before Michal grabbed his arm and pulled him back.

"Stop, Jackal!" he said. "What if you kill her and the prince returns?"

"If the prince returns, then he can carry away her corpse," he said.

"Aye, he may, but will he pay?" said Michal. "Besides, it is nearing sundown, and I am starved. Who will cook for us if she is dead?"

I was so consumed trying to breathe through the pain, I didn't know if Michal's words had swayed my brother, but in some ways, I didn't care. If this was to be my end, at least eventually, there would be no pain.

"Get up!" Jackal commanded suddenly, and I peeled open my eyes to find all three brothers standing over me.

I held my stomach tightly, fighting the nausea as I got to my feet.

"Feed us, wash the rug, fix the fence, and do not dream

of sleep until you are certain you are done, or I will have you dancing to your death in iron-hot shoes."

Jackal turned and entered the house. Michal offered me a strange look—not pity but interest. He'd never considered the possibility that I might bring them wealth. Hans spit in my face before he turned to leave, laughing maniacally as he headed into the house.

Once they were inside, I bent at the waist and vomited all over my feet.

CHAPTER THREE
The Fox and the Fae

SAMARA

 continued to feel nauseous throughout the evening and night. My stomach felt heavy; the ache was constant. I wondered as I worked to feed my brothers, clean the rug, and fix the fence if I would die by morning. Despite the pain, I smiled at the thought that my brothers would forfeit their payment of gold and silver. I wondered if this was what it felt like to have power, however little.

It was dark when I finished the fence, and I was frozen to the bone. I looked up at the sky, knowing I would see nothing but a dark void. The air was heavy with the smell of snow, crisp and crystalline. I took a deep breath, filling my lungs with it. The cold felt good despite the sharp twist in my gut, and my breath clouded the air as I exhaled. I looked toward the barn where Rooster and Mouse were likely asleep and considered staying there on my final night at home, but instead, I gathered my lantern and cloak close and walked toward Daft Moor.

The night was still as I took the familiar, winding path to the bog. I had once found such comfort in this short stroll. Now all I felt was dread, but it seemed important to say goodbye, whether I died or left with the prince tomorrow.

As I neared, my heart began to race, and something thick gathered in my throat. I was frustrated by these emotions, still just as fresh and violent as they were seven years ago. I knew the feelings would cease with death, but would they with distance? Time surely had not helped.

The path dipped down into a valley with great boulders on either side, covered in browning moss. It was here I first met the fae who had offered his hand and the knife that had changed my life. I paused on the edge of the moor. I paused on the edge of the moor where, the rich scent of dark earth reached me. It held so many memories, both terrible and thrilling. I could not decide how to feel, though I didn't know why. This place had been a source of misery, yet I felt a pang of sadness leaving. There were things here I still loved—the house my father built, their bodies in their graves, the animals both wild and tamed, even the fae who had given me the knife, as ridiculous as it was—but now it was time to let those things go. They were anchors to a past that kept me a breath from the surface, drowning beneath the weight of things that were nothing but dreams.

"I had never felt such hope as I did when you came to my aid until today," I said. "I can finally let you go."

The lie tasted bitter in my mouth, but if I said it enough, maybe it would be true. I took one final breath of cold, rich air and turned to leave when I caught sight of two glowing eyes. I gasped and stepped back, tripping on a boulder, falling against it.

The creature blinked at me twice and then slipped out from where it hid between two large stones—the same stones from which the fae had offered the knife.

It was a fox, a beautiful fox with orange fur and white and black paws. He shook his head, large ears flip-flopping before he sat, curling his fluffy tail around his feet, and stared at me.

"I did not mean to startle you," he said.

It was my turn to blink. "Did you—"

"Talk?" he asked. "Yes."

I pressed my palms to my face. "I must be dead."

The fox's beady eyes narrowed.

"Not yet, though you soon will be. Let me lick your hand, and you shall be healed."

I hesitated.

"Trust me, wild one. I am here to help."

"Why?" I asked.

"I must," he answered but did not explain.

I offered my hand and felt the rough brush of the fox's tongue against my skin once, twice, three times before the pain in my stomach eased instantly. I pulled my hand back, examining the spot the fox had touched, but there was nothing. Then I pressed my hand to my stomach. It was no longer tender.

"You healed me," I said in quiet wonder.

"I would not lie," said the fox.

"Would not or could not?" I asked. The fox tilted his head as if he did not understand the question, so I asked, "Are you fae?"

Fae could not lie—it was not a choice.

The fox bristled his tail as if he did not like that question.

"I am a fox," he said.

"I have never met a fox who could talk."

"I am a fox who can talk."

We were both quiet, staring at each other, and then a wave of guilt made my skin feel flushed.

"I'm sorry," I said. "Thank you for healing me."

"Do not thank me," he said. "Do as I say."

I frowned at his words, but he continued quickly.

"Tomorrow, the prince will arrive to take you away to his kingdom, but your carriage will be set upon by thieves. You must not move or make a sound, or they will kill you first. Wait, and you will be rescued."

"How do you know this?"

"I am a fox," he said.

"That hardly explains anything."

"It explains everything," he said.

"If this is true—"

"I would not lie," the fox reminded.

"Then perhaps I should not leave at all."

"You must," said the fox. "It has already been decided."

I did not know what to say, but the fox rose to his feet.

"Do not forget what I have said, or tomorrow, you will be dead."

Then he turned, tail swaying, and vanished into the dark between the stones. I stood there, staring, wondering what world I might find if I followed him.

Something cold touched my arm. When I looked, I saw snow melting on my skin. I lifted the lantern as icy crystals fell across the moor. The sound was silvery, beautiful like the laughter of the fae. It made me want to linger, and I did until the ground was covered with a thin layer of white I might have stayed there forever, under the spell of this magic until the blood froze in my veins, but a voice in the back of my mind was louder.

"Come away, Samara," it said. "There is nothing for you here but death."

I did not know who spoke, if it was my consciousness or the voice that called to me in my dreams, but it drew me away from the moor toward home.

The cottage was quiet and dark, save for the kitchen where the light from the hearth ignited the window, warm and welcoming. Anyone who passed would think it a quaint refuge from the cold, but it had been a long time since I'd felt safe beneath its roof. Instead of going inside to sleep, I made my way to the barn and rolled open the door, closing it quickly behind me.

When I turned, I found Rooster lying on a bed of hay. Mouse was curled up beside him sleeping. Rooster lifted his head and made a quiet, breathy sound as I approached.

I smiled and set the lantern down away from the hay.

"Hello, sweetling," I said, offering my hand, which he nuzzled before I caressed the space between his eyes, which fell closed. "It is good to see you. How was your day?"

He looked at me and then snorted as if to say *how do you think?*

"I know," I said. "My brothers are not the easiest to get along with."

Rooster blew out a harsh breath.

"I will take you from them someday," I said, pulling away. I sat beside Mouse and hauled her into my lap. She woke briefly, to meow and yawn, and then curled into a ball to sleep again as I rested my back against Rooster's flank.

This was the safest I had felt in a long while, though I could not escape the guilt, knowing what tomorrow would bring. At dawn, the prince would arrive, and I would leave Rooster and Mouse behind. My stomach churned. I should have asked for more from the prince, but that decision likely would have proven fatal for my two friends. I did not doubt my brothers' ability to kill the two creatures I loved most in the world as retribution for my newfound freedom.

It would be safer to come for them after I left—if I left at all.

There was still a part of me that doubted Henry's return.

"Rooster, I have to tell you something," I said. "A prince has offered for my hand. He says he will come soon to collect me, not a moment before sunrise. I do not want to leave you—"

Rooster interrupted, making a sound deep in his throat and throwing his head back.

"I know it is a chance at a different life," I said. I did not want to say a *better* life, because I did not truly know that. "But I will never forgive myself if they harm you while I am away."

Rooster's neigh was quiet and deep, as if to say *do not worry about me*, but I would until I saw him again. I could not help feeling I was abandoning them to the cruelty of my brothers.

"I will ask the prince to send for you as soon as I am able," I promised.

He nuzzled my hair, and my eyes grew heavy, surrounded by their warmth. Finally, I fell into a deep sleep, unhindered by the haunting voice that had lulled me into slumber the last seven years.

———

I was roused by Mouse, who rubbed her head against my hand, purring loudly.

"What is it?" I asked, still half-asleep.

Rooster neighed deeply, and I had no choice but to get to my feet as he rolled to rise. I rubbed my eyes and realized why they were so alert—someone was coming. I could hear the rhythmic clop of hooves, and suddenly, my heart was pounding. I went to the door and pushed it open. It was still dark, but a faint orange light burned on the horizon. It reached far enough to glint off an approaching golden carriage pulled by four black horses.

My prince had come.

I watched as the coachman made a wide circle and came to a stop before my small, ruined cottage, now covered in fresh snow. Two footmen stepped down from the back, each dressed in regally cut coats the color of midnight and trimmed in glinting gold. One opened the door while the other pulled down a set of gilded steps, and then the prince emerged, dressed far more finely than he had been the day before. His surcoat glittered as the morning sun sliced across the yard, and his cloak was lined with fur as white as the snow on the ground. His eyes gleamed when he saw me, and he reached for my hand.

"Samara," he said, pressing his lips to my knuckles.

I could not help it. The corners of my lips lifted.

"Prince," I breathed.

His fingers tightened around mine, but a sharp sound drew our attention from each other to the door of the cottage where my three brothers stood.

"We had a deal, Prince," said Jackal.

Henry released my hand and stepped in front me as if to shield me from their sight.

"And I have honored it," said the prince.

Just then, the footmen rounded the carriage, heaving a massive chest that they dropped halfway between us and my brothers before opening it to reveal a towering pile of gold and silver. Michal's and Hans's eyes sparkled, but Jackal seemed unaffected by his new wealth, his hateful gaze boring into mine.

"Well?" Henry demanded.

Finally, Jackal's attention shifted to the prince. "I expect you will welcome us to your castle. We would very much like to visit our dear sister."

"Of course," said the prince, though tightly. "You shall be guests of honor at our wedding."

For a moment, no one spoke, and then the prince took a step back so that he stood beside me.

Even he did not trust my brothers enough to give them his back.

"Say your farewells, my darling," said Henry. "We are running late."

I did not move, only stared at my siblings, who had made my entire life up until this point completely miserable.

"Farewell," I said, but then I turned to Rooster and Mouse, who lingered in the doorway of the barn, and went to them. I scooped Mouse into my arms and held her close as I hugged Rooster's neck and whispered to them both. "I will return for you soon."

"Darling," the prince said.

Pressure built behind my eyes, but I refused to cry.

I turned toward the prince and met him at the carriage door.

"Do not fret," he said. "The misery ends today."

He took my hand and helped me into the carriage, and as I sank into the seat, I was surrounded by rich, red velvet. I had never seen such expensive fabrics or felt anything so soft. I clasped my hands between my thighs to keep from touching everything around me.

The prince sat across from me. He was so tall, our knees touched.

"Tell me now before we depart, did your brothers harm you in the night?"

I held his pretty, blue-eyed gaze and answered, "No, my lord."

It was an easy lie, because I had told it so often.

The prince stared at me, and I knew he did not believe me, but he also did not argue. He rapped on the ceiling, and I was jolted as the carriage surged forward. I stared out the large windows, watching my brothers as we passed, eyes connecting with Jackal's long enough that the coldness of his gaze froze my very blood. If he could have killed me then, he would have.

I turned my head away to look out the other window, spotting Rooster and Mouse watching our retreat, and pressed my hand to the window.

"I can send for your animals," said the prince.

I met his gaze.

"My brothers will demand a trade."

"Of course," said the prince. "I shall make the exchange tomorrow. Three fine stallions and seven feral cats for your one. Will that please you?"

I smiled at the thought of the prince unleashing seven feral cats on my brothers.

"I have never been asked that before," I said.

The prince smirked. "I shall ask it often."

A flush unfurled in my chest, warming my throat and face. I dropped my gaze to my hands, still clasped between my legs.

"Well?" asked the prince, and I looked at him. "You did not answer. Will that please you?"

I was quiet for a moment and then answered in a whisper, "Yes."

He grinned and seemed to relax.

We rode in silence for a few minutes as the carriage bounced along the winding snow-covered path. I kept my eyes focused outside, on the ominous tree line of the Enchanted Forest, near which we were currently traveling. I wondered how long we would be within her shadow.

"You look troubled," said the prince.

"I am only thinking of the forest," I said. "Do the fae go as far as Rook?"

"No village is safe from the creatures who reside within the Enchanted Forest," he said. His eyes darkened as he spoke, and his mouth tightened. "Their magic is strong, and their presence is a plague."

"You are angry," I said, voice quiet. I could not help the hint of fear that rattled my spine.

"Not at you," he said quickly. "Oh my dear, not at you. My kingdom has long been at war with the forest, for you see, my sister was taken by the fae, and in her place, they left such an awful child. A changeling so cruel she has been imprisoned within her room until the true princess can be found."

"How terrible," I said. "I am so sorry."

The prince offered a small smile.

"Stop apologizing for things you did not do."

I started to open my mouth, but the only thing on the tip of my tongue was an apology, so I decided to change the subject.

"What will happen once we arrive at the castle?"

"You will be taken to your rooms, where your ladies-in-waiting will bathe and dress you, and then I shall present you to my father and mother, and we will feast with the court to celebrate our engagement," he said. "Tomorrow, we shall marry."

The shock of his words hit my chest, making me sit straighter.

"You said we could wait to wed until I was ready."

"My darling, it is hardly appropriate for me to take you from your family and not marry you quickly, and I cannot leave you at the castle unwed while I am gone."

"Gone?" I repeated, another wave of surprise striking deep in the pit of my stomach.

"I take no pleasure in leaving you so soon after the wedding, of course," he said. "If I could delay it, I would, but you must understand, when I stumbled upon you in the forest yesterday, I was in search of my brother."

"You have a brother too?"

"I have two," he said. "But one went in search of a tree with golden apples somewhere within the Enchanted Forest and has not returned."

I sat quietly for a few moments, my emotions warring. I did not know what to think of the information the prince had just chosen to impart to me. I did not know how to feel about marrying him so soon and then being left alone. What if his mother and father were not so kind?

"Why did your brother go in search of a golden apple?"

"He wished to marry his beloved," he said. "But her father, the king of Holle, has demanded a golden apple in exchange for her hand. Of course, my brave brother was more than willing."

"If your brother has not returned, will you?" I asked.

He tilted his chin down and leaned forward, lowering his voice as he spoke. "I will, so long as I know you are waiting for me."

His words made my chest ache, and I swallowed hard as a strange tension filled the space between us. I wanted to look away to regain my composure, but I couldn't.

"Samara." He said my name, warm and breathless, then his eyes fell to my lips, and I was spellbound as I waited for him to kiss me, but then the carriage came to a hard stop, and I was thrown forward into his arms.

Outside the carriage, there came a thud, a scream, and then a shout.

"Run, Your Highness!"

I felt an overwhelming burst of fear. It was sudden and hot and made my heart race. I pushed away from the prince, meeting his gaze. He did not appear to be afraid but angry, his mouth tense. Suddenly, I remembered the fox's warning from last night— *Tomorrow, your carriage will be set upon by thieves. You must not move or make a sound, or they will kill you. Wait, and you will be rescued.*

The memory was hazy, as if it had been a dream, but here it was happening.

I started to speak, to tell the prince what the fox had said, but before I could, the carriage door flew open, and the prince spoke. "Take what you want, but do not harm—"

His words were cut short, and I found myself splattered with something wet. I blinked, temporarily blinded by it, and wiped my eyes, only to see red stain my fingers.

Blood.

I looked up to see that the prince was dead, an arrow embedded in his eye socket. He fell back against the seat limply.

My mouth opened in silent horror as panic flooded my body.

I wanted to scream as fear clawed at my chest, but I could only think of the fox's words, so I stayed silent and still, even as the thief pulled me from the carriage by my ankles to the ground, where I hit hard, head ricocheting off the earth.

I bit down on my tongue as pain exploded behind my eyes, and still I did not move, even as the thief straddled me. I expected him to do something terrible, but he only frowned as he stared down at me. He was a grisly-looking man, large with dark, stringy hair and a wild, unkempt beard.

"Oi! What is it, Peter?" a voice shouted.

"Oi, Arthur!" said Peter. "This girl, she is as still and silent as a statue!"

"Oi!" said another voice. "Perhaps she is dead."

Peter stared down at me. "I don't know, Puck. Her eyes are open."

"People die with their eyes open!" he argued.

Peter put his ear to my chest. I was repulsed by his sour smell and where we touched. Everything inside me was desperate to shove him off, yet I remained still, as if the fox's words were magic and froze my limbs.

After a few seconds, Peter straightened. "No, her heart is beating!"

"Maybe she is mute!" Arthur called.

"Are you mute?" Peter asked.

I did not move, not even to shake my head.

"She isn't answering!" Peter said over his shoulder.

"Perhaps she cannot hear you," said Puck.

Peter looked down at me and then yelled. "Can you hear me?"

I just stared at him.

"Oi, you idiot!" Arthur said. This time when he spoke, he sounded closer. "If she cannot hear, she will not understand you!"

"How do you know?" asked Peter. "She might read lips."

After a few seconds, the man I presumed was Arthur came into view. He was equally as repulsive, but his hair was shorter, and he had a mustache that was so long, it curled into his mouth. Then another joined. This must be Puck, the third thief. His hair was red and stood on end, and while he was clean-shaven, I suspected it was because he could not grow a beard.

"Where did she come from?" asked Puck.

"I pulled her from the carriage," said Peter.

"She was with the prince?" asked Arthur, as if he did not believe it could be true.

"Oi, I *just* said that," said Peter.

"She does not look like royalty," said Arthur, scanning my clothes.

"Perhaps she is his whore," said Puck.

"She doesn't seem afraid," observed Peter.

"That has nothing to do with being a whore," said Puck.

"No, but I don't like it," said Peter.

"Nor do I," said Arthur.

Then they all shivered violently.

"Did you feel that?" asked Arthur.

"I did," said Puck. "What was it?"

"I believe it was…a…shiver," said Peter.

"A shiver?" Arthur question.

"Surely not!" said Puck.

"We would never fear such a frail thing—and a woman at that!" said Peter. "It is impossible!"

"But just to make sure," said Arthur.

"We should kill her," they all said together, and then they looked down at me.

In the seconds that followed, there was a strange sound I couldn't place. I thought maybe it was one of the thieves unsheathing their weapon, but then I noticed blood soaking the collar of Peter's shirt, and his head slowly slid off his neck, bouncing as it hit the ground. His body followed, revealing a towering figure with hair as dark as midnight. His brows were lowered over shadowed eyes, his cheeks high but hollowed with anger. He was dressed in fine clothing, finer than the prince of Rook, but I could focus only on the long sword he wielded, dripping with the blood of the thief.

He was fae, and he was beautiful.

For a few seconds, terror rooted me to the spot, but when his gaze shifted to mine, his violent eyes a stunning shade of lilac, I found my footing and scrambled to my feet. As I turned and ran, the two thieves bolted past me, screaming.

Arthur went down at the edge of the forest, a dagger in his back. The other made it into the thick of the wood, and I followed.

I ran so hard, it felt like my bones were splintering. The only thing I could hear was the rustling of flora as the remaining thief and I barreled through the forest to escape the warrior fae.

Beyond the blur of trees, I could make out the thief's retreating form as he stumbled over the ground. His mistake was looking back, though I suspected there was no escaping the fae.

"No! Please!" His voice rang with fear. "No!"

A bloodcurdling scream followed his final words, and then there was silence, save for the sound of my own breathing. I kept running, vaulting over a large branch. I halted and lifted it from the decaying leaves, holding it like a club in my hands as I hid behind an ancient tree, its shallow roots making it hard to stay upright.

It wasn't long before I heard footsteps. I held my breath and waited until they drew near before I stepped out from behind the tree and swung the branch with all my might. It flew through the air and landed a few feet away, not even grazing the head of the fox from last night, who sat patiently before me with his tail curled around his feet.

"What are you doing here?" I asked, relieved to see him and not the fae.

"Your aim was off," said a voice from behind me.

A strangled cry escaped my mouth as I turned and came face-to-face with the fae. I took a step back and fell. Spotting another branch, I tried to reach for it, but it crumbled in my hands, so instead, I squeezed a handful of the decayed limb and threw it at the creature.

I didn't wait to see if I hit him. I got to my feet and ran, but I didn't make it very far before his arm snaked around my waist and he pulled me against his hard body. His hand clamped down on my mouth, silencing the shriek that bubbled from my throat.

"Is that any way to treat your rescuer?" he asked. His breath was warm, and his lips brushed the shell of my ear.

I shivered and closed my eyes, readying myself for the sting of his killing blow, but it didn't come.

"I am a little disappointed you aren't fighting," he said.

I opened my eyes and then jerked away, snatching a limb from the ground. It was a poor weapon in the face of his blade, but it was something. I turned to face him. He looked at the stick and smirked before he met my gaze.

"You had better be careful, Lore," said the fox. "She is a wild one."

"I have no intention of killing you," the fae said.

I narrowed my eyes, suspicious. "Then why did you chase me?"

"I didn't," he said. "I chased your attackers."

"You put your hand over my mouth!"

"You were going to scream."

"Because I thought you were going to kill me!"

"You should not assume," he said.

"You *killed* three other men!" I snapped.

"They were men and thieves," he said. "Are you a man or a thief?"

"Do I look like a man?"

The fae's eyes dipped to my breasts, and he smirked. I swiped at him with my stick. It sounded like a whip as it cut the air toward him, though he caught it easily with one gloved hand and yanked it from my hands.

I recoiled and covered my head with my hands, preparing for his blow.

But nothing came.

Slowly, I straightened, letting my arms fall to my sides. I kept my gaze lowered, unable to face the fae. My cheeks burned with embarrassment.

"What did I tell you, Lore?" said the fox. "This one will break your heart."

I wasn't sure what the fox meant by that, but for some reason, it made me feel worse.

"Look at me, wild one," said the fae.

For some reason, that name only made my face burn hotter. The fae—Lore, according to the fox—took a step toward me, which finally drew my attention to his face. Again, I was struck by his beauty and the strange color of his eyes. I thought that perhaps he was an elf of some kind of status, given the point of his ears and his dress.

"I will never hurt you," he said.

His choice of words were interesting. It implied something beyond this present moment.

"People with kinder eyes have hurt me before," I said.

His gaze remained steady, but his mouth tensed.

"I cannot lie," he answered.

I'd heard that before but never truly believed it, and I didn't now. I considered saying as much, but just as I opened my mouth, I was interrupted by the sound of my name echoing in the Enchanted Forest.

"Samara!"

I whirled in the direction of Michal's voice, but I could not yet see him through the thick brush of the forest.

Panic rose inside me as I looked for a place to hide.

"Do you want to be found?" Lore asked.

My breath seized in my throat as he once again spoke against my ear. He moved so soundlessly, I had not heard him approach. Despite my heart pounding in my chest at the thought of being discovered by my brothers, I hesitated to answer—to trust him. While he had said he had no intention of killing me, there were always worse things.

A shuddering breath escaped my mouth, and I shook my head once.

Suddenly, roots shot from the ground, twisting around us.

Magic, I realized as I craned my neck and turned, watching them close over my head to form the trunk of a tree. My feet slipped on the uneven ground, and I fell against the fae. He caught me, and I tried unsuccessfully to straighten, my hands pressed flat against his chest, but I only managed to step on the fox's tail, and he emitted a horrifying, almost human yelp.

"Sorry," I breathed quietly, still trying to find my footing, but then Lore's hand came around my waist, and he pulled me against him.

I looked up at him, frustrated.

"This is easier," he said.

I glared, though it was hard to keep his gaze, not because his eyes were strange but because he was so beautiful.

This is how mortals die, I thought. *This is how I die.*

He did not seem to have any issue staring at me, his eyes illuminated by a blade of light streaming in from a gap in the twisted trunk.

"Couldn't you have made a larger tree?" I asked.

"Are you going to complain about everything I do?" he asked.

I opened my mouth to apologize, but he put a gloved finger to my lips and hushed me. I let my hands shift down his chest to his sides and held him tighter. This felt safer, though I did not know why.

I watched Lore's face as he turned into the blade of light and eyed my brother's approach.

"Samara!" Michal's voice erupted again, close this time. He was right outside the tree.

I jumped, and Lore held me tighter. I wasn't sure if he intended to comfort me or keep me close so he could silence me if needed.

"Shut up, you imbecile!" Jackal hissed.

At the sound of Jackal's voice, I began to tremble. I curled my fingers into Lore's tunic, trying to force myself into stillness, but it didn't work. Lore continued to hold me, and I made no move to push him away. I thought about how often I'd wanted someone to hold me like this and the irony that it was happening while I was trapped in the trunk of a tree, hiding from my brothers.

The sound of Michal's voice startled me again. I turned my head into a beam of light and realized there was an opening for me to see through too.

I leaned close to peer out. At first, I could only see Michal. Then a pebble flew through the air and hit the back of his head.

"Ouch!" Michal seethed and whirled to face Hans, who snickered as he also walked into view. The two were dressed for a hunt, in their darker clothes and leathers, which I found odd since Prince Henry had left them rich men.

"What?" he snapped. "She can't have gone far."

"Even if she didn't, what makes you think she would come running to us?" asked Hans.

"She will if she is smart," said Michal.

"She didn't leave on her own, idiot!" said Hans.

"How can you tell?"

"You don't really think she killed the prince and the thieves?"

"Have you seen her gut a pig?" Michal asked.

Lore gave a quiet laugh that almost sounded like a scoff. I glanced at him. He seemed amused. Maybe he found it hard to imagine I had gutted anything.

"Well, the prince wasn't gutted, and neither were the thieves, were they?" asked Hans. "They were sliced clear in half!"

Hearing that sent a shiver down my spine. Hesitantly, I glanced up at him again. I don't think his gaze ever left me. He didn't speak, but he lifted his hand to my face, brushing my cheek with his thumb. I held my breath. His touch was gentle, as if he were telling me in a different way that he would never hurt me.

I hated that I didn't believe him and turned away from his touch. He dropped his arm from around me, letting me lean closer to the opening.

Outside, my brothers still argued.

"If she didn't kill them, who did?" asked Michal.

"Perhaps she has had a secret lover who helped her escape," said Hans.

"But we have only her footprints and those of a fox," said Michal.

A heavy silence followed, and then suddenly, Michal and Hans looked up, as if they might find me in the trees. Only Jackal remained still and quiet, eyes narrowed and searching, and as I peered between the crack in the tree, his eyes met mine.

Fear ricocheted through me, and I inhaled an audible breath, which I immediately regretted. I covered my mouth with my hands and retreated, tripping over the fox, who let out a sharp yowl. Lore caught my arm before I could fall and dragged me against him. This time, his hold felt like an iron band around my back.

"Did you hear that?" Michal asked.

"It sounded like it was coming from inside that tree," said Hans.

I could see my brothers begin to circle the trunk, and Lore unsheathed a small blade. I wasn't sure what he planned to do with it, as it did not seem like a weapon that could take down any of my brothers but then again, he was fae and they were not. Still, I gripped his forearm, and he looked at me, his eyes searching mine.

"Please," I mouthed, though I did not know why I stopped him. Did I want to protect my brothers, or was I too afraid of being discovered? Truly, I did not know, but I also could not think. The fear was pounding through my veins.

Lore continued to stare, studying my face with a frown.

Then there was a sharp blow to the trunk of the tree. It caused the wood to vibrate around us and the air to fill with dust.

Hans was using his axe to chop the tree.

"Who cares about a fucking fox?" Jackal hissed suddenly. "Who cares how the prince was killed or even the thieves? What matters is that the prince of Rook is dead, and his kingdom will likely offer a great reward to the one who brings his murderer to justice."

"But we do not know who murdered the prince," said Michal.

"No, but our dear, dear sister does, and once we find her, we will surely learn the truth, and we will either present her or her supposed lover to the king as the assailant. Either way, we will be rich."

My brothers were quiet as they processed Jackal's words. Hans chuckled and then Michal. Their laughter rose, echoing all around me, making my ears ring, but it grew fainter and fainter as they retreated, returning, I guessed, to hide the bodies of the thieves.

"Well, aren't they pleasant," said the fox.

His words broke through my fearful haze, and I released Lore's forearm. My fingers ached from holding him so tight. I ignored the embarrassment I felt at having done so and peered out the hole in the tree, suspicious that my brothers were still near, waiting to pounce.

But then the tree disappeared, and I yelped as I fell to my hands and knees. I hurried to my feet and turned to face Lore as he sheathed the knife he'd drawn earlier.

He continued to look unhappy, and I wondered what I had done wrong.

"Your brothers are idiots," said Lore.

"They are heroes," I said. "Without them, my village would starve."

His eyes flitted down my body. I didn't like the way he looked at me, like he was frustrated with what he saw.

"What about you?" he asked.

"What about me?"

"What happens to you without them?"

My mouth parted, my answer poised on the tip of my tongue.

Then I am free, I wanted to say, but that was just a dream, and dreams were only achieved by wishing, and no one wished in this land—not without consequences.

"I suppose I would die," I said.

Lore stared at me, his eyes like violet fire.

"Within seven days?" he asked.

"What?" I asked, confused by his question.

"If you are without them for seven days, will you die?"

"Well, no," I said. "Of course not."

"And you said her brothers were idiots," said the fox.

I looked at him, narrowing my gaze.

"What's going on? First you come to me at the moor and warn me that my carriage will be attacked, and now you are here with the fae who saved me. Was this planned?"

I felt silly saying it aloud. Why would either of them make a plan to save me?

Lore and the fox exchanged a glance before returning their attention to me.

"Your brothers hired the thieves to attack your carriage. I believe their intentions were to kill the thieves and pose as the hero to the king of Rook but…Prince Lore got to you first."

My gaze snapped to the fae's.

"Prince?"

Lore raised a dark brow. "Yes?"

"You did not say you were a prince," I said.

I had tried to hit him and thrown wood in his face.

"We hardly had time for formal introductions," he replied. "Besides, I am not the first prince to make your acquaintance."

"Do not let him fool you, wild one," said the fox. "He was quite miffed over that."

Miffed?

Over me?

I had to be dreaming.

I closed my eyes and opened them again, but the fox and the fae still remained, watching.

"Perhaps I am dead," I said.

"You are very much alive," said Lore. "At least you have promised to be for the next seven days, which will bode well for me, since I am in need of a mortal, and you are now in my debt."

I swallowed hard, looking at him.

"Excuse me?"

"I saved your life," he said, as if that explained everything.

I stared at him and then asked, "Did I ask you to?"

He blinked. "What?"

"You say I owe you a debt because you saved my life, but I did not ask you to save my life."

Lore tilted his head as if he did not understand me. "Are you saying you did not want to be saved?"

"I don't know," I said. I could not remember what I had

273

been thinking before he killed Peter. "The point is that I did not ask, and how can there be a debt if I did not ask?"

The fox made a strange, high-pitched sound, a laugh, I realized. "Oh, she is a clever thing," he said. "If I did not know better, I'd think she were fae!"

Lore scowled and took a step toward me. I curled my fingers into fists.

"It does not matter that you didn't ask," he said. "You are obligated to repay me however I choose, and I *have* chosen."

I did not understand.

"Why me?" I asked.

"Why *not* you?" he asked.

"I am…worthless," I said.

I had no skills, save keeping house, and still, as my brothers often reminded me, I managed to fail at that every day.

Lore studied me for a few quiet seconds, and in that time, I felt like the only thing in existence. He lifted his hand but did not touch me, only let his fingers mimic brushing my skin. I could feel their heat, even gloved. It was enough.

"You do not get to determine your worth to me," he said and dropped his hand.

I stared at him, considering my options, though there truly was only one—to follow him and fulfill my debt. It was not as if I could go home.

"My brothers will come for me," I said. "They have hunted and survived this forest many times."

"So have I," he replied. "I will keep you safe."

A thrill went through me, warm and pleasurable. I longed to contain it, because I did not want to feel it. Fae would say anything to get their way, and I doubted this one was any different. He had, after all, saved me for a purpose that only served him. I would have to remember that if I was going to survive this.

"And after seven days?" I asked. "What happens to me if I have not managed to repay you?"

"Nothing," he said. "You will be free."

I almost laughed at his words but stopped myself. He did not understand—he did not know. I might be free of him, but I would never be free of my brothers.

Lore frowned and then asked, "Do you desire something else?"

I held his gaze as I answered in a hushed tone. "I have never desired anything else."

"Truly?" he asked, his voice just as quiet, and I refused to think about the fae I had loved and all I had dreamed for us.

"Truly," I said, glad that at least I could lie.

CHAPTER FOUR
The Cursed Prince

LORE

 oul humans with their foul mouths.

My hatred for Samara's brothers grew the longer I remained within the presence of this woman who flinched when I lifted a finger and looked at me as if I were the one who had harmed her.

It was a bitter irony given she was the one who had rejected *my* kindness, severing *my* hand with the very knife I had given her, a blade so sharp it could hew a stone in two.

That was seven years ago, and still I felt the pain of that day. It went beyond the phantom ache in my limb. This woman had carved her name in my heart long ago, and I still bled from that open wound.

She was my curse, and I wanted to be free.

"What did you choose?" Samara asked.

I blinked, so lost in my own thoughts, I had trouble tracking hers.

"What?"

"You said you had chosen how I will repay you," she said. "What did you choose?"

I watched her mouth as she spoke. There was something beautiful about the way words formed on her lips. It was not a helpful observation for my cock, which was growing inconveniently harder the longer I looked at her.

"Your Highness?"

I wanted her to say my name. I wanted to hear it in the dead of night while she lay beneath me, overcome with pleasure.

I ground my teeth, frustrated by my thoughts but it was also a reminder of why I'd rescued this woman and brought her into my world.

"I need you to break my curse," I said.

Before she could respond, I turned toward the fox.

"Lead the way, Fox. We only have seven days."

"As you command, Prince," said the fox, who rose and trotted off into the forest.

The trees were thick, their limbs heavy with thorned garland and wild grape vines. The ground was covered with an intricate tangle of tree roots, ferns, and wood anemone that bloomed white, stark against the sea of green. There were other flowers too, but they were not so dense—purple violets, pale pink gooseberry, and a colony of red bleeding heart. Their magic called to me like music, their petals like pretty bells chiming in the wind. Their scent was just as powerful. Some of it was honeyed and healing, and some of it was metallic and toxic, but nothing could overpower Samara, who smelled like sweet oleander. As enticing as it was, I was the Prince of Nightshade, and I knew that the sweetest things were sometimes the most poisonous.

With Samara, it had only taken a glance—a glimpse of her pale face, rosy lips, and coal-black hair—and it was done. That was how I knew I was cursed, because there was no such thing as love at first sight, yet here I was, completely ensnared and unable to escape her as she stumbled around behind me in an attempt to navigate the tangled wood.

Everything about her was *loud*. Her footsteps were like water crashing upon rocks, her breathing like the howling wind, and she was as slow as a snail. If this was to be our pace, I would fail to break my curse in seven days. I considered carrying her, but the thought of touching her made my body feel too warm and too tight. It was exciting to the point that it repulsed me.

"My lord?" Samara spoke softly but breathlessly.

I recognized her hesitancy as fear, and I did not like it, but I knew her brothers were responsible. They had been terrible since the moment I met her seven years ago. I would have killed them had she not stopped me. I did not understand why she protected them. I had killed my own brothers a time or two for far lesser offenses, though the action was futile. They just came back, worse than before.

I didn't look at her or ease my stride.

"You may call me Lore," I said, my voice tight. I wondered if it was a mistake to let her say my name, yet pressure built in my chest as I waited for her to speak it.

She didn't.

"May I ask you a question?" she asked.

I took a breath and let it out slowly, attempting to dispel the disappointment.

"You may," I said. As much as I dreaded what she might ask, I did not want to tell her no.

"Why are you cursed?"

"I looked at an enchantress, and now I cannot escape her," I said. It was close enough to the truth.

"It seems rather extreme to curse someone for staring," she said.

Ahead of us, the fox snorted. "His Highness has cursed many for far less."

I glared at the creature, thinking that I'd like to show him what it was to be cursed and sentence him to wear his fur inside out for the rest of his life, but I resisted the urge for vengeance. Samara was so used to horror, I did not want to become another monster in her eyes.

"Perhaps that is why you are cursed," said Samara.

Her comment frustrated me, and I paused, turning to face her.

"Are you implying that I deserve to be cursed?"

She ceased to breathe as I watched her, growing pale. I did not even know why it mattered what she thought; she was mortal and had no understanding of the world that flourished beneath the boughs of the Enchanted Forest. Still, I desired to know.

"No, my lord," she said.

"Then what are you saying?" I wanted to close the distance between us, but I did not want to watch her cower before me.

"Ignore me, my lord. I know not what I speak."

"Do you dislike my name?" I asked, tilting my head to the side as I watched her.

For a second, she looked confused. "No, my lord."

"Then why don't you use it?"

She opened her mouth to speak, but then she closed it and lowered her head. "I apologize...*Lore*."

"I do not want an apology," I said. "I want to know what you really think."

She watched me like prey shivering beneath the eyes of a wolf.

"I won't hurt you. I have promised, and I cannot break a promise," I said.

"It does not matter that you cannot break promises. I do not trust you," she said. "I will call you Lore when I trust you."

My chest felt tight, like she had taken a hold of my heart. I did not want to feel disappointed by her words. Lore was not even my true name, but that was not a name I would offer for the same reason, as eager as I was to hear her say it. It was a reckless thought. The gift of a true name was the offer of power. I could not deny her anything if she spoke it, though I knew I'd deny her nothing no matter what she chose to call me.

That was the danger of this curse.

I dipped my chin and held her gaze. "As you desire," I said. "And?"

"And what, my lord?" She used my title deliberately, as if to emphasize her point, her eyes alight with challenge. I wasn't even sure she realized it, and if I pointed it out, she'd likely crawl back into her shell, so I said nothing, only smirked, liking this peek at who she could have been—maybe who she still *could* be—without her brothers.

"You have an opinion on why I am cursed," I said. "I want to know it."

She took a breath, lifting her chin. She did not answer my question but asked one instead "Why do you curse people?"

I had not thought much about it. I suppose people just annoyed me, but I did not want to say that aloud.

"To teach lessons," I said.

It wasn't untrue, even if the lesson was leaving me alone.

"What kind of lessons?" she asked.

I hesitated. *Oh, she was challenging.*

"I suppose that depends on the offense," I said.

She watched me, and I waited, anxious for her approval.

"I do not think anyone deserves to be cursed," she said. "But if the purpose of a curse is to learn a lesson, what is yours?"

"I was not cursed to learn a lesson," I said.

There was no point in loving someone who did not love you back. Whoever had brought this upon me—likely one of my beastly brothers—intended one thing—*torture.*

I turned and began walking again.

"But isn't that how curses are broken?" she asked as she followed.

"Not this one," I said.

"Then I do not understand how I am supposed to break this curse."

"You aren't going to break it," I said. "You will wish it away."

It took me a moment, but I soon realized that Samara had stopped following. I paused and turned, but she was gone. Instantly, dread pooled in the pit of my stomach.

"Samara!" I jogged back to the place where I'd seen her last and looked in all directions but saw only dense, green foliage. It was as though she'd vanished. "Fuck!"

"You dimwit," said the fox. "You scared her!"

"I did not intend to!" I said. "She didn't even give me a chance to explain!"

"She told you she did not trust you," said the fox. "Yet you led with a wish!"

"I am aware," I snapped. I had a feeling she would remind me often, with her actions and her words, but if she'd given me a chance, I'd have told her about the wishing tree and its magic. "Fuck," I muttered again, scanning the ground for signs of her footsteps when I noticed a sprawling shrub with leafy, dark green vines. Purple flowers grew in clusters along their stems, and some had turned into bright red berries. It was bitter nightshade, and like all plants of its kind, they were singing.

> *There once lived a prince of poison*
> *Who marked a mortal as his chosen.*
> *But she did not want to be his wife*
> *So she severed his hand with a knife,*
> *And now his heart is broken.*

I ground my teeth. Despite my power, I often battled the singsong nightshades. The forest had influence first, and she

took great joy in taunting me, which had given me a specific reputation among the fae, since no one heard what I heard.

"I will poison you to the root if you do not tell me where she has gone," I growled.

The nightshade shivered, and their tune changed quickly.

Look close, Prince.
See our limbs, they are limp.
See our leaves, they are ripped.
Your lover, she came this way.
Your lover, she ran this way!

The bitter nightshade continued to repeat the verse as I followed the broken path Samara had left trampling through the forest to escape me.

Escape. That word twisted through me. As much as I wanted to be rid of this curse, this obsession, I wanted to be the one Samara never feared.

"Are you ever going to tell her?" the fox asked. He lingered behind me, trotting along as if nothing were wrong.

"Tell her what, Fox?" I asked, frustrated.

"Who you are," he said. "That you are the hand who offered the knife."

"Why would I tell her such a thing? She showed how she felt seven years ago," I said, not wanting to face her rejection again.

"Perhaps you are wrong."

"How can I be wrong when my hand is gone?" I asked.

"Her brothers, they are terrible things," said the fox. "Have you considered that they may be why you lost your hand?"

"Of course I have considered," I said. "But nothing changes that she held the knife."

"Surely, that is not true."

Honestly, I did not know, but it was easier to believe. She had already rejected me once, and I did not want to face it again.

"What I need most right now is to keep Samara from running so she can break my curse," I said. After that, I would be free, and so would she, and neither of us would ever think of the other again.

"Are you sure you are cursed?" asked the fox.

"Of course I am sure. She is all I ever think about!"

For the last seven years, she was all I ever dreamed about.

"Have you tried thinking of something else?"

"Of course I have!" I roared, annoyed by the fox's ridiculous words. I had tried to think of *anything* else. I'd gone to the very edge of the world and sat with the sun, moon, and stars and still thought of nothing but her. She was unmatched—brighter than the sun, more beautiful than the moon, sweeter than the stars. I loved her more than anything in this terrible world, and I hated it. "I cannot escape her."

"Apparently, you can," said the fox. "Or at the very least, she can escape *you*."

I growled low in my throat. "I hate you, Fox."

"Mutual, Prince," he said.

As we continued, a persistent thump echoed throughout the wood. At first, it was faint, but the farther we walked, the louder it grew, and so did my dread. It was soon joined by the sound of flutes and fiddles. It was the sound of fae revelry, and it had likely drawn Samara's attention, as it would many unlucky mortals tonight.

Just ahead, there came an old fae woman who was no bigger than a crow, her wings beating hard and fast. She wore a skirt of green grass and a shirt made from the petals of a poppy. She carried an umbrella made from maple leaves to keep the sun off her skin, which was so pale, it was almost translucent. Without it, she would surely burn to death.

"Fair maiden," I said.

"I cannot delay, my lord," she said, her voice high-pitched like a small bell. "For I must be off to the marsh where the night raven sleeps."

I followed beside her. "I will join you on your journey if you tell me from where that music comes."

"It comes from the elfin hill," she said. "The maidens are practicing their dances."

There were many elfin hills of varying sizes. Some were small and some were large, some housed tiny fae and some housed larger fae, and unless they were open, they merely appeared to be grassy mounds.

"For whom are they practicing?" I asked.

"Why, for the old elf king's honorable guests," she said.

"Would I know them, fair maiden?"

"I am certain I would not know," she said. "For I do not know you."

I gritted my teeth but tried not to show my frustration.

"If the maidens are practicing their dances and the old elf king has invited many distinguished guests, then there must be much to celebrate," I said.

"Oh, there will be, but only if every maiden ends the night betrothed," said the fae.

"Are there many eligible maidens?" I asked.

"Oh yes, for the music you have heard will only reach the ears of those who are unwed, even mortals."

I no longer had any doubt as to where Samara had gone.

"Tell me, fair maiden, who is invited tonight?"

"Anyone may come to the ball, which will take place after the banquet, but the banquet is only for the elf king's honorable guests," she said. "Now, I have delayed too long, and there is much still to do. I must be on my way as I have yet to send the invitations, and the night raven will wake soon."

"Fair maiden, you have been so busy. Allow me to assist you," I said. "If you tell me who is invited, I will go to the night raven for you."

"What a dear," she said. "If you will do me this favor, then you may come to the ball this night!"

"I am at your service," I said, bowing very slightly.

The old elf maid smiled so wildly and with much relief and then began speaking. "His first visit must be to Nereus and his daughters, who will likely not stay long, for they do not want to be gone from the sea. Still, we shall try to make them comfortable. We must ask the brownies, though it is nighttime, and they may not want to abandon their chores. Oh, and do not forget the trolls—not the giant ones, for they will stomp on the ground and cause much strife, but the ones with tails who are smaller and can fit beneath the hilltop."

The longer the fae rattled on, the more I regretted my decision, but I thought about Samara dancing beneath the moonlight for men who were not me, which reminded me why I needed to do this.

"I am hesitant to ask the ghosts, but I fear they will haunt our guests if I do not. But if we invite the ghosts, we must also invite the *gloson* and keep him well fed, or he will seek food among our guests."

"Of course, fair maiden," I said quickly, interrupting her before she could add more creatures to her list of guests. "Is there anything else you may need? You so smartly mentioned food. Perhaps there is something I could fetch for the old king's distinguished guests."

"What a blessing you are!" she said. "I daresay, our guests of honor—the goblin king and his sons—would enjoy a few rusty nails, but they must be from the foot of a bone horse, for those are a delicacy. If you return with them before sundown, you may have a seat at the banquet."

"Does the goblin king seek a wife?"

"For his two sons," she said. "Though they are rumored to be careless and rude."

"Pity the women they choose," I said.

"Nay, good sir," she said. "For the maidens shall become princesses, and their husbands will inherit many castles and goblin gold."

"I'd rather the castles and gold," I said.

"Well, perhaps the goblin king's sons will like the look of you, and then you will have castles and gold. Now off with you!" she said and called out as she turned. "The night raven will wake soon!"

There was silence for a few seconds, and then the fox spoke.

"Surely, a prince of your rank would be an honored guest? Wouldn't it have been easier to tell the old elf maid who you were?"

"No," I said. I was lucky she had not recognized me, and I hoped the same would be true tonight at the ball. Otherwise, I would fail to rescue Samara. "Trust me, it will be far easier to pry nails from the feet of a bone horse."

CHAPTER FIVE
The Elfin Hill

SAMARA

 ou will wish it away.

As soon as those words left the Prince of Nightshade's lips, I ran. I had made one wish in my life, and it had only led to horror. I swore I would never make another, and I certainly wouldn't for someone else, no matter the debt I owed.

He would just have to hunt me.

Though he may not get the chance if my brothers found me first, which was more likely now that I had fled from the prince's side. Despite the threat, I was willing to give the forest a chance. I doubted it was any more threatening than the men in my life.

I kept running, weaving what I hoped was a confusing path through the forest. I tore buttons from my cloak and pieces from my dress, leaving them scattered along a path I quickly abandoned for a new direction. Once I felt safe enough, I would stop and devise a plan.

I had few options. I could not go home or anywhere near Gnat. There were other towns within the shadow of the Enchanted Forest I might be able to reach, but then there was still the matter of the debt I owed to the prince and the lengths the forest would go to see that I fulfill it. Even with all this, I'd rather try something—*anything*. Even if I died in the process, at least it would be under my control.

As I ran, I glanced over my shoulder to see if anyone was following, when suddenly, my foot dropped into a hole and I fell, striking my knees on moss-covered rocks. Everything hurt, even my hands, which I had used to catch myself. Maybe I wouldn't have to worry about anyone finding me. Maybe the forest would swallow me whole.

I pulled my foot out from between the rocks. It hurt and was already swollen. I sat for a moment to catch my breath, my chest and ribs aching as I scanned my surroundings, realizing that what I'd thought was just a grassy hill was actually a slope covered in large boulders. Trees sprouted from between them, their branches like bony hands clawing at the air. They'd stopped growing long ago and now seemed to be frozen in time, covered in vibrant, green moss from which golden poppies grew.

It was beautiful, but the descent would be treacherous. I would have to change directions again, but as I got to my feet, there was a faint breeze. I had grown so hot from running, the sudden brush of cool air sent needlelike chills down my spine. Or perhaps it was not the wind so much as the music it carried. It was airy and soft, and I could barely hear it, but I couldn't let it go.

It was beckoning, and I wanted to follow it, which meant a descent through the labyrinth of boulders at my feet. The first step was the hardest and most painful. The second wasn't so bad, and by the third, I could manage the pain if I gritted my teeth hard enough.

There was no true path down, only a narrow space of

rocky earth that was sometimes overgrown with moss or ferns. Farther downhill, the boulders towered, and while the path was smoother, it was overgrown with flora. I had no choice but to wade through vibrant poppies as they danced in clusters around my feet. I thought they might be swaying to the music, which was closer now and more distinct. A drum had joined the ensemble, and I took a step with each beat. Soon, the pain in my ankle receded, but my eyes had grown heavy, and I suddenly had the overwhelming urge to sleep.

I stumbled and fell, finding that the earth beneath me was cushioned, far softer than anything I'd ever slept on in my twenty-six years. I tried to rise, but my body was too heavy, and my arms shook with the effort.

"Sleep," I heard the flowers say, their voices like a soft hum, a lullaby cradling my body. "We will keep you safe."

I opened my eyes, and I swore the poppies grew taller, blocking out the sun and sky and the twisted branches of the ancient oaks above me until there was nothing but darkness, and I fell asleep believing them more than I believed Lore.

───

Something poked me.

I woke instantly, heart already racing as I pushed myself up and scrambled away, expecting to see my brothers standing over me, but as my vision cleared, I realized it was not my brothers who had touched me but a fairy.

She was small, no taller than the poppy stem she gripped between her small hands. She looked as though she were made from a tree, with skin like bark and hair like braided vines. A dryad, I realized. She wore a dress made of dark leaves and rosettes, and the entire thing seemed to shimmer like dew in the early morning light, except it was not early morning at all. It was dusk, and the sky had turned orange in color.

"Oh," I said, rubbing my eyes. "I am so sorry. I thought… you were someone else."

She stared at me with her large, mossy eyes and asked, "Are you going to the ball?"

I blinked, confused. "The ball?"

"There is a ball down at the old elfin hill," she said. "If you do not hurry, you will miss the dancing!"

"That sounds lovely," I said. "But I am afraid I was not invited."

"You do not have to be invited, silly!" she said. "Everyone may come! The old elf king has declared it so!"

I hesitated again. "I would disgrace him," I said, looking down at my tattered and worn dress. It was the only thing I'd worn the last ten years. I had mended it to the point that it was now mostly thread and not cloth at all. "I have only these rags to wear."

"Then we shall dress you," said the dryad.

"Please," I said. "I would not ask that of you."

I did not feel comfortable with the thought of accepting such a gift, especially from the fae. Lore had already taught me that nothing was done out of kindness. Everything was an exchange, and I wondered what a pretty new dress would cost.

"You didn't," she said. "I have offered. All I ask is that you come to the ball."

I considered the dryad's offer, half-afraid this was a trap.

"What does one do at a fae ball?" I asked.

"What an odd question!" she said. "Why, dance and sing and eat until dawn!"

At the mention of food, my stomach rumbled. I could not remember when I had eaten last. Plus, I had never been to a ball before, and it sounded far more fun than wandering through the Enchanted Forest in the dark.

"And…will I be able to leave?" I asked.

"Mortals are so contrary," said the dryad, her brows furrowing. "Of course you can leave."

If that was the case, then I saw no harm in attending.

"Then I will come to the ball with you," I said.

The dryad smiled, pleased, and then leapt into the air, her wings glittering as they trilled behind her. "Hurry then! You must follow me!"

I rose from the flowers with no pain in my ankle and paused to inspect it. There was no sign I had injured it, no swelling or bruising.

"What's the matter?" asked the dryad, hovering near. "We must be on our way!"

"I am only amazed," I said. "Before I fell asleep in the flowers, I had injured my foot."

"The poppies must have healed you," she said. "For that is what they do, either heal or kill."

She zipped away then, somersaulting through the air, and I followed, again falling into step with the music, which I now felt vibrating in my veins. Before long, we emerged from behind the final row of boulders where the forest was open and endless. When we stepped beneath those ancient and heavy limbs, hundreds of lights ignited within the trees.

"Oh," I said, breathless, awed by the beautiful display.

As I looked closer, I saw that there were hundreds of fairies in the branches, holding lanterns.

"We will carry the lanterns to the elfin hill," said the dryad. "Come, or we will be late!"

I followed her past many trees until we came to the largest one. It was bigger than any tree I had ever seen. Perhaps it was the oldest within the Enchanted Forest, though I doubted anyone could say for certain. Its branches were dense and heavy with many needles and red berries.

"Old Mother!" called the dryad, knocking on the trunk. "Old Mother! I have a mortal here in need of some clothes!"

It took me a moment to realize that the tree was moving.

Suddenly, an arm broke free from the trunk and then a leg, and before long, an entire creature made of wood stood before me. She was about my height and had deep eyes, a wide nose, and a frowning mouth. Moss and mushrooms grew on her head and arms, trailing down her trunk.

"A mortal, you say?" asked Old Mother. She leaned in to look at me, creaking like long limbs in the wind, her empty eyes unblinking. "What a pretty, pale thing. Are you sure she is not a ghost?"

"I am not a ghost, Old Mother," I said, though my voice was quiet.

"No?" asked the old dryad. She lifted her limb-like hand to my chin, and I stiffened at her touch. "Your eyes say otherwise. Your eyes say you want to disappear."

I'm not sure why I blushed. Perhaps it was because she had seen to my soul. I did not know what to say, so I did not speak. Instead, I dropped my gaze.

"It is all right, pretty thing," she said. "Tonight, you will know what it is to be admired."

I started to protest. I did not need to be admired, but Old Mother stopped me.

"Ah, ah, ah," she said. "I will not hear it. You shall be the belle of the ball."

She reached behind her head, broke something off with a quick snap, and offered a walnut.

"Open," she instructed.

I looked at Old Mother and then at the nut. I did not want to insult her, so I took it, feeling strange as I bit into the woody shell and then pried it apart to reveal a bundle of white fabric. I pulled it out, dropping the shell, and found that it was a beautiful gown.

"Oh, Old Mother," I said, holding the dress to my chest. "I have never had anything so beautiful!"

"Put it on! Put it on!"

My eyes widened, and I glanced around.

"Behind my tree, pretty thing!" she said.

I hurried around the yew and found an opening in the bark that was just big enough for me to fit. A strange excitement went through me as I undressed. I had not had anything new in such a long time, much less something so beautiful.

As I slipped into the new dress, I was surprised by its softness and how perfectly it fit. The skirt was frilled but light and airy, like gossamer floating in the wind. Lace threaded with silver and garlands of pretty white roses dangled from the waist at different lengths. The bodice was corseted and cut like the top of a heart, embellished with the same lace and roses. The sleeves were nothing more than long ribbons of gauze fabric tied on my shoulders.

"Pretty thing, are you ready?" called the younger dryad.

"I...I cannot lace the back," I said.

"Come, pretty thing, and I will do it for you."

I stepped out from the cover of the tree to find the dryad hovering, wings beating fast.

"Turn around, pretty thing," she said and then pulled the laces of the corset tight. When she was finished, I turned to her, burying my hands in the skirt of my new dress. I did not think I'd be able to stop touching it.

"Oh, you are a vision," said the dryad. "Old Mother is never wrong! You shall be the belle of the ball!"

I smiled because I could not help it. I was going to a ball!

"Off with you now!" Old Mother said as we rounded her tree. "Off to the ball, pretty thing!"

The dryads descended from the canopy above, their lanterns flickering as they flew. I smiled at Old Mother and then followed the light. It was like running beneath the stars. As the dryads lit the way, they seemed to draw all manner of creatures from the dark—fairies with butterfly wings and brownies in strange hats, dwarves dressed in fine jewels. There were also nymphs, small ones and tall ones, some with wings and some without, some with white hair and some with brown.

One danced up to me, her arm laden with floral crowns, and placed one upon my head before twirling away. Another came up to me and took my hand in hers, giggling and smiling as she pulled me along. We skipped to the music, which was closer now than before, a soft but warm and rich sound that was deeper than bells but higher than drums. The melody was hypnotic, and my body was buzzing.

I had never been so happy, and I did not know what spurred it, the feeling of being included and seen or some other kind of magic.

The dryads parted in the air, forming two lines that looped and then tangled in the trees as we spilled into a meadow, already packed with all kinds of creatures and mortals alike. There were even more fairies and nymphs, some so small they flitted through the air like gnats, others taller than me. There were goblins with long teeth and sharp nails and trolls with tails, centaurs with hooved feet and long beards and fauns with short legs and horns. I had never seen so many creatures before, and there were even more I did not recognize, but they were all soon forgotten as I was pulled into a dance by the nymph who had taken my hand.

As we formed a circle, I looked at her, her eyes so bright, they were like glowing stars.

"I have never danced," I said.

"It is easy. Follow my lead!" she said and pulled me to left and right, skipping as she went. Our circle tightened, and the nymphs beside me raised my arms high, releasing them to clap and spin before we joined hands to do it all over again. By the third turn, I was moving with an ease I'd never felt before and smiling so wide my face hurt. I felt like I could dance forever, even as I grew breathless and hot beneath the dryads' glimmering lights.

The music continued, transforming into something far faster. The nymphs kept hold of my hands, our circle shrinking as a larger one formed around us. I was unprepared as I was jerked to the right, the fae beside me skipping quickly, and then suddenly, they released my hand to take a step and turn. I followed their lead and joined hands with a man, or I thought he was a man, except that his eyes were yellow and his irises black slits.

I held his gaze for a moment, unnerved by those strange eyes set within such a handsome face, until I found myself in the larger circle and pulled again to the right.

We continued like that, coming together and then apart, and I thought that I had never been happier, but as I moved to take another's hand, I realized the dancers were being watched, though that might not have bothered me if it wasn't for one set of eyes.

Lore.

Now that I was aware of him, I didn't know how I'd gone this long without feeling his gaze upon me. It was heavy and dark and...*angry.*

He sat stiffly at the end of a long banquet table, which was positioned beneath a hill that looked as if it had been propped up with grand posts, wound with green garlands. One of his hands rested on the table, gloved fingers tapping but not to the music. He was dressed differently, not in his leather and armor but in a silver tunic with sterling clasps. He was crowned with pale white branches, and his long, silky hair fell over his shoulders.

He was stunning but also terrifying, and the sight of him halted my steps, and then suddenly, no one was dancing, and everyone was staring at me and the Prince of Nightshade.

"My lady?" a voice asked.

It took me a moment to disengage from Lore's stare, a moment to prepare myself for what it would feel like to have his gaze burning up my body. Finally, I turned my head and met the pale yellow eyes of the man I'd first traded places with during the dance.

"Perhaps you would like to rest?" he asked. "Allow me to escort you."

He offered his hand, and I took it, not knowing what else to do. I did not think I could continue dancing now that I knew Lore was here and watching.

The stranger led me from the center of the meadow to a stack of stones that acted as a table and chairs. When I was seated, the music began again.

"Here you are, my lady," he said, handing me a large leaf with which I could fan myself, though I did not think it would help. My body wasn't hot from dancing anymore. This heat burned low and hot in the pit of my stomach.

"Thank you," I said, but the man did not seem to hear me, because he was waving over a servant carrying a tray upon which were a number of silver goblets. He took two and handed me one. I did not know what was in the cup, but I sipped it anyway and found that it was sweet.

The man did too and sat opposite me at the small round table.

"You are human," he said.

I hesitated. "Yes," I said. "Is it so obvious?"

"Only because you cannot dance," he said with a chuckle.

I blushed and took another sip of the sweet drink.

"Do not be embarrassed," he said. "I find it endearing."

I had never been called that before, and I found myself wondering if that was a good thing. It almost felt like being called naive, which I didn't like, though I knew it was true, especially when it came to survival in the Enchanted Forest.

"And you? Are you…human?" I asked, knowing he was not.

He held my gaze and smiled faintly before looking toward the dancers.

"My mother was human," he said. "My father was a goblin."

That explained his eyes.

"Are they still with you?" I asked.

"They died a very long time ago," he said.

It took me a moment to respond. I considered only saying I was sorry, but apologies were strange when the topic was death.

"Mine too," I said.

"Then we both know grief," he said.

I nodded, and we were quiet for a few moments.

"Tell me something about them," I said. "Your mother and father."

I couldn't place the look on the half goblin's face.

"Only if you want to, of course," I added, feeling silly.

"I want to," he said. Then he took a breath and looked away again. "My mother used to sing to me. She had a beautiful voice. Sometimes I think I can still hear her, but only when it is very quiet and the world is still."

"That is not often," I said.

He laughed. "No, not often at all."

"My mother liked to sing too," I said, and I could not help smiling as I remembered the sound. "She was terrible, but she loved it."

The half goblin laughed.

"Do you sing?" he asked.

My smile faded at his question. I did not expect it to be painful, to remind me that I had not sung since my mother died and that I had not felt happy enough to even try.

"I haven't in a long time," I said.

"You sound so lovely when you speak, I am certain you must when you sing."

"I am certain you are wrong, my lord," I said, growing uneasy beneath his praise. I looked away, regretting it instantly when I found Lore staring. He had not moved, and he still seemed angry.

The half goblin must have noticed how I stiffened and followed my gaze. He turned back to me, our eyes meeting.

"Do you know the Prince of Nightshade?" he asked.

"We are acquainted," I said, not wanting to disclose that I was in the prince's debt. "But I would not say I know him."

The half goblin studied me. I did not think he believed me.

"I am surprised he is here. He is not usually welcomed by the fae outside his kingdom."

My chest tightened. "Why?"

"They say he talks to himself and hears things no one else can."

"Is that all?" I asked, frowning. "It seems cruel to exclude him for something so...harmless."

"Is the way he looks at you harmless?"

I didn't know, though he had promised not to hurt me, so maybe it was.

"He is angry with me," I said.

"That is not anger," replied the half goblin.

Before I could ask what it was, a dwarf approached to whisper in his ear. The exchange was brief, but then he turned to me.

"I apologize," he said, rising. "I have been summoned away."

"Of course. Thank you for keeping me company."

"May I?" he asked, holding out his hand.

I hesitated for only a moment but accepted, his fingers clasping mine. He bent and brushed his lips across my skin.

"It was a pleasure," he said. There was an intensity to his gaze that made me blush, and I watched him as he retreated toward the banquet table, though it was not long before my gaze drifted to Lore again. This time, however, he was gone. My heart began to beat fast and my ears started to ring, but

before I could scan the crowd for him, a voice interrupted my alarm.

"I hope you did not give him your name, wild one," said a familiar voice, though it startled me. I looked down to find Fox sitting stoically at my feet.

"He did not ask," I said. "But why should I not?"

"Names have power," said the fox. "You do not want to give away your power."

I frowned. Another thing that required an exchange.

"Why are you here, Fox?" I asked.

"I should ask you the same thing, wild one," he said.

"The dryads invited me," I said. "They said all were welcome."

The fox's eyes narrowed, and he tilted his head. "Did they tell you anything else, wild one?"

Dread crept into my chest at his question.

"That I could leave," I said.

"One thing you must learn about fae is that just because they cannot lie does not mean they tell the truth."

"I do not understand—"

"Perhaps you may leave," said the fox. "But only if you are engaged before sunrise."

"What?" I asked breathlessly, shock striking my heart.

"You are dressed as a maiden seeking a husband, clad in white and crowned. Someone here must ask for your hand. Otherwise, you will spend a year inside the elfin hill."

"That cannot be," I said.

"It is," said the fox, his gaze moving past me. "Though you may have no trouble leaving. It seems the goblin king has taken a liking to you."

"Goblin king?" I asked, peering over my shoulder to find the half goblin from earlier standing at the banquet table beside a very small elven man who was so wrinkled, he looked as though he'd melted on the stack of pillows beneath him. They were watching me.

I turned back to the fox. "You must help me," I said. "I do not want—"

My words died on my lips as someone approached, and I looked up to meet Lore's violet eyes.

"Wild one," he said.

I swallowed hard. Up close, he did not look so angry, but his eyes were still bright, burning like an ethereal fire.

"Prince," I said and slowly rose to my feet.

He offered his hand. "Dance with me."

I hesitated, uncertain, given what he wanted from me.

"Samara?" he said. The name was low, barely a whisper. It felt strangely like a spell, and I thought about what the fox had said, about names having power.

I gave Lore my hand, and he led me to the edge of the meadow. We stood apart and the distance felt strange.

"I do not know how to dance," I said.

"You seemed to know earlier," he replied. "Though if you find you are lost, look for me."

The music began, and he bowed his head. I looked about, finding that the ladies curtsied, so I did the same. We rose and circled each other, only to repeat the same move, our eyes never leaving the other.

"You ran," he said.

"I will not wish for you," I said.

I noticed his mouth tighten, but then we turned away from each other, moving in a wide loop until we came face-to-face again. He held out his hand, and I took it as we stepped together and apart.

"I am not asking you to speak it into the ether," he said.

"Then what are you asking?"

We paused as we made another loop around each other, but this time, Lore took another fae's hand while I dipped beneath their arms. I looked at the other dancers, feeling ridiculous as I danced this strange dance, but I remembered Lore's words and turned to him.

He took my hand again.

"I am asking you to accompany me on a quest to find the wishing tree upon which golden apples grow," he said. "When we find it, you must pick one and only take a bite to wish me free. It is that simple."

It sounded too wonderful to be true, which had been the

case for everything in my life so far. The fae who had offered the knife, the prince who had offered for my hand.

"You cannot think I believe such a thing exists," I said.

"I cannot lie."

"Perhaps you cannot lie, but you do not have to tell the truth."

Lore's eyes narrowed. "Did the fox tell you that?"

I did not answer, but it was easy to avoid as we turned away from each other.

"I am telling you truthfully, the wishing tree exists," he said when we met again. "But its magic only works on the first night of the full moon."

I did not want to believe him, but he spoke with such sincerity, not only about the tree but also his curse. He seemed desperate to be free.

"That does not explain why I must make the wish."

"You must make the wish because I am unworthy," he said.

I stumbled, and Lore caught me. I righted myself, but he didn't let go, his hands braced on either side of my bare arms. It occurred to me that he had yet to take off his gloves. I considered asking him why—though embarrassingly, it was only because I wondered what his skin would feel like against mine. If his palms burned now, would they set me aflame uncovered?

But something he'd said disturbed me more.

"Who says you are unworthy?"

He stared down at me, brows lowered. I couldn't help watching his mouth and the way he frowned. I decided I did not like it, that I preferred when he smiled, even if the things that came out of his mouth were frustrating.

"No one must say it for it to be true," he said.

"Then it can just as easily be false," I said.

"It isn't," said Lore.

His words frustrated me, and I looked away. "I cannot

imagine why you would choose me," I said. "If we are speaking of worthiness, then I—"

"Your brothers are wrong," Lore said, interrupting. "It is they who are unworthy. They who do not deserve you."

"Just because you believe that doesn't make it so," I said.

We had stopped dancing, but the fae still moved around us, and I became highly aware of our proximity and the way I had to tilt my head all the way back to hold his gaze. I did not want to feel the desire curling in the bottom of my stomach. I did not want to like how his hands felt on me. I did not want to think about how his lips would feel pressed against mine.

Except that I wanted all those things. I just didn't trust Lore enough to give them.

His gaze shifted to my mouth.

"It seems we are at an impasse, wild one," he said.

"It would seem so," I said.

Slowly, the elven lord lifted his hand, and I took a deep breath as his fingers brushed lightly over my cheek.

"Come with me," he whispered. "I will show you your worthiness."

I closed my eyes, unable to face him. I desperately wanted to believe him. His words were familiar, like those that had called to me in my sleep.

"Samara," he whispered again.

His lips were so close to mine, I could feel their heat. It rushed down my throat and warmed my chest. I held my breath, trying not to think about what it would be like to close the space between us, to press my lips to his, to tease this passion burning inside me.

And just when I was decided, a rapid clink broke us apart. I turned to find the dwarf from earlier tapping a spoon against a glass.

"His Majesty wishes to speak!" the dwarf declared, continuing to hit the goblet so hard, I thought it might break. Soon, he had drawn everyone's attention, and still the goblin king looked at me.

"Fae-kind," announced the old elf king. "The goblin king has chosen a bride!"

There was a mix of quiet murmuring and applause as everyone looked around in an attempt to guess who among them it would be.

I thought my heart might burst from my chest.

"It seems though that he is not alone," the old elf king said, drawing out the sound of every vowel in every word. "And another is vying for her hand."

A noise came from behind me that sounded a lot like a growl, then Lore stepped in front of me to block me from view.

"There is no competition," said Lore.

The goblin king stepped forward. "You know the rules, cursed prince. If you want to lay claim to my intended, then we must duel to the death."

I could not tell what I was more shocked by—that things had escalated to death so quickly or that these two were now arguing over who I belonged to.

"If you want to duel to the death, I am happy to oblige, but it will not be for this woman. She is already mine."

"Silence!" said the old elf king. "Intended, what say you? Which of these fae do you belong to?"

"Neither," I said, though I wondered if I had made a mistake, given what the fox had said about leaving betrothed tonight. "I belong to no one."

"If you belong to no one, then someone must take you," said the king.

"That is ridiculous," I said.

Another round of gasps, louder this time. I spoke over them.

"I am allowed more than two choices," I said.

"More than two? You want more than two men?" The old

elf king's brows rose almost to his hairline, which had receded nearly to the middle of his head, though the crowd did not seem so opposed to that, their gasps morphing into more of an agreeable hum.

"I do not *want* anyone," I said.

"But you are wearing white," said the old elf king. "And you have apple blossoms in your hair."

I reached for the crown and pulled it off, tossing it to the ground.

The fae gasped, offended once again.

"What I wear says nothing about what I want," I said. At least I did not know it when I put on the dress or the floral crown.

Finally, there was silence after I spoke.

"I like you, mortal," said the old elf king. "If you will not choose a suitor, then you will reside here with me."

"Your Majesty—"

"You desired a third choice, and now you have it," said the old elf king. "Now, who will you choose?"

"This is obscene," said the fox. "This woman cannot choose between you three."

"And why not, Fox?" asked the old elf king. "Do you want to throw your hat in the ring?"

There were laughs, but they did not last long, for the fox spoke quickly.

"She cannot choose because she is in mourning, for her intended, a mortal prince, died this very day," said the fox. "It is only proper that she delay her choice for at least a year."

The fae muttered to one another, though I didn't catch what they were saying, hopeful that the fox's words had freed me from this terrible situation. Despite having accepted Prince Henry's proposal and my desire to kiss Lore, I did not want to marry. I wasn't sure I ever would.

"You make a good point, Fox," said the old elf king. "It

is settled then. We shall delay for a year, at which point the maiden shall make her choice."

My relief dwindled.

With that, the music began again, and the revelry continued as if nothing had gone awry. I turned to Lore, who was scowling.

"Would I have been such a terrible choice?" he asked.

I was startled by his question but recovered quickly. "It has nothing to do with you," I said. "A true choice offers the option of freedom."

Lore's features softened.

"Apologies, wild one. It was all I could manage for you," said the fox as he trotted up.

"Do not apologize," I said. "I am grateful to you, Fox...but must I really return in a year?"

"Yes," he said. "You have entered into a bargain with the old elf king, and if you do not honor it, the forest will seek vengeance."

I frowned, feeling defeated, and looked at Lore. "Is the same true for debts?"

He studied me with a strange heat in his eyes. It reminded me of where we'd left off—too close and on the very edge of a great mistake.

I was glad I had not kissed him, or so I told myself as my eyes dropped to his lips.

"No one escapes what is owed," said Lore. "We all pay, with our time or with our life. There is nothing else."

I did not like his words, but that was not unusual. I disliked a lot of things that came out of his mouth, and I had only known him for a day.

"If that is the case, then I suppose we should be on our way," I said. "I would hate to waste more time."

I thought that Lore would be pleased that I had finally agreed to his demands, but his expression remained tense.

"My lady," said a voice.

I whirled to find the goblin king waiting.

Lore offered an unpleasant growl, which was growing far too common.

The half goblin ignored him, holding my gaze. "I respect your decision," he said. "Allow me to offer you a gift."

"Oh," I said. Again, I found myself in a situation I had never experienced before. It had been a long time since I'd been gifted anything that didn't turn out to be some sort of trick planned by my brothers.

The goblin king produced a small, black box that he opened to reveal a comb.

It was a fine piece of jewelry, made of gold and opal.

"May I?" he asked, taking it in hand.

I was very aware of Lore's gaze and also his anger, and I did not want to make it worse given that I now faced spending the next six days crossing the Enchanted Forest by his side.

"Allow me," I said, taking it from him and slipping it into my hair.

The goblin king's eyes were sad as he watched and then met my gaze. "Beautiful," he said. "Perhaps in a year, you will find your voice and sing for me."

"Perhaps," I said quietly, almost a whisper.

He smiled faintly before turning to leave, and I felt like I could breathe again, until I turned to Lore. His eyes focused intently on the comb in my hair.

"H-how does it look?" I asked.

"Terrible," he replied before he turned, stomping away into the darkness of the forest, leaving Fox and I behind.

"What did I do?" I asked, confused.

"Trust me when I say, wild one, absolutely nothing."

CHAPTER SIX
The Kingdom of Larkspur

comb.

I gave her a knife, and she cut off my hand.

The goblin king gave her a comb, and she put it in her hair.

I stomped ahead of Samara and the fox, breaking branches and cutting down thorny vines. It allowed me to channel my frustration but also made the path easier to follow for Samara, who could not see like I could see in the dark.

What use was a comb? I thought.

It certainly was not as helpful as a knife, especially one that could cut anything in two, yet if I had given her a comb seven years ago, perhaps I would still have my hand and a shred of dignity among my six other brothers, who all found it immensely entertaining that I had given my beloved a weapon to use against me.

But they had not watched her toil in the mud and cold of a bog for hours. They had not heard how her brothers berated and belittled her. They'd not listened to her in the dead of night when she divulged her desires. They did not understand, because they had never sacrificed themselves for anyone or anything.

I could not wait until they fell in love, though it was rumored that Casamir, my seventh brother, had taken the beast we sent his way, the woman who had killed our sixth brother, as his bride.

She had been an angry and lonely thing, but she had fallen in love with him and broken his curse.

I was not so lucky.

Samara did not love me. She did not even know I was the one who had given her the knife. But she was the apple of my eye, and because of that, she was the only one who could make the wish that would free me from the curse of love.

"I know you are eager to find the wishing tree," said the fox, walking up beside me as I slayed another shrub. "But your lover is dead on her feet."

"Do not call her that," I snapped.

"Do not call her what, Prince? They shall both be true, one sooner than the other, depending on you."

I glared at the fox, but I could not help glancing over my shoulder to see her stumbling about, barely lifting her feet from the ground as she followed far behind me.

"She struggles, yet she says nothing," I said. "I cannot decide if she is brave or afraid."

"She is both, Prince," said the fox. "She does not tell you because she is not used to anyone caring about her pain."

"I am not her brothers."

"Right now, you are like them," said the fox. "You are angry with her, and since you left the elfin hill, you have pretended as though she does not exist."

There was no pretending.

I couldn't escape her. Even as she walked behind me, I knew she was there. I was attuned to every move she made—every small breath and every beat of her heart—but the fox was right. Shame poured over me, heavy and thick. I slowed beneath its weight until I stopped, turned, and went to her.

Her heavy eyes lifted to mine and widened as she came to a stop.

"I'll be quicker, I promise," she said, taking a step back.

The alarm in her voice was upsetting, because I had scared her. In the face of her fear, my frustration was not important.

"You do not have to be quick," I said. "Let me carry you."

"I do not want to be a burden," she said.

"You have been awake too long, and you need rest. We will not reach a safe place to stay for another few miles," I said, having already decided that I would venture into my brother's kingdom, the Kingdom of Larkspur. I dreaded the visit, but the fucker had soft beds and breakfast, two things I doubted Samara had in a long time. "Let me carry you."

I waited for her response, overwhelmed by the urge to touch her.

Finally, she nodded and held my gaze as I shifted closer. When I placed my hand on her back, she felt rigid.

"Be at ease, Samara," I said. "I am not angry with you."

"Perhaps not this second," she said. "But you are angry."

I said nothing, because that was true.

"Put your arms around my neck," I said as I bent and picked her up. Up until this moment, I had been able to mostly ignore the phantom pain shooting from my stump up my right arm in favor of my anger, but now it was all I could feel—that and the fact that Samara's face was only inches from mine. It made me think of how close I'd come to kissing her beneath the elfin hill, something I had dreamed about for seven long years.

Something that had cursed me for just as long.

Maybe holding her was a terrible idea.

"Are you okay?" she whispered.

My brows rose, surprised by her question. Looking at her now, I could not figure out why I'd been so angry with her.

"I am okay," I said. "Why do you ask, wild one?"

"Because you are staring," she said.

I smiled a little. "I am just admiring you."

She said nothing, but her expression was suspicious, as if she believed there was nothing about her to appreciate. I did not know how to help her see herself the way I did—beautiful and kind, someone worthy of more than I was even capable of giving.

"Sleep, Samara," I said. "I will take care of you."

She watched me for a few more minutes before closing her eyes, and I started our journey again, the fox trotting ahead. I was conflicted as I held her, torn between comfort and anguish. My body had yet to let go of the feeling she'd stirred up in the grove, and having her this close only brought everything rushing back.

I had wanted to kiss her, but I could not bring myself to do it, too afraid I would scare her away, but my greatest hesitancy was that she did not know who I was.

She did not know that I was the hand with the knife.

"In the grove under the elfin hill," she said.

Her voice sounded like a scream in the quiet night, and her eyes remained closed. I did not know if she could no longer keep them open or if she did not want to look at me as she spoke. My heart raced as I waited for the rest of her words, realizing that she too was thinking about the same thing.

She continued, "When we danced and you said my name… was that a spell?"

"A spell?" I was confused and also disappointed.

"Fox said that names have power," she explained. "When you said my name…I felt…like I had lost control."

I swallowed hard. I had felt that way since I met her.

"No," I said. "It was not a spell."

Her body felt heavier after that, as though she had finally given in to comfort.

There came a point in our journey when I turned from the fox's path toward the Kingdom of Larkspur, where Cardic, my second brother, ruled.

He was exactly as his name suggested—a dick.

"Prince! That is not our way," the fox said.

"It is our way now," I said. "We will rest for the night."

At least Samara would rest. I did not trust my brother enough to sleep in his territory.

"Are you certain, Prince?" asked the fox. "This will be unpleasant for you."

I was very aware, but as I held Samara in my arms, the desire to give her comfort exceeded mine. "I am certain."

Though with each step, the dread of our arrival grew and grew.

Ahead, I could see glimmering lights in the trees. They were the warmly lit windows and flickering lanterns of the fae who resided in Larkspur, the kingdom in the trees. A bridge marked the start of Cardic's realm, and I walked it as it twisted through the branches. It was a slow climb to his palace, past homes belonging to many kinds of fae—dryads but also wood elves, green men and goblins.

Something zipped past me, striking my face.

I knew what it was the moment I heard the distinct whir of their wings.

"Fucking pixies," I growled.

Cardic used their mischief and turned them into weapons. They attacked anything that came near him, even invited guests. He found it humorous, and the pixies enjoyed pleasing him, likely because they were in love with him.

I wondered what would happen if they discovered he was incapable of love.

Another pixie raced by. This time, I could feel her claws cut my face.

I ground my teeth as anger bloomed in my chest. I wanted to snatch them from the air and crush them into a nasty pulp, but as it turned out, I didn't have to, because as soon as another flew by, Fox jumped, capturing the pixie in his mouth.

He swallowed it whole.

That was the end of their attack.

Finally, Cardic's palace came into view. I was only relieved because my phantom limb had started to burn. Despite having no fingers at all, I could feel the fire in each digit. I grit my teeth against the pain, as I usually did, and I started up the many steps leading to its entrance. His home was crafted and carved into a great, ancient oak that seemed to reach to the stars, vanishing into the darkness above. Over time, the sturdy branches had grown thicker and fuller, further encapsulating the stone facade of his castle. It had many open windows and great balconies, overrun with trailing vines and dangling moss, though to my great delight, I spotted a familiar vine with tear-shaped leaves. It was poison ivy.

I willed it to grow wilder, to creep into my brother's castle.

I hoped he would handle it and then pleasure himself.

It filled me with glee to think about the pain such a rash would cause him even as I approached the open, arched doorway of his castle for refuge. My legs and lungs burned, and I was hot and breathless, two things I despised unless I was having sex, something I had not done in a very long time, not since I had looked upon Samara. It was another side to the curse. I could be nothing but loyal to her. The very thought of fucking anyone else was…unimaginable. After tonight, I doubted we shared the same feeling. I wondered if she dreamed of the goblin king.

I held her tighter at the thought, my gaze falling to the comb he had given her. I wanted to pluck it from her hair and throw it into the dark abyss below my brother's kingdom.

"Do not do it, Prince," said the fox.

"How do you know what I am thinking?" I snapped.

"Because you growl more than me when you are angry," he replied.

I set my teeth, hoping to keep myself silent. Soon, we came to the final few steps, but before I could reach the top, something flew over my head.

I ducked and looked over my shoulder to see a dagger land and skid down the steps.

It seemed my brother had already been made aware of my arrival.

"You ill-bred, liver-eating bastard!" he shouted. "Give back my fucking fairy!"

"Shh!" I commanded as I lay against his steps, the edges digging into my ribs. I would right myself, but I was preparing for more daggers to be thrown my way.

"Are you…are you *shushing* me?" Cardic demanded. "On the steps of my own kingdom?"

"Shut up, you dull-headed, cunt-bitten coward," I said, my voice a raspy whisper. "Or you'll wake her!"

"Wake who, you spitting, ill-tempered fool?"

I peeked over the final step to see my brother at the entrance of his palace, cast in shadow from the bright light behind him.

"Swear you will throw nothing my way," I said. "For what I carry is precious."

"No," said Cardic.

I scoffed. "You are a dick."

"And you are a bore," he said.

"Fuck you, dick," I said.

There was silence.

"Are you quite finished cowering?"

"I am not *cowering*!"

"Yes, you are."

The comment came from the fox, who was sitting above my head on the top step.

"Fuck off, you miserable excuse for a cat. He should throw daggers at you. You're the one who ate his fairy!"

Suddenly, the fox made a strange sound, almost like a gulp. Then he began to cough until at last he heaved, and the pixie he had swallowed burst from his mouth. She landed a few feet away in a pool of yellow bile. She rose, coughing and sputtering, and then burst into tears before flying away.

"There is your pixie," said the fox. "Now, will you welcome us in? Your brother has been carrying his mortal for quite some time."

"His *mortal*?"

Finally, I rose to my feet with Samara in hand.

"What is *that*?" Cardic asked, as if he were disgusted by the sight of Samara.

I bared my teeth. "Watch your tone, dick."

"Is this the girl you have pined over for seven long years?" he asked, his amber-colored eyes sparking with delight. After a few minutes, however, a slow smile spread across his smug face. "The one who cut off your hand and never spoke to you again?"

I wanted to tear out his throat, but I decided against it. I did not want to chance the retaliation of his pixies with Samara so near. My scowl deepened, and Cardic began to laugh.

He laughed so hard, he bent at the waist, bracing his hands on his knees.

He laughed so long, he turned red in the face, and I thought he might suffocate.

To my great disappointment, he didn't, and he soon composed himself, wiping at the tears on his face.

"I can't believe I almost killed you and missed this," he said, still chuckling between words.

"You didn't almost kill me," I muttered as I stepped past him into his palace. I made myself at home, turning to the right and walking along a robust bough that acted as a floor. I ducked beneath low limbs and dodged clusters of leaves. Hanging among the branches were round beds, shrouded in sheer, gauzy fabric. I chose one closest to the ground since Samara could not fly and knelt to lay her on the soft mattress before covering her with a blanket.

As I did, the fox hopped onto the bed.

"What do you think you're doing, Fox?" I asked.

"I am going to rest, Prince," he said. "Be at ease. I am just a fox."

The creature curled up, resting his chin on his tail. I glowered, my eyes falling to Samara, who had slept so soundlessly from the moment I took her into my arms in the Enchanted Forest. I marveled at how peaceful she looked. This was her, unburdened by worry or fear, and it was beautiful.

I brushed a stray piece of her hair from her pretty, rosy lips, and then she sighed and turned her head away.

I glared at the fox.

"You had better just be a fox," I threatened.

He opened his eyes long enough to roll them and then went back to sleep.

I left, turning to find my brother watching.

"So how did you come into possession of her?" he asked.

I ignored him, making my way back down the hall.

"Did you slip her belladonna and steal her away?"

"I did not slip her belladonna, and I did not have to steal her away," I snapped. "I rescued her from thieves outside the Enchanted Forest."

Cardic pursed his lips. "Well, that isn't very exciting."

"Luckily, I do not exist for your entertainment."

"You exist for nothing, Lore, save this girl. Perhaps now that you have her, you can become interesting again."

I ignored him.

"You used to be an adept hunter," he continued. "Do you even remember how to string a bow?"

"Would you like a demonstration?" I asked. "I'll send an arrow right through your eye."

Cardic scoffed. "Even your insults have gotten dull."

I walked ahead of him, back through the foyer of his palace and into the adjacent hall. I started to open doors.

"What do you think you are doing?" Cardic demanded.

"Looking for wine," I said. "You have to have it here somewhere."

"Don't open that!"

But it was too late. The door was open, and I was surprised. I turned to my brother and pointed at the room.

"Why do you have a library?"

It was a nice library, with rows of floor-to-ceiling shelves and leather-bound books.

"Because I *read*," he said.

"Since when?" I asked. I had never seen Cardic with a book in my entire life, not even when we lived with Mother and Father in the Elder Kingdom.

"Since...a while," he said.

I narrowed my eyes, and he crossed his arms over his chest.

"I have hobbies, Lore. I am a multifaceted being."

"Multifaceted?" I asked. I'd never heard my brother use such a word in his entire life.

"You are just jealous because you are...*boring*!"

"And you said my insults were dull."

I looked at the library and then back at him, narrowing my eyes.

"Are you... Did you meet someone? Are you in love?"

"What?" Cardic asked. "No...no. I am most definitely not."

I raised a brow.

"Fuck off," he said, and I grinned as he walked past me. I turned to follow.

"So," I said. "Tell me about her."

"No," he said, throwing open a door on his left.

"So you *are* in love with someone?" I asked.

"I am not in love!"

"You are lying," said a voice.

Cardic had entered his study, where a jagged piece of mirror hung over the fireplace. It had once been whole and displayed in my father's grand hall, but before his death, he shattered it into seven pieces and declared that whichever brother assembled it first would be king.

Only one of our brothers cared about becoming king, and that was Silas, yet none of us wanted to give up our piece of the mirror because of its magic, which showed us anything we desired.

The downside was that the mirror also talked.

"Shut up!" Cardic said. "Or I will shatter you into a million pieces!"

"Shatter me," said the mirror. "I will merely speak a million times more."

"Has he asked to see her? This woman he desires?"

"Of course," said the mirror. "Just as you have asked to see yours."

It was true that I had asked the mirror to show me Samara, but in my defense, I was cursed.

"Why can't you keep secrets?" asked Cardic.

"Because I am a mirror," the mirror said.

"Show me this woman," I said.

"Don't—"

The mirror rippled and gave way to a scene that shocked me even more than the library. I expected Cardic's love interest to be…well, like him, immoral and unholy, but the woman in the mirror was the opposite.

"Are you in love with a nun?" I asked.

I was pretty sure the woman I was looking at was a nun. She wore a black frock with long sleeves and a cowl on her head. Every part of her was covered, even her ankles, and she was sitting!

"She is not a nun!" he snapped.

"She looks like a nun," I said. "She is wearing a veil."

"She is not a nun!"

"She is *praying*, for fuck's sake, Cardic! You cannot have a nun!"

"Don't tell me what I can and can't have, you self-rutting, churlish...*bastard!*" he yelled, and then he punched me in the face.

I heard the mirror sigh.

"I knew you didn't read!" I shouted as I charged at him. He swung at me again, but I grabbed his arm with my hand and turned away from him, bringing my other arm down hard on his elbow.

Cardic howled.

I shoved my knee into his stomach, but he caught my leg.

"I fucking read!" he said as he bit my thigh.

I screamed and then shoved him away. He fell to the floor. I pounced as he tried to get to his feet, grabbing his ankle to jerk him back. He collapsed to the ground and rolled as I climbed over him, my hand going for his neck.

I didn't even know if I could choke him with one hand, but I was going to try, and I didn't know why—because he refused to acknowledge that the woman he wanted was a nun?

I started to laugh.

I laughed so hard that I could no longer fight, and when my brother pushed me off him, I didn't care. I fell onto my back, still laughing.

"I'm glad my pain amuses you," he said, which only made everything much funnier, and though Cardic pouted, it wasn't long before he laughed too.

"I can't believe you're in love with a nun," I said.

"I can't believe you brought the woman you've pined after for seven years to my palace," said Cardic.

"I can't believe I have to bear witness to this," said the mirror.

We both glared at the glorified windowpane, but as we settled into silence, a different sort of emotion consumed me. It was heavier than sadness, worse than dread.

It was sort of like grief because the moment Samara partook of the golden apple and wished me free, I would have nothing, and I was just starting to realize that at least loving her from afar was *something*.

CHAPTER SEVEN
The Curse of
True Love

SAMARA

 *woke to something tickling my nose.*

When I opened my eyes, I found three pixies staring back at me. I startled for a moment, surprised by their presence, and rose to my elbows, but they also seemed surprised and darted back, their small wings whirring behind them. They had large eyes and long pointed ears, both seeming too large for their small, delicate faces. Each of them wore a tattered-looking dress made of oak leaves. One wore the cap of an acorn as a hat.

"Hello," I said, though I was slightly apprehensive, wondering what sort of mischief they might intend, but before I could say anything else, the fox leapt into the air and captured them in his mouth.

"Fox!" I shrieked. "Let them go!"

I scrambled after him. I wasn't sure what I intended to do, perhaps shake him until he opened his mouth. I grabbed his tufted tail, but I wasn't prepared for the bed to sway. I fell forward, and he slipped out of my grip.

"Fox!" I growled as I followed him over the edge of the bed, where I found him crouched down, his mouth vibrating, as if the pixies were fighting to get out. "Spit them out!" I said.

The fox opened his mouth, and out flew the three pixies. I could hear their high-pitched voices but understood nothing as they zipped around my head before darting off.

Finally, in the quiet, I put my hands on my hips and glared down at the fox.

"That was horribly rude," I said.

He coughed, and blood sprayed the floor.

"Fox?" I asked, taking a step closer and kneeling.

He coughed again and then sneezed, shaking his head before sitting back and looking at me.

"If you think that was rude, then you don't know pixies," he said.

He licked his paw while scrubbing his face.

I studied him for a few seconds more before letting my attention drift to my surroundings. In the chaos of waking, I hadn't had time to think about where I might be, but now I saw that I was in a tree. Sunlight streamed in through the surrounding branches where round beds hung, some small, some large.

I had never seen anything so strange.

"Where are we?" I asked.

"We are in the Kingdom of Larkspur," said the fox. "In the palace of Cardic, the second brother."

"Lore's brother?" I asked.

"Unfortunately," replied the fox.

"Why?"

"Who can say what the Prince of Poison was thinking," said the fox. "But I suspect he thought you would be more comfortable sleeping in a bed than on the forest floor."

That was…thoughtful given that the last thing I remembered before drifting off was his anger. I lifted my hand to my hair, touching the comb the goblin king had given me.

"Keep it, wild one," said the fox. "You will need it."

I wanted to ask why exactly I would need a comb but decided against it. I was rarely ever given anything, and I did not want to throw away the gift from the goblin king anyway, even if it did upset Lore, which I still did not understand.

Would I have been such a terrible choice? he'd asked, but was it that he wanted to be my betrothed or that he wanted to ensure I would journey with him to the wishing tree?

Speaking of the Prince of Nightshade…

"Where is Lore?" I asked.

"Either dead or alive," said the fox. "Which, I do not know."

The fox's answer was unhelpful, but I suspected he knew that as he rose and trotted off down the hall. I followed him, entering what I guessed was the main entrance of Cardic's castle. It was beautiful. The walls were carved with intricate designs, with careful attention to the windows and doors, which were framed with leaves and flowers. A set of stairs was carved into the trunk, spiraling up and around. I craned my neck, wondering how far they went and what might dwell on the other levels of the palace, but dizziness overwhelmed me. I looked down, where the fox waited at my feet.

"Does Lore have a castle?" I asked, curious.

"He does," the fox confirmed.

"What does it look like?"

"I am certain I do not know," replied the fox.

I was surprised.

"If you have never been to his kingdom, how did you meet the prince?"

"We crossed paths while he was hunting. When he took aim at me, I asked him not to kill me, and in exchange, I would help him obtain his greatest desire."

I did not need to inquire after his greatest desire, because I already knew.

"Breaking the curse," I said.

The fox said nothing.

We continued down the adjacent hall. I considered shouting Lore's name, but that did not seem appropriate inside a castle, though neither did wandering around its halls without permission.

I paused at an open door to look for Lore but instead found rows of shelves that were packed from floor to ceiling with books. They were beautiful too, leather-bound with gilded spines. I had never seen so many. I took a step toward the room but stopped abruptly.

"What's wrong, wild one?"

"I don't want to intrude," I said, "or make anyone angry."

"They are just books," said the fox, skipping ahead.

I looked down the hall to see if anyone was coming before I stepped into the room. It smelled earthy and rich, and as I walked down one of the many aisles, I read the gilded titles and recognized none. I wondered what kind of books they were, if they belonged to the mortal world or the fae.

I started to reach for one, eager to hold it, to breathe in the scent of its pages, to read a story that would take me far from this place, when I heard a noise from somewhere in the room. It sounded like silverware clanking, which was odd given that this seemed to be a library.

I pulled my hand back and crept down the length of the aisle until I came to the end of the shelves, peeking around the corner to find a man sitting at a round table before a large set of arched windows. He looked like Lore but also didn't.

He was in the middle of biting into some kind of tart when he looked up at me, his eyes a stunning shade of amber.

When he saw me, he froze for a moment and then decided to bite into the tart anyway.

"You must be my brother's beast," he said as he chewed.

"I am not a beast," I said, stepping out from the cover of the shelves.

"I was talking to the fox," said the man. "Though perhaps I should be talking about you."

I did not know what to make of this man who was like Lore but also not.

"You must be Lore's brother," I said.

He rose from his chair and bowed, still holding the half-eaten tart in his hand.

"I am Cardic," he said. "Prince of Larkspur, the second brother."

My brows furrowed. "Why did you say that?"

"Say what?"

"Introduce yourself as the second brother?"

"Because the number designates our place in line," he replied. "Lore is the third brother, in case he did not tell you."

"To be king?"

"No, our father chose a different method for that. When we were together, it established who would eat first, who got the best horse, the nicest clothes. *Everything* other than the crown."

"And now that you are apart?"

"It reminds us of our resentment," he said, then gestured to a chair beside him. "Please, sit."

I hesitated and looked down at the fox, who was sitting patiently at my feet.

"Where is Lore?"

"Don't worry. When he discovers you are not in the bed where he left you, he will come looking for you. In the meantime, you should eat. I hear you have quite the journey ahead of you."

I shifted closer to the table. "You know about our journey?"

"Oh yes. You are going to break my brother's curse," Cardic said, though he was far more amused than I expected.

I sat down slowly. Cardic poured tea and then slid the cup and saucer closer to me.

"You…do not sound like you believe he is cursed?" I said.

Cardic held up a bowl in one hand and a pair of silver tongs. "Sugar?"

I hesitated, assuming he was ignoring my question.

"I…yes," I said. "Please."

He dropped a cube into my tea. "One or two?"

"One is plenty," I said. "Thank you."

"There is milk too," he said.

"Thank you," I said again. In the quiet that followed, I poured milk into my tea and stirred it with a polished spoon. Cardic was choosing pastries from a tiered tray.

"Do you like warm apples?" he asked.

"Yes," I said, thinking it strange that the Prince of Larkspur was serving me.

After a few seconds, he handed me a plate he had piled with fruits, sweet breads, cheeses, and meats.

"Thank you," I said again.

It was more food than I had ever seen in my life.

"You're welcome, beast," he said.

I looked down to see Fox again at my feet, and I bent to pick him up so that he could sit in my lap and share my food.

Cardic scowled. "Rats do not belong at the table."

"He is not a rat," I said, my tone bordering on terse. "He is a fox, and he is helping us on our journey."

The prince's mouth quirked. "Ah yes, the journey," he said. "To answer your question, I believe Lore thinks he is cursed."

"So…he isn't cursed?" I asked, confused.

Cardic shrugged. "Who is to say where love is concerned?"

"Love?" I asked.

"You do not know? He is cursed to be hopelessly in love with a woman who does not know he exists."

I could not describe the feeling that twisted through me, but it was violent. I dropped the piece of bread I'd just broken off. The fox was quick to devour it.

"What?"

"I see you did not know," said Cardic.

"He said he looked too long at an enchantress," I said. "I thought...I thought you could not lie."

"He isn't lying," said Cardic. "He fell in love at first sight."

"Why would he...not tell me?" I asked, but what I really wondered was why he would almost kiss me beneath the elfin hill. Why had he spoken of admiration while he carried me to Cardic's kingdom so I could sleep in a soft bed?

"Because he is embarrassed," said the prince.

Well, that made two of us.

"Who is she? This woman he loves. Is she truly an enchantress?"

"None of us know," said Cardic. "But he has loved her for the last seven years."

I sat quietly as pressure built behind my eyes. I realized it was ridiculous. I had not known Lore for long, but he had been kind, and I was so alone, I'd let him stir up feelings inside me that I should have kept locked away. This was just another reminder that no one would ever love me—and how could they? As my brothers had often said, I was nothing.

"Eat, beast," said Cardic. "I know you are hungry."

But I did not feel so hungry now.

"Do you know much about the wishing tree?" I asked.

"I know as much as anyone," he said.

"Can more than one wish be made?"

"If you can manage to pluck another apple from the tree," said Cardic.

I frowned. "What do you mean?"

"They say it is guarded by a fierce raven with silver claws and a beak as sharp as a blade."

"Did Lore know this?" I asked.

"I imagine he did," said Cardic. "We all know it."

Except me. I wondered when he was going to tell me. More, I wondered what he expected of me when we reached the wishing tree. He had made it sound as simple as picking an apple. Now, that did not seem to be the case.

"Oh dear," said Cardic.

I shifted my gaze to his.

"Have I hurt your feelings, beast?" he asked.

"I do not think you care whether you have hurt my feelings or not," I said. "Much like your brother."

"That is quite a rude assumption," said Cardic.

I held his gaze. "Then tell me it is a lie," I challenged.

The prince narrowed his eyes, though a smile played on his lips.

"I see you have learned some things during your time in Fairyland," he said.

"Not enough," I said. I should have known to guard my heart against the fae.

"Well, this is quite cozy," Lore said from behind me.

I did not turn to look at him but gritted my teeth at the sound of his voice.

"You look terrible," said Cardic.

"Fuck you, dick," said Lore as he came to sit beside me.

I hated the awareness I had for him as he neared. Everything in my body went rigid—my back straightened, my thighs pressed together, and a dizzying heat swept through my body. I took a breath and worked to reel these feelings in, like yarn on a spindle, trying not to look at Lore, though it was impossible not to notice things about him when he sat right beside me.

The laces at the collar of his tunic were undone, exposing his chest, and his hair was mussed. It reminded me of how Michal looked in the morning after a night spent with one of the many women who warmed his bed.

A shock of jealousy tore through my chest, which only made me angrier.

There was an awful silence that settled between the four of us now that Lore had joined. He reached for a piece of bread. Instead of using a knife, he dragged it through the butter and then brought it to his mouth.

"Please continue," he said before he took a bite. "Do not let me interrupt your conversation."

I wondered how much he had heard but also decided I did not care.

"How did you sleep?"

It took me a moment to realize Lore was talking to me. I met his gaze reluctantly, growing frustrated by the look in his eyes. His expression was so tender. I had to wonder if it was all an act.

"Fine," I said, my answer short. I was too afraid to say more. I did not want my voice to quake or my eyes to water.

"Only fine?"

"What more do you want me to say?" I asked.

He studied me and frowned but did not answer.

Another bout of silence followed.

Cardic took a deep breath as if he were inhaling the most savory of scents. "Well, this is just *lovely*."

"Shut up," said Lore, his frustration obvious and a complete change from only a few seconds ago when he had inquired after my sleep.

"You shut up," said Cardic. "No one invited you to eat with us."

The two brothers glared at each other, and a different sort of tension built between them. It made my heart race. I recognized it as the calm before the storm—the quiet that settled thickly between me and my brothers before one of them snapped.

"Why do you hate each other?" I asked, relieved when my question ironically seemed to ease the tension between them.

Both brothers looked at me, but I kept my eyes on Cardic. It was easier to look at him, despite the fact that Lore's gaze was burning me up inside, as always.

"What is there to like?" asked Cardic.

"Surely, you can find something you like about each other," I said, though I could not deny that I was finding it hard to decide what I liked about either of them at this point.

"Can you find something you like about your brothers?" asked Lore.

I glared at him. His question *hurt.*

"At this moment, I like them more than you," I said.

Lore's eyes widened, and I thought that he looked a lot like I felt.

Good.

Cardic chuckled. "Oh, you are a beast indeed."

Lore's mouth tightened. "We were not raised to be siblings like mortals," he said. "We were raised to see each other as competition, to fight for the top despite the order in which we were born. *That* is why we hate each other."

I stared down at my uneaten food.

"Wild one," said the fox, breathless. "You are squeezing me to death."

I released him, unaware that I had been holding him so hard.

The fox expelled a heavy breath.

Just then, there was a sudden disturbance as several pixies rushed in through the windows behind Cardic. The fox growled, but I held him close as they spoke in voices too high-pitched for me to understand, but I watched Cardic's and Lore's faces as they darkened with anger, and I knew something terrible had happened.

They both rose to their feet at the same time.

"What's wrong?" I asked. "What happened?"

They exchanged a look and then left the table.

"Where are you going?" I demanded, rising with the fox in my arms.

I followed them as they headed down the hall and entered an adjacent room.

"Mirror, show us the three villains the pixies have seen," said Cardic.

Three villains? I held my breath as the mirror rippled, and a scene formed before me of my brothers—Hans, Michal, and Jackal. They appeared to be walking through the Enchanted Forest, where I could not say, though I assumed they were close if the pixies were warning Cardic.

I heard Lore growl.

"Do you know these three mortal men?" asked Cardic.

"They are my brothers," I said and looked at Lore. "I told you they would come for me."

"Do not fret," said Cardic. "They will not get past my pixies."

"Pixies will not stop them," I said. "They have hunted in this forest for seven long years, and nothing has harmed them yet."

Cardic looked at Lore and then asked, "What changed seven years ago?"

"They came into possession of a knife," I said. "A blade so sharp it could cut through bone."

As I spoke, I was unable to tear my eyes from the mirror as I watched my brothers stomp through the forest, their expressions equally terrifying and bloodthirsty.

Lore stepped in front of me, blocking my view.

"That's enough, Mirror," he said, and the image vanished.

I managed to hold his gaze.

"I will not let them hurt you."

"You cannot promise that," I said. "You cannot promise unless they are dead."

"I would have killed them before, but you begged me not to," said Lore. "Are you saying you have changed your mind?"

"Lore," I whispered, my eyes filling with tears.

Do not make me decide, I wanted to say.

"Your brothers might be hunters, but they are terrible at hunting you," said Cardic. "My pixies were able to lead them west. For now, they are ahead, and you are behind."

That gave me little relief. What happened when they discovered they had been deceived? I knew Jackal well enough. He was making a list of everything that was my fault and assigning an appropriate punishment.

"Perhaps, beast, it is time you become the hunter and they become the hunted," said Cardic.

"If they die, many will suffer," I said.

"And if they don't?" asked Lore.

"Then only I will suffer."

"Are these people you are trying to save worth all this pain?" asked Cardic.

"No," I admitted. It felt terrible to do so, but no one in that town had ever tried to save me, though they knew how horribly I was treated.

"Then why do you care if they live or die?"

"I care because I will be blamed," I said. "I care because if I am blamed, the people of Gnat will destroy my home."

I cared because my home was where my mother and father had lived and the only place where I could still feel their love, despite all the bad that had happened since their deaths.

The brothers were quiet for a few moments, but then Cardic was the first to speak.

"Perhaps it is good that you are going in search of the wishing tree," said Cardic. "By the time you reach it, I hope you will find the courage to wish that your brothers no longer exist."

CHAPTER EIGHT
The Nixie

SAMARA

 waited for Lore at the entrance to Cardic's palace with the fox at my feet.

I worried about what lay ahead, both because of my brothers and because I was about to be isolated with Lore as we crossed the Enchanted Forest on an errand to free him from the curse of true love.

My fingers curled into fists. I clenched my jaw so tight, it hurt.

He was in *love*. He was in love, and he had tried to kiss me. At least I thought he had. I could still feel the press of his forehead against mine, the warmth of his breath on my lips.

I could still hear the way he said my name.

It shivered through me and then heated me up, and I was *so* angry.

Ladies do not get angry, I thought. *Ladies do not get angry.*

Usually, my mother's words would quell my emotions,

because I would remember how her warnings about my behavior made me feel—ashamed and embarrassed—and while I felt that way now, it wasn't because of my anger.

It was because of Lore.

"Goodbye, beast," said Cardic as he came to stand beside me.

I jumped, so lost in my thoughts, I hadn't heard him approach.

He smiled at me, though it was teasing. "I'll keep your bed warm in case you get bored of Lore."

"I'm not sure your nun would approve of you offering beds to young women," said Lore.

I turned to look at the prince who had suddenly appeared behind me. He looked more composed than earlier and now carried a linen bag, the strap across his chest.

"Did you just say nun?" I asked.

"Ignore him," said Cardic, glaring at his brother. "He knows not what he speaks."

"I appreciate your offer, Cardic," I said, looking at him again. "I will keep it in mind."

I ignored the low rumble that escaped Lore's mouth as I walked ahead of him, following the fox across the terrace, down the palace steps and the spiraling bridge as it descended through the boughs of other oaks, ash, and yew.

None of us spoke, not even as we left Larkspur and entered the Enchanted Forest.

"Where exactly are we going?" I asked Fox, trying to keep pace with him.

"We must continue through the forest and over the river until we find the witch of the wood," he said. "She has eyes everywhere and can tell us where the wishing tree will be."

"A witch?" I asked. "Are you certain a witch can be trusted?"

"It is not about trust, wild one," said the fox. "It is about the trade."

We continued, but I soon found it too difficult to keep

up with Fox and fell behind, walking beside Lore. Our hands brushed, and I pulled mine away, blushing fiercely, though I wasn't sure why. I was frustrated with his closeness and how I couldn't stop *feeling* him. I knew he could walk faster than me and wondered why he wasn't.

"Did you mean what you said?" he asked.

I glanced at him. "What do you mean?"

"You told my brother you would consider his offer of a warm bed."

The crunch of our footsteps filled the silence as we passed over fallen limbs and scattered acorns.

"Does it matter?" I asked.

"Yes, it matters," he said.

"I don't know if I meant it," I said. "But I appreciated the offer nevertheless."

"You know it wasn't out of kindness that he offered," said Lore. "He did it to fuck with me."

"I do not need a reminder that I am being used," I said, stopping to glare at him. "I understand perfectly well I am a pawn in everyone's game."

"That is not what I meant," he said.

"I don't care what you meant," I said. "You talk about your brother as if you are somehow different, but you are both the same."

Lore's features hardened. "Did I do something wrong?" He paused and then seemed to come to a realization. "What did Cardic tell you?"

"Nothing," I snapped, storming away.

"Samara!" Lore called after me, but I didn't stop. I continued forward, disappearing into the trees after the fox.

I had every intention of proceeding with my rampage, except that as I broke through the curtain of foliage, I couldn't move, and I found that the fox hadn't either. He sat, staring in horror at the same thing I was—dead animals dangling from the trees.

There were rabbits and deer, coyotes and boars, even foxes.

This was the work of my brothers.

"Samara, I—" Lore fell silent behind me. "What the *fuck*."

Panic erupted inside me in seconds, and all at once, the world was closing in on me. Everything blurred together, and I lost my ability to breathe, though I tried desperately. I nearly collapsed, but then Lore was in front of me, his hand on my face.

"Look at me," he said. "Look at me and breathe."

I couldn't.

My chest felt paralyzed, my throat swollen.

"Samara," Lore said. Dropping his hand to my forearm, he rested his forehead against mine as he had done in the meadow beneath the elfin hill. "You are safe," he whispered.

I had been so angry with him before this, but I was too afraid to be angry now.

I closed my eyes and managed a shaky, shallow breath. Then Lore wrapped his arms around me tight, as if he thought he could keep my body still, and I rested my head against his chest. I could hear his heart beating, an easy thrum. I wondered how he could be so calm before such horror, but it was likely not the first time he'd seen something so terrible. I had certainly butchered animals before under the orders of my brother, but this…this was different.

After some time, my breaths matched Lore's, and I felt less unsteady on my feet.

"My brothers did this," I said as I pulled away from him.

"I guessed as much," said Lore.

"Cardic said they were ahead," I said. "What if they circle back? What if—"

"Samara," said Lore, leaning forward to kiss my forehead.

His lips were warm, and they lingered as he spoke against my skin. "I will *never* let them harm you again."

Now my heart was racing for a different reason.

He pulled away and slipped his hand in mine.

"We cannot linger here," he said, pulling me along.

I dug in my heels. "We cannot leave them like this, Lore."

"If we stay, there is a greater chance they will find us."

"Lore," I whispered, desperate. "This will haunt me."

I was sure that was what my brothers intended.

Lore stared down at me, his gaze hard and his jaw set. After a few seconds, he turned to observe the animals. It was evident they had been here for some time, because their blood had ceased to drip. All of it pooled on the ground beneath them.

"We do not have time to bury them," he said.

"Then we will lay them in a line on the ground," I said. "It is better than where they hang now."

He studied me for a minute, and I wondered what he was thinking. Perhaps he was trying to decide if he could live with disappointing me.

I hoped he couldn't.

"The moment I hear so much as a twig break or a pebble roll, we depart," he said. "No matter who is left."

I nodded vigorously in agreement.

Lore turned, and I watched him climb up the nearest tree as if it were a ladder, arms braced around the trunk, his toes digging into the bark. When he reached the first bough, he pulled himself up and walked gracefully along its length like it was nothing but flat ground. He stopped when he reached the first animal, a rabbit that twisted this way and that. Lore knelt and drew a knife. As soon as the blade touched the rope, it was severed, reminding me of the knife I was given seven years ago—likely the very one Jackal had used to carry out this massacre.

With the rope cut, the rabbit fell, hitting the ground with a grotesque thud. I covered my mouth with my hand, unprepared for the sound or the additional horror of watching these animals abused in death.

I knew my brothers were cruel. They had often threatened to hurt Mouse and Rooster, but they usually took their anger out on me instead. Was this what happened when they couldn't?

My stomach revolted at the thought.

It wasn't until I tried to move the rabbit from where it landed that everything I'd eaten for breakfast came back up. I only made it a few steps before I vomited, my eyes blurry with tears.

This was horrible, and my brothers knew it.

They wanted me to feel responsible for each one of these deaths, and I did.

As I straightened, Lore handed me a waterskin.

"It's wine," he said. "But it will get the taste out."

I let the bitter drink flood my mouth before spitting it out, handing the container back to him.

"Perhaps you should pick some flowers," he suggested.

"I can do it," I said. "I want to help."

"Fox can move the bodies," he said.

I looked to see him already dragging the rabbit to the middle of the grove, and I felt my stomach revolt again.

Lore shuffled to the side to block my view.

"If we cannot bury them, at least they will have some kind of adornment," he said. "Flowers will help."

"Okay," I said.

"Don't go beyond the tree line," Lore warned. "And avoid the bell-shaped blooms. They are poisonous."

I nodded, and he returned to work. I tried to keep my back to him as I picked flowers, but I could still hear what was happening, and that was just as terrible.

When Lore was done and the bodies were lined up, he let

me place the flowers on each rotting corpse. I did so with a knot in my throat, and when we were finished, we left without a word, continuing through the forest on our journey to a tree that did not exist.

I expected that we would travel late into the night, since the animals had taken most of our day, but when we came to a wide river, Lore stopped and began searching for a place to camp out of sight.

"Shouldn't we keep going?" I asked.

"Normally, I would say yes, but I am eager to bathe after handling dead flesh."

I swallowed, both at the mention of the animals and at the thought of Lore naked.

"You intend to bathe in the stream?" I asked.

He was bent at the waist, clearing leaves and branches from under an alcove of tree roots. He paused to look at me, amused. "Yes."

"Naked?"

"That tends to be how bathing works," he said. He was smiling more now.

I liked when he smiled. He almost looked like a different person.

"You should probably bathe too," he said.

My mouth dropped open. "Are you saying I smell?"

"No," Lore said.

"Yes," said the fox.

I glared at both of them. Lore glared at the fox.

"I am only telling the truth," Fox said as he sat with his tail curled around his feet. "If your brothers could not trace your tracks, they could follow your scent."

I turned away from them and sniffed myself, wrinkling my nose.

The fox was right. I needed a bath.

I wandered to the edge of the river. The shore was rocky, but the water was clear and grew darker toward the middle where it was deeper. I dipped my fingers into it and found that it was cool.

"Do not wade into the water alone," said the fox.

I jumped, not realizing he had wandered up beside me.

I looked at him, confused.

"Why not?"

"The fae are not relegated to land," he said. "Some of the most vicious reside in water."

His words sent a shiver down my spine. I pulled my hand out of the water and straightened. It should not surprise me that the water, which appeared so serene, would actually be infested with nefarious fae.

"Then how are we supposed to bathe?"

"They will not bother you while the Prince of Nightshade is near," said the fox.

I turned to look for Lore and found that he had pulled a blanket from the bag he had packed at Cardic's and was attempting to secure it on a branch near the riverbank.

"What are you doing?" I asked.

"I am trying," he said, grunting as he struggled, "to give you…some privacy."

The blanket slipped and fell, half in the river and half on land.

"Fuck," Lore hissed.

I giggled as I went to him and picked the blanket up from the ground, wringing out the part that had landed in the water. I held it up by the corners and handed it to Lore.

"This will suffice," I said and started to remove my dress.

"I take it you've decided to bathe," he said from the other side of the blanket.

"I do not think I have a choice," I replied as I reached behind me to untie the laces at my back. I thought that they had been tied into a bow, but I found instead that they were in a tangle, and I had only made them worse. I dropped my chin to my chest, twisting both arms behind me, trying desperately to claw at the knot.

"Does it usually take you this long to undress?" asked Lore. "I am certain I could make quicker work of that dress."

"I do not want to hear about your conquests, Prince," I said, offering a frustrated growl.

Lore dropped the blanket.

"What are you doing?" I asked.

"My arms are tired, and you are not naked," he said. "Turn."

I glared at him, and he tilted his head back, looking over my head with squinted eyes.

"Is that a fly?"

He swatted at it.

"There's another!"

I scowled at him. "Fine!"

I turned, giving him my back. I wasn't sure why this made me feel so exposed. Maybe because I was about to wade into a river completely naked in front of a man, and I had never done anything like it before.

Lore was the first man who had ever kissed me, and he hadn't even touched my lips.

I wonder if he knew.

He could probably guess, given his years of experience.

"Thank you," I said.

"For what?" Lore asked.

"For letting me rest," I said. "You did not have to make yourself miserable. I am used to sleeping on the ground."

"You needed real rest," he said. "We still have five days of travel."

We were silent. I could feel him fiddling with the laces.

"Where did you sleep last night?" I asked.

I tried to keep my voice light, but I wasn't sure I succeeded. His hand stilled. "What?"

My face grew hot, and I couldn't decide if I should abandon this line of questioning or plow ahead.

"Where did you sleep last night?" I repeated.

"I didn't sleep," he said.

My brows lowered as I considered the implication. "Oh."

"Why do you ask?"

"No reason," I said quickly, realizing how great a mistake this was. "I was just curious."

"Why are you curious about where I sleep?"

"I'm not," I said.

"But you just said you were curious about where I was last night," said Lore. "There must be a reason."

"There isn't," I said. "Have you finished? I thought you were adept at removing gowns."

"Samara."

I turned to face him, frustrated. "Because of the way you looked when you came into the library this morning."

He tilted his head to the side, the corner of his lips curved. "And how did I look?"

I shook my head and shrugged my shoulders at the same time. I think the reaction was more for me—a kind of surrender. It was too late to back out now.

"Like you had slept with someone," I said.

"What makes you say that?" he asked.

"I *know* what men look like the morning after sex."

My face was so hot I could barely stand it. I was going to have to jump in the river just to cool down. Perhaps I would also drown, and then I could escape this humiliation.

Surprise flitted across Lore's face before he grew rigid with anger. He took a step forward. "How would you know that?"

"Do not condescend," I said. "I am not ignorant."

"I have never for a moment thought you ignorant," said Lore. "So you think I spent the night with someone?"

I tilted my head back, holding his gaze.

"And that bothers you?"

My eyes widened. "No, of course not."

"Then why did you ask at all?"

"I told you I was curious," I said.

"So you are saying if I *had* slept with someone, you wouldn't care?"

"No, I wouldn't," I said.

He stared at me, smirking.

"I think you are a liar, Samara of Gnat."

"Don't call me a liar!" I said and shoved him.

He stumbled back and fell into the river. The only problem was that I also fell, slipping on the roots at my feet.

I was barely able to hold my breath as I hit the water. Lore's arm fastened around my waist as he righted us and pushed us to the surface. I coughed and spit water from my mouth as it ran out of my nose before I smoothed my hands over my face and through my hair.

I found Lore standing over me, and I couldn't look away.

I forgot how imposing he could be, but in this moment, there was no denying it. He towered over me. His tunic stuck to every muscle and made me realize just how broad his shoulders were. I wanted to touch him.

"You are most certainly a liar," he said, smoothing a strand of my hair behind my ear.

I closed my eyes at his touch, but it was not out of fear. A different emotion shuddered through me, and I swallowed hard before I looked at him again.

"Perhaps I am a liar," I said. "But what good comes from knowing the truth?"

Lore's finger trailed along my jaw to my chin. "I suppose that depends on how I feel about it."

"And how do you feel?"

He leaned close, his lips hovering so close to mine.

"I like it," he said. "I like it very much."

Then he kissed me.

It was soft, a slow press of his lips against mine, and when he broke away, his forehead rested against mine.

"And you?" he said, his voice a quiet whisper. "How do you feel about it?"

He pulled back to look into my eyes.

"I like it," I replied. "I like it very much."

Lore smiled and offered a breathless laugh.

His hand slipped into my hair as he kissed me again, longer this time. He shifted closer, our bodies flush. I let my hands move and twist into the fabric of his tunic. I didn't know what to hold on to or how to touch him. I hated that I was so aware of my inexperience when something this wonderful was happening, but I could not help feeling clumsy and awkward despite the heat surging through my body. I wondered if Lore could tell, if he thought I was terrible at this.

Then something changed, and Lore's arm tightened around my waist. He pulled me closer than before. His body was hard, and I gasped at the feel of him. I thought I'd felt desire before, but it was nothing compared to this. My body suddenly felt heavy, and I was desperate to be touched in places only I had explored.

I wrapped my arms around his neck. I wanted to be closer, even if it wasn't possible. The friction of his body provided a shred of relief as my breasts flattened against his chest and his arousal pressed against my stomach. I was no longer thinking about my inadequacies but how it would feel to have him inside me. I had never known such pleasure, and I had only dreamed of it with one person—the fae who had offered me a knife.

But all those feelings were ripped away from me as Lore abruptly ended the kiss and tore away from me. He took a few steps back, breathing hard.

"I'm sorry," I said, because I didn't know what else to say.

"Why?" he asked.

My eyes widened. I didn't really know why.

"I…didn't mean for this to happen," I said.

Lore's brows lowered. "What do you mean? You said you liked it."

"I did," I said. "I *do*. You're the one who stopped."

Now that I had distance from him, the cold reality of why he had stopped settled in. I crossed my arms over my chest, feeling exposed and terribly embarrassed.

"Why did you stop?"

"I had to," he said.

"Because you are in love?" I asked.

Surprise flitted across his face. "What?"

"Cardic told me," I said. "You are in love, and you think you are cursed."

"I *am* cursed," Lore snapped. "You do not know how I have suffered. This yearning…it has torn me apart."

"Yet you touched me," I said, my voice taking on a tone I didn't recognize. "You kissed *me*."

He just stared at me. I wanted him to feel as embarrassed as I did now that he knew I was aware of his secret, but instead, I thought he looked devastated, which I found even more infuriating.

"You aren't cursed, Lore, Prince of Nightshade," I said. "You are a coward."

I turned and climbed out of the river, using the half-drenched blanket to cover myself, trying hard to subdue the pressure building behind my eyes as I realized that my brothers were right.

No man would ever want someone like me.

Cold and wet, I curled up near the fox on the pallet Lore had made beneath the roots as quiet tears streamed down my face, and I eventually fell asleep.

I woke suddenly to the sound of music.

It was an airy melody, beautiful but haunting. I rolled onto my side and gazed out at the night, but there was nothing near as far as I could tell, save moonlight bouncing off the rippling river. I sat up and listened harder, realizing that someone was also singing.

> *There once was a girl with brambles in her hair.*
> *Beauty they called her, she was so fair.*
> *But she danced to music no one could hear,*
> *Wounding her feet, which were small and bare.*

I rose and followed the sound, my own bare feet sliding over stone as if it were nothing more than sand. I wandered down the river's edge, past large trees and small trees and shrubs with flowers so white, they seemed to glow in the night. The singing grew louder as I neared, and the foliage became denser. I was forced to elbow my way through thick shoots of green while the ground grew softer at my feet.

> *From quiet village to mountains gray,*
> *Beneath starry sky and burning day.*
> *The grass grew green where she bled,*
> *And fairies followed where she led.*
>
> *She danced until she wished to die*
> *And came to a place where spirits lie.*
> *Beneath that barren ground, there lay*
> *Witches' bones and evil fae.*
>
> *Soon a handsome prince walked along,*

Drawn by the elves' silvery song.
So smitten was he with the dancing maid,
He promised to save her and drew his blade.

But when his feet brushed barren ground,
He began to spin and dance around.
The fairies clapped, their laughter rang,
Their voices rose, and they sang—

Finally, I pushed aside a curtain of greenery to spy the source of the singing. Two women sat on rocks in the middle of the river. One played a flute while the other sang and brushed her long yellow hair. They were lovely, dressed in white, and beneath the moon, they too seemed to glow.

The woman with the brush turned her head toward me and smiled, beckoning. She had strange features—large, round eyes and glittering scales on her temples. I thought that perhaps she was half human, but I was not afraid. I waded through the water toward them as she finished her song.

There once was a girl with thorns in her hair,
Who danced to music no one could hear.
And when a prince came along,
He swore to save her, but he was wrong.
They danced until their hearts gave out
And died upon the barren ground.

She paused and turned to the other woman.

"Look, Elke, we have brought our own beauty here," she said. "Perhaps we can make her dance." She turned her pale eyes to me. They were yellow in color and flickered like lantern lights. "Do you dance, beauty?"

I shook my head.

"Do not worry, beauty. We will teach you," she said. Slipping off the rock, she entered the water with me and brought her hand up to my face but did not touch me. "Beautiful," she said, and then she circled me, and I followed. The woman smiled. "Now we are dancing, beauty."

Then she took my hands and held them aloft, stepping into the left side of my body and then the right. I followed, unable to look away from her face. She was so beautiful, and her smile was so sweet.

"You are dancing, beauty," she said, leading me around in a circle, and then she let go of one of my hands. "Twirl."

I did as she commanded.

"Beautiful," she said when I faced her again, continuing to smile.

I smiled too.

"What…what are you?" I asked, spinning again at her direction.

The woman laughed, and it sounded like chimes. "Why, I am a nixie, and so is my sister," she said. "This river is our home."

"I do not have a home," I told her. "Well…not anymore."

"Poor beautiful creature," she said with a frown. "Elke and I will take you. Would you like that, beauty?"

Before I could answer, there was a terrible scream, and I looked to see the other nixie, who had been sitting on the rock, playing her flute, fall back into the water, a knife lodged in her eye socket. Then the woman in front of me hissed. My eyes connected with hers as she changed before my eyes, her teeth growing sharp and her hands webbed as she gripped my wrists.

"Mine!" she growled.

I screamed.

"Samara!"

Lore bellowed my name just as the creature yanked me into the water. I fought with her, clawing at her face as her hands fastened around my throat. Then suddenly, she was off me, and

I was able to rise to my feet, choking on water as I gasped for breath and Lore fought with the monster.

"The comb, wild one!" said the fox. "Throw the comb!"

The comb? I had forgotten about the comb. I could feel it in my hair, and though I had no idea how it might help, I obeyed the fox's orders, but it was so badly tangled, I couldn't get it free. I tore at the wet strands while Lore grappled with the snarling creature before me, but even he struggled. She was slippery and wet, but her grip was strong, and soon she was able to throw the Prince of Nightshade off with a guttural scream and dive into the water toward me.

Panic filled me as I yanked at the comb, ripping hair from my head in painful clumps. Finally, it tore free just as the monster broke the surface of the water and launched itself at me.

I threw the comb, and when it hit the water, it turned into a thousand spears. The nixie's glowing eyes widened, and she kicked her arms and feet as if she wished to swim away, but it was too late. She gave a short, high-pitched cry before she was impaled on the sharp spikes, and then there was silence, save for the sound of her blood dripping into the water.

In an instant, Lore was beside me, his hand on my face.

"Are you hurt?" he asked, but I really couldn't think, and I didn't answer him.

Instead, I turned to look at the nixie again, who was bent in half, a hundred spears piercing her body. Before, she had seemed to glow beneath the moonlight, but now her skin was dull, and her hair fell over her face in a cascade of yellow.

"Cut off the nixie's hair," said the fox. "And it will turn to gold."

I looked at the fox and then left Lore's side, wading to the nixie with the knife in her eye and pulled it free.

"Samara?"

I ignored Lore and went to the nixie with the yellow hair, took it into my hand, and cut it with his blade. As soon as the hairs were severed, they became glimmering, golden thread. I turned to Lore with his knife in one hand and the gold in the other.

"I'm fine," I answered, even though I was not, and gave him the knife.

I climbed out of the river and followed Fox back to camp.

CHAPTER NINE
Dreams Do Come True

LORE

 ***walked behind Samara as we made our way*** through the forest, pelted by icy rain. She was not fine, and she was cold, shivering so hard she could barely walk. I had tried to offer her my cloak, but she had shoved it off and left it on the ground, charging ahead wrapped in the wet blanket from the river. It was frustrating that she was so stubborn, that she would sacrifice her comfort just because she was angry with me.

I could fucking kill Cardic.

I would when I saw him next.

Why would he tell her I was in love when I could not tell her *she* was who I loved?

It didn't matter that she had kissed me back or that she had liked it. What mattered was that she did not know the truth of who I was, and I did not want to tell her, because I didn't want to watch as she realized her mistake and rejected me a second time.

She was right. I was a coward.

We continued to make our way through the forest, but soon even the fox slowed, his fur weighed down with ice.

"We must find shelter," I said.

"I know of a place," said the fox. "It is not much, but it is not far."

I did not care what it was so long as Samara was out of this weather.

The fox led us on, twisting through trees and down slippery hills until we came to what I could only describe as a lean-to. It was basically a room with three walls and a thatched roof, but it had an iron stove. Inside, the ash was nearly solid. I scraped it onto the floor, uncaring of the mess I made, highly aware of how deeply Samara was shivering. Once it was clean, I rose and headed out into the rain.

"Where are you going?" Samara asked.

It was the first time she had spoken to me since last night.

"To find wood for the fire," I said.

"It's raining," she said.

"There is still a chance I can find dry wood," I said. "I will return. Fox will keep you safe."

I wandered out again and searched high and low for dry wood. It was harder to find with the forest so wet, but there were dead branches tangled in the canopy above that had managed to stay mostly dry. I also gathered a few larger logs, as it was possible to split them into smaller, dryer pieces.

When I returned, I found Samara curled in the corner and the fox lying on her feet. They were both shivering. I set to work with a sense of urgency, picking pieces of thatch from the roof to use as kindling. I pried apart the logs with my knife and shaved away pieces of dry wood.

Once a fire blazed in the stove, I turned to the opening of the lean-to and summoned my magic. Thorns sprouted from

356

the wood, and vines burst from the ground, weaving through one another and blossoming until the lean-to was closed off from the outside. It wasn't necessary to keep the space warm, but I thought Samara might prefer it.

When I was finished, I turned to find her watching me.

"Sorry," she said and cleared her throat. "I just…haven't seen you use your magic before."

"I don't mind when you watch me," I said, even though she dropped her gaze after.

I took off my cloak and hung it from a knot on the wood and then pulled off my tunic, which was mostly dry, far dryer than Samara's wet blanket and dress.

"What are you doing?" she asked.

I looked at her, disliking how alarmed she sounded.

"You need to change into something dry," I said.

"But what about you?"

I smiled faintly. "While I would not mind you naked, I imagine you prefer otherwise."

She stared at me, then stood, slipping the wet blanket from her shoulders.

"Change in front of the fire," I said.

I took the blanket and tried my best to hang it so that it could dry while she changed. I wasn't prepared for how I would feel seeing her in my clothes. The tunic hung to her knees, and the collar was low, dipping between her breasts. I tried not to stare, but she noticed, because she gripped the front closed.

I cleared my throat and willed my cock to settle down, but my mind was already running wild with fantasies of how it would feel to have her legs wrapped tight around my waist while I buried myself deep inside her.

That was what I wanted, and that was what I would never have, which was why breaking this curse was so important.

"What happened to you?" she whispered.

Now I understood her expression a little better—she was alarmed by the scars on my body. I had a few lashes across my back, one of which curled around my shoulder to my chest.

"I was struck with a whip by a dullahan," I said, though a little reluctant to approach this subject.

"A dullahan?"

"It is a type of hobgoblin. They are nasty spirits who desire the taste of blood, but only from headless victims."

"And you encountered one?"

"I have encountered many," he said.

"Are there a lot here in the Enchanted Forest?" she asked.

I realized my mistake, and I did not want her to be afraid.

"Not really. I went looking for them," I said.

"Why would you go in search of a dullahan?"

I was quiet because the answer was…her. I went in search of them because the only time I never thought of her was when I was fighting for my life.

"Lore?"

"I'll take that," I said, changing the subject and reaching for her dress.

Once it was hung, I opened the satchel and pulled out the only dry blanket we had and handed it to Samara. She took it and slipped it around her shoulders.

"If you sit near the stove, your hair will dry faster," I said.

She shifted closer as I sorted through the food I'd stolen from Cardic's pantry—dried meats, fruit, and bread. I organized everything on top of the satchel so Samara could graze.

When I was finished, I sat with my back against the wall and bit into a hard roll. I tried not to look at her, but it was difficult. My eyes drifted to her constantly. When she caught me staring, I looked away.

"Why do you not want to be in love?" she asked.

I clenched my jaw. My chest felt tight as I took a breath.

"I would not mind it if it was returned," I said.

She said nothing.

"Did you love the prince?" I asked.

"No," she said. "I had only just met him."

"But you agreed to marry him?"

"I agreed to leave with him and go to his kingdom," she said. "He told me he would give me time to fall in love with him, but once we were in the carriage, he said we were to be married once we arrived."

There was a part of me that was glad the thieves had stopped the carriage and a part of me that knew I wasn't being fair. I could not expect Samara to never fall in love. I could not expect her to never marry.

"So he lied," I said.

She nodded. "He said his brother had not returned from the Enchanted Forest, and he would have to leave to search for him. He was also looking for golden apples. It seems you are not the only one who desires to make a wish."

I was not surprised to hear it. I didn't think there was a person alive who did not want their greatest wish granted.

"What would you wish for?" I asked. "If you could do so without consequence?"

She shifted, drawing her knees to her chest. She looked so small and so frail, but I knew she was strong and unshakable.

"I would wish that no harm would ever come to Mouse and Rooster again."

"Mouse and Rooster?" I asked.

"Mouse is my cat, and Rooster is my stallion," she said. "My brothers are terrible to them just as they are to me."

It did not surprise me that she would think of others before herself.

"And what would you want for yourself?"

"I used to think that I wanted to be loved," she said. "But

now I think that maybe love cannot exist without pain, and I have had enough of that."

"I don't think that is true," I said.

"If it isn't, then why are you wishing it away?" she asked.

I had no answer, and after a few quiet seconds, I cleared my throat. "You should get some rest. I am sorry I cannot give you a more comfortable place to sleep."

"It's all right," she replied. "I am used to the floor."

She folded the blanket in half and lay down.

I wrapped the food and put it aside so I could roll up the cloth satchel.

"Here," I said, sliding it under her head to use as a pillow.

"Thank you," she said.

Our eyes met and held for a few quiet moments. I wanted to kiss her so badly, the desire tightened my whole body, but I knew after what had occurred between us at the river that I would never have the chance to touch her again.

"Get some sleep," I said instead, returning to my place against the wall but I did not sleep.

———

The next morning, the rain continued to come down in icy sheets and I let Samara sleep.

"Are you sure, prince?" asked Fox. "Staying will set us back another day."

"Do you want to venture out in this?" I asked. "As I recall, you could barely walk, your coat so weighed down with ice."

"I have no desire," said the fox as he circled his spot before laying down again.

It was a while before Samara rose and when she did, she sat up fast. I thought she might run, but her eyes darted around the small room until they found mine.

"Bad dream?" I asked.

She swallowed, shaking her head. "No, I...thought you left without me."

I was taken aback by her admission.

"That sounds like a bad dream to me," I said.

She frowned and then rubbed her eyes before speaking again. "What time is it?"

"I believe it is well past noon," I said.

Her eyes widened. "Noon? Why didn't you wake me?"

She threw off her blanket and rose to her feet.

"If we were leaving today, I would have," I said. "But the weather has not changed, so I thought it best that you rest."

"Oh," she said. "But then you will only have—"

"Three days," I said. "I am aware but the journey is pointless if you die from the cold."

She settled again, taking her place in front of the fire, pulling the blanket around her shoulders.

"Thank you," she said.

The word set my teeth on edge, not because I didn't appreciate hearing it, but because choosing to stay was no grand act of kindness. It was required if we were going to have any chance at reaching the wishing tree.

"How did you sleep?" she asked.

I smiled a little. "I didn't."

She blushed, and I knew she was thinking of our conversation at the river.

"I'm sorry," she said.

"You are sorry for so many things and none of them are your doing," I said.

She dropped her gaze from mine, holding the blanket tighter.

"I suppose I am used to being blamed," she said.

"I am not blaming you," I said.

We were quiet after that, and Samara laid down again.

When I was certain she was asleep, I pulled off my gloves and then my prosthetic. It had been carved by dryads and given the illusion of realness by the blue fairy, but even with magic, it still made my limb hurt and sweat. A wave of relief I could not describe came over me as I removed the cloth layers I used to cushion my limb. It had hurt since yesterday, worse than usual because of the weather but I hadn't wanted to take my hand off earlier, too afraid I might fall asleep without it.

I sat, staring down at it, remembering the horror of losing it.

Nothing had prepared me. It had been there one day and was gone the next. I was initially shocked. The more I struggled with things that had once been simple—like using a knife to spread butter on bread or unsheathing my sword—the angrier I became, particularly because I could still *feel* my hand and all five fingers. At first, I tried desperately to keep it a secret, especially from my brothers, but in the end, they did not care that I lost my hand. They cared more about *how,* and the truth amused my brothers to no end.

I could handle that.

I could handle learning to live differently within my world. I could handle everything taking longer. It was the pain that made it hard, and it worsened throughout the day. It was like holding my fingers near a fire, drawing closer and closer until they were consumed, except it was all in my head, because I had no hand.

Even now, I kept my jaw tight as wave after wave of pain coursed down my arm, straight to the tips of my nonexistent fingers. I took a deep breath and closed my eyes, resting my head against the hard wall of the lean-to.

I don't know exactly what woke me, but when I opened my eyes, it was to Samara. For a brief second, I thought perhaps I was still dreaming, except that in my dreams, she never stared at me like this—her eyes wide with shock, her mouth parted as if she wanted to speak but had found no words.

Then I realized she was holding my hand, and that look on her face meant she knew exactly who I was.

"Samara," I said, sitting up. Inside, I felt frantic to explain myself.

"It's you," she said, dropping my hand and taking a step back. "You are the one who gave me the knife. I…I don't understand."

"Samara—"

She shook her head. "Why is it you?"

"Why not me?" I asked, though I didn't exactly know why. She had every right to ask, though in some ways, I felt defensive.

"Because you left!" she said, her eyes burning with anger and hurt. "You left seven years ago!"

I was surprised by her words, given she had cut my hand off.

"I never *left*," I said.

"You're lying, and if you're not, then I hate you," she said. "Where were you when I needed you? When I *wanted* you?"

Wanted me? When had she wanted me?

"I tried to help you," I said, rising to my feet. "Why do you think I gave you the knife?"

"You mean the knife that ruined my life?" she snapped.

"*Your* life?" A hot wave of anger erupted inside me, and I held up my arm to show her my hand was no longer there. "What about *my* life?"

She paled and averted her eyes before turning her back to me. I couldn't decide what her reaction meant. Was she ashamed, or did she find me repulsive? Though I abandoned that line of thinking quickly when she started to take off the tunic I had lent her for the night.

"What are you doing?" I demanded, though it was mostly because I was flustered, both because she was about to abandon me and because she was naked. She had undressed with little hesitancy, exposing her entire body to my starved eyes.

When I had first looked upon her, I'd never seen anyone so beautiful, and that remained true now, though it seemed wrong to be aroused in the middle of this fight. I tried hard to stay focused on her face, but my gaze slipped, especially when she turned around to throw my tunic at me. I caught it and dropped it on the floor.

It was the least interesting thing in this room.

"I am leaving," she said, turning to pick up her gown.

I drew nearer. She was like a flame, and the closer I got, the hotter I burned. I also didn't want to scare her.

"Samara," I said, hoping my voice sounded calm and quiet. "Look at me."

She froze. I didn't think she would listen, but maybe she was inclined because she felt vulnerable, cornered and naked before me.

That was not what I wanted, but I did want her to listen.

She straightened and looked up at me. I was so close to her, I could feel her breasts brush my chest as she breathed. It was sweet torture.

This will be my punishment when I die, I thought.

Or maybe it would be looking down into this beautiful face and seeing her eyes glistening with hurt.

"You left me," she said, and despite the threat of tears in her eyes, she spoke between gritted teeth.

"I thought that was what you wanted," I said. "You cut my fucking hand off!"

"Well, I didn't, you *fucking* idiot," she said. "Jackal held my hand around the knife. It was he who took your hand and ruined your life."

I straightened, and she took a step back. "You think losing my hand ruined my life?"

She blinked, obviously feeling like that was the worst thing that could have happened to me.

"I could have borne losing my hand far easier if it wasn't for you," I said, inching toward her until she could go no farther, her back pressed into the wall, though she didn't look afraid. She looked angry. "You. You have stolen everything. I have had no peace since I looked upon your face. You haunt my every step. You linger in my dreams. I can do nothing without thinking about you, yet you say I have ruined *your* life!"

"I loved you!" she seethed, rising onto the tips of her toes. "I loved you, and you left me!"

For a few quiet seconds, I couldn't move or breathe. Her words had stunned me.

"You loved me?" I asked. I could not believe it. I needed her to say it again, but she didn't speak.

I shifted closer, though we hardly had any space.

"Do you still?" I asked. I was on the verge of panic.

"You were the only thing I had to look forward to," she said, her voice trembling.

"That isn't what I asked," I said, frustrated. "Do you still love me?"

The first tear trailed down her cheek, then another. I took her face between my hand and limb, brushing them away.

"I want to hate you," she whispered, her voice thick.

"*Do you love me?*" I asked again.

I recognized it was selfish of me to demand a confession from her given the reason we were together, but I needed to know. I had to know.

She stared at me. There was so much between us—anger and frustration but also a deep and unyielding desire. I fought it now, on the very edge of breaking.

"Yes," she whispered, another stray tear sliding down her face. "I never stopped."

I kissed her.

I had dreamed of this moment for seven long years, and it

had finally come. Everything inside me that had wound so tight suddenly unraveled. It was like a release of its own, heady and thrilling. It only deepened my desire.

I let my hand tighten in her hair as I bent over her, exploring her soft skin with the blunt end of my wrist. She did not seem to mind as I made a slow descent from her neck to her chest, to the swell of her breasts and the hard peaks of her nipples. She gasped, and it made my cock harder. I let my tongue ghost across her lips, teasing and testing, and when she did the same, I slipped into her mouth, groaning at the feel and taste of her.

She was exquisite.

I left her mouth to kiss along her jaw and down her throat to her breast. Her hands moved to my head, and I teased her nipple with my tongue and sucked it into my mouth. She let her head fall back against the wall as she inhaled sharply, whispering my name on an exhale.

Her fingers were so tightly woven into my hair, my scalp burned, but I didn't care. I would let her hold me like this forever if this was what I got in return.

I moved to her other breast, aware that she was moving beneath me, widening her stance. It was an invitation I took, letting my hand graze down her body to the back of her knee. I hiked her leg over my hip and then ground into her. The friction numbed my mind and set my entire body on fire.

I choked on a moan.

Fuck. I was so desperate to come it was embarrassing, but I had waited so long for this—for her.

I wasn't sure I could handle much more.

But then, the fox cleared his throat. The intrusion wouldn't have bothered me, though, if it wasn't for Samara, who froze instantly at the sound.

"If you two are going to fuck," he said, "at least wait until I am asleep."

I could have fucking killed him.

I probably would after our journey was done, except that now that he had broken through my haze, I was reminded of why Samara and I were together at all, and suddenly, I was consumed by guilt. How could I want this when I knew that I was cursed to love this woman?

I pulled away and met her gaze. Her cheeks were flushed, and her lips were swollen. I liked the look, and I liked more that I was responsible, even though I shouldn't.

"You should rest."

She tilted her head a little, raising a dark brow.

"You want me to rest when we have just found each other again?"

Found each other.

She said it as if she'd been searching for me this entire time, which had never occurred to me until now. My chest tightened at the thought, and I leaned forward to kiss her again before taking her hand and leading her to where she'd fallen asleep earlier before the stove.

On the way, I picked up my tunic and handed it to her.

"I'm not opposed to having you remain naked," I said, glancing at the fox, who was curled into a ball facing away from us. "But you might be more comfortable if you wear this."

I retrieved the blanket, a little disappointed when she decided to slip into the long shirt, even though I was the one who suggested it. Still, there was something so fucking beautiful about the way she looked in my clothes. It made me feel like she really was mine.

"Would you like me to spread the blanket?" she asked, her voice quiet.

I wondered if she was asking because I only had one hand or because I had been staring at her.

"I can do it," I said, shaking it out before letting it rest on the ground. I walked around to pull it flat. "I can do most things. Sometimes it just takes a little more time."

"I didn't mean to suggest—"

"I know," I said quickly. I met her gaze and held out my hand. She took it, and I helped her sit, though she didn't need it. She drew her knees to her chest, hugging them close. It felt like a barrier, and I wondered if she felt shy now and a little afraid of what the rest of the night might bring.

I knelt before her.

"You have never…lain with another before?" I asked.

She shook her head.

"We do not have to do anything," I said. "I would be content to hold you until morning."

That was the most honorable thing I could do—the most right considering our circumstances.

"Maybe that is where we start," she said.

I nodded and then stretched out on my back while she lay on her side. Her head was on my chest, her hand on my stomach. If she grew bold and started to explore, she would find that I was aroused, my cock hard and heavy against my stomach. I doubted that would change between now and morning—or for the rest of this trip.

She was still to start, but then her fingers began to trace the faint scars on my skin.

"You never said why you went in search of the dullahan," she said.

I never said it because I dreaded telling her, but in this moment, I felt like a liar, so I told her the truth.

"I sought them out because I thought I could forget you."

She was quiet, her fingers slowly stopping their soft caress. I missed it.

"Am I so horrible to think about?" she asked.

"I wasn't trying to forget you because you were horrible," I said. "You are all I have thought about for the last seven years. I could not figure out where I went wrong, how I had managed to make you hate me so much that you would use my own knife against me. I thought it was part of the curse."

"I never hated you," she whispered.

I could tell she was close to crying again.

"My brothers grew suspicious, thinking my work seemed too easy, and followed me. They saw you give me the knife. They confronted me at the moor and forced me to give it to them. If I had known what Jackal intended…"

"I should have known it was nothing you were capable of," I said. "At the time, it made sense. I did not think anyone was capable of loving me."

She was quiet, but then she shifted onto her elbow and looked down at me.

"This cannot be real," she said. "I must have stumbled into a fairy ring when I ran from the carriage in the woods."

It was strange to hear her say what I was thinking.

"I can assure you, beloved, this is all very real," I said. I held her face in one hand, caressing her cheek. "The fae are too restless to maintain an illusion this long."

"Every day after you left was unbearable," she said.

"I shared in your misery," I said, brushing a stray piece of her hair behind her ear.

"I wish—"

She stopped short of speaking aloud, and I offered her a small smile.

"There is no undoing what has been done," I said. "I think all there is to do now is to forgive ourselves for what we did not know."

She shifted closer, her lips brushing over mine.

I held my breath to hold myself back. If anything more happened, I wanted her to lead. Then she slid her leg over my torso as she kissed me, and when she sat back, her heat settled over my sex. It felt glorious, even though I was clothed.

She froze, looking down at me, her hands on my chest. I rested mine under her knees.

"I have never done this before," she said. "But I feel like my body knows what to do."

"And what is that?" I asked.

We did not look away from each other as she moved, gliding over my cock. I tightened my hold on her, my hips rising, but she paused.

"Is this okay?" she whispered.

I swallowed hard. Of course it was fucking okay, I wanted to say, but all I managed was a nod.

She moved again, a slow pull forward and back.

It was the way she breathed that ignited me. The small gasp that came from somewhere deep in her throat. I tightened my grip under her knees and helped her move.

"Do you mind?" I asked.

Her eyes were dark and glittering as she shook her head, "No."

"Kiss me," I said.

She did as I commanded, and when our lips collided, I kissed her harder than before. We moved together, her hips grinding hard into mine. If I had been in control, I would have stopped to undress so I could feel her wet heat surrounding me, but there was too much momentum around what we were doing, and now all I wanted was to feel the pressure building at the base of my cock erupt.

"Have you ever come?" I asked.

I didn't know what she might have done alone in the dark, and I was curious.

"I…I don't know," she said, breathless.

"Do you touch yourself?" I asked.

"Yes."

Fuck. The bottom of my stomach tightened with her answer.

"Take off my tunic," I said.

She hesitated only a moment but did as I commanded.

"Fucking glorious," I said, squeezing one breast. My other arm remained behind her knee. "Now show me how you touch yourself."

Her fingers trailed to the curls between her thighs, but she stopped short of teasing herself. I wanted to put her on her back and suck her clit into my mouth, but I wasn't sure she was ready for something so forward.

"Kiss me again," I said instead, and when she bent down, I shifted my hands to her ass, gripping her as tight as I could, moving her over my cock. I felt her clit brush across the bottom of my stomach, and a delicious moan came from her mouth. The pleasure overwhelmed any reservations she might have had as she took the lead.

I watched her, awed by the beauty of this moment.

"Yes," I whispered, because the harder she chased her release, the faster she moved.

I lifted my hips higher and higher, ready to unwind.

The explosion hit like a physical blow. It was almost painful, the way my body tightened as it prepared to release another wave of pleasure.

When it was done, I opened my eyes and relaxed my jaw to find Samara staring down at me. I didn't know what to make of her expression. She looked flushed, and her eyes were glassy. Had she come? I was about to ask, but she spoke.

"Are you okay?"

I grinned. "I am more than okay," I said. "But how are you, beloved?"

"I am perfect," she whispered as she lay down beside me with her head on my chest.

In the quiet that followed, every rapturous feeling slowly left my body, replaced by guilt. I had let things go too far between us. It did not matter that she loved me or that my feelings for her over the last seven years felt real. The truth was my love for her was nothing more than a curse.

CHAPTER TEN
The Witch in the Wood

SAMARA

 amara," Lore said. *His voice was near my* ear, and his hand was on my shoulder. He nudged me gently as he spoke. "It's time to rise. We must be off."

"Go away," I said, burying my head under the blanket.

"Perhaps you should let her rest," said the fox. "You did keep her up half the night."

"Hold your tongue, Fox," Lore snapped before returning his attention to me.

"I agree with Fox," I mumbled. "Let me sleep."

"Has everyone forgotten that I too was up half the night?"

"Most men wouldn't complain," said the fox.

Lore growled.

"Don't you have a few rats to catch?" he snapped.

Suddenly, there was a sound like tearing vines, and a gust of cold air entered the small space.

"One would think you would be in a better mood given your night," said the fox. "Perhaps you should listen to your *beloved*. I think you could use a nap."

I sat up as Fox leapt out of the lean-to and into the gray morning to hunt for his food.

"That wasn't very nice," I said, meeting Lore's gaze.

"You are only saying that because he wanted to let you sleep."

"What is so wrong with sleeping a while longer?" I asked, but then my gaze fell to his mouth, and I leaned close, my lips brushing his as I spoke. "Or perhaps you are eager for something else?"

"Samara," he said, though I couldn't place the tone of his voice. It was almost pained, but that didn't make sense, not after the night we had shared. I closed the distance between us and kissed him. I was too new to feel very confident in how I moved, but I liked the way his mouth felt against mine, so I kept going, soft and slow, but then Lore kissed me back, harder this time and longer before pulling away.

"This is wrong," he said.

I couldn't quite describe how his words made me feel, but I thought that perhaps my heart was close to breaking. My chest hurt.

"What did you say?" I whispered, meeting his violet-eyed gaze.

"Samara," he whispered, pleading. "What happened last night cannot happen again. This love I have for you, it is a curse."

I knew I was Lore's enchantress, the source of his suffering, his so-called curse, but I thought after last night, he would realize the truth—he had never been cursed at all.

"You think what you feel for me isn't real?" I asked.

He just stared at me.

"You don't want to say, do you? Because the curse doesn't make sense if the feelings are real."

"I know you want things to be different," he said. "But I have told you the truth from the start."

I shook my head in disbelief and then rose to my feet. I crossed the room to change, pulling off his tunic as I went and tossing it to the ground. I slipped into my dress, turning to him as I tied the laces at the back.

"I pity you, Lore of Nightshade," I said. "Everyone in your life who was ever supposed to love you abandoned you, but it has made you so afraid of love, you cannot even recognize it when it's true."

If he wanted to continue this journey, then I would do that just to prove him wrong. I would waste a wish on a curse he had conjured in his mind to protect his heart. I would do it because I loved him, because despite how much this hurt, I wanted him.

———

We left the little shed behind not long after our fight.

I followed the fox into the forest while Lore lingered behind. There was a strange tension between us. It was nothing like I'd experienced before—not exactly angry, not exactly desire. For my part, it was a buildup of all the things I wanted to say but knew he would not hear.

I realized our beginning was full of horror, that for seven years, he had thought I had rejected him in the most violent way and assumed his love was not returned, but I had suffered as he had suffered. There were times when I too thought I was cursed.

But I knew deception. I had lived with it daily since the deaths of my mother and father, and this was not it.

"What troubles you, wild one?" asked the fox.

I did not answer for a few seconds as we made our way over the slippery ground. There was a fine mist in the air that kept everything wet, but it was nothing compared to the icy rain from yesterday.

"Lore prefers to think he is cursed rather than accept that his love for me is real," I said.

"That is the nature of curses," said the fox.

"What do you mean?" I asked.

"Anything can be real if you believe hard enough," said fox.

I didn't like the fox's words. "So you are on his side?"

"I am on no one's side, wild one," he replied. "But it will take more than just your love to break Lore's belief. It is not just that he believes he is cursed. He believes he is unworthy of love."

My throat felt tight as a wave of emotion crashed through me. I had forgotten, but the memories returned now.

Who says you are unworthy? I had asked.

He had frowned as if he did not understand my question, as if it was a universal truth that the Prince of Nightshade was not deserving.

No one must say it for it to be true, he had replied.

"How do I make him feel worthy?" I asked.

"You cannot make anyone feel anything," said the fox.

"You are most unhelpful," I said.

"Why do you love Lore?" the fox asked instead.

At first, his question felt overwhelming as I thought of all the reasons, but then I considered how my love for him had only grown since entering the Enchanted Forest. How it had begun to burn hotter, fiercer than ever before, and I realized why.

"Because...he makes me feel safe," I said, and because of that, I had been able to let go of other feelings like fear. "How do I make him feel safe enough to love me?"

"I suppose," said the fox, "you just keep loving him."

We were silent after that as we continued through the forest, and it was not long before we came to a cottage with a pitched roof covered in thatch. A little fence surrounded it, and a path wound through a healthy garden to the door. I had never seen such a welcoming place.

Smoke rose from the chimney, and the air smelled like roasted pork. It made my mouth water, and I thought about how long it had been since I'd had a warm meal. My stomach growled, just as eager.

I started toward the house, surpassing Fox, when I felt something tug my skirt. It was the fox, who had taken hold of my hem to keep me back.

"Take heed, Samara," he said. "For we are in the presence of a witch. Do not trust your eyes."

A sliver of unease shivered down my spine and then moved through my entire body. At the fox's words, my gaze returned to the cottage, which was no longer so pleasant looking but cast in ruin. The roof was buckling, the garden was wilted, and the smoke smelled more like burning flesh.

In the yard between the house and the wood, a woman was bent at the waist, cutting grass with a sickle. Everything about her was gray, from her head to her toes, with the exception of a pair of black gloves. They reminded me of Lore's, though I doubted she wore them for the reasons he did.

"Do not speak in front of the witch," said the fox. "For if you do, she will refuse us refuge."

I had no trouble remaining silent or distant.

"Good woman," said the fox as he approached. She did not cease slicing blades of grass. "We are told you have eyes everywhere and know where the wishing tree will grow on the night of the first full moon."

"Of course, good fox," she said. Her words were cut with the snick of her sickle. "I can tell you where the wishing tree will appear on the night of the first full moon, but you must do me a favor, or none of you will ever leave this forest alive."

The hair on the back of my neck stood on end. Lore shifted closer to me, and I felt myself straighten.

"What favor, good woman?" asked the fox without fear.

"I have only a glass ax with which to chop wood and require a rick before morning. Go now and complete this errand, and I will tell you how to reach the wishing tree, but if you return the ax broken, you will die."

"I shall complete your task, good woman," said the fox. "But would you be willing to give my companions a place to sleep for the night?"

"I have only one bed," said the woman. "But the maiden may have it if she will help me cook, and the prince may sleep on the hay in the stables if he will cut this grass with my sickle."

"Thank you, good woman," said the fox.

She straightened stiffly and dropped the sickle on the ground.

"Follow me, pretty thing," she said.

Fear gripped me instantly, and Lore could not suppress his growl, which made the witch's face change. It was the briefest glimpse at her true self, a snarling creature with sharp teeth and eyes like pools of midnight oil.

"A moment, good woman," said the fox. "I want to say farewell to my companions for the night."

"A moment, of course," she said. "But then you are mine." She left then and entered her cottage.

Once she was inside, the fox turned to look at us. I wanted to beg not to be left alone with her, but the fox was quick to advise.

"You will survive the night if you listen to me. The woman will try to offer you food and drink, but do not take it, or you will fall into a deep sleep from which you will not wake." Then he looked at me. "Before you lay down to rest, stretch seven lengths of golden thread across the floor from the door to the bed."

I nodded and did not question why. After what happened to the nixie, I thought it best not to know.

"I will," I said.

"Good. I will see you at dawn."

The fox walked up to the glass ax which rested against the fence. There was a small clink as he took it into his mouth by the handle and trotted off toward the forest.

I watched until he vanished into the dark between the trees. When I turned, I found Lore watching me.

"I don't like this," he said.

I held his gaze. We were so close, our bodies almost touched.

"I will be okay so long as you are near," I said.

His brows lowered, and his mouth hardened. I did not understand how he could look at me this way, with so much emotion in his eyes, and still say what he felt for me wasn't real.

"I will keep you safe," he said, brushing his fingers along my cheek. His touch drew heat from the depths of my stomach, and I closed my eyes against it.

When I opened them again, my gaze slipped past Lore to the cottage where the witch looked out from her window, pale and hollow-eyed. Then I blinked, and she was gone.

"Samara?" Lore said, his voice hushed, as if he did not want for anyone else to hear. Perhaps he didn't.

"I should go," I said.

"Wait," he said, and pushed something into my hand. It was the golden thread.

"Thank you," I whispered as I slipped it into my pocket.

I stepped around him and headed toward the cottage, following the cobbled path as it twisted and turned through the garden. Like earlier, the cobbles at my feet were polished and new and the garden green and lush.

Do not trust your eyes, the fox had said, so I didn't and focused on other senses.

The cobbles beneath my feet felt broken and uneven, and the garden smelled musty and sweet. The cottage steps felt too soft and creaked beneath my feet. The handle of the door looked polished and shiny, but it felt rusty and rattled as I turned it.

When I entered the cottage, there was a lovely kitchen to the left and a small sitting area to the right. Everything appeared tidy and pristine. A fire blazed in the hearth before a long wooden table where there was an array of vegetables, potatoes, and pork, and though the cottage smelled like burning cedar, it could not mask the rancid smell of rotting meat or the pungent odor of spoiled potatoes.

"Come, pretty thing," said the witch from behind me.

I jumped at the sound of her voice and the feel of her gloved hand on my arm, which was slimy and cold, though it looked perfectly normal.

She pulled me into the kitchen. "Help me cook for your beloved, for that is what he is, is he not? Your beloved?"

I did not answer her, because the fox had said not to speak before her.

"There is an apron for you near the fire, pretty thing. Put it on!"

I did as she instructed, knowing it was not clean though it appeared bright and white. As I slipped the strap over my head, I was overwhelmed by a wave of nausea. If I made it through this evening without vomiting, it would be a miracle.

"Now, pretty thing, there is a knife and a board for cutting. Slice the carrots and the mushrooms, and chop the potatoes and the pork."

I approached the table. The knife she referred to was more like a cleaver, and when I took it into my hand, the handle felt oily. I dreaded knowing the truth, what horror it might be stained with. I started with the carrots, but the first turned to mush in my hand. Bile rose in my throat, and I swallowed it down, reaching for the second carefully. The mushrooms were slimy, the potatoes were covered in sprouts and soft, and the pork was sticky and foul. My nose burned with the smell of it, and I gritted my teeth hard to keep from retching.

"Now, pretty thing, there is a cauldron over the fire. Fill it with water."

The water came from a barrel near the hearth. I was hopeful that it might be fresh, but when I removed the lid, it smelled like rotten eggs. Still, I ladled bowl after bowl until the cauldron was full.

"While you wait for it to boil, pretty thing, you can clean the dishes and scrub the floor."

I crossed to the sink where stacks upon stacks of dishes were piled. I wondered where they had come from, though I suspected the witch had many visitors, and not all of them had a companion like the fox. I tried not to think about what happened to those unsuspecting guests, the ones who trusted their eyes and not their guts.

The dishes were tedious, but I was used to the chore. I took my time clearing the sink so I could fill it with water, which I boiled in a heavy teapot. My hands burned as I worked, but I didn't care. The scalding water made me feel a little better about all the horrible things I had touched within the witch's house, though it still smelled like sulfur.

At least the sink was near the window, and in my periphery, I could see Lore slicing away at the grass in the field. He was shirtless and sweating, his muscles and scars on full display.

I battled a wave of electrifying lust, but it was too late. My mind had already wandered to last night when he lay beneath me. I thought of how he felt against me and how desperately I had wanted him inside me. I crossed my legs as the ache grew worse, which only seemed to heighten my need, and in some ways, I suddenly understood why Lore might consider this feeling a curse.

My thoughts were shattered instantly when something sharp sliced me. I gasped and pulled my hand out quickly to find a cut along my palm. It bled heavily and stung as soon as it was exposed to the air.

"Oh, pretty thing, look what you did!" said the witch.

Her horrible hand latched onto my injured arm. I bit my tongue, wanting so badly to scream no as she dragged me from the sink. She brought me near the hearth and retrieved a canister from the mantel, smearing something jelly-like over my palm. I thought it looked like honey, but it smelled sour. When she was finished, she wrapped it with a piece of linen she pulled from her pocket.

I squeezed my fingers into a fist, my stomach churning, both from the pain and the anxiety of what exactly the witch had used on my wound.

"The water is boiling, pretty thing," said the witch. "You must add the meat and potatoes."

I did as she said and finished the dishes, even with my wounded hand, then added the carrots and mushrooms before scrubbing the floor.

By the time I was finished, the sun was setting outside.

The witch was at the hearth, ladling stew into a bowl, which she placed on a tray along with a loaf of bread and a bottle of wine.

"Take this to your beloved," she said. "Be sure he does not leave a drop, and when you return, you may have some of your own."

I was suspicious of her instructions but relieved at the same time. I took the tray and carried it to the door. The smell of the stew made my stomach turn. Saliva gathered in my mouth, and I knew I was going to vomit. Thankfully, as soon as I was outside the cottage, the cold air washed over me, and the feeling lessened. I paused on the rotting step and took a deep breath before following the cobblestone path from the garden.

Lore was no longer in the field. I found him in the stables, having just spread a blanket on the hay-covered floor. He was still shirtless, still sweaty from his work in the field. He had tied his hair back, and the angles of his face looked just as fierce as his eyes, which raked down my body.

"Are you okay?" he asked.

I nodded, dropping my gaze to the tray. "I know Fox said not to accept food and drink," I said. "But the witch instructed me to bring you dinner. I thought perhaps we could share what food we already had."

"Of course," Lore said.

I set the tray down on a nearby barrel. When I turned to face Lore again, his eyes were on my hand.

"I thought you said you were okay," he said.

"I am," I said. "Mostly."

He crossed to me and took my hand, unwinding the bandage. He bent to smell the salve.

"I don't know what she used on it," I said.

"Nothing that will heal, certainly," he said. "Sit, and I will dress it."

I obeyed, only realizing now how badly my feet hurt. Lore retrieved the satchel and then came to kneel in front of me.

"How do you think Fox fares in the forest?" I asked.

"I am sure he is fine," said Lore. "Hold out your hand."

I did as he said. He scraped away what remained of the witch's medicine and then pulled the waterskin from the satchel and poured fresh water over the wound, squeezing it until it bled.

The pain was almost like being cut again, and I inhaled a breath between my teeth.

"I'm sorry," he said. "I just want to make sure it is clean."

"I know. It's okay," I said.

After he seemed satisfied with the cleansing, he placed his hand over a patch of ground, and beneath it sprouted a green stem with pointed leaves and berries that looked almost like black tomatoes.

"What is that?" I asked.

"It is called deadly nightshade," said Lore.

He let the plant grow until it was a few inches tall before he ripped it from the ground and then tore the leaves free, leaving only the stems, from which he squeezed a pulp-like salve onto the cut. When he was finished, he tore a strip of cloth from his tunic and wrapped it around my hand.

"Before you leave, I'll replace the witch's rag," said Lore. "She will be none the wiser."

The thought of returning to that awful cottage filled me with dread. "Do you think she will know if I do not go back?"

"We risk offending her if we do not do as she says," he said.

"She expects me to eat when I go back inside," I said.

"Then we will make it appear as though you have eaten with me," Lore said, handing me a piece of bread from our own supplies.

I took it, but I wasn't very hungry. The smell of rancid meat lingered in my nose, which meant I could also taste it in the back of my throat.

I ate the bread and then reached into the satchel for the other waterskin, which was full of wine. I downed a mouthful and then another. When I was finished, I found Lore watching me.

"I can't escape what I have seen and felt in that cottage," I said. "Everything looks pretty and clean, but my body tells me otherwise."

"If I could, I would take your place," he said. "But I suspect the witch does not like fae, especially elvish princes."

"I will be fine," I said, looking down at my hands. "I would do anything for you."

Slowly, I raised my head and met his gaze. My heart beat faster as I thought about the words I was going to say. Then they started to tumble out of my mouth, and they fell into the air between us where I could not take them back.

"You may think you are cursed," I said. "But my love for you is very real."

"Samara." My name slipped from Lore's mouth in a pained whisper. "Please, Samara."

"In two days, I will partake of the golden apple and wish you free of your love for me, but I will still love you. I will always love you. I deserve to know what it's like to be loved by you before it is too late."

My voice trembled. I could not tell if it was from anger or sadness. I felt overwhelmed by both at this moment. I rose to my knees and unlaced my dress, pulling it over my head and casting it aside. I sat there, kneeling naked before the prince I had loved for seven long years, waiting for him to say something—anything.

He stared at me, mouth tense.

Just when I started to think he would do nothing, the word *coward* poised on the tip of my tongue, he was on his knees in front of me. His hand tangled in my hair, and he guided my head back so he could look into my eyes.

"I always dreamed this moment would happen somewhere far nicer than the floor of a stable," he said. "You deserve more than this."

"I don't need anything else," I said. "I just need you."

He stared at me a few seconds longer. I think he was looking for any sign of doubt, but I had none. I had never taken what I wanted, but I was going to tonight.

I kissed him, and his hesitation fell away as his fingers fisted in my hair. My lips parted on a moan, and his tongue slid against my own, teasing before he kissed me long and slow and deep. My heart beat rapidly as my hands moved to his chest. I tried to guide him to his back, because all I knew was what we had done last night, but Lore stopped me, smiling as he broke our kiss.

"Be patient, beloved," he said. Tilting my head back, he brushed his thumb over the curve of my swollen lips. "I have plans for you."

I liked the look in his eyes. It was hunger, gnawing and deep. The kind that made you feel hollow. I had seen it in his gaze before but to a lesser degree. Tonight, it roared to life, and a thrill shivered through me, knowing that I was what he craved.

"I...don't know what to do," I said.

I didn't need to say it, but I felt like I had to provide some kind of excuse in case I was terrible.

"Samara," he said, resting his forehead against mine. "You are perfect."

He kissed me again and then guided me to my back. He didn't follow but stayed seated on his heels, staring down at me. I felt exposed and moved to cover myself, turning my knee slightly into the other, as if I could hide from Lore, whose eyes only darkened at the sight.

"I will have my face there soon enough," he said. "You might as well let me look."

"It is an easy request for someone who is still clothed."

The corner of his mouth lifted, but I knew by the gleam in his eyes he had taken my words as a challenge. I lifted myself onto my elbows as he rose to his feet and unlaced his trousers, pulling them off. As he straightened, my eyes roamed over his body but stopped at his arousal, which was thick and rigid. I blushed fiercely when I realized it was the only thing I was staring at, but I was also thinking about what it would feel like to have him inside me soon.

I don't know what possessed me. Perhaps it was just the way he was looking at me now, but I shifted to my knees again, my face level with his sex. I lifted my hand but didn't touch him, moving my gaze to his. I suppose I wanted permission.

"You can touch me." His voice was strained. I wondered if he felt like I had felt all day—wound so tight, I could barely breathe.

I turned my attention to his arousal and let my fingers drift from the crown of his cock to the bottom where his balls hung heavy between his thighs. He was soft, which surprised me. No other part of his body felt like this.

"Will I hurt you?" I asked.

"I will tell you," he said. "Wrap your fingers around me."

I did as he said, and then he wrapped his own around mine and moved my hand up and down, letting out a low breath as I followed his lead.

"And that feels good?"

"Yes," he said, breathless. "Very."

"What else do I do?" I asked.

Again, Lore let out another long breath.

"Sweet Samara," he said, and I was surprised when he pulled my hand away from him and then knelt in front of me. "Let me show you how good this can be for you."

"I want to please you," I said.

I did not want to bring up my brothers, but I knew how they talked about the women who frequented our cottage. I knew who had satisfied them and who didn't.

"Beloved, you please me simply by existing," he said.

He kissed me long and slow, guiding me until I rested on my back again. He remained upright, staring down at me.

"You are so fucking beautiful," he said, and then he placed his knee between my legs, nudging them apart. He settled into that space and then rested his elbows on either side of my head, continuing our kiss. At some point, he let himself relax fully and my breath caught in my throat. He was so warm, and his arousal settled against my heat, heavy and hard. I wanted to be full of him, and I reacted without thought, widening my legs and lifting my hips.

Lore groaned against my mouth and then dragged his lips along my jaw and neck. He trailed kisses down my chest, between my breasts, before taking each into his mouth in turn. He teased mercilessly, plying my nipples with his tongue and then sucking hard. It was a push and pull of overwhelming pleasure and dizzying relief.

I had some idea of what he intended as he pressed soft kisses down my stomach, but it was another matter entirely once he arrived at the apex of my thighs. The inclination to press my knees together overwhelmed me, but Lore was there, and he was looking at a part of me no one ever had like he looked at all of me—as if it was the most beautiful thing in the world.

He kissed the inside of my thigh as he met my gaze, and I swallowed hard as a fierce blush stained my cheeks.

"You are perfect," he said.

He continued kissing along my thigh and then the other before settling completely on his stomach and kissing my heat. He did it again, harder this time, burying his face between the soft mound of curls between my legs.

I gasped, pressing my head into the floor.

I didn't know what to do with my hands. At first, I let them twist into his hair. It felt safe because if I grew too insecure, I could pull him away, but then he used his fingers to part my flesh and licked along my heat, letting his tongue circle where I ached most. I let out a moan, my head falling back.

Lore pulled away. "Is it good?" he asked.

"Yes," I breathed. My eyes were closed, and my chest rose and fell heavily. I had held my breath the entire time. "Yes."

He licked me again, and then his mouth closed over my clit. He sucked gently, and I thought I might die. I dug my heels into the floor but couldn't go anywhere, because Lore's arms were locked around my legs to keep me still, his face pressing harder into my sex.

When he let me go, he exhaled deeply, and when I looked at him, his lips were wet with my arousal. A wave of embarrassment burned through my body, but the corner of Lore's mouth lifted, his eyes dark with lust.

"There is no room for shame here, beloved," he said. "It's okay to love this. I do."

He turned his attention to me again. This time, his fingers trailed along my opening, deepening as he moved through my heat until one finger slipped fully inside. I instinctively tightened at the invasion, but then his mouth was on me again, and I was able to relax. Soon I felt molten, and he slipped another finger inside. The muscles in the bottom of my stomach contracted, and I gripped Lore between my thighs, unable to do anything else. It felt instinctual, and it gave me what I wanted, heightening the pressure and pleasure in a way I hadn't felt before.

Lore pulled away long enough to let out a low curse. Then he was back, but this time with a steady and unending rhythm. His fingers curled inside me while he licked and sucked my clit, and my legs pressed into him so hard, I shook. Inside, I was rising higher and higher, the pleasure moving from the depths of my stomach straight to my head until it unraveled.

The cry that left my mouth scraped against my throat. I could not even open my eyes. It felt like my body had pulled everything inside me to a single point between my thighs. If it wasn't so pleasurable, it would have been painful. I curled into myself as tremor after tremor shook my entire body. When it lessened, I could relax, but my eyes were heavy.

He had taken all my strength in a matter of seconds.

I heard him chuckle, and I opened my eyes enough to see his smug expression.

He was proud of himself.

He kissed the inside of my knee.

"How did that feel?" he asked.

"You know how it felt, arrogant prince," I said. "Is it a requirement to praise your mouth before we continue?"

He grinned and then shifted, resting one elbow, then the other on either side of my stomach. He kissed his way up my body. I felt warm and relaxed. I felt ready for him, even surer when his cock came to rest against my wet heat.

As quickly as he had brought me to release, the desire ignited again. It was a strange type of torture but one I was desperate for.

I held Lore's gaze as he brushed strands of hair from my face.

"I love you," I said, unable to bring my voice above a whisper. I was a little afraid he would recoil at my words, but his expression only grew softer.

"What I have felt for you these last seven years, it borders on obsession. I have never felt anything like it. I never will again."

I was surprised by his words but also confused. It was a confession of his feelings for me but also an acknowledgement that it would end.

He kissed me though, and I was reminded of why I had made this decision. I loved Lore despite everything, and this was what it was like to be loved by him.

When he pulled away, he let his nose drift down mine.

"Are you ready?" he asked.

I nodded, because I couldn't speak.

He shifted his weight to one side, reaching between us to guide the head of his cock through my heat before resting his forearms on either side of my head.

We were both a little breathless, though nothing had happened yet.

He kissed me again, once hard and deep, once soft and slow, and as he broke from my lips, he rocked his hips into mine. I let out a breath. There was no pain but a sweet pressure, and I widened my legs preparing to take more of him, though I found it difficult to relax. The anticipation kept me rigid, my heels were pressed into the floor, my back arched into him.

He kissed my forehead, one of his arms resting beneath my head.

"Wrap your legs around my waist," he said.

I followed his instructions, and the tension in my body lessened, then he drove into me again, this time to the hilt. I took in a sharp breath, but not because it hurt. It was because I was surprised.

Lore kissed my face and my neck and told me to breathe. I held his gaze. I had dreamed of so many aspects of what this moment would be like, but the one I could never have imagined was how close I would feel to him. This went beyond the way our bodies were connected. It was another level of existence, and within this space, I knew I would never love another as long as I lived.

"How do you feel?" he asked.

"Like I am dreaming," I said, slipping his hair behind his ear. "You?"

He gave a breathless laugh. "I feel like I might die if I do not move soon."

"I'm ready," I said.

He studied me, kissed me again.

"You are everything," he said.

His words twisted inside me. They were so close to the ones I wanted to hear but still so far away, but there came a point after he started to move that I no longer cared how he told me he loved me, because I could feel it in every part of my body. It was like he had taken ahold of everything inside me. My head fell back, and my hands slid over his back to his ass. I gripped him hard and pulled him into me. I wanted as much of him as I could get.

"Samara," he whispered my name as he kissed along my throat, matching the pace I desired. "Beloved."

He buried his face in the crook of my neck and held me tight as he rocked into me over and over, faster and faster, until his breath caught hard in his throat and his entire body tensed as he came. I could not describe the euphoria I felt, knowing that part of him was inside me, and I knew I'd been right to ask for this.

"Are you okay?" he asked as his body relaxed against mine.

"Yes," I said. "I am perfect."

"There is nothing truer," he said, his lips teasing mine.

We kissed and explored each other in the aftermath of our coupling, but there came a point when I knew I had to go. It was strange rising from where we had made love. I felt different, renewed in a way I never expected, and so in love my heart ached.

Once I was dressed, I turned to find Lore watching me. His stare was hard, and his brows were lowered. My heart ached suddenly, afraid that he had already decided to regret what happened between us. I decided I wouldn't ask, because I didn't want to know. I would show him soon enough that we were meant to be together, that his love for me was just as real as what we had shared tonight.

"Here," he said, wrapping the witch's ragged bandage around my hand to hide his work. After, he picked up the bowl of stew. "Rub some of the juice around your mouth, and pour it on your apron. I know it will be awful, but she will think you have eaten with me."

I took the bowl in hand, but before I could complete the task, Lore tilted my head back, and his mouth came down upon mine. I wanted so badly to stay with him, but there would be other nights, I told myself, knowing I was trading this one for hundreds more after.

"Get some sleep, wild one," Lore whispered when he pulled away.

I held my breath as I smeared the horrible stew around my mouth and poured it on the apron the witch had given me before leaving the barn. I paused at the door to look back at Lore.

"I love you," I said, because I did not think I could say it enough, but I turned before I could see his expression and hurried to the witch's cottage where a pretty orange glow filled the windows, though I knew it to be from the fire upon which the rancid stew still boiled—and likely many other terrible things.

I tried to prepare myself for what I would hear and taste and smell on the other side of her rotten door, but knowing what to expect did not make it any easier.

I cringed, turning the rusty knob, and a wave of nausea hit as I pushed the squealing door open. The witch was sitting in a chair, rocking back and forth, knitting with a pair of long needles. As she worked, they scraped against each other, and I ground my teeth harder and harder with each pass.

"You have been gone for quite some time, pretty thing," said the witch. "Your dinner has gone cold."

I glanced at the table and saw that she had prepared my bowl. There was a glass of wine and a loaf of bread too. When my gaze returned to the witch, she had moved and stood only an inch from me. I was glad that I'd clenched my jaw so tight. It kept me from screaming at her nearness, but I did stagger back. She gripped my wrist as she seemed fond of doing and dragged me close, taking a deep breath.

"You smell like the prince," she said. "But it seems you are full. Full of the prince and full of stew. Now it is off to bed with you."

She turned and dragged me into the dark of her cottage, to a room with an iron bed. It was neatly made, with many pillows and a coverlet edged with lace. A candle sat on a table nearby, but it had burned low and would soon go out.

The witch let go of my hand and pushed me farther into the room. I stumbled but caught myself before I could fall.

"Rest, pretty thing, for your belly is full. Nothing will harm you tonight, unless you wake before daylight."

She slammed the door, and the candle went out.

Alone, I placed my hands on the bed and recoiled instantly.

The coverlet was damp, and so were the pillows. I would not rest there and instead lay down on the floor by the bed. It was like sleeping in the kitchen at home, and I suppose it was that familiarity—and my exhaustion from the evening spent with Lore—that helped me sleep despite my awful surroundings.

———

I was torn from slumber by a sudden, sharp kick to my side. I woke trying to catch my breath and full of terror as a terrible shriek filled the room and the witch crashed to the floor beside me. With horror, I realized I had forgotten the fox's final task. I had failed to stretch seven lengths of golden thread from the door to the bed.

Still gasping for breath, I rolled onto my hands and knees and tried to rise to my feet, but the witch wrapped her hands around my ankle, and it was then I realized that she had claws, for they were sharp and cut into my skin. I screamed as the pain sliced through me and she pulled me to the ground.

I fell flat, and my lungs felt paralyzed in my chest. I couldn't even scream as I lost the ability to take in air.

I tried to rise again, but the witch jerked me toward her.

"Pretty creature, full of vicious fae," the witch seethed. "I will cut them out of you. I will drain you dry, but first I will take your eyes."

I rolled onto my back. Though the witch still had her claws in my leg, my other was free, and I used it to kick her. I wasn't sure where my foot landed, maybe her hands or her arms, but she screamed and screeched and finally let me go. I scrambled to my feet, but my leg gave out as I tried to run, shredded by the witch's claws. I rose again and stumbled into the hallway, hitting the wall.

"Lore! Lore, please, help me!"

My scream broke into a sob.

"He cannot hear you, pretty thing," the witch sang in a shrill voice. "He is dead, dead asleep!"

But I knew otherwise. He had not taken her food or drink. "Lore!"

My hand had just brushed the door when the witch's claws cut into my arms. I screamed as she threw me to the ground but was quickly silenced as my head struck the edge of the wall. My vision swam with explosions of black, and my stomach turned violently. I rolled onto my side and vomited.

"That is what you get for not listening, pretty thing. You are a fighter, and you are a liar," said the witch.

Her claws sunk into my wounded leg, and all I managed was a short wail. I did not fight her as she dragged me closer and closer to the hearth where a fire still raged.

When she dropped my leg, she turned her back to me, and it was then I caught sight of something glimmering on the floor.

It was the golden thread.

It must have slipped from my pocket.

I don't know what came over me, but something dark took hold, and all I felt was rage—rage toward everyone who had ever hurt me. It was like all the anger my mother had locked away inside me had suddenly been unleashed, and I felt…violent.

I reached for the thread and rose to my feet, stumbling toward the witch, whose back was still turned to me. With each step, I wound the thread around my hands and pulled it taut. As I came up behind her, I looped it around her neck and pulled it tight. I had meant to strangle her and was prepared for the struggle that would ensue, but the thread cut right through her, and her head slid completely off, falling into the empty sink. A second later, her body fell heavily to the floor.

My breathing was ragged and my ribs hurt, but I stood there numbly with the bloody thread dangling from my hands until I caught movement in the distance. Fox popped out from between the darkness of the trees, the glass ax clasped between his teeth, and Lore opened the stable door just as the sun peeked over the horizon.

Together they made their way across the freshly trimmed field toward the cottage.

I left the sink and went outside, making my way down the steps and to the edge of the garden. Lore raced to my side. He touched my face and then backed away to look at me from head to toe. I think he expected me to burst into tears, but right now, I was beyond that.

"Where is that fucking witch?" he hissed, reaching for his blade.

"She's dead," I said. "I killed her."

Lore's anger melted into shock. The only one who did not seem surprised was the fox, who turned his head to the side as he maneuvered the glass ax to the ground and propped it up against the fence.

"You did not listen, wild one," he said.

"No…I didn't," I said, and then I looked at Lore. "I'm sorry. I know how much you wanted to find the wishing tree."

Lore's brows slammed down over his eyes, and his jaw ticked. He didn't like what I'd said, but I assumed it was because he had not yet realized the witch could not tell us where the wishing tree would appear.

"Do not be so quick to presume," said the fox. "The witch can still show us the way to the tree, but first we must harvest her eyes and her claws."

I looked at Lore and handed him the thread.

CHAPTER ELEVEN
The Final Night

LORE

 it, wild one, and let me lick your wounds," said the fox as I made my way up the dilapidated steps.

I ground my teeth, needlessly jealous. I should be grateful that the fox could heal Samara, but all I felt was anger. As much as I wanted to be the one to nurse her back to health, I was the reason she needed it. I had promised to keep her safe, and I had failed miserably.

I was a terrible lover but a worse protector.

That reality struck even harder as I entered the witch's cottage and was overwhelmed by a foul stench. I could not place it exactly, but it was sickly sweet and burned my nose. Bile surged into the back of my throat. It was so instantaneous, I choked as I swallowed it down.

If Samara had managed to spend hours in this cottage, I could stay for a few seconds.

I stepped into the kitchen. There was a trail of blood on the floor between a rotten wooden table and a large blazing hearth over which a cauldron boiled fiercely. Seeing it filled me with dread. What had the witch had planned for my beloved?

I found her body just beyond the table and her head in the sink. Her face was gray and waxy, but her eyes were open, and she stared back at me just as she had in the field.

I shoved my thumb into the corner of her eye, and when her eye popped from its socket, I tore it loose. I did the same with the second.

After it was done, I stared down at her face before catching sight of a row of knives laid out neatly on the counter, and an anger unlike anything I'd ever felt burned through me. I reached for one and before I could think twice, I shoved it deep into the witch's face. I jerked it loose and did it again.

And again.

And again.

I slammed the blade into her until I couldn't breathe. When I was finished and her face was nothing more than a bloody pulp, I screamed until my voice gave out, dissipating into silence.

"Feeling better?" asked the fox.

I wondered at what point he had decided to join me.

"No," I growled. I scooped up the eyes I'd removed from the witch and threw them at the fox. "Here are your fucking eyes."

They landed at his feet. He watched them roll away until they disappeared under the table and then looked at me.

"They are your eyes, Prince of Nightshade," said the fox.

I knew it, but I did not want it to be true. At this moment, I could not understand my own actions. I did not know why I had sent Samara back to this cottage, especially after the night we had shared. I had made love to her. I had made love to her, and no one else had before, and I had let her leave my side to sleep in a house of horror.

I should have kept her by me. I should have spent the rest of the night inside her.

Instead, I had traded all that for a pair of eyes I could barely look at.

"She apologized to me," I said, grinding my teeth so hard my jaw ached. "She, bloody and broken, apologized to *me*."

"What do you expect from a woman who is used to abuse?"

My eyes burned.

Only one thing was clear to me now. Cursed or not—I did not know anymore—nothing changed the fact that I was unworthy of Samara's true love.

"We had better be on our way," said the fox. "Find her eyes, and cut her nails. Tonight, we will find where the wishing tree will grow."

The fox turned and left the cottage, and I followed soon after, but not before dropping the witch's head into her boiling cauldron and setting her cottage alight.

———

We traveled until the sun went down. Fox led the way, and Samara followed. As usual, I lingered behind, carrying the satchel, which felt strangely heavy, weighed down by the witch's eyes and her long iron claws.

Though I desired to walk beside my beloved, it felt like a reward I didn't deserve, so I kept my distance, and she kept hers. I wondered how she felt about me now, in the aftermath of my failure. Did she regret giving herself to me? Did she love me less? Did she love me at all?

The questions gnawed at me the longer we went without speaking, but I could not bring myself to ask. I was afraid and ashamed.

Coward, I thought.

The sun was setting when we stopped at the base of a hill where there were many trees, and the foliage was dense.

"This will do," the fox announced. "Make a fire beneath those shrubs, and burn the witch's eyes. The ashes will tell us where to go."

I hesitated, watching Samara continue on, up the grassy hill and out of sight. I dropped the satchel to the ground and started to follow her, but the fox stopped me.

"Where are you going, Prince of Nightshade?"

"I no longer care about the eyes or the wishing tree," I said. "What value do they hold when all they will do is take my beloved from me?"

"Are you saying you no longer believe you are cursed, prince?" he asked. "Or are you saying you are content to be cursed?"

I hesitated. I did not know exactly what I was saying, I only knew that when I thought of a life without Samara, it was not a life I wanted to live.

"Think carefully before you choose to end this journey," said the fox. "For your beloved has made sacrifices in your name. Would you have her do so in vain?"

"Of course not," I said, frustrated by the fox's question.

"Then burn the eyes, Prince of Poison."

I ground my teeth and set to work, building a small fire beneath the thickest green shrubs, hoping to conceal most of the smoke. I had no idea where Samara's brothers might be in relation to us, and despite having set the witch's cottage on fire, I did not want to give away our current location. While I had failed to protect her from the old woman's evil, I would not fail to protect her from her brothers.

Once the fire blazed, I tossed the eyes into the flames. They were still sticky and wet, and they sizzled until they popped. The fire hissed in retaliation, and the smell made my stomach turn, but I watched them until the fire died. When they were cool, the fox instructed me to pour water over them.

As I did, he watched.

I wondered what he saw in the remains, because all I could make out were ashes swirling. After a few seconds, he gave a soft hum and spoke.

"The wishing tree will appear in a valley surrounded by the Glass Mountains."

I could not deny the dread I felt at the mention of the Glass Mountains, and it reinforced my belief in my curse. The mountains were vengeful, and they had cursed many of my brothers. Why would I be any different?

"Which valley?" I asked. The Glass Mountains went on for miles and miles.

"The moon will let us know," said the fox. "The question you must answer, dear prince, is how will you spend this final night."

Final night.

Those words tore through me.

I did not want a final night with Samara. I wanted many nights—many like the one we'd had last night, but would that be possible on the other side of this broken curse? Right now, I could not imagine feeling anything less for Samara than I felt now. I could not imagine a world without her. She was everything to me—the sun rose and set with her, and the moon waxed and waned with her.

She was the love of my life and even if she broke the curse, that would still be true.

The fox curled up on the ground to sleep while I made my way up the hill where I found Samara sitting, her knees pulled tight to her chest. She was surrounded by tulips, the petals of which seemed to glow pale blue beneath the starlight. As I stared at her from a distance, I remembered the day I'd first laid eyes on her and how she had ensnared me. It was not even her beauty, which was so plainly evident, that hurt my heart. It was what radiated from within her—a kindness I had never seen, a patience I had never endured. Still, she showed these things to me, though I did not deserve them, but tonight I was going to ask for both again as I approached and sat down beside her.

She did not look at me, keeping her head tilted toward the sky.

"Have you learned where we will go next?" she asked, her voice light.

I did not know what to make of it, but I answered her question.

"Yes."

She said nothing, and in the quiet that followed, I gathered the courage to speak.

"I do not want to find the wishing tree," I said.

She looked at me. "Why?"

"Because I do not want to live without you," I said.

She smiled at me, but there was no humor in her eyes or in what she said. "You are a beautiful man," she said. "But you are very stupid."

I frowned. "I am telling you that I do not want to live in a world where I do not love you."

"I know what you are saying," she said. "But you do not seem to understand the point. You still believe your love for me is a curse, which is why we must continue to the wishing tree."

"Why does it matter? I love you now," I said, frustrated.

"It matters because you are afraid of what comes after the wish is made," she said, and then she moved suddenly, shifting into my lap. She wound her arms around my neck, her breasts pressed against my chest, and I tilted my head back to hold her gaze. "But I am not afraid. I am not afraid at all."

Then her mouth was on mine, and something inside me broke open. It was like all the hope I'd locked away within me was suddenly free, pouring into every part of my body, and for the first time since I'd started this journey, I thought that perhaps I had a chance at true love, but with that feeling rose doubt.

"I failed you," I said, breaking our kiss. "I should never have sent you away last night."

"Nothing would have happened if I had listened to the fox," she said.

"It is not about whether you listened," I said. "I chose the quest over you."

Samara's brows lowered. "Do you really believe that?" she asked. I was surprised she didn't.

"You would never have sent me into that cottage if you thought I was unsafe," she said. "I know that to be true."

It wasn't untrue, certainly.

"It was not fair to you," I said. "I should have kept you at my side, I should have made love to you all night."

"Should have, would have," she said. "There is nothing for you to do except make up for it tonight."

I shook my head, wondering how I had been given such a gift. "You are incredible," I said.

"I love you," she said, as if she were answering why.

Our lips collided, and I let my hands side up her thighs and beneath her dress. I gripped her ass and pulled her over my arousal.

She pushed me down into the flowers with a firm hand on my chest but did not follow. I stared up at her with a raised brow.

"Samara," I said.

"Yes?" she asked, grinding against my cock.

I let out a hissing breath. "I want to be inside you."

She laughed.

"Do you find pleasure in my torture?" I asked.

She made another breathless sound and then bent to kiss my chest.

"No, but I fear I am being selfish tonight," she said. "For I very much desire to taste you as you tasted me."

I groaned and felt my cock tighten a little more, her body grazing me as she kissed down my stomach. It took everything

to keep still as she unlaced the ties of my trousers. I distracted myself by removing my prosthetic. It was easier to move without it, but also, my stump was far softer.

My arousal sprang free and the cool air was a welcome relief, but not for long, because soon Samara's hand was wrapped around me, and her thumb was teasing the crown of my cock.

"I should have known from the start you were a siren," I said.

"I am no siren," she said, not looking at me but at my arousal. "I do not even know how to do this."

Even if she did nothing else, I would be content, but then she bent and licked the come from the tip of my cock.

I groaned. "What has made you so bold, wild one?"

She smiled a little. "Curiosity," she said, and then she swirled her tongue around me. "Do you like that?"

A strangled laugh left me. I could barely think. "Yes, wild one," I said. "I love it."

She did it again but continued to explore me with her tongue, running it along every part of me—beneath my crown and along the veins, down to my throbbing balls. I was in disbelief as I watched her. There was a joy to the way she teased and tested, and it was far more arousing than anything I'd ever experienced in my life.

Finally, I could take it no longer, and I pulled her away.

"Enough, wild one. I want to be inside you before I come."

She crawled up my body and straddled me, her mouth closing over mine before sitting back. Then she pulled her dress over her head and tossed it aside. Her skin was pale in the moonlight but marked with bruises. They scored her skin, a map of where I'd explored her last night. It seemed fox's healing had not reached them.

She stared down at me, hesitant. It was the first time since starting this that she didn't seem too confident.

"What is it, beloved?" I asked.

"I...how do you want me?"

"What a wild question," I said. "Any way I can have you, beloved, but I think that tonight, you should stay just where you are."

She looked down, as if she were trying to figure out how we were going to make this work.

"Lean forward a little," I said. "And guide me inside like last night."

She did as I instructed, obedient as ever and eager to please. A wave of heat rushed straight to my head as the crown of my cock sank into her wet heat.

"That's it," I whispered, wanting more of her. My hand smoothed over her ass, gripping her flesh.

She pushed against me, taking me little by little. When she finally sat back, I slid fully inside her, and perspiration had broken out all over my body. I wanted to take a deep breath, but I couldn't until she stopped adjusting to me. Finally, with her hands planted on my stomach and her breasts crushed between her arms, she looked at me.

"Are you okay?"

My laugh was short and hoarse. "I am fine, beloved. Are you?"

She nodded, and I rested my hand and limb on her thighs. At first, she only rocked her hips back and forth, but as she became more comfortable, she started to move up and down my cock, and her breasts bounced. I reached for them, and she bent forward so I could take them into my mouth. I sucked her nipples hard, and she moaned, grinding against me.

I fell back into the flowers and brought her with me, tightening my arms around her and rolling, pinning her beneath me. She anchored her legs around my waist as I thrust into her. I had no thoughts. My only guides were her body and breath as I chased the pressure building at the base of my cock, and when she tightened around me, I came.

I collapsed on top of her, my body shaking. She kept herself wrapped around me, her fingers threading through my now-damp hair as I listened to the beat of her heart. My eyes grew heavy, and as I drifted off to sleep, I thought I heard Samara singing.

CHAPTER TWELVE
Apples Dipped in Gold

SAMARA

 *terrible sound startled me awake. I lay there* for a few seconds on my side, my back to Lore's chest, listening as my heart raced in my chest. Then I heard it again. It was a cry, short and pained.

"Did you hear that?" I whispered.

"Ignore it," Lore replied, his voice still groggy from sleep. His grip tightened around my waist. He didn't even react when the scream sounded again.

"Lore!" I snapped, elbowing him in the stomach. "There is a woman in trouble!"

He groaned and released me. I sat up.

"It isn't a woman," he said, "It's the fucking fox."

"What?"

"It's about time you two woke up. I have been screaming for half an hour."

I looked ahead to see the fox sitting amid the tulips, staring at us.

"Fuck you," said Lore.

"I am only fulfilling your demand, prince," said the fox. "Tonight is the first night of the full moon and your only chance to end your curse."

"A choice I am regretting by the second," said Lore.

"Take heed, Prince," he said. "Without me, you may have never even met your beloved."

"By all means, Fox, take all the credit."

"I will wait for you at the bottom of the hill," said the fox.

I turned and looked at Lore. He lay on his back, staring at the sky. It was barely morning, but thick clouds hung heavy overhead, and the air smelled like rain.

I moved over him, though I questioned if it was the best decision. His arousal was hard beneath me.

"Are you okay?" I asked.

His violet eyes met mine, his stare striking deep.

"I don't want you to do this," he said.

I was glad he did not lie.

I leaned over him and kissed him softly, whispering against his lips.

"I know."

———

We dressed and headed down the hill where Fox was waiting as promised.

Without a word, he led us up another hill. This one was taller, and once we reached the top, he paused and nodded toward the horizon. Despite the dreary day, I could just make out a faint glimmer in the distance.

"Can you see them?" asked the fox. "Those are the Glass Mountains."

"They seem so far away," I said just as the wind picked up. A chill shivered down my spine.

"Those are the tallest peaks," said Lore. "The range is much closer."

"You have been before?" I asked.

"Regrettably," he said. "The Elder Kingdom lies beyond them. It is where I grew up."

I was surprised. "I didn't realize… But then…how are you Prince of Nightshade?"

"I was designated Prince of Nightshade by my father," he said.

"And where is your father?" I asked.

"He is dead."

The news gave way to a new worry. "I thought fae could not die."

"They can if they choose," said Lore. He paused and then met my gaze. "If anything happened to you, I would choose to die."

I didn't know what to make of his words.

"Don't say that," I whispered.

He was quiet, and there was a sincerity in his eyes that twisted in my gut. Then he slipped his fingers between mine and held my hand as we continued down the other side of the hill and into the forest ahead, though we could not maintain our connection long. The forest was too thick, the underbrush a tangle of brambles and green briar, which not only covered the ground but grew upward into the trees. The stems were impossible to escape; even when I thought I had avoided the sharp thorns, they still managed to scrape across my skin. In some places, the vines were so thick, we had to find a way around.

As we continued through the wood, a horrible smell reached us. It was distinct, putrid and vile, worse even than the witch's cottage.

"What is that horrible stench?" I asked.

"It is the dead," said Lore.

"The dead?" I asked, feeling the blood drain from my face.

"There are dead at the base of the mountains," said Lore. "Many have tried to scale them, and many have failed."

I considered asking why so many had tried to climb the mountains, but I guessed it was likely for the same thing we were after—wishes.

"You do not have to do this, Samara," Lore said.

"I know," I said. "I am choosing to do this, Lore. I will be fine. Fox has not led us astray yet."

At least, that is what I kept telling myself.

That, and I was closer than ever to the truest love I had ever known.

It was nightfall when we broke through the final row of trees. My calves stung, and my skin was shredded and bloody. I was so exhausted, I wanted to collapse, but the moon was out, and she had cast a silver beam of light upon the earth just as the fox had said, only it was guiding us over the first mountaintop, which, as I tilted my head all the way back, seemed to nearly touch the sky.

The height was daunting, but so were the bodies at the base of the mountains, just as Lore had said.

"Fasten the witch's claws to your hands and feet," said the fox. "And you will be able to scale the mountains."

Lore pulled the satchel over his head and withdrew the claws. They were still bloody. I did not have the heart to ask if it was mine.

We each took four and did as the fox instructed. With two remaining, Lore slid one in my hair as he leaned in to kiss me.

"Just in case," he murmured against my lips.

Our gazes locked as he pulled away, thumb brushing over my cheek. His eyes were dark, almost swallowed whole by his pupils, and there was a tightness to his mouth that made me think there was more he wanted to say, but I would never know what was poised on the end of this tongue, because his body jerked suddenly, and he roared in pain.

"Lore!" I screamed, fear pounding through my entire body as he reached behind his shoulder and snapped off the shaft of an arrow.

My heart raced at the sight of the familiar fetching. It was Michal's.

I whirled, finding my brothers standing before us.

It had only been seven days since I last saw them, but in that time, they had grown far more severe. Anger settled deep in the lines on their faces, and they looked worn and haggard, their cheeks and lips chapped.

They'd had no one to care for them, and they looked every bit as wretched as they were.

The only one I cared about was who stood behind them—Rooster, my sweet and beautiful stallion.

"I cannot believe it is true," said Hans.

"The little whore really did run away with her lover," said Michal.

I glared at them and stepped in front of Lore, though he quickly pulled me back.

My brothers laughed.

"It seems he has made her brave," said Hans with a laugh.

"I have seen that look before," said Michal, lifting his chin. "It is his cock has made her brave."

A low growl escaped from Lore's mouth, but the sound only made Hans and Michal laugh. Jackal was quiet, but his eyes were full of hatred, and his mouth curled in disgust. It was his silence that scared me the most, his silence that made me wary of what he had planned.

"You think you can battle us, demon?" asked Michal.

Hans chuckled, eyes sparking with humor. "We have hunted and survived this forest for many years."

"So has he," I said through gritted teeth.

Hans and Michal exchanged a look.

"We have a lot to beat out of her," said Michal.

"Where do we start?" asked Hans. "With her lover?"

"No," said Jackal. His tone was too calm for what he intended. He drew his knife—Lore's knife—and grabbed Rooster's reins.

"No!" I screamed, lurching forward, only to be held back by Lore.

The stallion jerked sideways, but Jackal yanked him closer, moving to thrust his blade into Rooster's neck, but all of a sudden, Fox was there. He launched himself at Jackal and bit down on his forearm.

Jackal screamed, and Hans and Michal turned in surprise just as Rooster kicked his front feet. The two stumbled back to avoid his strike.

"Samara," Lore snapped, his hand on my forearm. "Climb!"

I hesitated, desperate. I did not want to leave him and Fox to face my brothers.

"Please," I begged, finishing my plea in my head. *Do not leave me.*

It wasn't that I did not trust Lore's skill, but my brothers were motivated by a will to see me suffer and it made them strong.

Lore gripped the back of my head and pressed his lips to my forehead. "I know," he said. "Now go!"

With a final look, I turned and raced to the foot of the mountain, piled high with a mix of bleached bones and swollen and rancid bodies. I retched as I navigated the climb, battling maggots and flies and slipping on loose flesh. My eyes watered from the stench, and my throat burned. I did not know how I made it to the top, but the horror of it all made me desperate to put distance between myself and the corpses.

I pressed my hands against the smooth surface of the glass

and then slammed my right foot into the mountainside. The witch's claw sank deep with a strange clink, then I lifted my left hand and stabbed the other claw into its surface. With two secured, I began my climb. It was tedious and terrifying. I hated the strange grind of metal sinking into glass. I gritted my teeth with each movement, sure that by the time I reached the peak, I'd have ground them to dust.

It wasn't long before my hands began to bleed. At first, it was only a few drops, but soon it spilled down the side of the mountain in rivulets. My breathing became ragged, and my body shook. I was tiring quickly, and I had not even made it halfway.

As my will weakened, so did my hope.

I looked down, eyes searching the ground below for Lore, who was locked in battle with Michal. Rooster had Jackal cornered near the base of the mountain, but my sweet stallion kept his distance, too afraid of his weapon, Lore's gleaming knife, to get close.

I turned my attention back to climbing, but I had only made a few more feet when I heard a terrible yelp from below. I looked down despite a wave of dizziness barreling through me to see the fox lying on his side. Hans stood over him, and I screamed.

"No!"

My brother whirled, grinning wildly.

"What's the matter, little whore? Did I kill your pet?" he yelled back, his terrible laugh echoing around me.

A terrible pain ripped through my chest, but as I watched, I noticed something strange. The fox's fur was fluttering, as if caressed by the wind, and then suddenly, he transformed into a human man. He was naked and he had a swath of reddish hair. His eyes blinked open. He lay there for a moment and then reached for a nearby rock. Rising to his feet, he slammed it against Hans's head.

My brother went rigid and fell down dead.

The fox, who was now a man, looked up at me.

"Hurry, Samara!"

It was then I looked to see that Jackal had begun to climb the mountain behind me. Panic shot through my limbs, and all of a sudden, I felt numb. I looked up, still unable to see the top of the Glass Mountains, but the fear of Jackal catching up to me spurred me on. It was fuel that did not last the higher I climbed.

My mouth grew dry, and my lips chapped. I found it hard to swallow, and each attempt to move higher made my entire body shake. Then I felt the brush of fingers against my foot. I looked down to see that Jackal had caught up with me.

It was the shock I needed.

"Don't fucking touch me!" I screamed, scrambling higher.

"I gave you a place to sleep and food to eat," Jackal said, his voice trembled with anger. "I gave you more than you deserved and it was still not enough."

"I gave you everything!" I yelled. My breaths came in wild, wheezing gasps as I tried to climb, though everything in me wanted to stop. "I gave you soft beds and warm rooms, I gave you hot meals and cold beer. I washed your clothes and cut your hair. I kept house like mother did—"

"Do not speak of her!" Jackal yelled so loud, the mountains shook beneath me. "You may look like her and sound like her and move like her, but you are not her. You could never be!"

"Fuck you," I said, and as I looked down at him, I spit in his face.

Jackal roared. "You forget your place, fairy fucker!"

"You're wrong," I said as he neared, pausing my ascent. He glared at me, his teeth bared. "I found my fucking place."

His eyes, full of rage, widened with fear as I let myself drop, smashing my feet into his face. His screams echoed as he fell until his body slammed against the mountain slope. He landed with a final crack atop the pile of corpses at the bottom.

In the silence that followed, all I could hear was my ragged breathing, and then I opened my mouth and began to wail. I had never uttered such a sound, but it came from deep inside me, tearing at my lungs and my throat, and when I could no longer make it, I sobbed.

I don't know how long I clung to the side of the mountain, but I felt unable to move. My hands were sticky but also dried with blood, and the parts of my skin that touched the mountain were raw. I felt as though I was melting, fusing with the glass beneath me.

My thoughts turned to Lore and the fox and Rooster. I could no longer see the ground, as thick clouds had gathered below me. I wondered if they were alive. I prayed that they were, though I had never really believed in a God.

My eyes grew heavy with exhaustion.

"Samara!"

Lore's voice echoed around me. It sounded so far away, I thought I had only imagined it. Perhaps I had started to slip into a dream or maybe even accepted death's embrace, but then I heard it again.

"Samara, beloved, I am coming!"

Hope swelled in my chest.

He was alive! He was alive, and he was coming for me!

"Lore! Lore, I am here!" I called. "I am waiting!"

I could have cried with happiness, but I had no tears left. The feeling was short lived, however, as a massive shadow passed over me. I looked up to see a large, black raven circling overhead. I had forgotten Cardic's caution, about the raven who guarded the wishing tree and his iron talons.

He gave a sharp cry and then sank his awful claws into my shoulders.

"Lore!"

My scream curdled even my blood as the raven carried me higher and higher, his claws digging deeper as he rose over the mountain's peak. My terror gave way to wonder as I came to see the silver beam of moonlight flooding the valley below.

Where the light touched, everything was green, not glass, and at its center, I saw it.

The wishing tree.

It was more beautiful than I had imagined.

The trunk was massive and the roots were deep. The branches too were long and thick and dense with evergreen foliage and large golden apples. They were so bright against the dark leaves, they almost blinded me.

The raven carried me near, but panic rose inside me as I realized I couldn't let this creature take me any farther, but I had no idea how I was going to get down with his claws locked so keep inside me.

"Please," I tried to speak, but my throat was so dry, I could not raise my voice.

Then I remembered the claw. The one Lore had threaded into my hair as he kissed me goodbye.

I reached to pull it free, screaming through the pain as I hacked at the raven's feet. The bird gave a harsh cry and released me just as he flew over the wishing tree.

I fell, hitting the branches as I landed hard on my back.

I knew I was broken as I lay there on the ground, yet I felt no pain, only wonder as I stared up at the emerald canopy, heavy with golden fruit.

Something dropped near me, and I turned my head to the side. An apple had fallen within reach. I stretched, grazing its smooth skin with my fingertips, rolling it closer until I could take it in hand. I held it against my heart, and closed my eyes, wishing that Lore was no longer cursed.

Then I took a bite.

The skin was crisp and broke easily, flooding my mouth with sweetness.

It was the last thing I remembered and nothing more.

CHAPTER THIRTEEN
True Love's Kiss

 amara!"

I don't know how many times I screamed her name and waited for a reply, but nothing came.

Still, I continued, clinging to the hope that she was alive on the other side of the mountain. I did not even care if she'd found the wishing tree. I did not care if she had eaten an apple or made a fucking wish.

All I wanted was for her to be alive.

"Why isn't she answering?"

"Do not think on it, Prince, just keep going," said Fox—or rather, Friedrich, who was not a fox at all, but a man cursed to live as a fox. After I'd managed to cut Michal's throat, I'd come face to face with him and punched him in the face.

"What was that for?" he'd demanded, holding a hand to his cheek.

"I warned you when you slept on Samara's bed that you had better be a fox," I said.

Now he climbed the mountain behind me, dressed in Samara's brothers' clothes.

"I heard her scream," I said. "I know the raven has taken her. Fuck!"

I wanted to stop. I wanted to beat my fist against this fucking mountain until I shattered it into a thousand pieces but that was not possible, so I kept climbing.

When we reached the very height of the Glass Mountains, the sun shone brilliantly on the horizon, and in the distance, I could see the dazzling turrets of my father's castle. It had been a long time since I'd looked upon his golden castle, though it held little interest as I hugged the narrow peak of the mountain, finally making it to the other side.

Relief washed over me as I observed the valley below, but I was soon overcome with panic as I saw Samara lying beneath the branches of a skeletal tree.

"Samara!" I screamed, but she did not move. "Samara! Fuck!"

I pulled my claws from the glass and sailed down the side of the mountain.

As I neared the bottom, I shoved them into the mountain to slow my descent. The sound tore at my insides, but again, I did not care. Once my feet touched the ground, I nearly fell as I raced to my beloved, falling to my knees beside her.

She was pale, her face void of color and her lips blue.

"Samara!" I breathed, shaking her before pressing my ear to her chest, but there was no heartbeat, no signs of life.

"No," I said as a keen wail tore from my throat. I gathered her into my arms, tucking her head beneath my chin, rocking her back and forth. "No, please! This cannot be. Please come back. Please don't leave me."

"Oh, Prince," said Friedrich as he approached.

I pulled away and stared at Samara's beautiful face through my tears.

"I love her, Friedrich," I said. "I love her, and I never told her."

"Tell her now, Prince," he said. "Tell her and kiss her."

I took a shaky breath and rested my forehead rest against hers. "I was wrong to never say it, wrong to never believe it. I love you, Samara. I love you more than anything in this terrible world."

I kissed her, though she was cold, and then I held her to me and willed her to be warm.

It was only a moment after that I felt her fingers in my hair and heard her speak my name. I pulled away to find her eyes open, her cheeks and lips as rosy as they were before.

"Lore," she whispered and placed her palm flat against my cheek. She looked at me in wonder, as if I were the miracle.

"Samara," I said, holding her face in my hands, marveling at the life in her beautiful blue eyes. "You are not a curse at all but a gift. You are my dream come true and my greatest wish. I love you. I have loved you since the moment I saw you seven years ago."

"I know," she said and smiled so sweetly, I could not help kissing her.

She pulled away and gasped, looking over my shoulder where I knew Friedrich stood.

"Who are you?" she asked.

"I am Fox," he said, bowing. "Or Friedrich if you'd like."

She opened her mouth to speak, but I stopped her. "Pretend he doesn't exist," I said and kissed her again, longer this time. I was slow to stop, letting my lips linger against hers.

"Marry me, Samara of Gnat," I said when I pulled away.

She smiled and answered, "No."

"What? Why not? We love each other, do we not?"

"I will marry you eventually," she said. "But only after you have lived with me in my quiet cottage by the moor for at least a year."

"Beloved," I said, nuzzling her nose with mine. "Your heart is my home. I will go wherever you lead."

AND THEY LIVED HAPPILY EVER AFTER.

THE END

Author's Note

Hello and welcome to my TedTalk—as you are all probably used to by now, I have a lot to tell you about the fairy tales that influenced this story, and like *Mountains Made of Glass*, there are many.

First, I want to say this story was far more complicated than *MMOG* for a variety of reasons. I tend to write first books in a series as more straightforward romances and I thought every book in this series, since they all feature a different couple, would be just as simple…but I was wrong. This one took a toll on me mentally, and I think a huge part of that was the abuse Samara suffered, particularly at the beginning of the story. Abuse—mental, physical, sexual, and neglect—is prevalent across fairy tales. It is said that the Brothers Grimm were the first to include these themes in literature to reflect the historical and social context of the time. I do want to note again that the Brothers Grimm collected fairy tales, they did not write them, so this suggests only that they chose to include fairy tales with child abuse, not exclude them.

Abuse was also featured heavily in *The Hand with the Knife* by the Brothers Grimm which is the fairy tale that inspired most of *Apples Dipped in Gold*. In the story, a maiden is horribly abused by her brothers and mother and is forced to cut peat from the bog with a dull knife. An Elf falls in love with the girl and offers her a knife that can cut anything in two but when the girl starts to finish her chore faster than before, her brothers and mother grow suspicious. The brothers follow her and discover the hand with the knife. They force her to give them the knife and cut off the Elf's hand and he is never seen again.

I thought this was an intriguing beginning to a story and so, in my head, *Apples Dipped in Gold* is what happens in the aftermath. Though the events I just described happen before the start of his fairy tale, they are referenced heavily throughout the novel.

Other Grimm Fairy Tales

There are a few other Grimm fairy tales I referenced throughout the book. Notably, *The Nixie of The Mill-Pond* where a miller meets a woman in his mill pond. She had a beautiful voice and promised to make him rich if he brought her "the young thing which has just been born in your house." He agrees because he thinks that it must be a puppy or kitten, not knowing that his wife just gave birth to a son. The miller warns his son to stay away from the pond and he does, of course, until one fateful day hunting. When he vanishes, he has left behind his beloved who is given a golden comb and told to comb her long, black hair beneath the moonlight by the mill pond. She is given other tasks after this—play a flute, spin this spinning wheel. Eventually, her persistence pays off and her beloved rises from the pond. There is more to this story—the two forget each other and must remember but the themes here—the alluring voice, the comb, and later, moonlight—are obvious and appear also in *Apples Dipped in Gold*.

There is another story called *The Water-Nixie* which is about a brother and sister who are captured by a water-nixie who lives in a well. She forces them to work for her but after some time, they are able to escape. As they run from her, the children throw items at the creature to stop her—a brush, a comb, a mirror. Each item stops the nixie from pursuing them, though not as violently as I portrayed in *Apples Dipped in Gold* (though we know these fairy tales could be just as terrible).

One of the reasons I have the comb turned into a thousand spears is because in *The Water-Nixie* the comb is said to "make a great ridge with a thousand times a teeth."

The next fairy tale I want to talk about is *The Golden Bird*. In this story, there is a king and three sons who all try to discover who is stealing golden apples from a tree in the garden. Only the youngest is able to witness a golden bird pluck an apple from the tree. He was also able to shoot the bird, but only one of his golden feathers fell to the ground.

The feather was so valuable, the king desired the entire thing and so the sons set out to find the golden bird. Once again, the youngest is the only one who can accomplish the task, though he would not have done so without a Fox who counsels him along the way. The advice the fox gives is always very straight-forward. For example, at one point he tells the brothers "this evening you will come to a village in which stand two inns opposite to one another. One of them is lighted up brightly, and all goes on merrily within, but do not go into it; go rather into the other, even though it looks like a bad one." Of course, two of the brothers enter the "good" inn and the youngest enters the "bad" inn.

Later, the fox will tell the youngest son to walk straight past a regiment of soldiers and into the castle where the bird is held.

While there is an empty golden cage, the boy is warned to keep the bird in the "common cage." The young prince does not listen and as soon as he tries to move the bird from cage to cage, he squawks and wakes the soldiers.

The young prince's journey continues after that with the fox advising and while he has not been proven wrong by the fox's guidance, he continues to ignore it for some reason. It's very frustrating. Finally, though, at the end of the story the fox asks the youngest son to kill him and chop off his head and feet. The prince obliges and when he does, the fox becomes a man and of course, he, too, is a prince.

Obviously, you can see the parallels between the fox in *Apples Dipped in Gold* and the fox in *The Golden Bird*. He advises as if he already knows how everything plays out. There is no explanation for why he has this knowledge, and no one ever questions it, though as soon as he is not obeyed, there are great consequences as we saw with Samara and the witch.

Hans Christian Andersen
As I indicted in the author's note of *Mountains Made of Glass*, Hans Christian Andersen is noted for creating his own fairy tales, but they also have similar tones and themes.

The fairy tale I used most in *Apples Dipped in Gold* is called *The Elf-Mound*. I highly recommend reading it after you have read this retelling not only because it is fun, but you will see the parallels.

The story is initially observed from the point of view of the lizards who see that something is taking place at the elf mound. They were kept awake all night by a grand commotion and are discussing it as an 'old-maid elf' emerges from the elf mound. She is hurrying to see the night-raven and invites him to the mound if he will do them a favor and deliver invitations. She goes into a very long-winded explanation about who can come to the ball and banquet and who should be invited and why or why not. I used this same behavior pattern when Lore encounters the old elf maid in *Apples*.

In the exchange, the "old-maid elf" invites "the old man of the sea and his daughters" which I took as a reference to Nereus who is named by Homer as, "Old Man of the Sea." His daughters would be the Nereids, or sea nymphs. She also invites the "grave pig" which is the ghost of a pig buried in a church yard. I called this creature a gloson in the book. It is the same creature, though I felt there were more details under the name gloson than grave pig.

The gloson is said to have a razor-sharp saw sticking out of its back and it will charge at its pray and cut them in half.

Anyway, we later learn that the reason there is such a stirring at the Elf-Mound is because the old elf king is receiving the goblin chief of Norway as he desires to find wives for his two sons who are said to be "rough and rowdy." The old elf king tells his daughters, "they'll improve when they get older. It's up to you to polish them." I referenced this exchange when Lore comments to the elf maid, "pity the women they choose."

The expectation that the women are responsible for their husband's behavior is obviously not new—in fairy tales or the modern world.

Andrew Lang

The Yellow Fairy Book by Andrew Lang includes two stories I used in *Apples Dipped in Gold*—*The Glass Mountains* and *The Glass Axe*.

In *The Glass Mountains*, a princess has been trapped in a golden castle at the top of the Glass Mountains for seven years. A golden apple tree grows before it, and it was said that whoever picked a golden apple from the tree would gain entrance to the castle. Many had tried and failed, to the point that corpses had piled out at the base of the mountains. One day, a young boy appears and desires to rescue the princess, so he cuts off the claws of lynx and begins to scale the mountain. It is a rough climb. Eventually, he is attacked by an eagle who guards the tree. The youth grabs onto his feet and the eagle carries him high over the mountain top. When he is in view of the tree, he cuts the eagle's feet off with a small knife. Though he is injured during his fall, he is able to eat one of the golden apples and heal himself.

In *Apples*, I did not use the claws of a lynx but instead the claws of a witch which is a reference to the Grimm fairy tale, *The Goose Girl at the Well* in which a father warns his sons, "beware of the old woman. She has claws beneath her gloves. She is a witch."

The other fairy tale is *The Glass Axe* in which a young Prince is kidnapped by a fairy queen. She orders him to cut down all the trees there before sunset using only a glass axe. The first blow he strikes shatters the axe into thousands of pieces. It turns out, the fairy's daughter has been exiled to the woods as well. She finds the young prince and offers to help him with his task. Of course, she has magic and reassembles the glass axe and completes the task.

I had the witch task the fox with a similar favor—a rick of wood by morning—because I needed Samara and Lore alone so they could have sex, LMAO.

Other Themes

Samara has a bit of a "Cinderella" moment when she is found by the dryads and given a dress so she can go to the ball. In Apples, Old Mother gives Samara a walnut. Inside, there is a beautiful dress. This is a reference to a few Grimm fairy tales, *Allerleirauh*, *The Two King's Children*, *The Iron Stove*. In each, a princess is given nuts (usually three) with beautiful dresses inside.

I am sure you can pick out a few themes from *Little Snow White*. Samara is made to work hard for her family, and she has black hair and rosy lips. She is also poisoned at the end of the book by an apple. These themes aren't really themes exclusive to Snow White, but the title is a reference to the poisoned apple in *Little Snow White*. In *Apples Dipped in Gold*, it was technically Samara's wish that poisoned her. She wanted Lore free from his curse and the only way to do so was to die and be awakened by true love's kiss. This is more-so a reference to Disney's version of Snow White, since in *Little Snow White*, she was awakened after the apple was dislodged from her throat.

It goes without saying the overall theme of this novel is the concept of love at first sight. I presented this in two ways within *Apples Dipped in Gold*. One was with Prince Henry who decides to marry Samara at first sight, commenting that she is too beautiful to die. He also adds that "beauty is genius" which is a reference to *The Picture of Dorian Gray*. The actual quote is, "Beauty is a form of Genius—is higher, indeed, than Genius, as it needs no explanation." The irony here is that *The Picture of Dorian Gray* is a story about the corruption of beauty. The beautiful are easily forgiven and easily loved by society.

Because Samara is beautiful, the prince decides she is worthy of his attention, his love, and the title of princess. She thinks he is an idiot, but she is desperate to leave her situation.

On the contrary, we have Lore who does not think that love at first sight exists which is why he believes he is cursed. He can acknowledge that Samara is beautiful, and he is captivated by that beauty, but grows more frustrated the longer he cannot disentangle himself from his feelings. This spurs the entire journey to the Glass Mountains which, at the end, is where he is convinced his love for Samara is real but only after she sacrifices herself.

And yes, Lore is an idiot, but there is something to be said about people who believe in something so much, it becomes true.

If anything, I think these retellings just point out the far-fetched nature of the source material while also shedding light on what society values. There is nothing more disturbing than seeing your world within the pages of two-hundred-year-old fairy tales and realizing it hasn't changed.

As always, I hope you enjoyed this tale because Cardic and his nun are next.

Much love,

Scarlett

Read on for a sneak peek of
Scarlett's latest book

CHAPTER
ONE

Ritual was teeming. Glossy tables and velvet couches were already overcrowded, leaving people standing shoulder to shoulder beneath pulsing blue and purple light as they waited for the entertainment to begin.

They would come from above, the aerialists, their red silks unfurling in the dark like ribbons of flame, hypnotizing the audience with their strength and grace as they soared, suspended in the smoky air. It was a popular attraction in Nineveh. Those who came down from the other four districts would have the church believe it was this tame performance they'd come to see, but we all knew otherwise.

Their descent began like clockwork. On Friday at three, Procession Street, the only road in Eden that connected all five districts, would fill with bumper-to-bumper traffic. The onslaught started with the financiers from Hiram, then the industrialists from Temple City, the merchants from Galant, and the artists from Akkadia. Though once they crossed the border into Nineveh, where they were from didn't matter. They were all just hypocrites.

Crits, the locals called them.

Most spent the weekend roaming from club to club on Sinners' Row, returning to their respective districts to worship at temple early Sunday morning. By Monday, they would be cleansed and forgiven, ready to live piously until the weekend.

Forgiveness is an invitation to sin. It will be our ruin.

I ground my teeth as my mother's words came unbidden, roaring to life in my mind. Her doctrine was etched into my memory, conditioned to surface anytime I came into contact with anything that contradicted her teachings, though this was one of few I actually agreed with.

Forgiveness *was* an invitation to sin. I witnessed it every week, which was why I'd decided a long time ago that I did not care to be forgiven.

I'd rather be a sinner than a hypocrite.

I wove my way through the flock dressed in red, as vibrant as the aerialists' silks, but unlike them, I went unnoticed. It was a choice. I could draw attention if I wished, but among those present, I had yet to spy anything of worth.

And tonight, I needed something expensive.

Rent was due, and my landlord had just hiked the price again.

My roommate, Coco, short for Colette, had gone into work down the street where she danced at Praise. She'd asked me to stay home, but only because she didn't like the way I managed to make ends meet.

I was a procurer of goods, usually of the religious variety, but I wasn't picky. I'd sell anything if I could get a good price. The issue was, my job was technically illegal since the church prohibited the sale of holy items.

Coco called my methods stealing, but I called it using my resources, which just so happened to be *magic*.

Honestly, I wouldn't need to if Zahariev, the head of the Zareth family and the district of Nineveh, would let me dance at one of his many clubs, but he refused.

You would start a war, Lilith, he had said.

I rolled my eyes. *You are dramatic, Zahariev. No one has to know who I am.*

You are the daughter of House Leviathan, he said, as if that explained everything. *Besides, I like my balls, and your father would cut them off and feed them to me if he found out I let you dance.*

Let me.

Zahariev.

Zahariev.

Zahariev.

He was a beautiful, frustrating man. I had known him my entire life. He was eight years older than me and had ascended to the head of his family after his father died five years ago. He had always been quiet and controlled, mostly unemotional, as were all Elohai. That was the name of the bloodline that gave each family magic and, with it, the right to rule.

Except that was all really bullshit, because the blood of the Elohai—the blood of God—only gave magic to *women*. It made *us* powerful, a power we could not even utilize because we were subservient to men.

It is what we deserve for tempting the First Man, my mother would say.

She liked to quote the *Book of Splendor*. It was the religious doctrine that ruled our society, that said men should be wary of women.

It also meant that unlike Zahariev, who had been trained to ascend to the head of his family, I had been trained to be a wife, and since I was the only child of my house, my father would choose my husband, the next head of House Leviathan.

I fucking hated it, but that was why I'd run away.

And while Zahariev might not let me dance, he did let me take refuge in his territory.

A hand snaked around my waist, and I was pulled against an older man. I put my hands out, flat against his soft chest. He wore a buttoned shirt, open at the collar and sweat stained. His forehead was shiny, his hair thinning. He chuckled as he drew me closer.

"Where are you going, pretty girl?" he asked.

I narrowed my eyes and glanced at his person. His suit jacket hung off the back of his chair. It was cashmere, evenly stitched, and accented with genuine animal horn buttons. The man was obviously from Hiram, the financial district. I was more than familiar with the area. I was born and raised there.

It was also where my father, Lucius, governed as head of the Leviathan family.

The man looked me up and down before his gaze settled on my breasts. They weren't really that big, but in this dress, a sheath with thin straps, they swelled over the neckline.

"They don't make them like you anymore," he said.

I raised a brow. "Say that again," I said. "*To my face.*"

The man lifted his gaze, a thin smirk curling over his mouth. I had felt his lust from the moment he drew me near, rampant and dark, but now I could see it. His pupils were blown, swallowing the color of his irises, his skin was flushed, and his cock was hard, straining against the fabric of his dark trousers.

"Defiance," he said, a thin smirk curling his mouth. "I like it, but you'll never find a husband with it."

I kept my hands planted on his chest, both to maintain distance between us even as he tried to pull me closer and to give me more control over his arousal.

"Let me tame you, sugar," he said. "I'll be real good."

A violent shudder went through me, and I suspected few

women ever left this man's clutches alive.

I let one of my hands drop to his thigh, the other remaining at the center of his chest. His lips pulled back from his teeth as he chuckled in triumph, but I was reaching into his energy, seeking the parts of him that fueled his sex drive. I knew his by feel—a dizzying, nauseating force. I pulled it into the space between us. Outside his body, it no longer had purpose or intention—it was just fuel I could use to kill his sex drive.

"Let go," I said, imbuing my command with magic.

He dropped his hand, and at the same time, his cock deflated as if pricked by a needle. His slimy smile fell, and his pupils constricted so that I could see the color of his eyes, a dull gray. Now pale, he looked far older than before, almost frail.

It felt like a just punishment.

References

Andersen, H., Walker, D. and Tegner, H. (2012) *Hans Christian Andersen: Best-loved fairy tales*. New York: Fall River Press.

Carruthers, Amelia. *Snow White and Other Examples of Jealousy Unrewarded*. Cookhill, Alcester, Warwickshire: Pook Press, 2015.

Grimm, J., Grimm, W. and Hunt, A.W. (2021) *The Complete Grimm's Fairy tales*. Translated by Margaret Hunt. New Delhi: FingerPrint! Classics.

Grimm, Jacob, Wilhelm Grimm, Jack Zipes, and Andrea Dezsö. *The Original Folk and Fairy Tales of the Brothers Grimm: The Complete First Edition*. Princeton: Princeton University Press, 2014.

Grimm, J., Grimm, W. and Mondschein, K. (2011) *Grimm's Complete Fairy Tales*. Translated by Margaret Hunt. San Diego: Canterbury Classics.

Lang, Andrew. *The Yellow Fairy Book, by Andrew Lang*. New York, NY: First Racehorse for Young Readers, 2020.

Treasury of Irish Fairy and Folk Tales. Barnes & Noble Inc, 2016.

Acknowledgments

My experience with limb loss is secondary. My sister lost her leg below the knee a couple of years ago and the toll it has taken on her emotional, mental, and physical health has been more intense than anything I have witnessed in my life, and yet, she has handled the transition with such grace despite the world catering to able bodies. As I wrote Lore, the other thing I learned is that language is also ableist and I must give credit to my friend and former co-worker, Dave Brown, who answered so many questions about navigating the world with one hand.

Of course, I wouldn't have gotten anything done if it wasn't for my editor, Christa, who graciously opens her home and she shed to me when I find myself stuck and pushing against a deadline. When you reached out to me via email in July of 2021 about joining Bloom, I never guessed I would not only gain a new friend but an entire family. Thank you for welcoming me and my Adie girl.

Thank you to my agents, Caitlin and Alyssa, and my best

friends, Ashley and Molly, for giving me the space to write and encouragement along the way, even when I stop being so responsive. Your support is endless and keeps me moving forward.

Last, but not least, none of this would be possible without my husband, Armand, who keeps the house clean, cooks, takes care of Adie, and drives me everywhere I need to go when I am on deadline. There is no one in the world more dedicated than you. You are unwavering, even in the face of my chaos. I love you.

To every reader who has read *Apples Dipped in Gold* and loved it as much as I do—thank you from the bottom of my heart for taking a chance on a ridiculous novel. I'm glad you're on this journey with me.

About the Author

#1 *New York Times* bestselling author Scarlett St. Clair is a citizen of the Muscogee Nation and the author of the Hades X Persephone series, the Adrian X Isolde series, Fairy Tale Retellings, *Terror at the Gates*, and *When Stars Come Out*.

She has a master's degree in library science and information studies and a bachelor's in English writing. She is obsessed with Greek mythology, murder mysteries, and the afterlife. For information on books, tour dates, and content, please visit scarlettstclair.com.